HER BILLIONAIRE'S BEST-FRIEND TRILOGY

LEXIE MIERS

MY DAD'S BILLIONAIRE BEST-FRIEND

1

CHASTITY

"W*ow*. Who's the guy? Your boyfriend? He's unbelievably hot!"

I flinched as a new college friend sidled up next to me and sat down on the ledge I'd been occupying.

The man she was looking at was a chick magnet, it was true. With dark, short, styled hair, figure hugging jeans and a washed out vintage band t-shirt a size too small that showed off his ripped muscles.

He lifted his arm and waved at me, a huge smile causing him to flash his pearly whites at me.

I waved back, shaking my head. He wore what he liked, but sure didn't look like my friends' fathers.

"Not my boyfriend, my dad," I said, matter-of-factly as I stood and slung my bag over my shoulder and grabbed my suitcase. "Have a great break."

I walked away from Claire, whose mouth was still hanging open as she continued to stare at my father. I knew all the questions that would be running through her mind. First and foremost, would be, "How old was he when you were born?" I'd been asked the question a thousand times before.

"Hey, Chastity, how was your week?" he asked, leaning casually against his red convertible, like an old re-run of Magnum, PI.

I narrowed my eyes at him. "Seriously, Dad. Can't you wear normal fitting shirts like everyone else's father?"

He laughed and pushed off from the car, his big arms encircling me and squeezing tight. "I've missed you."

I let my eyes close as I inhaled his scent. The spicy Polo he'd been using since I was little engulfed me and made me yearn for Friday night movies and popcorn that had been our tradition. "Me too." I stepped back and he held open the passenger's side door for me. *Always a gentleman*, as my mother would say. Pity she hadn't held on to him long enough for us to be a real family. "Thanks." I slid into the small, older BMW and he got in the other side after closing my door and walking around hood.

"Do I really embarrass you?" Dad asked, his huge biceps flexing as he turned on the ignition and grabbed the gear shift.

I rolled my eyes at him in an exaggerated way. "Some of my oblivious friends think you're my boyfriend when they first see you. They're shocked when I say you're my father."

He chuckled and pulled into St. Pete traffic. "Not my fault I take care of myself and didn't age as well as your mother."

Age as badly, you mean. "Hey, leave her out of it. She doesn't have the time you do to spend hours in the gym, you know," I shot back and then had to work hard not to laugh when he gave me a side-eye look that said, "You know what I mean." I sighed and glanced out the window, watching the palm trees fly by.

My dad wasn't *that* young. I was born on his twenty-first birthday, and he always said I was the best birthday present he ever received. The problem was, I was now twenty-one, and instead of looking forty-two like he should, my dad looked thirty. Maybe thirty-five, if you looked really close at the crow's feet around his eyes. But his body was better than any thirty-year-old I'd ever seen, and his naturally thick and dark hair took a decade off his age.

"Mom isn't that bad," I defended, and my dad didn't say anything, diplomatic guy that he was. "She just looks her age." *Or a few years older*. She worked hard as a high school algebra teacher and was always stressed. *Next topic, please...*

"Anyway, sweetheart... how have you been? I feel like we haven't caught up in forever."

We hadn't. It had been far too long between dinner dates with my dad, which is why I was so happy we were going to spend a whole week together over the Christmas break. "Awesome. I got some incredible news, actually." I turned towards him to talk as he drove.

His gaze flicked over to me, his lips lifted in a smile. "Tell me."

"I got accepted into Sherman."

"For chiropractic?"

"Yes!" I squealed and then swallowed hard to force myself to calm down.

His contented sigh and smile said it all. "Oh, Chastity, I'm so proud of you. That's fantastic news."

Neither of my parents had finished college. When they'd gotten pregnant with me, Dad had dropped out to get a job, but they'd spilt up by the time I was two. Luckily Mom had managed to finish her teaching degree when I got older, but they both missed out on some pretty major opportunities in life, thanks to their promiscuity. And stupidity.

One of the main reasons I did not sleep around. Quite the opposite. "I couldn't have done it without you, Dad."

"Naw... don't be ridiculous. You're a star. And you should shine."

Both of my parents had helped me enormously through

school with living expenses, since I'd earned a full financial scholarship for tuition, but my father was always my biggest cheerleader. "Without your help, I could never have studied so hard, Dad. I want you to know how much I appreciate it."

His cheekbones were looking suspiciously pink now and he brushed the back of his free hand against his eyes. "I'm just glad you used that brain of yours for something good. And I hope that means I get free adjustments for the first five years?"

"More like forever!" I beamed at him. I could never repay the help he'd given me, but I'd make sure his spine was in tip top condition for the rest of his life.

He chuckled and turned the car off the street and into the gym parking lot near his apartment.

I glanced up at the large signage. *All Day Health.*

Dad had managed to work his way up through the commercial construction company he worked for and now had an office job preparing quotes and building specs for large projects. He had a nice apartment in an upscale part of town and worked out at an exclusive gym.

"Do you need to lift again before we get home?" I joked as he parked and turned the ignition off.

"Uh, not exactly. I've got a casual meeting of sorts inside. This investor is really difficult to pin down, so he invited me to have a chat after his training. It's a new business venture I'm looking into. Do you mind if we stop here for twenty minutes before we go home?"

I did mind a little bit. I wanted to spend time with him, not sit in the car by myself. "Sure, but can I come inside with you? I don't feel like sitting in the car and frying in the sun."

He laughed that deep, carefree laugh he'd always had. "Of course. There's a café and an area to relax if you want to play on your cell for a bit. I'll show you."

"Perfect." I grabbed my bag and we both got out of the car.

When we walked inside, the air conditioning hit me in the face like a snowstorm. "Whoa, it's freezing in here."

Dad chuckled and indicated I should follow him, so I did.

We walked through a second set of doors and into Nirvana, where the coffee was grinding, soft music played, and I couldn't stop myself from sighing.

"This is awesome." Nothing like the basic gyms Mom and I had frequented over the years.

My father smiled again at me, then stepped over to the counter and spoke to the pretty woman working there. She nodded and he came back to me. "I just spoke to Martine, and she'll take care of you. Order anything you want. I won't be long, Chas, I promise. You all right here?"

In the lap of luxury? Absolutely. "Yeah, sure, Dad. Go. See you in a bit."

He disappeared through the frosted glass doors, and I suppressed the urge to squeal. I'd spent the last few weeks cooped up in a small dorm room studying for finals. This was heaven in comparison.

"Would you like something to drink?" the pretty blonde called out and I walked over to the bar.

"Sure. I know this is a strange request, but a hot chocolate, if you've got it?"

She nodded and went over to the coffee machine.

I turned and leaned against the bar, letting pure happiness filter over me. *When I'm a Doctor of Chiropractic I'll belong to a club like this. One day.*

Growing up with a mother who had very little, we'd never gone on vacations. My father had helped the best he could, and I'd never wanted for anything I actually *needed*. But now, I could see my future ahead and I was sure my mom would love to join a place like this too. I owed her everything. I'd find a way to make it up to her. All the sacrifices she'd made for me. Just four and a half more years of school and I'd be able to buy her all the extras she'd missed out on.

The frosted glass doors that led into the interior of the health club opened and my gaze swung towards them, half expecting my dad to walk back through. My belly tightened and clenched with an intensity I'd never experienced. *Wow.*

The man who walked through the door was sex on legs. Literally. You could feel the intensity of his power like a radiant wave of heat.

Whoa.

His gaze turned my way and sparks sizzled between us. I couldn't move and I couldn't look away as heat simmered through me.

His lips lifted in a smile as he hefted his sports bag onto his shoulder. He seemed to be going for the doors that led to the outside, but then he turned and headed over to the bar near me.

"Hiya, Axel. Ice water?" the blonde woman asked him, her voice strong and overly friendly.

He winked at her and nodded. "You know me well. Thanks, Martine."

I shivered. The timbre of his voice was perfect. Deep and rich. Strong and sexy.

He turned towards me, his perfect white teeth glistening in a smile as his blue eyes sparkled in response. "Here to work out?"

Me? I struggled to think of a response. My gaze was drawn by the thin sheen of sweat on his bulging biceps and I wondered how sweet he would taste. His physique wasn't exaggerated like some puffed-up body builders. But God, did I want to bite those biceps. I shook myself. "Uh, me? No. Just getting a hot chocolate and waiting for my dad." A warm drink may have seemed odd in this heat, but Christmas was approaching, and it was my holiday go-to.

His eyebrows lifted high on his forehead, slight wrinkles at the edge of his eyes indicating he'd be about ten years older than me. Perhaps a little more.

Nothing like a hot, older guy to teach you a few things. Which I needed desperately.

"They sell hot chocolate here?" he asked skeptically.

I laughed. "Yeah. She said they did, anyway."

Martine slid a mug across the counter towards me. "We don't get many orders for it, but I always have some in stock."

"Why wouldn't they have it?" I asked, lifting the mug to my lips, and taking a big sip. "Hmm... Yum."

The man in front of me laughed. "Ah, because this is a health club and most the women here are terrified of sugar."

I shrugged. "Not my problem." I probably carried a bit too much weight by most people's standards, but I did laps at our school pool when I found the time and generally ate well. My life didn't start or begin with my weight. I didn't even own a scale.

He stared at me for a moment, as though assessing my soul. Something I wasn't afraid of, because I was a nice person. Or I certainly tried to be.

I stared straight back at him, feeling a strength building within me. I'd gotten over the initial shock of his devastating appearance, and now I wanted to know if he had some brain cells between his gorgeous ears.

"Yes? Was it... Axel?"

He shrugged. "Alternative parents."

I rolled my eyes. "Yeah... I know the feeling."

He stuck out his hand. "Axel Patterson. Pleased to meet you...?"

"Chastity," I answered and wasn't surprised when he burst out laughing.

"Really?" He grinned, his gaze running up and down my body. "Is there a metal belt hidden under those jeans?"

I'd been asked similar questions in the past, and always tried to have a smartass answer in response. "Of course, I do. After all, we are the names our parents gave us, aren't we? So, tell me, Axel... Do you stick your arms out and act like an axle for the wheels in your car?"

He froze for a moment, his eyes widening in shock before he burst out laughing.

Martine pushed the tall, icy glass at him, her interested gaze swinging between us.

He picked up his drink and downed the whole thing like a thirsty pelican. When he put it down, he was still smiling. "You're the most interesting person I've met today, Chastity."

I snorted. "That doesn't say much for the people you work with, then."

His blue eyes sparkled even more as he stared at me and my gaze swung down to his left hand, bare of a wedding ring. "No. No it doesn't."

2

CHASTITY

Axel flicked his wrist around and checked a very expensive looking watch. "Damn, I've gotta go. But I hope we meet again."

That was very doubtful since I was only here on my father's dime. "You probably won't see me again, Axel. But thank you for the chat."

I gave him my biggest smile and he walked away, shaking his head as though he couldn't believe the things I'd just said to him. The front doors opened and let him back into the sunshine. I dragged myself back to the bar and my drink. He was way out of my league. *As if he'd ever be into someone like me.*

Next to my hot chocolate mug was a large smart phone in a black leather case resting on a black mat. Impossible to see unless you were right next to it. "Shit." I grabbed it up and bolted to the door, stepping out into the sunshine and chasing Axel to his car. His very expensive car.

Fuck. Is that a Lamborghini? Yep. Sooooo far out of my league.

I cleared my throat then forced myself to speak when he didn't turn around. "Um... Axel?"

He turned, keys in hand and a gorgeous smile on his face. "Yes?"

I held the phone out to him. "I think you forgot this."

His eyes widened in surprise, then he took it from me and slipped it into his bag with a sigh. "Thank you very much. I would have been totally lost without that. Damn. I'm not usually so thoughtless."

I waved my hand at him and began to back away. "No worries, you just enjoy your day."

He stepped towards me. "So, you're beautiful *and* honest. Any other attributes I should know about?"

I laughed. "Uh, not beautiful. But thanks, anyway."

"I'd like to see you again."

I'd like that too, but how? "When?"

"Any time. Hang on, let me grab my card." He opened the shiny black car with a button on his keys, leaned inside and came back out holding a small, white card. "Here. Please call me. I want to take you out for dinner and get to know you better."

I took the card and stared at the embossed writing. "CEO of a management company? No offense, Axel, but I don't think you're going to find me very interesting." I had to be honest because seriously, I didn't think we had a single thing in common. Least of all, our exercise habits.

"I think you're wrong. You're a breath of fresh air to me."

I snorted, not sure if that was a compliment. "Yeah, my mom would say something similar. She's always telling me to think before I speak, but my mouth can't seem to slow down long enough for that to happen."

He continued to stare at me as though he'd never seen a person like me before. Perhaps he hadn't.

"Well... I better get back inside." My father may be looking for me as we speak.

He reached out and grabbed my hand, pulling me closer. His

fingers were hot and slightly rough against my hand. Strong. "Please say you'll go out with me."

My breath hitched in my throat. He couldn't possibly be serious. But as he waited for my response to his absurd question, my heart began to race inside my chest. I swallowed hard and tried to ignore the way my nipples tingled beneath my plain t-shirt. "But you are so far out of my league," I blurted out, then wished I'd kept my thoughts to myself.

He cocked his head to the side. "You'd prefer me poor?" he asked, kinking one eyebrow up.

I huffed out a laugh and pulled my hand out of his grip. My fingers ached to run alongside his hair and pull him into me for a kiss. It had been so long since I'd felt anyone's lips on mine, and he was attractive in every way possible. "No... it's just—"

He cut me off, not that I had a proper answer to his question. "It's just *nothing*. Go out with me. Your choice. Anywhere you want."

I lifted my gaze and met his solid blue stare. That sounded like a challenge. "Anywhere I want?"

He nodded and butterflies fluttered inside my belly. This could be fun. "All right, I'll go out with you, then. But it's my choice."

He gave me a huge smile that made my knees weak. "You're so delicious, I just want to devour you."

I giggled, unable to help myself as a heated flush raced up my cheeks. "You sound like the big, bad wolf."

His grin was the sexiest thing I'd ever seen, and I staggered sideways, catching myself on a conveniently located pole.

"You all right?" he asked, his smile conveying his humor at the situation.

"Yeah, thanks. I better go." I began to back away, glancing towards the gym, but my father was nowhere to be seen.

"When are we going out for dinner?" he called out, ever persistent.

"I didn't say it was dinner," I responded, laughing inside. As if I was going to take advantage of some rich guy. I'd been taught better than that. Plus... if I even had a chance with a man like him, I wasn't doing what every woman had done before me. I wasn't going to be boring.

His eyebrows drew down in mock outrage. "When?" Axel repeated.

I thought quickly. Dad always worked weekends, even when I was with him. Maybe I could sneak out for a few hours in the afternoon? "Tomorrow too soon?"

"Definitely not. What time?"

I loved how he let me choose everything. For a man who obviously had total control of his life, it was a lovely gift. "Three? I can meet you here if you like."

His lips quirked a little, but he didn't ask anything else. "Done. I will see you, gorgeous girl, tomorrow."

I nodded and took slow, careful steps backwards. I clung to his card like a lifeline. I was not letting it go.

He gave me one more killer smile that made my insides clench and tighten in a way I hadn't felt before. Then he got in his car and drove away.

I wandered back inside in a daze, reaching out for my now barely warm hot chocolate with a stupid smile on my face.

"What happened?" the woman behind the bar asked. She was eyeing me in a way that reminded me of a jealous bitch I'd once known in high school. Her hackles were raised, and her eyebrows were lowered. Not a good sign.

"Oh, nothing. Just gave him back his phone." I wasn't telling her anything. Her mood had changed substantially since my interaction with Axel, and the last thing I wanted was some blow-up from her in front of Dad. I finished my drink and pushed it over the counter towards her. "Thanks so much." I wandered over to the couch and settled down just as I heard my dad's voice over my shoulder. I twisted around to see him deep in conversation with an older man with silver streaks through his hair. They shook hands and the man left.

Dad walked over to me; his smile full of happiness. "Hey, sweetie. I'm sorry that took a little longer than expected. You ready to go? I hope you weren't too bored while I was gone."

I got up from the couch, slipping Axel's business card into my cell phone case. "Nah, of course not. Looking forward to a night of Chinese food and movies, though."

He put a comforting arm around my shoulders and tugged me in the direction of the entrance. "You were? Perfect! Because so was I."

3

AXEL

I tapped my fingers along the steering wheel of my car, a strange excitement bubbling in my gut. I hadn't done anything this impulsive in too long. I'd forgotten how good it felt.

A movement caught my eye and I turned to see Chastity walking into the gym's parking lot, dressed in the simplest of clothes. Blue jeans. A plain, red tank top. Flat shoes. Her long, blonde hair pulled up into a high ponytail. She looked about sixteen, and I hoped to God she was older than that.

A smile tugged at my lips as she glanced around for me. I dated models. And actresses, and basically women who were professional sex objects. They knew the score, and marriage was not on the table. Money, fun, and sex were. And that had been enough for me for a long time. But as I stared at the beautiful, natural girl before me, my heart yearned for more.

She twisted around and spotted my car, her face transforming into a huge smile. She rocked back on her heels and walked over.

I opened the car door and got out, my hands itching to grab her. Pull her close and kiss the living daylights out of her.

"Hey," she said casually as she walked over, a hint of cleavage catching my eye above her red tank top.

"Hey, yourself." I licked my lips and gripped the car door to stop myself from devouring her on the spot. She made my heart pound and my cock ache. That delicious skin surely needed my lips upon it. *And how beautiful would she look spread out beneath me?* I shook my head to clear the erotic thoughts and forced my mind back to the present. "So where are we off to? A late lunch?" I asked, still confused about the time she'd chosen for our first date. Three p.m. was just... odd.

She cocked her head to the side. "Why? Are you hungry?"

In truth, I wasn't. "Not really, but I gave you carte blanche on our activity." And if this were any other woman I knew, we'd be sitting at the most expensive restaurant in the city, drinking French champagne for the rest of the day.

"Good. My dad's in meetings for a few hours, so I have some time. Can we go drive to the beach and have ice cream?"

I didn't know which shocking piece of information I needed to tackle first. "Your dad?" How old was this woman that she still lived with her parents? And did I need to drive her home like... now?

"Yeah, we're spending the weekend together since I don't get to see him much."

Family-oriented was good. I hadn't had a lot of that growing up. "And you want ice cream?" *Of all things?*

"Yes. Is that okay?" she asked, her slow smile making me want to grab her high ponytail and drag her in for a kiss.

"Absolutely. The beach is twenty minutes away. That gives us a bit of time, I suppose." I was supposed to be working myself, but if she had a few hours free to eat ice cream and talk, then I was clearing my schedule. "Jump in."

She walked around the car, nothing in her hands, and jumped in.

"Don't you have a bag?" I asked her. What woman went anywhere without her makeup, phone and purse? And whatever else women hid in those things.

Chastity reached behind her and grabbed a phone and some cash from her back pocket, placing them both on the dashboard. "Got what I need."

I could only nod as I stared at the crumpled twenty-dollar bills and the typical smart phone with a spangly pink case. "I'm not sure I'm going to like the answer to this question, but how old are you, Chastity?" She had to be twenty-one. *God help me if she's not.* I started the car, and she looked my way with a devilish grin.

"How old do I look?'

I groaned. *Oh, fuck.* "About sixteen."

She laughed, loud and hard. "That's good to know."

I waited, but she didn't answer. "No, seriously. How old are you?"

"I'm twenty-one. How old are you?'

Relief flooded me. That wasn't too bad. Legal, at least. "I'm forty." Which was old enough. Too old, if you asked me.

She laughed a bit softer this time. "You don't look forty."

I winked at her. "I work pretty hard at that, so thank you." I ate clean, worked out hard, and was embarrassed to admit that I owned more vitamins and supplements than the local health food store.

"I would have said closer to fifty myself," she said calmly, not a bit of humor written on her face.

I spluttered as I stared at her, my mouth hanging open. "Huh?" Was she serious? How could she possibly think I was fifty?

This time she burst out laughing so hard I saw tears at the edges of her eyes. "You should see your face. Honestly, you've gotta lighten up, Axel."

I pressed my foot to the accelerator and turned the car into traffic, heading for the beach as requested. I hadn't been teased in far too long, and the uncomfortable feeling was like spiders crawling on my skin.

"Axel, you okay?"

I think so. I didn't like to think I was vain... but dammit. Fifty?

"Yeah, fine. I just..." I swallowed hard. Humble pie tasted like shit. "I haven't had anyone tell me I look older than I am... ever, I don't think."

She shrugged. "Well, I hate to tell you, but you need some teasing. You take yourself too seriously."

We pulled up at the first set of lights and I turned to study her face. "Well, that's what happens when you run a billion-dollar company."

Her eyebrows shot up in the air and her bare shoulder shuddered. "That must be stressful," she said, not sounding very interested.

Didn't she know what that meant for my life? Or what that could mean for her in the future if we continued to see each other? "It means I can do anything I want, anytime."

She snorted. "Really? Can you go on a three-month trip around Europe? And I don't mean to work. I mean like... travel. Relax. Vacay."

I eyed her carefully, then set off again as the light turned green. I wanted to watch her face during this conversation because I had a very strong feeling that I was going to keep this girl around for a lot longer than a few nights. And I wanted to know how much my money mattered. "If I set things up properly, then yes." *Sort of.*

She snorted again. "No, you can't. And if I ever went overseas, I'd want to backpack through Europe. No swanky hotels, no plans. Just set off and go. Stay as long as I want in any place I liked. No computers, no phones, just adventure. I bet you couldn't leave your billion-dollar company long enough for that."

This conversation had taken a weird turn. "You want to travel rough?" Did women still do that?

"Of course. I want to do everything."

"So, you don't come from money then?" I swear, I felt about five years old when she lifted her chin and stared down at me over her nose.

"My parents worked their asses off to put me through school. Am I looking forward to becoming a chiropractor and paying them back for all their support? Absolutely. But do I think money buys happiness? Absolutely not!"

I continued to glance over at her as we drove. My heart had begun to pound like it was readying itself for a run. I liked this girl. Her conviction, her naivety. Everything about her screamed pure and good, two things I hadn't had much of through my life. The silence stretched until I decided to continue the strange conversation. "It sounds like you had a great childhood, unlike mine."

She relaxed back into the seat, picking up her phone and stuffing the cash into the case. "Oh, it wasn't amazing... but it was okay. My parents split before I even remember, so I was always shuffling between two houses, which was hard. But both of them made it work as well as possible, and I was always loved."

"Hmm, that's better than mine." *What are you doing?*

"How come?" she asked.

I wanted to bite my tongue off. What was I doing, exposing all my history to the poor girl? "Uh, nothing. Tell me more about your parents."

"No, I want to know. Tell me."

I considered the wisdom of my next move. Exposing anything about myself was never a good decision, but being honest was probably the best way to go with a woman like this. I shrugged as

I drove, trying to make light of a pretty dark topic. "I barely saw my parents growing up. They had too much money and no time for me. Now they live in London most of the year and I hardly see them."

"So, most of your money is inherited?" Her tone was cold as she asked.

I grunted. "Hardly. My parents believe in making your own fortune. They paid for a good education, then said, 'You're on your own.' And I've been working hard ever since."

She seemed to relax at hearing that. "I like that," she said, then sat up straight and waved her hands. "Not the part about your parents being assholes... that's crap. But I like that you've made your own way. I think that's important."

The atmosphere inside the car relaxed and Chastity stared out the window as we neared the beach. "Could we park near the shops on Gulf Boulevard? There's an ice creamery there that I love."

"Sure." I followed her instructions and pulled the car into a spot near the beach. My breath whooshed out of me as I stared at the crashing waves. The sunlight dancing off the never-ending blue.

She reached over and squeezed my hand. "Haven't been to the beach in a while, huh?"

"Nope. Not in months." Longer actually, but I wasn't admitting to that.

"Great then. Let's go."

She released her hold on me and I gasped from the strength of the tingles on my skin. *Ridiculous.* I shook myself as I got out of the car.

She walked ahead, stepping up in front of one of the small shops and ordered a big waffle cone with three scoops of ice cream.

Damn. The calories...

She'd paid for herself before I'd had a chance to notice.

"What do you want, Axel? My treat."

I wanted to scoff at her, but I could see from her clear eyes, she wasn't joking.

"Uh... what do you recommend?"

"Oh, everything, but this chocolate one is my favorite." She stepped closer and held the cone up to me to lick.

I felt like an idiot but did what she asked. I leaned forward and licked the chocolate ice cream. Dark, rich creaminess exploded across my tongue. I swallowed hard as her pupils dilated. "Yum."

She turned towards the man behind the counter. "Double scoop in a waffle cone, please."

I went to protest but she waved her hands at me, and I was soon holding exactly what she'd ordered for me.

When the guy handed her back her change, I pulled my wallet out.

"No. Here." I thrust some money at the man who'd scooped our cones. "Give her money back, please."

The guy held up his hands in surrender, chuckled and walked away from me.

Chastity grabbed my sleeve and tugged. "Not a chance, I've been coming to this place for ten years and your money's no good here. Let's go for a walk."

The man behind the bar gave me a sympathetic smile and I tucked the cash away.

Fucking hell, that's a first. I stumbled onto the beach, my Italian leather shoes stiff and annoying.

"Let's go closer to the water, the sand's harder there. Easier to walk on."

I followed her like a puppy, unable to resist. *What sort of magic was at work here?* "So, now you've got me here, what are you going to do with me?" I asked her.

She grinned and kept licking her ice cream. "I don't know yet."

A growl rolled through me, and I reached out and grabbed her hand, pulling her closer so that our pelvises met, and I could slide my arm around her waist.

She stared up at me, our gazes connecting like two live wires.

"You are far too much to resist, you know that?"

She swallowed hard. "No one's ever said that to me before."

"Well, they're idiots."

I couldn't resist any longer. I dropped my head just as she lifted her mouth to mine. I pressed my lips to hers and moaned as her heat touched me. The attraction between us roared to life like a log igniting on smoldering kindling.

I tightened my hold on her with the hand that wasn't holding the ice cream and slid my tongue into her mouth, tasting her sweetness. The coldness of the ice cream offset the heat of her mouth and I pulled her even closer, wanting her naked and writhing in pleasure.

I dragged my lips away. "Come home with me."

She blinked a few times then stepped away, her head down.

"What's wrong?" I asked, suddenly regretting showing my hand so early. That wasn't like me either.

She tilted her head to the side. "Let's walk."

She stepped closer to the crashing waves, and I trailed behind her, the cold trickle of melting ice cream flowing across my hand.

"What happened?" I asked. One minute she was as hot as the sand, and the next she was freezing me out.

"I don't think going back to your place is appropriate yet."

"Appropriate?" I parroted. I hadn't heard words used like that in forever.

She turned to me and rolled her eyes heavily. "I met you yesterday. We've spent an hour in each other's company, total. Is it really your normal practice to take a woman to bed that quickly?"

On occasion... "No, but I thought the attraction between us was exceptional. That you wanted the same thing I did."

"I do... but we shouldn't do that yet."

She was shifting and fidgeting like a kid caught with her hand in the cookie jar and I started to smell a rat. "Look, if this is some sort of play, Chastity, I'm not into games."

"What are you talking about?" She was glaring at me now, but the warning bells were peeling madly.

"If you like playing the role of cock-tease, I have to tell you that's not something I'm into. I like my women willing." Anger was building in my gut like a storm, hot and fast.

"No. It's not that," she said, her voice sounding a little hurt.

"Then what? Because I thought you were different from the other women I've dated. But if different translates into a better liar, then I don't want anything to do with you." Why did they all play the same games? It made no sense. Why couldn't they just be honest?

She sighed and her gaze dropped, as did my gut.

I should have known better than to act upon my lustful thoughts. Served me right to think I'd found someone unique for once.

4

CHASTITY

Fear poured through me like hot rain, making my heart pound and my stomach tighten. He wasn't going to want to speak to me after he learned the truth. *No way.* "I don't like saying it," I managed to get out, clinging to the cone in my hand.

"You don't like saying what?" he ground out. Everything about Axel had changed and I hated it. His mood. His face.

Why was I suddenly the bad guy here? Obviously, he was used to getting what he wanted, when he wanted it, and screw anybody else. I heaved a sigh and put my ice cream to my lips, licking the rivulets of heaven up with my tongue. A fun date had just taken a terrible turn.

"Maybe we should just go back to the gym, Chastity," Axel said, his voice hard now.

"Okay." I nodded and began walking back to the stupidly expensive car. Why was he so angry with me? I walked past a trash can and threw my still beautiful ice cream in, my stomach rolling over and twisting like tumbleweed. What a waste of money and time. I could have just stayed at home and eaten out of my dad's freezer. He wouldn't have been angry at me.

When I got to the car, I turned around to see Axel still standing by the trash, holding his cone and staring inside the can as though wondering if he was going to throw his out too. "Are we going back or not?" I called out and he suddenly dropped his ice cream into the trash and stormed over to me. "What's wrong now?" I asked, stepping back and away from his unwarranted anger.

"I want to know where I went wrong. Tell me. Please. You seemed so natural and different from all the other women I've met. How could I not know that you were just a tease?"

I put my hands on my hips and glared at him. Obviously, the poor guy had been duped by far too many gold diggers in the past, but I was allowed to say no to sex without being accused of being like them. "I wasn't lying. What are you talking about?" He was just being plain stupid now.

"I mean this," he waved his hand back and forth between us. "The sweet smile, paying for our ice cream. All so you can reject me when I fall for your act. I don't get it."

Now I was getting angry. "Look. Just because I don't want to jump into bed with you after one kiss, does not mean I'm a cock tease, okay? Who the hell do you think you are? Some sort of sex god?"

"No, of course not."

"Then why take such offense because I asked you to back off for a bit?"

"Because I know women. And you had all the hot signals on."

I laughed in his face and squared myself up to glare at him. "You know women, huh? What a crock of shit."

His eyebrows shot up. "I do," he declared.

"How much do you want to bet?"

He pulled back and looked me up and down, no desire or heat in his expression now. "A thousand bucks."

Easy. "Done. Tell me how many lovers I've had."

His eyes narrowed and his mouth flicked into an odd smile. "You won't tell the truth about that even if I do guess correctly."

I leaned forward, connecting our gazes as tightly as I could so he'd see if I lied. "How many men, Axel?"

His posture relaxed and he finally said, "Three."

I kept our gazes locked. "Really? You think I'm some sort of amazing cock tease, but I've only had three lovers? That doesn't add up."

His shoulders slumped a little and his gaze slid sideways. "I didn't say you were experienced; you just seem to know how to play the game."

I put all my anger into my gaze and spoke slowly. "Look into my eyes when I say this Axel, because I know you can tell when someone is lying. You wouldn't be filthy rich if you couldn't. Nod if you agree."

He nodded.

"Look at me."

His gaze slid back to mine, and I was beginning to see the start of regret in his eyes, but I was too angry now.

"I. Have. Never. Had. A. Lover." I took a deep breath. "*Ever*."

His eyes went wide, and he stepped back, bumping into his side mirror.

But I wasn't done. I put my hands on my hips and glared at him. "And just because I don't want to fuck you right now, doesn't make me a cock tease, it makes you an arrogant asshole." I waited for that to sink in before putting my hand on the car door handle. "Now unlock the car, I want to go home."

"Chastity... I'm so sorry."

"You should be. Because I *am* different and special. I've always known it and so has anyone else who's bothered to spend more than an hour with me. So please open the car door and take me home."

He nodded, pressed a button that unlocked the car, and I got in.

I focused on my phone the whole drive back and didn't look at him once. *What a fucking waste of time that was.*

When we finally pulled into the gym's parking lot, I opened the door with a grunt and got out as fast as I could. Dad's house was only a block away and I needed the walk to let off some steam. Pity I couldn't go into the gym and beat up one of the punching bags.

"Chastity, please stop."

I turned around and crossed my arms over my chest. "What?" If he thought I could be sweet talked out of this, then he was seriously mistaken.

"I'm so sorry I accused you of playing me. I know you weren't."

Oh, so now you're sorry? "Yeah, now you say that because you know I'm a virgin. But guess what? I don't care. You're nothing but a spoiled little rich kid who expects to get everything he wants, when he wants it. Well, let me tell you, I'm not for sale." I turned around and stomped off, anger filling my hands and fists. How could he be so stupid? How could I? I knew better than to trust a guy with so much money and so little heart.

"Chastity, I..." Axel stopped, then held up his hands, palms up, as though he'd given up.

"What?" I demanded.

He pulled out his wallet. "I owe you a thousand dollars. That was our bet, right? I would never have guessed that you were a... were a..."

"Virgin!" I exploded at him. "I'm a virgin, you can say it. You were too, once upon a time."

He pulled out a wad of notes and handed them to me. "Here you go."

I took the money, more because I was confused rather than anything else. "What do you mean? Oh my God. You carry a thousand dollars around with you?" I held it up with both hands. "Wow." This was a month's rent for my mom, and he'd handed it over like it was nothing. Which to him, it probably wasn't.

"I'm sorry, again." Axel said, stepping back.

I groaned, rushed him and pushed the money back into his shirt breast pocket. "I don't want your money."

"Then what do you want?"

The question hung in the air, and I found myself struggling to stay angry at him. "I want... I want to walk home. Thank you for the crappy date. Amazingly, it wasn't my worst, by far."

5

CHASTITY

I turned on my heel and started marching through the parking lot, then down the street. Stupid, idiotic man! He could have called me dumb, or ugly, or… lazy! None of which I was, but still… I would have taken less offense to all those words. But cock tease? He couldn't have been further from the truth. The sound of a car's idling engine hit my hearing and I turned to look behind me.

"Jump in. I'll drive you home."

I shook my head and kept walking. "No thanks. My dad's place is only five minutes from here."

"You didn't answer my question!" Axel shouted out his window.

"Which one was that?"

He stopped the car and got out. "What do you want? If you don't want me for sex or money, what do you want?"

The insult in those words was too enormous to process properly, and yet most of it was directed at himself.

I frowned at him as he stepped closer and swallowed hard. It was difficult for me not to stare when I looked directly at him. He was so gorgeous; he made my brain function in slow motion. "I don't know," I said, not sure what he wanted me to say. When he turned away as though disappointed, I grabbed his shirt-covered arm and turned him back. "But you shouldn't categorize women or yourself in that way. It's degrading, mostly to you."

He narrowed his eyes at me. "What do you mean?"

I rolled my eyes. "Are you serious?" I huffed out a sigh and decided to be embarrassingly honest, which for me was par for the course most of the time. I didn't believe in beating around the bush. "You are insanely hot. And way before I saw your car or your business card, I wanted you to kiss me."

He turned back and slid his hand around my waist, tugging me close. "Then why... I know why." He sighed too. "I'm sorry I tried to rush you."

I cupped his face in my hands. "You are someone I want to get to know, but you need to realize that I've never done any of this before. And I don't want you for your money. Or status. Or whatever. I'm going to make my own money, just like you."

He grinned. "A doctor of Chiropractic, huh?"

I grinned at him. "You a fan?"

He nodded. "Yep. Got my weekly adjustment booked in for Monday mornings, seven a.m."

I threw myself at him, hugging him tightly. I didn't know why, but I had to hold him. I didn't know him very well, but now all I could see were the vulnerabilities he obviously tried hard to hide.

He was sexy, successful and forty. But had he ever been married? Kids?

His parents hadn't loved him, so had he ever let anyone else?

I pulled away and he stared down at me, his eyebrows lowered over his eyes. "Uh... what was that for?"

I swallowed the lump in my throat. "Um... I just wanted to."

"Does this mean I'm forgiven?" he asked.

I bit my lip. "I suppose so." After all, could I really blame a guy who obviously had more scars than a pro football player for assuming I was like every other woman? But I wasn't. And he needed to know that. "But no more second guessing my motives. I'll be honest with you. I promise."

He inhaled sharply. "Okay. So... you don't want to come back to my apartment then?"

I was surprised by the question, but then he followed it with the most gorgeous grin, and I knew he was joking, so of course I had to tease him. How could I resist? "I will... but only for an epic make-out session. Think you can handle the blue balls?"

His mouth dropped open.

I laughed. "Another day, maybe?"

He ran a hand through his disheveled hair and huffed out a laugh. "I can handle the blue balls, but I'm not sure I can keep my hands to myself. I'd want to feel you come around me."

It was my turn for my mouth to drop open.

Axel grinned. "Yeah... exactly."

I pressed my lips together, trying not to laugh. What a thing to say! "Well, how about we try again?" I asked. "Another date? Maybe dinner this time?"

He nodded, straightening up and looking more confident by the second. "Tonight?"

I laughed and shook my head. "Already got plans with my dad. "How about tomorrow night? Or Monday, even."

"Tomorrow," Axel said. "Definitely."

I smiled, then found myself staring at his lips and aching to kiss him once more. "My dad's apartment is just down the block, but..."

"I'll walk you."

"Okay."

We turned and started ambling along the sidewalk.

I took his hand, because... why not?

He stared at me a moment when I did but didn't shake me off. Instead, he gripped my fingers tighter, and my breath caught in my throat.

I was in so much trouble when it came to this guy. He was too beautiful, genuine, raw, and so different from anyone else I'd ever met. But was a mutual attraction enough to keep us together when we were leagues apart in every other way?

We walked the final half block and suddenly we were standing outside my dad's massive apartment complex, and I was thinking of reasons to delay going back inside.

"Well, uh..."

Axel slid his hand up my arms until he finally cupped my face and lifted my chin, so I was staring up into his gorgeous eyes. "I'm going to kiss you goodbye."

I nodded, lifting my arms to encircle his neck and drag him closer. But the kiss was a chaste one, a mere brushing of his lips against mine before he was pulling back. I groaned. "Now, you're teasing me."

He laughed and slowly stepped away. "I'm seducing you. There's a difference."

I pressed my lips together, trying to hold onto his taste forever. "I better go up. Dad will be done with his meetings by now most likely. I'm assuming you don't want to come up to meet him?" I waggled my eyebrows at the billionaire, as the man ran a hand over the back of his neck and stared at his shoes.

"Nah, it's okay."

I laughed aloud at that one. "Too early?"

He nodded and lifted his head to meet my gaze. "Yep. A bit." Then he stared up at the building. "My best friend lives here, actually. It's a small world."

I shrugged. There were hundreds of units in this complex. "Well, next time you're here visiting him, come by."

He nodded, his eyes blazing with promise. "Will do." He

began walking backwards, a smile still glued to his luscious lips. "I'd better get going."

I watched him go, loving how young and silly he seemed as he stumbled across the street and walked back to his car. If only his business partners could see him now, all relaxed and embarrassed and unsure. I kinda loved it. "Bye!" I waved at him with my arm over my head.

He chuckled to himself, turned, and walked away.

Damn, he had a fine ass. No man should be that handsome and that rich. It wasn't fair to the rest of the world. With my heart singing, I practically skipped into my dad's apartment building and zipped up to the tenth floor where he lived.

I didn't knock on the door. I could hear him talking inside, through the door, and he had his business voice on. I pulled out the single key in my back pocket and slid it into the hole.

Dad raised his hand in greeting as I stepped over the threshold, then turned back to his phone call.

I went to the bathroom and stared in the mirror, taking note of my shining eyes and my too red lips. "You're in way over your head with this guy," I said to my reflection. And yet I found myself laughing, bubbles of happiness floating to the surface. I shook my head, still staring in the mirror. "This is crazy." I needed a shower or something to distract me and use up all this excess energy. So, I stripped out of my clothes, and climbed into the shower, the hot water beating down on my hair.

"Hey, sweetie!" Dad called into the bathroom, the door only opened a crack. "How was your date?"

I laughed at how excited he seemed. "Been waiting to ask that question for a long time, haven't you?"

He chuckled. "Well, you work too hard. You deserve some fun, too."

I was in total agreement. Squeezing the shampoo into my

hands, I worked it into a lather, then started scrubbing my head. "It was okay... but it was just ice cream."

"So? Are you gonna see him again? Or cut and run?"

I weighed how much to tell my dad, thinking about the age difference. Not gonna happen.

"Of course!" Dad said. "I'm surprised you didn't organize something for tonight."

I smiled as I rinsed off the shampoo. "No way. I'm looking forward to our night." I couldn't see his smile, but I could imagine it.

"Thai takeout for dinner?" he asked. "Or you wanna go out?"

"Thai is perfect," I said. "And a movie, maybe?"

"I'll see what I've got. Take your time."

He disappeared, leaving me to think about Axel once more. I'd never met anyone like him. He was extremely intelligent and successful, that was obvious. But he'd worked his ass off to get there, which I liked.

He was also the hottest man I'd ever seen in real life. It was definitely in the body and the gorgeous face, but what I really loved about Axel was his confidence—the way he looked at me. Then, what made me want to curl up in his lap and stay there forever, was his honesty. His vulnerability.

Everyone always said they wanted a bad boy, but that just wasn't right. Girls wanted a bad boy who would change, just for her. That never worked out well.

Axel was definitely a bad boy with the stupid expensive car and black book a mile long. He'd probably had more sexual encounters than I'd had hot dinners. And yet that didn't put me off, somehow. It made me wonder how the hell I was going to compete in his bed and his heart when I had next to zero experience, but I wasn't one to be put off by a challenge.

I conditioned, brushed all the tangles out of my long hair, then got out of the shower to inspect myself in the mirror once more. Being too thin was not a problem for me. My boobs were big, and so was my ass. But if the way Axel looked at me was any indication of what he'd like to see in bed, then he was gonna see plenty of it.

I wrapped my hair up in a towel, my breath hitching in my throat. Damn, I was excited. And I hadn't felt this truly elated in a long time. My focus was so intense at school, I really hadn't stopped to smell the roses much this year. Not ever, really.

Well, Christmas was a week away, and I had a few weeks during winter break to have some fun. Now to work out just how much fun I truly wanted to have with a guy twice my age. I giggled as I wrapped myself in a towel and darted out of the bathroom and to my room. The answer was... plenty. I wanted to have as much as possible, and damn his age, experience, and his money. This was fate, and I was going to ride this rollercoaster out.

6

AXEL

I was an idiot. I had to be. Maybe I should get my doctor to do a psych evaluation next time I had a physical? Because this was a first for me, on so many levels.

I was standing outside a restaurant where Chastity and I decided to meet, waiting for her to arrive. This was not the way I dated. I'd pick my woman up, lavish her with attention and expensive meals, whatever she wanted. They knew the score. That nothing else was on the table except for exactly what I was offering them. A small amount of my time, fun, and sex

With Chastity... I shook my head and chuckled to myself just thinking about her and her name. How apt it was. The girl was a virgin and almost half my age. I should be running for the hills. Scrolling through my list of available lovers and picking one off the menu. I shouldn't be here, waiting, for a young woman to arrive who made me as nervous as a twenty-one-year-old, myself. It was embarrassing and stupid and—

"Hey!" Chastity's voice sounded as she walked towards me, her smile as bright as the sun.

It lit me up and reached all the dark and ignored parts of my soul. I couldn't believe she could make me feel so much. "Hey, yourself," I growled at her, grabbing her hands, and hauling her into my body.

Her arms went up around my neck and she pressed her soft breasts into me, giving me a huge rush of lust, then her lips met mine. Her taste was so sweet. So perfect.

I pressed deeper, grabbing her ass, and pulling her into the cradle of my hips while her tongue swept out to meet mine. I pulled away and stared down at her. "Damn, you burn hotter than any woman I've ever met."

She laughed and dropped her head, then did the strangest thing. She put her arms around my waist and snuggled into my chest.

I put my arms around her back and hugged her. And we stood there like stupid teenagers in love. *Whoa. Back the fuck up there. It's your first official date. Don't go falling in love with a girl who technically could be your daughter.*

"Should we go inside? You hungry?" I asked, beginning to feel even more like a fool for my over-the-top reaction to her.

Chastity pulled back and smiled again. "Starving, actually."

I stepped out of the circle of her arms entirely, tugged on my fitted shirt and grinned at her. "Let's go, then."

She nodded, then her hand slipped into mine and I was right back to where I started. With a clingy teenager who had the ridiculous skill of making me feel like a clingy teenager also.

7

AXEL

Not wanting to shake her hand off, I instead rearranged her arm, so she held my elbow instead and escorted her into the restaurant. Holding open the glass door for her, I followed her inside the most expensive restaurant this side of the city.

"This is more highbrow than I expected," Chastity whispered, staring into the dimly lit space.

I looked around and smiled. There were only about fifteen tables in total, which made it quiet and private. Add in the candlelight, soft, classical music, and expensive furnishings, and yeah... I could see why Chastity thought it was special.

"The food is amazing," I said, nodding at the maître d who recognized me who then took us to the table I'd booked. An intimate table for two in the back of the restaurant.

The maître d inclined his head and seated us.

Chastity stared at the place settings and ran her hand over the white tablecloth. "This is way too fancy for what I'm wearing."

She wore a spectacular white cotton dress. It wasn't expensive, that was obvious, but it hugged every curve and highlighted her naturally gorgeous skin and youth.

"You could be wearing a burlap sack and still be the most beautiful woman here."

Her gaze flicked to mine, and a quiver of a smile lit up her perfect mouth. "I wanna say thank you, but I don't know what a burlap sack is."

I couldn't stop the laugh that bubbled out of me. *Oh my God... the age gap. I'm an old man.* "Definitely take it as a compliment."

She grinned at me, pink coloring her cheeks. "Okay."

Our waiter approached the table. "Can I start you off with drinks and appetizers this evening?"

I glanced over at my date. "Let's order now so that we can have a conversation while we wait."

She nodded, and we got into the menu. Chastity ordered a salad, pasta, and asked if dinner included bread and that made me like her even more. She hadn't been lying about liking her food and not caring about the calories.

I'd dated women who said they weren't concerned about their weight, but their clothes, their makeup, their eating habits all belied what came out of their mouths. Actions truly spoke louder than words.

Once the waiter left after taking my order, I sat back and stared at her. "Tell me about yourself."

She shrugged and the creaminess of her skin in the candlelight once again caught my eye. "What do you wanna know?"

I inhaled deeply. "Well... may as well dive in the deep end. I feel totally out of my depth with you anyway, so—"

She laughed and interrupted me. "I doubt that very much."

I held up my hand. "See? Even that. I don't remember the last time anyone interrupted me." Not my family, not my friends, certainly not my work colleagues.

She giggled and reached for her glass of water as the waiter delivered our salads. "Sorry. What did you want to dive into?"

I raised an eyebrow at her as I hesitated a few seconds until he left the table. "I want to dive into you... but that's not on the table at the moment."

She burst out laughing, chuckling so loudly everyone around us started to stare.

But I didn't worry about their looks. Instead, I found myself puffing up my chest in pride, since I was the one sitting there with such a beautiful young woman.

When she finally stopped laughing, she ended up taking another gulp of water and wiping the tears from her eyes. "You're relentless, aren't you?" She tucked into her salad, obviously enjoying it, if the expression on her face was anything to judge by.

I nodded, sobering. She had no idea. "Yes, I am. You should know that. It's part of what makes me successful." The greens I started to chew didn't affect me the same way. Chastity was my sole focus.

She nodded, smiling brightly. "I must admit I've been told I'm the same. No one thought I'd get into college, and now chiropractic school. Being stubborn and relentless regarding things that are important, is... well, important."

I nodded at her. I'd never heard anyone so young speak so maturely. "Absolutely."

Our main courses were served a few minutes later and the waiter poured us a glass of red wine each.

Chastity took a sip, then picked up her fork, digging into her gnocchi with a satisfied groan. "God, this is delicious!"

"Told you the food was amazing."

She sprinkled parmesan cheese over her dish then raised her eyes to mine again, "You still haven't told me what you wanted to dive into."

I picked up my knife and fork to start on my filet, deciding to once again jump in the deep end and start the conversation with the only topic I had any interest in. "I want to know why you're still a virgin."

8

CHASTITY

I reached over and picked up my glass of red wine, taking a slow sip before setting it back down again. I was thrilled that I did it without spilling a drop, though I barely tasted the alcohol as I swallowed it down.

Could he have possibly chosen a more embarrassing topic? *Because he's a horny man! Why else?* "Uh, why?"

He cut into his steak and chewed, appearing thoughtful. "What do you mean why? It's a pretty important question, I think."

I shrugged. "It's not that interesting."

His eyes gleamed as he ate, and I wondered what he was thinking but was afraid to ask. He'd probably tell me sooner rather than later. The guy didn't exactly have any shame.

May as well tell him the truth. "Well... I suppose I never met anyone I wanted to go to bed with."

Axel gave me a look that reminded me of a principal who wasn't impressed with his student. "I find that very difficult to believe."

I reached for the wine again, this time taking a longer sip and enjoying the foreign taste and slight burn. "Well, look. I've never really over-analyzed it, but it probably has something to do with my parents."

"How so? Are they extremely religious or something?"

I laughed at that. "Hardly! No, it was just... they got pregnant with me when they were young, and it wrecked a lot of things for them. Dad didn't get to finish college, and neither of them ever married again or had any other kids. I just feel like... you shouldn't have sex with someone unless you're willing to pay the ultimate price of that mistake."

When I saw Axel's gaze become shuttered and his head bent to focus on his food, I knew I'd said too much.

I rushed to reassure him. "I didn't mean it like that."

"Like what?" he asked.

"Like... that I won't have sex with you unless you're willing to have a baby with me. That just sounds crazy."

Axel picked up his own wine glass, his eyes shimmering with an intensity I couldn't quite make out. "What do you mean then?"

I sighed. "Look. I take sex seriously because it's something serious. The consequences can be extreme in some cases. And I'm not an irresponsible person. I'm sorry if you find that a turn-off." I set my glass down and pushed my unfinished meal forward. Why did every conversation with this guy turn into something uncomfortable?

"I think we need to get out of here," Axel said suddenly.

I glanced up. "Are you serious?"

He nodded, "Just for a minute. Would you come outside with me?"

I nodded, my face heating with shame. What the hell was wrong with me? Why did I have to be so fucking honest all the time? I could have just said that all the guys at school were creeps, and I was waiting for someone who at least turned me on enough to part with my virginity.

I stood up and heard Axel say to one of the staff, "We're just stepping out for a moment, we'll be back in a few minutes."

Then he set his hand on the small of my lower back and escorted me out of the restaurant and around the corner.

9

CHASTITY

"I'm sorry... really..." I began to explain, but as soon as we'd stepped into the alley next to the restaurant and no one could see us anymore, Axel was pushing me up against the brick wall, his delicious body pressing into mine.

"Do you know how fucking hot you are?" Axel ground out, his lips speaking directly into my ear.

He slid his hand up my ribcage, grazing my breasts, then moving up my neck until he gripped my jaw and held my head in his hands.

I swallowed hard, feeling trapped. Possessed. And in need. "I thought you didn't like what I said," I whispered back.

He groaned aloud this time and thrust his body against mine. "A part of me didn't. That educated, damaged, hardened part of me that's been screwed over by women time and time again is telling me that this is just a game you're playing. That you're really saying that if I take your virginity, then I owe you. Marriage, children, money—whatever it is that you really want."

Tears sprang to my eyes, and I swallowed hard before I could speak again. "That's not true. You're the one chasing me, not the other way around."

"I know," Axel said into my ear. "And if you can't feel how much I want you, then something's wrong."

He thrust his hips against me again, and heat unfurled inside my belly. Oh, I could feel it. The hard-on was obvious.

"Then how come—"

"Because that's only one voice in my head. The other part of me, and the part that I'm more inclined to listen to at the moment, loves the fact that you are so fucking honest. And sincere. And responsible, and unlike any other woman I've ever known."

I nodded, not sure what to say but hoping he'd keep talking.

Axel pressed closer, sliding his thigh between mine and pressing on my clit with perfect precision.

I gasped and grabbed for him, wanting to thrust back against him but afraid of setting fire to my panties in the process. "Then why..."

"Why, what?" he repeated. "Why don't I just take you home and fuck you right now? I'd love to, as you can tell."

"No. Why did you seem so angry inside?" I whispered, turning my face closer to his, needing to be kissed.

He pulled back slightly so that I could see his eyes and he stared at me. "I'm not angry with you, I'm intrigued by you. I'm confused by you, but I'm not angry."

"But why—"

He kissed me so hard and fiercely; I lost my breath.

Then I was kissing him back with all the pent-up passion in my soul. I thrust my tongue into his mouth and opened my mouth for him to kiss me deeper.

He held my face and I grabbed at his waist, wanting him naked, wanting to touch his skin. Then he stepped away from me, and he was breathing like he'd just run a marathon. His hair was disheveled as he ran his hand through it, and my mouth felt swollen and bruised. He stumbled back another step. "Damn woman, what are you doing to me?"

I took his question to be rhetorical because I didn't have an answer for him.

"I just want to ravage you... you have no idea."

I did have some idea. My panties were soaked, and my heart was thumping in my chest. I wanted him so much it shocked me. "I'll go home with you tonight, if you still want me to."

Axel stared at me, his eyes blazing with heat. Then he stepped back into the darkness with me and kissed me again.

10

AXEL

I kissed her gently this time. Sipped from her lips as though drinking a fine wine. I had to calm the fuck down. She'd just offered to come home with me, and I knew what that meant. She was offering me her virginity, which I couldn't just take.

She'd waited this long for a reason. She'd hadn't thrown it at her high school sweetheart, nor fallen into bed with some drunken frat boy at school. She'd wanted her first time to be special, and I needed to work out how serious I was about this girl before I took something from her, I couldn't give back.

I drew back and stared down into her dazed eyes, then slowly pulled right back. "Should we go back in and finish our dinner?"

She nodded and I reached out and took her hand. She intertwined our fingers, and we walked back into the restaurant, finished our main courses, then moved onto dessert.

We avoided any heavy topics, talking only about college and travel. She had done practically none, so I told her about Paris, Italy, and Spain. We chatted and laughed, ate our decadent desserts, and I couldn't remember feeling so happy in a long time.

When I'd paid we walked out into the cool night air. "So, what are your plans this week?" I asked as we moved towards my car.

"Nothing much," she said. "I'm on Christmas break for a couple of weeks, so I'll just alternate between Mom and Dad's places, see some friends, then it's back to school for my final semester."

So, I only had a few weeks with her before she disappeared forever. "Do you want to go out tomorrow? Maybe we could try the beach and ice cream date again?"

She grinned. "I'd love that, but what about tonight?"

Her eyes were so big and hopeful, I knew I had to be extremely cautious about how I said this. The last thing I wanted was for her to feel rejected.

"I think tonight I should take you home..."

Her face fell like I'd kicked her puppy.

I gently grabbed her chin and tilted her face so she could look into my eyes as I spoke. "Listen to me, beautiful girl. I want to get to know you, and I want you to get to know me. If I take you to my bed, I never want you to regret it."

"I wouldn't," she assured me, shaking her head.

"You would if the next day we decided to end it, wouldn't you?"

She bit her trembling lip, then nodded suddenly. "Yes."

"So before either of us commits to this any further, let's hang out a bit more, okay?"

"Okay," she whispered.

"Hey," I said to her, needing her to understand. "I'm not saying no. I'm just saying not yet. We have two weeks before you head back to college, yeah?"

She nodded.

I grinned at her. "Do you think I'm worth waiting two weeks for?"

The question should have been ridiculous but instead, she pouted. "Don't wait the whole two weeks, because then we won't have more than one or two times. I'd rather we start sooner so I can get good at it."

I groaned and pressed her into the wall. "Fucking hell, beautiful. You'd test the patience of a saint. Maybe taking you back to my place wouldn't be such a bad idea."

When her face lit up, I knew I'd said the right thing. *Fuck.* "But we are not having sex, got it?"

"Everything else, though?" she asked, throwing her arms around my neck, and clinging tightly to me.

Oh my God. I don't have the strength for that.

I nodded. I'd keep my pants on. That would be the only way to make sure that I didn't take her. Though, even that was going to be pure torture. Penance for the sins of my past. Would she like my fingers? Or my mouth on her pussy more? Or would she only come on my cock?

Heat flushed over my whole body, making my face burn and my cock throb, and by the time I'd gotten her into my car, I was going out of my mind wondering how she'd look stretched out on the bed beneath me.

I grabbed her hand and tugged her away from the alley. "Time to go."

"How far is your place?" Chastity asked as we took off in my car.

I reached over for her thigh, gripping her warm skin, and squeezing gently. "Not far. Ten minutes, maybe."

She shivered and clung to my hand as we drove.

We didn't speak, and it only built the tension higher. Tighter.

How was this the same girl who'd rejected my advances yesterday? Had so much changed between us that she was now willing to jump into bed with me?

I glanced across at her, afraid to speak in case I broke the unbearable tension aching between us, but I had to know.

"Why now?" I put on my signal and turned on to my street.

"What do you mean?" she asked, glancing across at me.

"Yesterday you were horrified by my suggestion we should go to my place. What changed your mind?"

She glanced out the window, then back at me. "Well... I think it's the fact that I've never wanted anyone the way I want you. And I always promised myself that if I felt this way, I'd go for it, and I wouldn't let fear hold me back."

A strange lump formed in my throat. The trust she was offering me was insane. "Thank you."

She grinned at me. "Don't thank me yet, I haven't done anything worthy of it. Not so far, anyway."

My cock throbbed at the mere mention of what was to come.

11

AXEL

I drove into the parking lot and pulled into my spot. "We're here."

She nodded. "Okay." She opened her door and got out of the car before I was able to get around the hood to her. She shivered in the cool air of the parking lot. "I know this is all swanky and nice, but don't you ever want to live in a house?"

I locked the car, wrapped my arm around her and hustled her over to the elevators. "A house? As in..."

She laughed. "As in a house. With land around it. A fence. A backyard."

"In the suburbs?" I asked. "Not really."

When the elevator doors opened, I hustled her inside and we rode up to the top floor of the building.

"The penthouse? Really?" she asked, gaping when she stepped out of the elevator and straight into my apartment. "This is unbelievable." She walked around the open plan living area with the huge leather couches and high-end, modern kitchen.

"It's just an apartment."

"Really?" she asked, her eyes wide and disbelieving.

"If you don't like it, we can go to another one. There's a few vacant."

"And you own all of them, I guess?" she asked, her tone teasing.

I didn't respond because the problem was, I did own them all. I'd built them.

Her gaze snapped to mine, then her mouth dropped open. "You're kidding me?"

I shrugged. "Told you I was rich."

She groaned and covered her eyes with both hands so she couldn't see me anymore. "What am I doing? You are so out of my league."

I laughed at her and tugged at my tie. It was time to get naked. "Not tonight, I'm not."

Dropping the tie to the floor, I slowly unbuttoned my shirt, not breaking eye contact with her the entire time.

She licked her lips as I tugged my shirt off and tossed it over the nearest couch.

The way she looked at me with eyes as big as saucers and yet with a hunger that was so honest and pure was like a gut punch of the best kind. My breathing became ragged. I kicked off my shoes, then stopped undressing. My control in bed was superb, but I could already tell this girl was going to be the death of me.

She watched me walk towards her, her gaze scanning me like she'd never seen a half-naked man before. And she probably hadn't.

"Like what you see?" I asked, reaching for her, and pulling her into my arms.

Chastity's hands went straight to my chest, laying her hot little palms against my pecs. She grinned at me. "You know you're gorgeous. You must get told that all the time."

I did, and it meant nothing to me. I grabbed her ass and pulled her into the cradle of my hips, wanting her as close as possible. "I want you to want me, Chastity. I don't give a flying fuck about what anyone else thinks. What do you think?"

She giggled and pressed her lips to the base of my throat. A groan escaped me as she whispered, "I think you're the most beautiful man I've ever seen."

Well, what was a man to do when a woman said something like that? I swept her up into my arms, ignoring the squeal that echoed through the living room, and walked her down the hall to my bedroom.

"Where are we going?" she asked, grabbing tightly to my neck.

"My room." Enough talking for the moment. I took her lips in a kiss to keep the fire burning between us. It had been a very long time since I was with a woman as inexperienced as Chastity. Probably twenty years. I set her on her feet, so she was soon standing in front of me again. "Your turn."

"My turn?" she repeated, her eyebrows raised in silent question.

I nodded and slid back until I hit the end of my king size bed and sat down on the luxury mattress. "Yes. Your turn to strip. Show me that gorgeous body of yours."

She covered her face with her hands as though embarrassed.

I waited because I was convinced that she would do it if I waited long enough.

Eventually her hands came down and she took a deep, steadying breath. "Okay." She started to unbutton her cotton dress, one slow button at a time.

I wanted to reach forward and yank the thing off her, but instead I leaned back on my hands and watched the butterfly emerge.

Chastity looked down at her feet as she slipped the dress off her shoulders, then flicked off her white sandals and stood in the middle of my bedroom in only her underwear.

There's a joke that goes, "If you get a woman naked and she's wearing sexy, matching underwear, then sex was her idea, not yours." Well, beneath her gorgeous cotton dress, Chastity wore the most perfectly virginal set of matching lace panties and bra.

And the fact that she may have planned for the night to go exactly as it was about to go wasn't a turn-off. In fact, it made me want her even more.

12

CHASTITY

I was quivering, quite literally, standing in the biggest bedroom I'd ever seen, in my underwear. I'd worn the nicest bra and panties I owned, and they felt as odd and uncomfortable as a thong up my butt. I wanted to take them off. Now. I took a step towards Axel where he sat on the bed, his hot gaze on my body. He was the sexiest man I'd ever seen, leaning back on his arms, displaying his chiseled chest and arms for me to see.

He seemed completely unaffected by what we were doing, whereas inside my belly, I was a quaking mess. Taking another step closer, I moved between his spread legs.

He sat up, putting his hands on the sides of my thighs, running his warm palms up to my ass.

Setting my hands on his shoulders and staring down into his dark eyes, I forced myself to breathe. To not freak out. I was finally here. With a man I lusted after so much I wanted to go to bed with him. For a moment I wondered how he felt about me then quickly dismissed that thought. The only thing I ever wanted for myself was to not regret my first time, nor the person it was with. And with Axel, I knew it would be perfect.

He grabbed my ass tighter with his hands and I leaned down to kiss him, moaning as he lifted his head and met me halfway.

I kissed him, loving the way his strong lips met mine, then he took over the kiss, pressing my lips apart and tasting me with his tongue. The need to get closer took over. I pulled back and lifted my legs to either side of him so that I could straddle him and wrapped my arms and legs around him.

He grinned like he'd won the lottery and wrapped his arms around my body, taking my mouth in another kiss.

This went on and on, his hands roaming all over my body. He cupped my ass, then moved around to my breasts, tweaking my nipples, and teasing my skin with long touches until I was wiggling and thrusting against him, anxious for a deeper touch.

He spun us around and I ended up on my back, him between my thighs, bearing me down.

This was exactly what I needed.

He moved down and away, then stood up.

I got up on my elbows, wanting him back down on top of me. "I hope you're not planning on stopping there?"

He shook his head, the cheekiest grin on his lips. "Hardly. I just want you comfortable, so how 'bout you shuffle up and put your head on the pillow?"

I nodded and did exactly what he suggested, scooting up the middle of the huge bed until my head rested on a pillow and all I could hear in the room was the thud of my heartbeat in my ears.

He prowled across the bed towards me, but instead of laying back down over me like I was hoping, he reached out and grabbed my panties by the waistband.

"These are sweet, but I'd rather see what's underneath," he said, a deep growl beneath the words making me shiver.

My comfort level was faltering. In fact, I opened my mouth to ask him to turn the lights off, but I silenced that insecurity with an internal whack, swallowing down the protest. Instead, I lifted my hips and let him pull my panties down over my hips and thighs, then lifted my feet as he pulled them off completely and tossed them over his should in a totally slick move. "Done that a few times before, have you?" I asked, then instantly wanted to slap myself in the forehead. "I'm sorry... no, don't answer that."

He grinned and didn't say anything, which niggled in the back of my head. But then again, would I really want some forty-year-old virgin introducing me to the pleasures of the flesh? Probably not. I forced myself to concentrate not on Axel's past but instead, our mutual future.

He slid down onto his muscled abdomen and crawled up over me, kissing my lips then my neck, groaning in my ear. "God... you feel so good."

Then he was gone again, trailing kisses down my chest, over my belly and between my legs. *Oh, shit!* I reached down to grab hold of his hair, to drag him back up and away from there.

But he didn't move as I tugged at him. Instead, he pushed my thighs apart and licked me.

Pleasure shot through me unlike anything I'd ever felt. Then he did it again, and I fell back on a moan. "Oh my God." I felt more than heard him chuckle as he pushed my thighs apart, and this time I let him.

He kissed the inside of my thighs, the fluttering of his tongue over my clit very much like a butterfly.

I gasped and moaned, then covered my mouth with both of my hands to smother all the embarrassing noises. But Axel didn't stop. Instead, he added his hands into the pleasuring mix and slid a long finger up inside me, making me scream out.

But I didn't want him to stop. No... I *needed* him to keep going. Keep feeding this flame of passion inside of me.

Axel drove his finger up inside me over and over again, mimicking the action I assumed his cock would one day make.

"Ahhh!" I called out as my stomach tightened and my legs

began to tingle. I was going to orgasm, and I'd never done it with another person in the room before. I didn't know how to let go, how to do this.

Then Axel looked up and grinned at me. "You going to come for me soon?"

I nodded and he dropped his head, suckling on my clit and stroking those places inside of me no one had ever touched before. I crested up to that pleasure palace, then fell again. Everything tightened inside of me and released. I groaned in frustration, unable to hit that elusive level of ecstasy.

But Axel didn't stop. Instead, he seemed to add another finger, stretching me and thrusting in and out of me. His tongue was magic, working over my clit until finally... finally... my legs tightened.

I grabbed for his head and held on tight as my pleasure crested and crashed, and everything went silent and still and tight. And then I was shaking, and coming all over his hand and face, unable to stop the moans or sobs coming from my own mouth.

When it was over and I was left as nothing more than a shivering pile of jelly on his bed, Axel slid up the mattress and pulled me into his arms, my head on his chest, and his arms around me.

I closed my eyes and listened to his heart beating, feeling his warmth around me, and I went to sleep.

13

AXEL

I ran my hand down Chastity's body, enjoying the softness and the sheer lushness of her curves. God, she was so damn hot. And not in a way I normally experienced. She was so honest about her passion. Guileless. She wasn't trying to be sexy; she just was. She wasn't trying to impress me, she was just...Chastity. And she was perfect.

I glanced down at her face where she rested on my chest, surprised she wasn't complaining about the beating of my heart. It must sound like a jackhammer beneath her ear. Pushing back her hair from her face, I glanced down at her again to see her eyes closed and her mouth slightly open, and I had to stop myself from laughing aloud. She was asleep!

The urge to laugh was strong, but I didn't want to wake her. Instead, I'd lie here with throbbing blue balls. A laugh stuck in my stomach, making me gasp for breath. Fuck, she was funny. I lifted my hand and stroked her hair again, closing my own eyes for a moment. I never slept next to the women I had sex with. I had a separate bedroom exactly for this situation.

Sleeping next to those hook-ups was an uncomfortable

complication I didn't need. Not to mention I couldn't get a decent night's sleep. I'd tried several times before, and it always ended the same way. With me getting up at four a.m. because I'd barely slept a wink.

My routine was consistent. I'd get up, take a shower, say good night, and settle into my guest bedroom. I wasn't rude enough to ask them to leave. They were always blissed out and comfortable, so I just left them there.

But this was nice. I didn't feel that urgent need to climb out of the bed and run to the shower. I felt content, considering nothing had happened for me except pleasuring Chastity. And, God, had that been amazingly hot. Incredible, actually.

Smiling, I relaxed into the pillow, letting myself enjoy the feeling of her sleeping on me for a minute. I promised myself I'd get up and move soon, but for the moment I wasn't going anywhere.

WHEN I WOKE up in the morning, I was confused. I was lying on my side, the blankets covering me, and in my arms was Chastity. My arm was wrapped around her waist, and her naked body was pressed against me. I froze. How on earth had that happened? Surely, it couldn't be morning. I must have just dozed off for a few hours, and the light in the room was coming from the bathroom or something.

I lifted my head and looked across Chastity's naked shoulder and peered at my alarm clock—six forty-nine a.m. *No way.* I let my head fall back onto the pillow, an avalanche of emotions pummeling my system. What did this mean? Surely, it was just a mistake. A coincidence. This couldn't be the woman I was meant to be with. It was impossible. She had her whole life ahead of her. School. Travel. Work. Kids.

I'd done it all already, except for the marriage and kids part. I'd skipped that intentionally, and I wasn't sure it was a life goal I had anymore. I lifted my arms from her warm flesh and slowly rolled away.

Part of me had always thought that the woman I could sleep next to all night would be the woman destined to be my wife. After all, for me, being able to sleep next to a woman meant I trusted her. It meant that I was safe to relax around her. And that had—literally— never happened with another woman.

I grabbed my cell phone and moved to the bathroom, scrolling through my hundreds of emails, texts and messages. It was Monday and I had to work today. In fact, I was already late for my training session at the gym.

I went to the toilet and jumped in the shower, scrubbing myself clean. What was I going to say to her this morning? I had no idea. I couldn't give her my normal "Thanks, see you around" speech. For one thing, I hadn't had enough of her yet. Yes... yes... that was it.

This uncomfortable feeling was only because I hadn't fucked her yet. Once I did—well, maybe more than once—I'd feel better. As though I could let her go and not look back. The feeling of being out of my depth was unusual. It didn't happen in business, and certainly not in my personal life.

The bathroom door opened, and Chastity suddenly walked in. The cotton dress she'd worn last night had been donned again, and I felt an instant kick of disappointment that she'd covered herself up.

I poured some shampoo into my hand and started scrubbing my hair. "Take your dress off and jump in. I'm sure you could use a shower after last night."

She wrapped her arms around her torso self-consciously and stared at the tiles on the floor. "I am so sorry about last night. About falling asleep. I can't believe I did that."

I laughed. "It was a compliment, don't worry. I was glad that I could pleasure you like that."

Her head came up and she stared at me as though assessing my honesty. Then a small smile curled up her lips. "Well, I owe you an orgasm."

I burst out laughing. Damn, she was refreshing. So honest. So open.

"Deal," I said, gesturing to her again. "You sure you don't want to join me?"

She shook her head. "No. I've gotta get home, actually. My mom and I have plans today, so I better run."

That was usually my line—not the part about parental commitments—but I was definitely the one who would normally be running in the opposite direction after a one-night stand.

"Well, when am I going to see you again?" I persisted, walking over to the open doorway in my shower.

Chastity's eyes ran greedily over my naked body, lingering on my cock so long that I started to thicken and harden in response. She took a step backwards and her gaze flicked up to mine. "Um... when do you want to see me again?"

"Tonight?" I asked, mentally screaming at myself to stop plowing forward so hard at this woman. I was acting like a bull in a China shop.

Then she smiled, and I forgot why I was trying to play it cool. "Okay. I'd love to."

"So, I'll pick you up?" I asked, trying to remember what I had planned tonight. Nothing I couldn't reschedule, I hoped.

She nodded. "Okay. But I'll be at my mom's place, which is about twenty minutes from here."

"I think I can manage that," I said. "Dinner?"

She chewed on her lips. "Uh... I think Mom wants to have dinner and celebrate my getting into Sherman. How about drinks after?"

I crossed my arms over my chest, loving the way her gaze kept wandering over my body. "Sure. I'll pick you up around nine, nine-thirty. Can you text me the address?" That would give me enough time to finish whatever work I needed to get done today.

"Sure."

"Do you need a lift home?" I asked, glancing at my watch. I needed to get moving.

"I'm fine. I called for an Uber already." She nodded and opened the door further so she could leave. "Thank you for last night. It was amazing on so many levels. I didn't know I could feel like that."

I walked across the bathroom tiles and cupped her face. "That's only the beginning, beautiful girl." I kissed her goodbye and she fled, leaving me with a raging hard-on and a head filled with excitement for what the night would bring.

14

AXEL

I'd had one hell of a day and when I'd finally scarfed some dinner down, the last thing I'd wanted to do was get back in the car and drive out to the suburbs to pick up my date. But this wasn't just any date, it was Chastity, so I'd hauled myself into the shower, put on a fresh shirt and black jeans, and got in the car.

If it had been any other woman, I would have delayed. But instead, I pulled out my cell phone and sent a text apologizing for being late. I wanted to see her, and even after a shit day, I still wanted to. That said a lot about how much I was beginning to like her. A fact I both found amazing and wanted to ignore.

I pulled up outside a tiny little cottage about twenty minutes out of the city and sighed. I was tired of working so fucking hard every day. Success and enough money to have a comfortable life were always the goal, and now I was missing out on a lot of the "life" side of things. It was probably time to look at my business structure again. See what I could back off.

I got out of my sports car and walked up to the door, texting Chastity as I went.

The red door opened, and behind it stood a woman about forty.

My age.

She had shoulder-length blonde hair and lines around her eyes that spoke of stress and hard work.

"Hi. I'm—"

"Axel. Yes, I know," Chastity's mom said, interrupting me.

I grinned at her. She obviously hadn't gotten the memo that people didn't interrupt billionaires. And I liked the fact that she hadn't. "Yes, that's me."

"I'm Katherine," she said, holding the door open, but not inviting me in. "Chastity! He's here!"

I almost laughed but didn't. The tone spoke of long-suffering, though I don't know what she would have suffered with a good girl like Chastity as her daughter.

Then Katherine turned to me, her gaze narrowing in an assessing look I'd seen too often on her daughter's face. "Do I know you from somewhere?"

I looked at her again, something niggling in the back of my head as well. "I was actually going to ask you the same thing. You look familiar to me."

Katherine nodded. "Me, too. But I doubt we've ever hung out in the same circles."

I nodded and hummed in agreement. She was probably right. A single mother who hadn't gone to college. Not the type of woman I would have dated, thank God. Because that would have been awkward as hell.

There was something strangely familiar about her, though. I felt like I'd seen her before, when she was younger. Or maybe I was just confusing that thought with how much she looked like Chastity? Weird.

"Hey!" Chastity suddenly stuck her head in the doorway, her hair freshly styled and her face full of makeup.

I blinked. "Wow. I don't think I've ever seen you so done up."

Her mom growled. "That's what happens when she spends too much time at her father's. She forgets how to be a girl."

I reached out a hand to her, and she took it. "I kind of like you better natural." And I did. The makeup added years to her face. She had such beautiful, clear skin beneath the foundation. It seemed strange to me that her mother would try to hide that.

"Thanks." Chastity said, beaming up at me. "Give me two seconds." She squeezed my hand, then raced off, back into the house, leaving me standing on the doorstep with her mother. Again.

"I might wait in the car," I said, nodding to her. "It was nice to meet you."

She gave me half a smile in return. "It was nice to meet you too... and I'm sure it'll come to me when you leave where I've seen you."

"Good night," I said in return and fled to the car.

People tended to say that if you looked at the mother, that was who your woman would turn into in twenty years' time, but I wasn't sure I believed that. Katherine had an edge to her that I hoped Chastity would never develop. It spoke of heartbreak and disappointment.

When I got to the car, I turned around just in time to see Chastity kiss her mom on the cheek, and with a bag now casually hanging over her shoulder, she came running at me. I held out my arms and laughed as she jumped into them, hugging me tightly. I didn't lift my gaze to look at her mom, though I could feel the heat of her stare boring down into me. "Shall we go?" I asked.

"Yes!"

I held the door open as she climbed into the passenger side.

Once I'd shut the door, I waved to her stony-faced mother and jogged around the car to get into the driver's seat.

Once inside the car I glanced at her face again, relieved to see her fresh, bright face once more. "You got rid of the makeup," I said, turning on the ignition.

She grinned. "Hell, yeah. I hate that crap."

"Then why wear it?" I asked, pulling into traffic, and sliding my hand over her bare thigh. She wore a denim mini skirt and a white tank top. Extremely causal and too sexy by half.

"Because my mom kinda makes me." She shrugged. "She likes me to dress up if we go out, and since we went out for dinner, it was expected."

I nodded, not sure how to broach that one. "Are you and your mom close?"

She sighed. "I know what you're thinking."

"No, you don't," I said, turning the car onto the main road.

"I do. You think she seems like a bit of a bitch, and I suppose to some people, she can be. But she's been a good mom."

I nodded. "That's great, I'm glad you had her. But, yeah, she does have an edge to her that I didn't expect. You're so relaxed and open."

She laughed. "That's because I'm more like my dad. You'd like him, I think. He's fit, like you. And funny. He doesn't take life too seriously."

I grinned. "Definitely sounds like my kind of guy."

And considering how old he'd be, I didn't really want to think about it. I'd always assumed my father-in-law would be at least twenty years older than me. If this relationship got to that point, that was not going to be the case.

I shook myself and took my hand off her thigh and put both hands on the steering wheel. *Fucking hell. Father-in-law? Seriously? Get your head in the game and out of the clouds.*

"So, what are we doing tonight?" Chastity asked.

"Anything you want." I said, grinning at her. "I was thinking we could have a few drinks, then back to my place maybe?"

She reached over and ran her hand over my denim clad thigh. "I think that's an awesome idea."

Blood throbbed in the lower regions of my body, and I groaned. "Now I want to pull over and ravish you in the car."

Chastity looked up and down and around the car, then sat back and laughed. "Uh... yeah... no. This car was not meant for ravishment."

I chuckled at that. I wasn't going to tell her that the seats reclined and if she got on top, I was pretty sure we could manage it. Because if I did, the cheeky girl would want to know how I knew that, and I wasn't telling the truth about that, either. "You're right," I admitted. "My bed would be a lot more comfortable." So, I focused on getting us back to my apartment.

We passed a busy area of exclusive, boutique shops and I slowed down. "There are some nice bars around here. How about we grab a cocktail or something before we go home?"

Every woman I'd ever met would have agreed to that. This part of the city was ritzy and expensive, and she would have jumped at the chance to get free drinks and be seen on my arm. I was photographed regularly around here, unfortunately, and the gold-diggers loved that sort of publicity.

So, when she screwed up her face and said, "No thank you," I was shocked. And that was an understatement.

"You sure?" I asked again.

She slid her hand over my thigh. "The only cocktail I want is in this car. Are you going to let me drink that one?"

I glanced over at her face, and she looked utterly serious.

Heading to my building, I pulled the car into my parking lot and didn't utter a word until I'd parked in my reserved spot, turned off the car and twisted around in my seat to look at her.

Had she just said what I thought she said? "Um... could you repeat that please?"

Her eyes lit up with mischief before she glanced down at where her hand still lay on my thigh. "I was hoping you'd let me play with you tonight, like you did with me on Sunday night."

I swallowed hard. Part of me was excited that she wanted to play with my body at all, but another part of me didn't like the idea that she wanted to take over the evening's activities. I'd been hoping for a repeat of the other night, minus her passing out. "You'll need to be specific here," I said, licking my lips. "My imagination is spiraling out of control."

She flicked her gaze up to mine and smiled shyly. "You gave me the most incredible night, and I want to return the favor. Teach me what you like."

"So... you don't want to have sex tonight, then?" I asked. "You want to just play some more?" I was feeling totally out of my depth once again, a feeling I was beginning to uniquely pair with Chastity.

"If you don't mind waiting a little longer?" she asked, her tone hopeful. "There's no rush, is there?"

I took a long breath, then shook my head. "No, of course not."

"Good," she said, grinning now. "So, let's go upstairs and you can show me all the things you like, and what you want me to do to your body." She opened the door and hopped out of the car, but I was frozen in place.

She wanted to give to me? Since when did that happen? I shook my head and joined her in the parking lot.

We walked over to the elevator and made our way up to the penthouse, where I was about to give a lesson, I never thought I'd give. This girl was going to be the death of me, I was sure of it.

15

CHASTITY

I could tell I'd shocked him, which had been the plan. The man obviously didn't have enough joy in his life, and he deserved to be spoiled. I shook my head at my own thoughts. Of course, he was already spoiled. Or was, if you asked anyone with eyes. And yet, I had the feeling that he wasn't spoiled in the way I planned. I wanted to give to him and receive absolutely nothing in return other than the pure happiness that would come from seeing him fulfilled.

He'd given so selflessly to me last night, I intended to return the favor. In truth I wanted to see him lose his mind with pleasure, wanted to see him lose control. This guy had way too much control over his body, his food, his business, his life. And honestly, he seemed to lack fun despite the wealth, the women, and the toys.

The elevator took us up to his expensive apartment and as we walked into the room, my breath caught in my throat, excitement filling me up.

"A drink first?" he asked, leading me into his plush living room. "Or..."

I took his hand and tugged him towards the bedroom. "I think I choose the or option." He chuckled as he let me pull him into his bedroom and shut the door. Not that I thought anyone would walk in on us, but I wanted him to stay and not leave me. "You're going to have to tell me what you like," I said, forcing myself to speak through the nerves that closed off my throat. I had butterflies the size of elephants flapping around in my belly. "Because I literally have no idea what I'm doing."

I reached for the buttons on his fitted blue shirt and slowly began pushing them through the holes. I heard him inhale, and a similar gasp caught in my own throat. He didn't answer my question, so I didn't stop with my unbuttoning. I just kept my gaze and my focus on the buttons in front of me.

Another one popped through, then another one, revealing his gorgeous body. A body that he obviously worked very hard at, because the muscles beneath the shirt were not ordinary muscles. They were simply perfect. "God, you're a masterpiece," I whispered as the shirt slid to the floor and I was able to run my hands over his smooth, warm skin. His huge pecs, his thick arms.

He hissed as I stroked his abs, dipping my fingers into the grooves between each of his muscles. The man was so defined, he was breathtaking.

I sighed happily and enjoyed the luxury of the time he was affording me. Being able to just touch him. No rushing forward to the next step. I glanced up at him through my eyelashes and found him staring down at me. "Is this, okay?" I asked.

He jerked out a nod.

"What's wrong?" I asked, not sure if I should continue with my seduction or not.

"I have no idea what we're doing," he bit out, sounding angry.

My arms fell. "I just wanted to pleasure you."

He grabbed for me, dragging me closer against his body, and that's when I felt his erection digging into my stomach.

At least he's turned on.

"I want to take you to bed," Axel purred into my ear. "I want you to come all over me again."

I groaned. *Damn it. Why did he have to make this so difficult?*

I pulled back and stared at him. "You're not used to being told "no," are you?"

He stopped growling and grabbing at me, then his arms dropped away as though I'd offended him. "Uh..."

I took his hand in mine again and led him to the bed. "I want you to teach me everything you like. How to touch you. How to kiss you. Everything." *How to lick you and suck you,* though I couldn't say it aloud. I swallowed hard against the insecurities that rose. "Unless me being so inexperienced is a turn-off and you don't want to teach me."

"No, no, no. That's not it. I just..." Axel sighed and lifted a hand to run his fingers through his hair.

His muscles flexed and bulged with the movement, and I groaned as I wrapped my arms around his torso and pressed my lips to his bare chest. "Damn, you're gorgeous," I said against his skin, kissing him.

He sighed and cupped my face, tilting my chin so I looked up at him. "You're going to drive me to distraction. I'm not sixteen anymore." He paused, and I waited. "But if you really want to do this, Chastity... then, yeah. I can teach you."

I almost clapped with joy but restrained myself. Most likely the juvenile move would probably kill the mood.

I mock frowned at him. "Then please, get naked."

Stepping back in an obvious move to watch him, his jaw practically dropped open. I loved it. The man I'd met in the gym a few days ago had been ultra-confident about who he was and in the appeal of his body. But the man who stood before me now didn't grin or smirk. He stared at me with an intensity that made my breath catch in my throat. There was true vulnerability in his eyes, and beneath that was the man I really wanted to know.

"Please?" I whispered, begging now.

He finally moved, with sharp, jerky movements. Reaching down, he undid his belt, then unbuttoned his black jeans with a flick of his wrist. "You get naked too," he growled.

Not quite sure that was a good idea, I decided I'd meet him halfway. "Well... last night you kept your pants on." I pushed my denim skirt to the ground. My panties would stay on, but it would be amazing to be almost naked with him.

"More," he demanded, and I laughed.

So impatient.

I pulled my tank top over my head, and his eyes flared with lust. Feeling confident now, I unclipped my bra and let everything fall around me. The panties stayed on, though. There was no way I could part with them tonight. This was meant to be about his pleasure, not mine, and I was one hundred percent positive that if I took them off, we'd be going all the way.

Axel continued to stare at me, and my nipples tightened and tingled under his gaze.

I didn't cover up, though I was tempted. Everything about this man made me nervous and insecure and excited all at once. But the other night had proven to me that he found my curvy body attractive, so I flicked my hair over my shoulder and lifted my chin.

Another growl sounded, and this time I got to watch him kick out of his shoes and socks, then push his jeans to the floor and stand up again. He was as naked and as glorious as the morning I'd seen him in the shower. But this time, I wasn't running off home, I was here to devour him.

I dropped to my knees and crawled over to him on the plush carpet, wanting to pleasure him in a way I'd heard of, and even seen in X-rated movies but never actually done. When I came close to him, I pushed up and knelt before him, staring at his cock and swallowing hard. Damn, it was getting bigger by the second. I put my hands on his thighs, feeling the heat of his skin and loving the way his muscles bunched beneath my palms. "So? How do I do this?"

He groaned, the sound seeming like it had been ripped from his chest. "You don't know? You've never...?"

I shook my head. I hadn't. I'd gotten close, but most guys wanted everything or nothing, so those nights had ended more abruptly than expected.

"Oh my God." Axel moaned, covering his face with his hands.

I frowned. "If that's an issue, I can..."

He dropped his arms and one of his hands tangled in my hair, gripping the back of my head. "It's not an issue. It's too fucking hot for words."

Pleasure tightened my chest. "What do you mean?"

He sighed. "I'd like to think I'm a modern man. I accept everyone has a past and have never before been turned on by the idea of a virgin before. But knowing that this mouth—" He ran his free hand over my face, his fingers brushing my lips. "—has never been anywhere else... Fuck, I feel like a caveman with how possessive I'm feeling towards you."

I liked the sound of that. "Because you don't want me to do this to anyone else?" Hopefully my assumption was on target.

He didn't answer, he just shook his head.

Good. I didn't want to do this with anyone else either, though I knew he didn't want to hear those words. We had no commitment to each other and on a rational level, I knew that I would have another lover after Axel. Probably more than one. But in this moment of perfection, Axel was mine. And I was his. And I didn't want to think about tomorrow.

He grabbed his shaft and held it in his hand. "The head is the most sensitive part. It's the same cells that your clit is made from. So, concentrate on that part with your lips and tongue."

I nodded and leaned forward, pressing a kiss to the big, bulbous head. It was so much warmer and smoother than I thought it would be. Opening my lips, I pulled the head into my mouth, licking it and sucking at it, trying not to use my teeth.

Axel's hand was still in my hair, but he wasn't moving me or guiding me in any way.

I rocked backwards and looked up. "Is this okay?"

He nodded, his face flushed with heat. "You can use your hands too, if you want."

As I nodded, he let go of himself, reaching for my hands and guiding me up to grip his shaft. "Just... suck the head, and move your hands up and down."

I did as he said, gripping the thick shaft that was getting thicker by the minute, loving the feel of the softness of the skin. Silk over steel. I moved my hands up and down, having down that part before, then sucked on the head again. Damn, this was hot. But what else could I do for him?

I began to explore him a little more, running one hand down his thigh and up again, venturing between his legs to softly cup his balls and stroke through his legs to cup his ass. So many places to kiss. Once again, I pulled off and glanced up at him. "Can you lie down? I want to do more."

16

AXEL

More? She wanted to do more? She was fucking killing me. Slowly, deliciously, killing me with that mouth of hers. And she wanted to do more? "Um, sure. Where do you want me?"

"Lie down on the bed."

Fucking hell. I turned around, crawled onto my bed—my domain, my pleasure sanctum—and lay on my back. Then I waited. Seriously, what was going on around here?

"Do you have any lube?" she asked suddenly, popping up next to me on the bed, her gorgeous boobs bouncing enticingly.

"Yeah. Top drawer," I said, pointing to the nightstand.

She hurried across the bed, pulled open the drawer, grabbed a tube then crawled back over, a huge grin on her face.

"Lube, huh?" I asked, lifting an eyebrow. "I thought you were a virgin."

She giggled. "Um... I go to college and have an iPhone. I've seen porn and have friends who are quite experienced and don't hesitate to talk about it. So, I know what goes where."

And from the look of her, she was trying to explore everything in one night.

"Well, I'm all yours," I said, putting my arms behind my head and relaxing into the pillows.

"Brilliant." Dropping the lube on the mattress, she swung her leg over my waist so that she was on top of me.

"Now we're talking," I said, grabbing her waist and thrusting up against her. She still wore her panties, but I was pretty sure I could talk her into taking those off.

Before I even had the chance to touch her, she shimmied down to lie down on top of me and kissed my lips.

I kissed her back but then she was gone, kissing down my neck and licking my nipples. "Oh, you don't have to do any of that." I didn't really like extra attention on me. It made me feel a bit... strange.

She glanced up at me, then narrowed her eyes. "You don't like it? Are your nipples sensitive?"

I shook my head. "No, not really."

She shrugged and put her head back down, flicking my nipples with her tongue and her nails, and causing sparks of pleasure to twirl inside my gut. That wasn't something I was used to. Then she sucked on one of them, and I gasped.

She looked up and grinned. "Just let me enjoy myself. It's my turn." She kissed all the way down my stomach, then pushed my legs up so that my knees were bent. What the hell was she going to do now?

"Have you done ass stuff before?" she asked, kissing my cock and nuzzling into my thighs.

"Some. Why?" Did she really want to know about other women I'd had anal sex with? That really wasn't necessary, was it?

She nodded and began to nibble and suck the flesh on the

insides of my thighs. Then she was touching me with her fingers, probing my ass.

"What are you doing?" I asked, looking down at her, my eyebrows halfway up my forehead.

She was kneeling now, squirting lube onto her fingers. "Ass stuff," she said simply. "You said you've done it before."

Holy shit! That wasn't exactly what crossed my mind when she'd asked about anal play.

But then she grinned, showing so much enthusiasm for what she was about to do, there was no way I was going to say no. "There's something I want to try. Is that okay?"

I nodded. "Yeah, of course, but..."

She bent her head and sucked the sensitive head of my cock into her mouth.

I groaned and clenched the sheets beside me. *You've gotta be fucking kidding me!* I was already too turned on. Her tenderness, sweetness and enthusiasm for my body were going to get me off too quickly.

Then her fingers began slipping between my cheeks, circling my asshole and pressing in.

"Oh, God." I groaned, sitting up, only to have her push me down with her free hand.

I grabbed onto her arm, needing an anchor of sorts. Suddenly things were unstable, the mattress felt like it was moving and shaking beneath me.

She sucked me and fondled me, then moved her finger in and out of my ass, sending wave upon wave of pleasure through my body.

"Fuck... I..." I couldn't talk.

Chastity never stopped. She pleasured me and attended to me like I was her sole focus.

My orgasm began to tingle at the back of my legs, and I forced myself to take deep breaths, slowing down my breathing.

But she didn't let me separate myself from what we were doing, and I didn't get a moments rest from the exquisite torture. She just kept sucking and licking and pleasuring me in ways no one had ever done before, which if I were honest, was one of the biggest turn-ons about her.

"Chastity... You've gotta stop." And she did. I was about to come in her mouth, and that wasn't something I wanted. Not for her, or me.

I wanted her closer, wanted her lips on mine.

"No."

I growled when she wouldn't stop. Sitting up, I grabbed her and hauled her up onto my body.

"I want to make you come." She pouted.

"Oh, you will," I gasped out. In fact... I rolled her over, so I lay between her legs, my aching cock pressed against her pussy. I grinded against her. "I want inside you so badly," I said, dropping down so that I was speaking directly into her ear.

"Can you come like this?" she whispered back.

I groaned. "Hell, yes. But you've gotta fuck me back."

She wrapped her arms and legs around me, arching up into me as I drove against her again and again, only one thin piece of cotton separating my cock from her pussy. She gasped and groaned and clung to me in a way that made me want her so much more.

My orgasm flared in my gut and this time I wasn't fighting it. The heat tingled up my back and roared down my thighs. My balls tightened and I thrust into the cradle of her hips one more time.

She turned her head and said in my ear, "I can't wait to feel you come."

And I lost it. I cried out like an animal, shooting my seed all over Chastity's panties and belly.

She held me through it, her fingers digging into my back and her heels digging into my ass, holding me as tightly as she could against her.

For me, the orgasm was one of those that go down in history as the longest, loudest, most drawn-out of pleasures. I couldn't stop the groans that flew from my mouth, nor the way I shuddered as my cock pulsed and spasmed between us.

When she turned her head towards me, I captured her lips with mine, partly to stop the noises that fell from me, but mostly because I wanted to kiss her more than anything in the world right now.

The blazing hot pleasure began to recede, and a wash of shame pushed at me. I should never have let her seduce me like that. At the very least she deserved an orgasm of her own. I pulled back to stare down at her, her cheeks flushed and hot with arousal. "Next time we come together."

She giggled and nodded. "Absolutely. But I have to say, that was fucking hot. We can do that anytime." She smiled up at me with so much pleasure that any feelings of regret began to recede.

Rolling onto my side next to her, I ran a hand over her sticky belly. "How about a shower? And I can make you happy with my fingers this time?"

She rolled onto her side to face me. "Yes, to the shower, but I'd rather wait for my next orgasm, if that's okay."

"Why?"

She shrugged her elegant shoulders. "Because this night is all about you. That's what *I* want."

I shook my head. "You don't make sense."

She sighed. "Look, I know you're used to being in charge, and giving everyone else everything they need."

I narrowed my eyes at her. "You don't know me well enough to say that."

She tilted her head to the side. "Am I wrong?"

I stilled, thinking about her words then realizing that for a woman who'd only known me a few days, she seemed to understand me better than people who'd known me for decades.

"No. You're not wrong."

She smiled softly. "Then let me spoil you. Let me pleasure you and expect nothing in return, just for one night. Because I know once we start having sex, we'll never be able to go back to these nights of amazing foreplay, will we?"

I chuckled. "No, I don't believe we will." I didn't want to admit it aloud, but I was pretty sure that her pussy was going to be as addictive and enticing as the rest of her. Glancing at the clock across the room I realized it was almost midnight. "So... what should we do? Showers, then take you home?" I didn't really want to let her go, but we hadn't discussed tomorrow yet.

She sat up and swung her legs off the bed. "Definitely showers, but I was hoping I could stay again. Then I'll Uber back to Mom's in the morning."

"Did you bring anything to stay?" I asked, getting to my feet as well despite the lethargy that tugged at me. *Damn, I could pass out this very minute.*

She grinned. "Yep. Toothbrush and clothes for tomorrow are in my bag."

I shook my head. *I've never met a girl who packed so light.* "Then you're set," I said, thinking about the guest bedroom that waited for me down the hall. I'd lie with her until she fell asleep and if I was still awake, I'd go to my own bed then.

"Shower time," she said, then my gaze caught on the clock next to the bed. One minute after midnight.

It was officially tomorrow, which meant it was *my* turn again.

17

AXEL

I followed Chastity into the ensuite, loving the way her generous ass swayed as she moved. She was all curves, and she was absolutely gorgeous. I flicked on the water and adjusted it so that it was soon steaming hot, and she moved beneath the spray. She was naturally, gloriously beautiful. Bright eyes, amazing smile, perfect skin. And her body was so inviting I couldn't wait to touch her again.

I watched her quickly rinse off, then when she turned around to smile at me, I moved in. My hands ached to touch her, and they weren't going to be denied. If she wanted to wait to have sex then I'd wait, but that was where following her lead ended.

I cupped her face and kissed her, stepping into the shower, and feeling the hot water washing over my face and body. She grabbed my waist and held me close, kissing me back with all the passion and need I'd hoped for.

My hands roamed her body, loving the smoothness of her back and the indentation of her tiny waist. I cupped her breasts because moving past them without touching them was impossible. Those fleshy globes were soft and full and filled my hands perfectly.

She moaned, arching back to give me better access.

I pulled away slightly, nibbling on her earlobe and whispering to her, "It's tomorrow, you know. It's not your turn anymore."

She gasped but pressed closer. "I don't want to—"

"I know you don't," I interrupted. "But you aren't going to sleep with that deep ache between your legs."

She moaned softly and thrust her hips against mine, my cock beginning to rouse once again. Poor bastard didn't know that sex wasn't on the menu tonight.

"You do ache for me, don't you?" I asked, loving the way her small hands grabbed for me, keeping me as close as possible to her.

There were no games with this girl. She didn't try to play hard to get or demand I jump through a hundred hoops to get into bed with her. She was panting and needy, and I wanted to give her the relief she deserved.

"Yes, I do," she said, moaning into my ear as I slid my hands down to her ass and pulled her tight against me.

"Then it's time for another orgasm. *Yours*," I said, pressing her back against the cold tiles and hearing her gasp once more. I tilted the shower head so that she had hot water pouring over her and she stared up at me, quivering with the dual temperatures. "Do you want me to?" I asked, wanting her consent for everything I was about to do to her.

She nodded. "Yes. How are you going to manage that here?"

My brain threw images at me of lifting Chastity up against the tiled wall and thrusting my cock up into her waiting pussy again and again until she cried out with ecstasy. I shook myself.

That wasn't the plan for tonight. I grinned at her. "Open your legs and I'll show you."

She nodded, her thighs falling open as she leaned back against the tiles, her chest heaving with arousal.

"Damn, you are the hottest woman I have ever known. How do you do it?" I demanded as I stepped closer.

She huffed out a laugh. "What are you talking about? I'm a mess."

I didn't know how to explain to her that her inexperience, her enthusiasm, and her beauty were an intoxicating combination. I bent my head to kiss her, and she wrapped her arms around my neck. My tongue slid into her mouth, tasting her sweetness as I moved my palm over her belly and ran my fingers over her mons.

"Oh, shit," she gasped out. "I want you so much, it's insane."

"Tell me more," I demanded, sliding my fingers over her swollen clit and parting the slippery folds.

"I... uh... want you inside me so bad..." Anything more eloquent seemed to fail her at that point.

I groaned at those words, finding her slick entry and sliding two fingers inside her pussy.

She clamped down at me, squeezing my fingers tightly.

"God. You're so perfect." I captured her lips with mine and there were no more words, only moans and groans. Gasps and cries of pleasure.

My fingers worked her body, making her climb higher and higher. And when she finally came apart in my arms, shattering into a million pieces, a part of me knew I would never be the same again.

"Bedtime?" I asked her when her shuddering had subsided and she was slumped against me, her head resting on my shoulder.

She nodded. "Yes, please."

Turning the shower off, I grabbed towels from the rack. "Here you go, beautiful." I wrapped the towel around her, and she sluggishly moved towards the bedroom once more.

"You okay?" I asked, chuckling at the way she staggered and stumbled like a drunkard.

She giggled as she dried herself, then flung the towel over the chair next to the bed. "I feel amazing. Drunk, but better." She pulled back the covers and climbed into the bed, crawling to the middle of the mattress and laying on the pillow as close to my side as possible. She reached out her arm and patted my side. "Come. Please."

I crawled into bed and lay down, facing her. "Sweet dreams, sweetheart."

She reached out, under the blankets and lay her hand on my arm. "Thank you for tonight. It was amazing."

I grinned at her. "It certainly was."

She nodded and closed her eyes, her little hand curled around my bicep.

I watched her fall asleep and everything in me was content. Happy. More than I'd been in so long, I couldn't even remember the last time I'd felt anything like it. Even with the women and the money. I closed my eyes and let myself relax into the pillow.

I'd had a shit day at work, and a brilliant session with her, but I was never going to be able to fall asleep. As soon as I closed my eyes, my subconscious would percolate up everything I worried about. And the downward spiral would begin. I began to pull away, determined to sleep in the room I reserved for these nights.

"Don't go," she whispered. "Cuddle with me." She rolled over, pushing her ass back into the cradle of my hips and nestling into me like a cat.

"I'll stay for a while," I said, sliding my arm over her waist and holding her close to me. I could think about work while I lay here. I didn't really need to go anywhere. "Sweet dreams, Chastity."

She sighed happily and I closed my eyes again. She was

warm, and soft. Inviting in a way that women who were too skinny just weren't. I was beginning to think that my taste in women was changing.

The software company merger... I tried thinking about the deal I had on the table, but my brain wouldn't grab onto any of the facts, and I slipped into sleep.

18

AXEL

Waking up with her in my arms again was startling. She was so hot and soft, draped all over me. I felt instantly overwhelmed and suffocated, though my stomach lurched at the idea of kicking her out so that I could get ready for work. I moved away from her and took a breath. This was too strange, too different. *How is this even possible?*

"Good morning," she said to me, rolling onto her back and stretching her arms above her head. The sheet slipped down to her waist, exposing her gorgeous, pink-tipped breasts.

My mood changed instantly, my half hard cock rousing to full mast. "You sure you don't want to change your mind about the timing of your next step?" I asked, running my hand over her tight nipples.

Chastity giggled. "Don't you have work this morning?"

I did. I always had work to do. "It can wait."

She laughed louder this time. "Yeah, right." She rolled out of bed and grabbed for her bag, pulling out the clean underwear she'd packed yesterday.

I sat up in bed and watched her get dressed, loving how free and relaxed she was. There was no darting to the bathroom to put on makeup, no covering up or turning away. It was almost too relaxed, too easy. And I didn't trust it.

"When are we catching up again?" I called out as she pulled on a simple sundress and started tying up her shoes. Damn, this girl did not mess around. I'd struggle to get ready so quickly.

She pulled out a hair elastic from her bag and swept her long blonde hair up into a ponytail. "I don't know. What sort of schedule do you have this week?"

"Terrible." I groaned. "Meetings every day, but I'm sure I can squeeze in another late date one night." Maybe. I had plans to wine and dine some international visitors, and some of my meetings would go into the early hours of morning.

"How about I pop by for lunch sometime this week?" she suggested, grabbing up her bag.

"Sure, but when are you going to stay over again?" I asked.

Chastity grinned. "I'm spending a few days with my mom and have plans with friends, since I only have a few weeks off. But how's the weekend for you?"

I frowned. "I have a party Friday night, but we could catch up after?"

She bit her lip. "I have plans Friday night too, not sure how late it'll be. Are you free Saturday night?"

I didn't really like the idea of waiting five days to see her again, but this week would fly with all the work I had to do. "I can clear the weekend for you." I said with a grin. Once I got her into my bed, I wasn't letting her out again for at least two days.

She walked over to where I lay on the bed and leaned over to kiss me sweetly, then pulled back with a smile. "I better get going. Thank you again for a great night."

"Have a great week with your friends," I managed to say, though the words sounded like sawdust in my mouth. *Fuck it.* I was jealous of anyone who got to spend time with her. What was wrong with me? I raised a hand and waved at her as she walked to the door. I was starting to think she was opposed to breakfast the way she kept running off. "See you on Saturday."

She grinned at me as she headed out the door. "Bye."

And with that, I flopped back on the mattress and covered my face with my hands. I had it bad. And unlike most of the women I dated, whose appeal lessened with every date, my attraction to Chastity was only growing. I sighed and hauled myself out of bed and headed for the shower. Why did I get the feeling that no matter how much time I spent with Chastity, I was never going to get sick of her smile?

19

CHASTITY

The plans I'd made with my mom suddenly seemed lackluster compared to what I would have been doing with Axel.

"What are you thinking about?" my mother asked me, looking over her expensive cappuccino. "You look a million miles away."

I picked up the little silver teapot in front of me and poured myself peppermint tea. "I don't know..."

"It's Axel, isn't it?" Mom asked, sighing heavily.

I rolled my eyes, immediately annoyed at her. "Why do you have to say it like that?"

"Honey, you're about to finish college and head off to chiropractor school. The last thing you need is to start some *relationship* that's never going to last."

I took a sip of my tea, though my stomach dropped with a lurch. Why did she have to be like that? "Why won't it last?" I asked, though I didn't want to know what she thought.

Mom had dated a few guys since she and Dad had divorced, but never been serious with any of them. Things just always "didn't work out" and I often wondered if it was them, or if she had some issues that she simply couldn't get past.

Mom sighed again. "Sweetheart, he's twice your age."

"And?" I said, annoyed that his age was the first and only argument Mom had with me. "I love how old he is. How smart and successful and fit he is. Guys my age are skinny, lazy, and horny, and just..." I shuddered. "Gross." They also weren't into serious relationships. They all wanted to screw around for a few years before they settled down, so a virgin like me was a red flag for all of them.

"Then find someone five or even ten years older," Mom said with a sigh. "Not twenty. People will think you've got daddy issues."

"Mom!" I groaned and pushed my half-eaten chocolate croissant away. She'd just ruined my appetite.

"It's true, Chastity."

"Well people can think what they like. I do not have *daddy issues* because I've always had my dad. He never abandoned me, never moved away, never stopped loving me." I huffed at her. No matter how many times she liked to complain about my dad, I wasn't disappointed in him. "He never got re-married, never had any kids..."

"Neither did I!" Mom defended.

I glared at her. "And I don't have any mommy issues either, so stop trying to put your shit on me."

My mother's eyebrows flicked up. "What's wrong with you tonight?"

"Nothing!" I said, annoyed now even though I was the one who had ramped up the fight. "I just... I like him, Mom. A lot. And I don't want you shading me or him when I've never even dated someone before. You just can't do it." I was so agitated, my arms were shaking, so I stuffed my hands into my lap and squeezed my hands into fists.

"Okay, okay. Chastity don't blow a gasket. Geez."

I stood up abruptly, afraid I'd start yelling if I stayed with her a moment longer. "I'm just going to the bathroom. Won't be long." I snatched up my cell phone, went to the ladies' room and sat down in a stall. I didn't need to go, but I needed a moment to myself, a second to breathe. I got my phone out and decided to message Axel. After all, why not?

Hey! How's your day been?

I sent it off, then decided to cruise Facebook for a minute before going out to brave my mom again. God, she could be such a drag. If I wanted someone to give me hope or support or love, she wasn't the one I went to. And that was kind of sad.

Hey, yourself. Day was busy but good. How about you?

I couldn't stop the immediate flush of happiness that permeated every cell in my being at his response. I giggled to myself, not caring if someone heard me and thought I was crazy.

Good overall. Mom's being a pain in the ass.

I bit my lip and waited for the response.

You okay?

Again, my heart took flight. Damn it, I was *sooo* into this guy.

Yeah, no problem. Just tired, I think.

I could almost hear his chuckle in my ear. He knew why I was tired.

We had a late night and an early start.

No regrets.

LOL. Never.

I wished I had a photo of him just so I could look at it for a minute. Definitely something I'd have to do next time we were together. And speaking of which.

I haven't got any plans for lunch tomorrow. Where will you be around 12? 1? Can we catch up?

He didn't respond right away, so I got up, left the stall, and washed my hands. I'd organized to catch up with some friends tomorrow, but I could push them back to the afternoon. My heart wouldn't be happy until I saw him again.

I could probably take half an hour off around 1pm. Though, can I confirm tomorrow? Meetings change last minute sometimes.

I dried my hands and picked up my cell once more.

Yeah, sounds great. Text me the address and I'll be there.

He did, sending me the address of a building right in the heart of the city. If Mom wouldn't lend me her car, I'd just take an Uber. Wouldn't be too expensive, hopefully.

I took a deep breath before heading out of the bathroom and walking back to the table.

"You're smiling again, that's good," Mom noted, still eating her grilled chicken salad.

"Yeah, everything's fine. Are you almost ready to go home, Mom?"

"Oh?" Her tone was filled with disappointment. "I was hoping we could stay out for a bit. Go for a walk. Catch a movie. Something."

I tried not to grimace visibly. "I'm starting to get a real headache mom. Can I take you out for breakfast instead? My treat."

Mom lit up at the idea of another meal out. I had money saved, and I had no issue spending everything on my mom. She and I might clash a bit, but in the end, I owed her for my life.

"Okay, sweetheart. Let's go home and put you to bed."

Mom tucked me up and took me home, and I curled into my tiny single bed and dreamt of the king size bed I'd slept in the night before.

~

The next day I took Mom out for brunch, had a long shower, braided my hair, and got dressed into some of my best clothes. Proper black pants, nice sweater. I was going into the city to meet Axel in his work environment. A denim mini skirt and flip flops would not cut it, I was certain.

I even tucked my long braids up into an elaborate design at the back of my head. I looked thirty. Maybe. I put on mascara and a rose-pink lip gloss and was ready to go. "You sure it's okay if I take your car?" I asked my mother as I grabbed the keys and packed my bag.

"Of course, hon. You won't be long, right?" Mom asked, walking out into the hallway. "Wow. You look nice. Where did you say you were going again?"

I didn't.

"Meeting Axel for lunch," I said with a brilliant smile and turned away with a wave before she could say something cutting about my extremely hot, pseudo-boyfriend. I didn't really know what to call him. "Bye, Mom!"

I ran to her car, got in, and started it. It had been ages since I'd driven a car since I didn't have one at school. I just didn't use it enough to justify the expense. I drove the half an hour into the city, hating the traffic and the inability to find parking, but at the same time, I couldn't be annoyed. I was so freaking excited to finally see him.

Luckily, I found a lot with a few spots open a block from Axel's building. I had about fifteen minutes to walk to his address, so I sent him a message.

Just parked. Will walk over and meet you where? Lobby? Outside?

I was almost at his building when the message came back.

I'm running a little late, so come up to the office and I'll order us in some food.

I wasn't going to argue with that. I arrived at the address and my mouth fell open. It was a fucking skyscraper! "Whoa." *Please let him have some little dinky office on the third floor.* Because the idea of facing the reality that Axel really was as rich as he claimed was finally sinking in. *He's a billionaire. A billionaire. Say it again.* "A billionaire," I whispered to myself as I stepped into the lobby and went straight up to the reception desk.

"Can I help you?" the smartly dressed woman behind the sleek desk asked.

"Yes, I'm here to see Axel Patterson. He said to come up to his office."

The woman smiled back. "Yes, Mr. Patterson said he was expecting someone. Go right over to those elevators. Forty-second floor."

"Forty-two?" I repeated, aghast. That was a little too high in the sky for me.

"Yes."

She returned to answer the phone and I headed over to the elevator and got in. "Holy shit," I squeaked to myself as the doors closed and I rode all the way up to Axel's floor. When the elevator doors dinged open, I was greeted by another reception desk. "Um, hello," I said to the woman behind this desk who looked about sixty and seemed like the kind of professional who should be running her own business.

"Can I help you?" she asked, staring down her nose at me.

"I'm here to meet Axel Patterson for lunch," I managed to say, standing tall and straight, and trying not to fidget.

The woman looked me up and down, and I wasn't sure she liked what she saw.

"Don't worry," I whispered to her, because I couldn't help but attempt to make her smile. "My mom doesn't like the fact I'm dating him either."

The old crone actually cracked a smile and walked around the desk. "Let me show you to his desk personally."

I didn't know why that sounded like a huge compliment, but I flashed the woman my brightest smile, and was led down an imposing, long hallway until finally I stood before two large, impressive doors.

The receptionist, who was probably the office manager, knocked and I heard Axel's annoyed voice call out, "I'm rather busy!"

I giggled and covered my mouth with my hand.

"Your name, dear?"

"Chastity."

The woman's eyes lit up with amusement. "Shall I send Chastity away, sir?"

There wasn't a verbal reply, instead, the door opened abruptly. "No. No, Cheryl. Thank you."

The office manager winked at me and walked away.

Axel turned to me with an awestruck look on his face. "How did you get that dragon to like you?"

I laughed, "By not treating her like a dragon, for one thing." I grinned at him and despite my better judgement, jumped at him and wrapped my arms around his neck. "Hey, you."

"Hey, yourself," he growled, and whisked me into his office, the door shutting loudly behind us.

20

AXEL

I kicked the door shut, the sound reverberating through the empty room. Then the little vixen moaned, and my cock swelled against my suit pants. Damn it. I could take her on the desk this minute if our relationship was at that point. So instead of lamenting the loss of the great sex that could happen, I put all my energy into the kiss. I thrust my tongue deeply into her mouth, tasting her sweetness and exulting in the groans that erupted from her throat.

She felt so good, a refuge in the storm of the day I'd had. Grabbing her ass, I kissed her hard, and for a few minutes I couldn't think of anything but her. It was bliss. When she finally pulled away, the euphoria eyes made me smile. "Hey."

"Hey," she said as she cupped my face and smiled.

Something strange winged through my heart at the look in her eyes. Was this what it felt like to be in love? To want someone in every part of your life, not just your bed? She'd already wrapped my dragon of an office manager around her little finger, and I could see myself meeting her for lunches and dinners, taking her home to meet my parents.

Holy hell. Slow the fuck down. I grabbed her wrist and pulled her hand off my face, suddenly irked by all the thoughts pulsing through my brain. "I ordered lunch. It should be here soon," I said, taking her hand and drawing her over to the leather couch against the wall.

She didn't sit down, instead disentangling our fingers and walking over to the window behind my desk. "Holy shit!" she gasped. "This view is insane!"

I shrugged. "Yeah, I guess so."

This has been my office for almost ten years now. I'd slowly but surely taken up more and more of the office building and the upper twenty floors were all my employees now.

She spun around. "And this office! Axel, you could play volleyball in here!"

I glanced across the expanse of my workspace and tried to see it how she did. To me, the large desk, visitors' chairs, bookcase, and couch were just props designed for ease of work and to impress people who walked in for a meeting. It seemed like she was impressed, which I supposed was the point.

"Not an activity I've considered," I told her seriously. Volleyball? I hadn't even looked at a net since college. And back then, I only played on the beach so that I could show off my upper body. That usually guaranteed me a woman or two in my bed that night. I hadn't had much back then.

She came back to my side and sat down on the couch. "So, what's for lunch?" She was all bright-eyed and bushy-tailed.

I tried to lift myself up to her level of excitement—but failed for some reason. Perhaps I was starting to worry if all my money and success were a major factor in her wanting to date me. "It'll be here in a moment." And as if my words had conjured the delivery, there was a loud knock at the door. "Come in!" I called out, and a young woman walked in with tray full of food from the restaurant downstairs.

"Hello, sir," she said with a polite bob of her head.

"Just put it all on the table," I requested, reaching for Chastity's hand.

But she jumped up and went over to the server, giving her a beautiful smile. "What did you bring us?"

The server glanced at me, then looked back at Chastity. "Well, there's a bit of everything for lunch. Both tuna and chicken salad in tomatoes, roast beef sandwiches with herbed cream cheese, cucumbers and greens, soup and fresh baked rolls with homemade butter."

"Sounds delicious. Thank you," Chastity said to her, and the woman all but lit up with her smile.

"Yes. Thank you," I added, realizing that I really didn't think twice about the people who worked for me, and how much like me they were.

The girl left and Chastity started uncovering all the dishes. "How's your day been, Axel?"

I leaned back against the couch and watched her taking in the spread before us with excitement.

"Honestly?" I asked.

"Yep. If you're having a shit day, you can tell me. You don't have to answer with the standard 'good.'"

I laughed. "Well, yeah, it's been shit. A merger I've been working on for a month is looking like it won't go through, and I've put in too many hours on it to lose now."

"Do you want a selection?" she asked, picking up one of the plates to start dishing out. "Or do you want to come choose?"

"A bit of everything is fine." I answered, not feeling hungry. I didn't eat well when I was stressed.

But she made us up two plates, then came and sat down next to me with a sigh. "This looks so good. Thank you."

She picked up half of one of the roast beef sandwiches and ate it with a moan.

My heart kicked out at me again. She was happy. Truly happy just to sit here with me, eating takeout from disposable containers with no one around to see us. Was it expensive takeout? Yes. Was my office a million-dollar space, yes? But perhaps that wasn't the reason for her happiness. If that were true, she would be truly unique.

"Enough about me. What about you?" I asked her, picking up one of the tuna-filled tomatoes and taking a forkful.

"I'm fine." she said. "Had breakfast with Mom this morning and catching up with some high school friends for dinner."

"Busy girl," I said with a grin.

She giggled. "Yeah, well, even though school isn't very far, I don't really hang out with anyone during the semester. I study hard and socialize when I can, but I generally wait until the holidays to really catch up with everyone."

I nodded, my memory casting me back to my college days. "One long party, right? College? Your weekends must be full."

She shrugged. "Not really."

I stared at her, not seeing any signs that she was lying. Damn, the girl was an enigma.

"You and your mother, okay?" I asked, "I got the vibe from your messages last night that you two weren't getting along well."

She tilted her head to the side and kept munching, and that's when I noticed how corporate she looked. Her hair was all tied up so I could barely see it, and she was covered from head to toe.

I frowned at the black pants. Nope. They didn't suit her or her laid back personality, either.

"We're okay," she said, "We're always okay. She raised me, so I don't think I'll ever let go of the feeling that I owe her for my life, but at the same time, we're very different, so we butt heads on occasion."

"And you butted heads over me?" I could imagine that to a

protective mother, a guy my age wouldn't look like the best prospect for her daughter.

She shrugged again. "Yeah, we did. I like you, and she thinks there's no future for us because you're so much older than me."

I opened my mouth to respond then slammed it shut again. *Whoa. That was a bit too intense for me.*

She laughed at me. "You look like I just proposed marriage or something. Relax. I just told Mom that we're having fun. I'm only here for a few weeks, anyway."

I nodded. "That's true."

Her statements made me feel better on some level, but they also tugged at my gut. I only had a couple of weeks with her before she headed off for her last semester before chiropractic school and possibly started a career in another state.

"Speaking of our limited timeframe, what did we agree to this weekend? Are we catching up Friday night?"

She looked out the corner of her eye at me and waggled her eyebrows. "Anxious to get into my pants, are you?"

I glanced down at the black slacks she wore. "Not these ones, I can tell you. Where are your normal clothes? Your dresses and skirts."

She raised an eyebrow. "What's wrong with my outfit?"

"It's so..." *Boring, conservative, old.* "Not you. I like how you usually dress."

She sighed. "And my hair?"

Hated it.

"It's pretty," I hedged. "But can you take it down?"

"You prefer it like that?" she asked, as though wanting to confirm my reasoning behind my statements.

I nodded. "Hell, yes. Can you take it down?"

She stared at me for a moment then nodded. She tilted her head forward, then painstakingly took out a dozen or more hair pins, which loosened the braids that fell, then she started to unwind them. "I thought you might like me looking a bit older. More mature. I was trying to fit in with your co-workers, so you weren't embarrassed by me."

I outright laughed at that one. "I don't want you to fit in, sweetheart, you were born to stand out."

She poked her tongue out at me for that one. "That is so cliché."

And the fact she didn't fall for cheesy lines like that made me like her even more. "Remind me again when you're sleeping over?"

She ran her fingers through her long blonde tresses then looked at me. "Better?"

I reached over and tangled my fingers in the strands, then cupped her head and dragged her mouth to mine. "Much better."

We kissed again, and this time I kissed her slowly, exploring her lips and inhaling her scent.

When we finally broke apart, my pants were tight once again. "So?" I asked, still nose to nose with her. "Friday night?"

She nodded. "Okay. After my family thing."

Oh, damn, I'd forgotten about my best mate's party. "Okay." I'd leave early if I had to. Patrick only turned forty-two once, sure, but having sex with a girl like this? It was a rare gift.

We finished our lunch and then I had to get back to work.

She left and I spent the rest of the day on a high, not allowing the people around me to stress me out like they normally would. I had a date to look forward to, and at this moment in time, it felt like the most important date in the world. Friday night.

21

CHASTITY

The next two days flew by quickly. I kept myself busy as I normally would, and messaged Axel any chance I got. He was always flirty and thoughtful, and it made me ache to see him again. But his workload was kicking his ass, so I convinced myself that it was better if I simply stayed busy and didn't try to sneak in an extra visit. The nights of kissing, orgasms and fun and foreplay were amazing for me. The best "almost sex" I'd ever had.

But from Axel's point of view, I was beginning to think that he was getting frustrated not being able to go all the way, which was expected really, considering he was a man who'd done it a thousand times. Probably more. It would be like telling a professional football player, "yeah you can play the game you love, but just until halftime, then you've gotta get off the field and go home."

But soon that would all change. He would make love to me, and my world would forever be different. I'd no longer be a virgin. And after waiting so long for the right person, it felt incredible to say that I'd found him.

"You ready to go?" My mom asked as she stuck her head in my room, wearing her robe and slippers.

It was finally Friday night, and I had my dad's faux-fortieth birthday party to attend, then I'd be heading out afterwards to meet Axel. He'd actually turned forty, two years ago, but thanks to a global pandemic that had us all avoiding parties like the plague, he was making up for it tonight.

"Yeah, I think so." I said, checking myself in the mirror one more time. I was an hour late because the hairdresser I'd gone to this afternoon had been running way behind and I'd taken way too long to get ready.

"Your dad's gonna have kittens over that dress," my mother said, giving me a visual once-over, though her smile said she liked the idea of my father being annoyed at me.

"It's the second anniversary of his fortieth birthday," I justified. "I have to look nice." And the fact that I'd bought a brand-new dress, and expensive underwear had nothing to do with the fact that I was meeting up with Axel later. *Nothing whatsoever.*

"You sure you don't want me to drive you?" Mom asked for the tenth time.

"Yeah. I'm sure. Though I can't wait to get my own car." In a few years when I had the money, and hopefully would have the time to drive around, I'd buy my own car.

"Well, have a good night," Mom said, her sadness eating at me.

I knew she wanted to come with me, but there was a toxic nature to my parents' divorce that I'd never quite gotten to the bottom of. Neither of them had ever re-married or had more kids, which made me think that perhaps they were destined to get back together. But then again, that was probably just some childish fantasy I held onto and shouldn't.

"You too, Mom. I love you."

"I love you too!"

My phone beeped. Uber was here. "Gotta go." I grabbed my jacket, covered up all the bare skin I was showing, and raced to my Uber. This dress was mid-thigh, skin-tight, and had spaghetti straps that barely kept it up. It was hot. And it was nothing like the clothes I would normally wear. But tonight was special. Tonight, I wanted to feel beautiful.

Dad's place was only twenty minutes away, and while I jiggled nervously in my seat, I messaged Axel but didn't get a response. He said he had to do something tonight. A friend's party, or something. I didn't know. And it didn't really matter, we were catching up at a club in the city tonight, then I'd go home with him. I just had to get through the family stuff first.

When we arrived, I paid and jumped out, grateful for the fact that I hadn't driven. The place was packed. It was Friday night and there were cars everywhere. I ran up to Dad's apartment and knocked on the door. A moment later the door flew open.

"Auntie Shell!" I flew at my dad's sister with my arms opened wide.

She laughed in my ear and hugged me back. "Oh my God, you are so gorgeous. Let me look at you."

We pulled apart and she held my hands, opening my arms wide. "You are freaking gorgeous! When did that happen?"

I laughed, knowing she didn't mean any offense. "I think you're being fooled by a nice dress and some makeup, Auntie Shell."

She smiled at me with a familiar grin. "You haven't lost your down-to-earth sensibility. I'm so glad." She shut the door behind me and took my coat. "I'm putting everyone's stuff on your father's bed. When you're ready to leave, you can grab it."

"Thank you! Do you know where Dad is?"

She waved her hand in the air. "In the middle of the fray. You know what he's like."

I grinned. I sure did. My dad was extroverted and single,

which meant he had a lot of friends, and from all walks of life. There would be people here from his work, his gym, his high school. He collected people and they stayed around forever, something I loved about my father.

I walked down the short hallway, grinning as the music began to pound through my chest. When I stepped into his large living room, there were people everywhere. Food was laid out in platters on the kitchen counters and some heads turned to look at me as I stepped forward. One head in particular. "Axel?"

It looked like he was mid-sentence when he stopped talking to a couple of guys and turned to look at me. His gaze raked me from heels to lips, and back again.

My belly tightened and heat coursed through me. He was seriously the most breathtaking man in the world to me. That smile... damn, the things I'd do to have him smile like that at me.

He said something to the people to whom he was speaking then walked over to me, a beer in one hand.

"What are you doing here?" he asked, leaning forward to kiss me.

I knew my dad had to be around here somewhere, so I dodged his lips and quickly kissed him on the cheek, but damn that was hard! He wore dark wash denim jeans and a fitted white shirt and looked just... fucking hot. There was no other way to put it. He looked lean and powerful, and I suddenly wished he could throw me over his shoulder and take me with him this very minute.

"Me?" I asked, giving him the same look he was giving me. "What are you doing here?"

"Chastity!" My dad yelled out, barreling across the room to grab me up into a hug, the scent of wine and whiskey wafting around him.

I laughed as he lifted me up, then put me down. "Happy birthday, Dad."

Axel's eyes goggled out of his head. "Did you just say *Dad*?"

I nodded. "Yeah, why?"

Axel glanced away, his jaw tight and angry.

"What's wrong?"

Dad put an arm around me. "Hey, sweetie, how do you know this big lug?"

"Ah..." Well, shit "I don't really. We, uh... met briefly the other week when you dumped me at that expensive gym of yours for an hour or so."

"I didn't dump you," my father corrected, rolling his eyes. "But I didn't realize you two had met."

"I didn't realize you two knew each other," I added, my throat tight and hot. I swallowed hard to push back the feelings of rising panic. "Are you two gym buddies?"

The expression on Axel's face was devastated, there was no other word for it. He looked ready to commit some sort of felony. "No," Axel said, gruffly. "We've known each other for years."

"Yeah, Axel's been my best friend for at least a decade, I can't believe you two have never met before."

"I've seen photos," Axel said, shaking his head, "But didn't connect the two."

I raised my gaze to his, pain shattering around my heart. "Yeah, he probably showed you some school pictures. I don't really look like that now."

Axel looked as if he tried to smile but it came out more of a grimace.

"Speaking of how you look... jeez, Chastity, you're more beautiful than any of the other women in this room. You know you're not supposed to show everyone else up if you can help it." He winked at me, and I tried to smile but I wasn't sure if I succeeded or not.

"Don't know if that's a compliment or not, Dad," I said, elbowing him in the ribs. "But thanks. I... uh... was going to meet up with someone after the party, so got dressed up for a date." My eyes met Axel's and for a moment I saw the burning lust I'd been hoping for, then he looked away.

"Well, he's one lucky guy," Dad said. "Hey, there's some kids here your age on the balcony if you wanna go chat with them. You don't need to talk to us old guys all night, you know."

I could almost see the knife Dad had skewered into Axel's heart. "Thanks, Dad, but I think I'll go catch up with some of the family. I haven't seen Aunt Shelly in years."

"You do that, beautiful. You know how proud we are of you. Did I tell you my girl got into chiropractic school?" my dad bragged to his best mate—Axel. *My date.* What a fucking mess.

Axel shook his head. "Nope, but that's probably not your fault. I don't always listen well."

Dad *tsked* good-naturedly. "Well, bachelors don't. Anyway, see you later, sweetie." And my father turned his back on me, dragging Axel away.

I stared after him, everything in me aching yet numb at the same time. What did this mean? Would Axel want to continue this two-week fling we planned, or had the fact that my dad was Axel's best friend truly fucked up any chances of us being together?

22

AXEL

"Hey, Patrick, gotta take a leak. I'll be back."

"Use my ensuite, if you want."

I nodded my thanks. "Yep, will do." I needed some space and some time to think before my head exploded. What the hell was I going to do now? The bathroom was through Pat's bedroom, so I walked around the bed and headed to the bathroom. I used the toilet, washed my hands and checked my phone.

One text from Chastity.

I'm in an Uber, headed to my dad's birthday, and omg I am so excited about tonight! What time do you want me to meet you?

I wanted to slap myself upside the head.

How did I not know? Well, how could I have known? "Her mother! That's where I know her from."

Pat had shown me photos of his ex-wife a few times. They hadn't really stuck in my mind too much, but when I'd seen Chastity's mom, Katherine. "Kaiti, he calls her Kaiti." Something about her had been familiar. And this was why. I texted Chastity back.

Um... you still wanna meet up?

I headed out of the bedroom, suddenly afraid that she'd come and find me and then we'd get totally busted. Patrick would have an absolute fucking conniption. At least I hadn't screwed his daughter yet... but damn, had I gotten close. And damn, did I want to. Even now.

What was with that dress? And her hair. She looked amazing tonight and had already admitted to her father that she'd dressed up for her date. *Our* date. *Her dad. Fuck!* I raced back to the safety of the gym crew, where they were talking about protein shakes and what shares were up at the moment. Boring, normal shit that soothed me a fraction.

I ran my hand through my hair, my nerves shot to shit. I needed to break it off. Tell Chastity that there is no way we could meet up tonight. And we certainly couldn't get into bed together again.

"You okay, Axel?" Danny, another guy from the gym, asked me.

"Yeah. Sorry, just had a big week." I managed to have another beer and found a spot in the corner, sitting at the table chatting with some friends who didn't need me to carry the conversation because I sure as hell couldn't talk like normal. My brain was ninety percent consumed with the girl who was currently flitting around the apartment as though nothing was wrong.

Chastity was talking to everyone, hugging anyone who came towards her, and serving food. The lady of the house. Her gaze occasionally caught mine, but then one of us would look away and the spell would be broken.

"Is that Pat's daughter?" Danny asked suddenly, pouring himself another whiskey.

"Which one?" I asked.

Danny grinned at me. "The one you haven't stopped staring at all night."

I looked properly at Danny this time. I'd never thought about him being that insightful or clever, but from the grin on his face, I wasn't going to be able to bullshit my way out of this one.

"Yeah, that's her," I admitted.

"She's beautiful," Danny said solemnly.

"Yeah," I managed to say, taking another sip of my drink.

"Do you know her?"

I stared at him for a minute, not sure how to answer. I didn't want anything getting back to Pat, but at the same time, damn, I could use a friend.

"Yeah... we met a few weeks ago. I didn't know she was Pat's daughter."

"And you two..."

I shook my head. "No. We just shared a few meals."

I'd gotten as physically close as possible to fucking her as someone could get without actually doing it. But Danny wasn't getting the details. No one was.

"So, what's the problem?" Danny asked.

"The problem..." I moved closer so the people around us wouldn't hear. "The problem is that I was hoping to meet up with her again. But I can't now. And that's fucked."

"Why not?"

"Why not?" I repeated, incredulously. "Because Pat would fucking kill me if he found out. She's his only kid. And she's..."

"What? Half your age?"

I growled at him. "Fuck you."

Danny laughed. "Look buddy, I've known you a long time. If she's special, and you think you could make it work long-term, go for it. But if you just want another toy in your bed, then yeah, let her go." He shrugged like it was that easy.

And, yeah, it probably was. My phone vibrated and I picked it up.

Yeah. I still want to meet. At the club like we planned? Or somewhere else?

I glanced around but Chastity was nowhere to be seen.

We can still go to the club, but how about you walk down to the cafe on the corner, and I'll pick you up and drive you.

It was risky. Someone could see her getting into my car, but I didn't want her to order a ride. We needed to talk.

When I looked up from my phone, Danny was staring at me. "You like this girl, huh?"

I ran a frazzled hand through my hair. "Yeah, I do." My phone vibrated again.

I've got my coat. Give me five to say goodbye and I'll meet you down the street.

I glanced up and saw her re-enter the room, all smiles as she hugged her dad and said goodbye to his family. She was just as beautiful as the moment I'd met her. All bright vivaciousness. Natural charisma.

When she headed out the door I glanced at my phone. "I'd better go. My car is parked at the far end of guest parking." It wasn't. I'd gotten a spot not far away, but I needed to go.

Danny held out his hand. "Nice seeing you, man."

"Yeah, you, too."

"Don't tell me you're leaving as well!" Pat said, coming up to give me a hug.

I hugged him back. "Happy Birthday, Patrick. but yeah. Got some late conference calls with Taiwan. Gotta head out." I hated lying to him, but the truth was gonna sting a lot worse.

"Cool. See you Sunday morning for a run?"

"Yes," I told him. It wasn't like I had plans with Chastity anymore. "See you then."

Patrick headed off, and I practically ran for the stairs. My heart was pounding now. I was excited. I could feel the edges of my mouth tick up. *Shit! No! You're going to break up with her. Don't get all excited to see her.* I tried to dampen down my enthusiasm as I ran down the stairs, found my car and drove to the end of the street.

But there she was, waiting for me, her black coat covering her gorgeous dress, and her long blonde hair flowing down her back. She turned at my approach and for once, her face didn't light up when she saw me. Instead, she simply nodded, walked over, opened the door, and got inside.

As soon as her seatbelt was on, I drove off, getting into the lane to hit the freeway, and the city. "You still want to go to the club?" I asked her.

She nodded. "Yeah. I want to dance. With you. Just once."

She sounded so sad I reached over the space between us and grabbed her hand with mine. "You okay?"

She twisted around to glare at me. "No! I'm not! This night was meant to be..." She growled and shook her head. Then she crossed her arms over her chest, effectively dislodging my hand.

I put both hands back on the steering wheel, pain in my gut now. She was upset. "Tonight was meant to be what?" I knew, but it felt like she needed to say it.

"Tonight..." She took a deep breath. "I thought we... Let's not talk about it. Let's just go and have a drink, and a dance, and—"

"And what?" I asked. "Say goodbye forever?"

She stared out the window. "We have to. There's no other way, is there?"

I gripped the steering wheel until my hands ached. We didn't talk for the rest of the drive, and I pulled into the closest valet parking. When I turned the ignition off, she unbuckled her belt and got out of the car without waiting for me to get her door.

I took a steadying breath. *You can do this.* I got out of the car, locked it, and handed the keys over to the valet driver. When I reached for her hand, she came to me, gripping my fingers and pressing into my side as we walked up to the front of the club.

"Do you think we could forget about my dad, just for an hour?" she asked. "I just want to enjoy *us* for a little bit more."

She sounded so depressed, I tugged her into my arms. "The world isn't ending, sweetheart."

She nodded then blinked, tears soon cascading down her cheeks.

Oh, crap. I kissed her quickly, unsure how to otherwise stop her crying.

She cupped my face, then wove her fingers into my hair, holding me tightly against her.

My cock throbbed and I pulled back. If we started fooling around, I was done for. There was no way I'd remember why we couldn't be together if she started touching me. "Let's go."

I knew the bouncer at the club, so he nodded at me as we approached and opened the door for us.

"Ohh, fancy," Chastity said as she went ahead of me.

I bit back my retort. I had more money than I knew what to do with, and no one to spend it on or enjoy it with. I could give this girl the world, if she wasn't the only person I couldn't have. And for the first time in my entire life, a saying that my friends had used all the time rang through my head: *"Sucks to be me."*

23

CHASTITY

I wanted to cry. I'd been holding it in all night, pretending to be happy and social. Filling the void of the wife-figure my dad didn't have. I'd served drinks and food, pandered to my aunts and uncles. And all I wanted to really do was bury myself in Axel's arms and cry my eyes out. But now that I had him all to myself for a very limited time, the last thing I should do was cry. I wanted to dance.

The music was great, playing some sort of deep-base techno with no words. Just a great vibe, dark lighting, and bars aplenty. I stopped walking and Axel slid up behind me, his lips at my ear and his hand around my waist, holding me close.

"Do you want a drink?"

I nodded and turned my head towards him so that our lips were only a few inches apart. "I think I need one."

"Me, too," he growled back, and pushed his hand into the small of my back. "Let's go to the bar."

I let him lead me through the throng of hot people pressed against each other. The music was so loud I was going to need to holler to be heard, and then I wouldn't be able to speak tomorrow. Or we could just not talk. What more was there to say, really?

Axel was my father's best friend. Dad would be horrified to know that I'd jumped into bed with him. And even if I could get over the link between them, there was Axel. I'd seen the look on his face. It was like he was suddenly disgusted by me. My age. Who I was to him now. His best friend's daughter.

He'd known all along how old I was and yet, there was nothing like realizing he was literally older than my father to put a damper on things.

"What do you want?" Axel shouted next to my ear.

"Something strong."

He leaned over the bar and spoke to the bartender.

A minute later, two shots of tequila and lime slices were lined up in front of me, and another two were lined up in front of Axel.

He turned to me, a shot held in the air, waiting for me to join him in drinking away our sorrows.

I picked one of mine up and we clinked them together.

He threw his back and grabbed the slice of lime to suck on, gasping as the gasoline-like quality of the straight alcohol hit him.

I did the same thing, wincing as the burn traveled all the way down my throat to my empty stomach. I'd barely eaten all night. The first shot down, I picked up the second.

Axel nodded and once again, we clanked our little shot glasses together and tipped back the fiery liquid.

As I gasped and sucked on the lime wedge, I wondered what we were toasting. The end of our relationship? Getting this far and finding out just in the nick of time that we really, really shouldn't be together?

"Thanks!" I yelled at him, already feeling the warmth of the liquor moving through my veins.

"Let's dance." He took my hand and led me to the dance floor.

Women stared at him as he walked past them, one girl practically falling over herself to come and speak to him.

I just gaped at her arrogance, whereas he shrugged her off with a tight, annoyed grimace.

Then he pulled me into his arms and everything in the world was right again, if only for tonight.

I put my arms around his neck and moved to the music, smiling and laughing as he grinned down at me.

The music changed into something faster, and I was shocked when he moved back and began to move his hips like a pro.

I put my arms up in the air and let the music take me.

We danced and laughed our way through so many songs I lost count. Until the tequila had made my head fuzzy and my heart sing, and my mind was struggling to come up with a reason we shouldn't do this every night.

I moved closer to Axel and wrapped my arms around his neck. Then I went up on my toes and lifted my face to be kissed.

He didn't hesitate, wrapping me in the tightest hug and kissing me until I was seeing stars.

When he lifted his head, I whispered. "Take me home. Please."

The cloud of lust that had been enveloping us seemed to vanish in a single moment. Axel lifted his head higher, further away from me. Then he gently but firmly pulled my arms from his neck and back down to where they came from.

"We need to talk. Come on." He grabbed my hand and pulled me through the crowd, towards a door at the back of the club.

"Where are we going?"

The enormous bouncer who stood at the door had a lethal expression on his face. But the moment he saw Axel, he stepped aside and opened the door for him.

"Ummm..." *Where are we going now?*

"Come on." Axel tugged me through the door, and up a flight of stairs.

My legs were not steady, and by the time we got to the final step, I almost stumbled. In fact, I would have fallen ass over tits in my very new and expensive dress if Axel hadn't swept me up into his arms.

"You, missy, are drunk," he growled at me, like it was my fault.

"Yeah, whatever." I wasn't impressed that he wanted to blame all this on me.

"Whatever?" he repeated, his eyebrows raising in surprise.

"Yeah. Whatever." I said again, flicking my hand dismissively. "I didn't eat at my dad's, and you know why. And then you gave me shots on an empty stomach."

He plonked me down on an empty couch, and that's when I glanced around. "Where are we? Some sort of private bar?" I couldn't see the club from here, but I could hear the music.

There were couches and tables around, but no one else in the space.

"Yeah. It's for VIPs."

I bit the retort that came out my lips at that. Was there anywhere he didn't go? Anyone he didn't know?

As though in answer to my thoughts, an older guy reeking of whiskey stumbled by.

He straightened when he saw Axel, then tugged on his jacket as though that would help his appearance.

"Axel. Haven't seen you around here for a while. What have you been up to, man?"

Axel's lips tightened and he held out his hand to me.

I didn't hesitate, I moved straight onto the couch next to him and he put his arm possessively around me.

"Not much." Axel said nonchalantly. "Work. Nothing new."

The guy unbuttoned his jacket and slid onto the couch I'd just been occupying. "This a new one?" he asked, nodding at me.

Axel stiffened beside me. "This one... is none of your business."

I couldn't read the room well, so kept my mouth shut. Their relationship seemed strange. Strained, as though they'd once been friends, but not anymore.

The man, whose name I still didn't know, laughed. "You mean this one isn't for sharing? Come on Axel, she looks hot."

He licked his lips and let his gaze roam over me like he had the right to look at me like that.

I shuddered and turned my whole body into Axel.

Axel's growl was almost feral as he reached across the small divide and grabbed the other guy by the tie, then hauled him off the couch.

"Get out of here," he snarled at the drunk. "Or I'll have you thrown out."

He tossed the guy to the side, then slid back onto the couch with me.

The asshole got to his feet and stuck his nose in the air. "No need to be so fucking pissy. If this one is special, you just needed to—"

"Sam!" Axel called, and out of nowhere, a huge, bald bodyguard appeared. Axel flicked his head in the idiot's direction, and he was escorted from the room by the bouncer.

I nestled closer to Axel, my heart hammering in my chest. "That guy was creepy."

Axel put his arm back around me and grunted. "He was a good man, once upon a time. We went to college together."

"What happened to him?"

Axel tightened his hold on me. "Divorce, business failure, normal shit. He's an alcoholic now, and a miserable bastard. I can't believe he got in here."

"Why?" I looked up. "Because this place really is for very important persons only?"

He crushed his mouth to mine, and I slipped my tongue between his lips, needing to get closer, to taste him. To be a part of him.

When he pulled back from the kiss, he sighed. "I would have killed him if he'd touched you." He pressed his forehead to mine.

"You mean you didn't want to share me with him?" I joked.

Axel grabbed me around the waist and hauled me over his body, so I was straddling him, my dress up around my ass, exposing my thighs and my underwear to him.

"Is that a 'no'?" I asked, breathless.

Axel ran his hands up the outsides of my thighs and stared up at me. "No. I would never share you. With anyone."

His words were clipped. Short. As though he were still angry.

I slid closer to him, pressing my panties against the crotch of his jeans. "Why won't you take me home, Axel?" Surely, he wasn't planning on having sex with me for the first time up here? It was nice, but privacy was definitely a problem.

He groaned and dug his fingers into my thighs. "Because if I take you home, I'll fuck you… and that's not on the table anymore."

Even though I knew it, hearing it come straight from Axel's lips made my heart sink. I'd been so close to getting what I wanted.

"I know," I said, slumping.

Then I glanced up and met his eyes again. "Do you think we could just have one night, tonight, then pretend we've never met?"

Axel stared at me for a long, intense moment. Then he shook his head.

I groaned like an impatient toddler. "Why not?"

He sighed. "Because I couldn't just let you out of my bed

after one night, Chastity. I just know it. I'll want you over and over again."

My pussy throbbed at the mention of all the sex I would have been getting if it weren't for the fact that my father knew Axel first.

"This is so not fair," I pouted, running my hands over his broad chest. "How well do you know Dad? I mean, is he just a friend you see once a year?"

"I have a key to his apartment."

Oh, fuck. I thought I was the only one except for my father's cleaning lady who had a key to his apartment.

"He loves you," I whispered.

He nodded. "And he loves you."

Tears gathered in my eyes, hot and horrible. "So essentially, we're fucked."

He pressed his lips into a thin line. "I think we'll break his heart and his trust if he finds out we're doing something like this behind his back."

Did we have to sneak around behind his back? Probably. Since this relationship was only destined to survive a few weeks at best, I couldn't exactly come out and say, "Hey, Dad, we're just fucking each other while I'm on summer break. Don't stress about it.'

"Is that what you want?" Axel asked, because I'd obviously been silent too long.

I shook my head, the tears were now falling down my cheeks. To hide them, I fell into Axel's arms and buried my face in his neck.

24

CHASTITY

The next day, I couldn't get out of bed. Just waking up hurt.

"Hey, sweetie! It's almost noon. You wanna go out for lunch?" Mom called through my closed door.

"No, thanks!" I called back. "But I'll get up soon." Then I pulled the comforter, quite literally, back over my head.

After we'd decided that it was probably best to quit while we were ahead, Axel drove me back to my mom's place. Neither of us had wanted to say goodbye, so instead we'd just held hands for a few minutes, then I'd gotten out of the car and run for my life. I didn't look back because my face was covered in tears, and I knew that Axel felt bad enough as it was. We'd made the right decision, but fucking hell, it was a bastard of a choice.

Then I'd officially had the worst night's sleep of my life, or at least in my memory anyway. Mom always said I'd been a terrible sleeper as a baby. It had taken me hours to fall asleep, then I'd been haunted by nightmares that had woken me up multiple times before I'd finally passed out from exhaustion after sunrise.

My head kept circling back to one universal truth. *It wasn't fair.* I'd waited patiently for the right guy to come along, for the man I finally wanted to fall into bed with, and I'd found him. The fact that he was my dad's best friend shouldn't have mattered, should it? But it did. I knew it did. It only highlighted our age gap, and how different our lives were.

Not to mention the fact that my father would be horrified. And although I was pretty sure that no matter what I did, I wouldn't lose my dad's love or our relationship, I was pretty sure Axel would lose his. I didn't want to do that to either of them. Not for the sake of a relationship that wouldn't last.

Of course, part of me wanted to yell that it could last forever if we both wanted it to work. But that was just the teenage version of myself talking. That tiny part of me that still believed in *happily ever after*. And love at first sight.

But I had to face facts. Axel had never said anything about a long-term relationship. If anything, he'd made it clear it wasn't on the table. And I was leaving for school soon too, so the likelihood of being able to make "us" last was minimal.

I sighed and pushed the comforter back off my hot face. It was lunchtime. I needed to get up and go out. Make some plans. I'd deliberately kept this weekend free for Axel. So that we could spend as much time together as possible, if we wanted to. Now I had days and days of nothing to do, except maybe getting ready for Christmas.

That thought got me moving, and I quickly jumped in the shower and got dressed. "Hey, Mom! Wanna go into town and do some Christmas shopping?"

"Sure," she called back, sounding happy at the invitation.

I tugged on a hoodie, not caring what I looked like today. "Great. Let's go."

25

AXEL

S*unday morning.*

I pulled on my joggers when I heard a knock at the door. "Coming!"

When I got there, I pulled the door open, a part of me secretly hoping it was Chastity. Damn, I missed her. "Oh, hey, Patrick."

"What's wrong with you?" Pat asked, handing me a blue Gatorade. "Hung over?"

He pushed past me into my apartment, and I groaned. *Thank God Chastity isn't here.*

"We were supposed to go jogging. Sorry man."

Patrick and I went running most weekends. He was a great training partner, fit and determined.

"All good," he said, cracking open his drink and taking a swig. "I ran here, so I figured you might wanna join me for a bit."

I definitely did. Something had to get me out of this funk. "Give me two minutes." I walked to my bedroom and pulled on some socks and shoes, then went in search of a tank that wouldn't irritate me while I ran.

"Hey," Pat called from the doorway. "You okay?"

"Yeah, why?"

He shrugged. "Don't know. You were a bit odd on Friday night, and now... I don't know. Just wanted to ask. Check in on you, because I know not many dare to ask." He grinned at me to show he was joking.

I sighed and ran my hand through my hair. "Yeah. I..." How much could I tell my best friend? "I started dating this girl a week or so ago."

"Oh, yeah? She screwing with your head already?" Patrick laughed.

My gut tightened. "Yeah, she is. But it's... I don't know. I like her. I just don't know if I can do anything about it."

"Hang on a second," Pat said, putting his hand up. "You actually like this girl? Since when do you get attached?"

I got to my feet and pulled on a thin, cotton white tank. "She's different."

Patrick laughed at me again. "And by that, do you mean she's a brunette rather than the normal blonde?"

I groaned and scrubbed my hands over my face. "You really think I'm a shallow asshole, don't you?" Which boded even worse for me if Chastity and I decided to date. Pat would never want me, with my history, anywhere near his daughter.

Patrick sobered instantly. "Hey, man, I didn't mean to offend you. It's just... hey, if you actually like her, I'm happy for you. I just never thought you'd find someone worth settling down for."

I grinned at him. "I didn't say that." Settling down was another chapter entirely. Then I shrugged and stood up. "I just like her."

"Then go for it," Patrick said, walking forward and clapping me on the back. "Any woman who has you distracted, forgetting your schedule, and tied up in knots must be worth chasing after. I've known you for ten years and never seen you like this."

I nodded my head, my heart sinking. "Yeah... maybe. You're definitely right about that run, though. I could really use a heavy training session."

"Let's go, then." Patrick put his Gatorade down on the table and dumped his keys and cell phone. "Can I leave all my shit here?"

"Yeah, of course. We'll just take a key." I left my cell phone in my room, just in case Chastity called or texted. She hadn't since Friday night, but it would just be our luck that the one time she did, her father would see it.

Once I'd stashed any potential evidence of Chastity away, we headed out. We took the elevator down, then started stretching and began our run. We jogged through the city and made it all the way to the beach. By the time we got there, I'd developed a good sweat, and my heart was pounding.

"Oh, yeah. That feels better," I said, bending forward with my hands on my hips and breathing deeply.

"So, where'd you go Friday night?" Patrick asked in between panting breaths. "You said you had a conference call, but I know you. Did you catch up with the chick you're hung up about?"

I nodded. "Yeah. Went to Chase's. But we pretty much ended it before it began. She's... too different. Young."

Patrick chuckled. "Half your luck, bro. Let's go."

We turned and headed back, running around each other, and sprinting along each street.

When we finally got back to my apartment, my legs were shaking. "Fuck, that was good."

Patrick nodded, red-faced and completely out of breath.

I went straight for the fridge, where I pulled out a couple of bottles of water and tossed one at him. "You got plans for Christmas next week?"

Patrick nodded, drinking the water and lifting his tank to

wipe away the sweat on his red face. "Yeah. Meeting my parents for lunch and having my daughter over for dinner."

My stomach lurched and I turned away to get something to eat. "You want some eggs or something?"

"Nah, I've gotta get back, actually. Got a date myself, for lunch."

I turned and stared hard at him. "A Sunday afternoon date? Who are you, and what have you done with my friend?"

Pat had been pretty burned by Chastity's mom, and I'd never known him to date anyone seriously.

He laughed at me. "Pot. Kettle."

"Touché."

"Maybe we're just getting too old," he joked.

That is very possible. I'm kind of sick of waking up alone.

He walked over and held out his hand. "Thanks for the run, Axel. You should get strung up over a woman more often. I haven't had that good a run in ages."

I slapped him on the shoulder. "You enjoy your lunch date. I hope she ties you up in knots."

Patrick huffed and headed out, whistling softly.

Wow. He actually sounds pretty happy. I shook my head, scrambled up half a dozen eggs, then dug into them. Damn, I was hungry. Then it was shower time. I was sweating from the back of my neck to the soles of my feet. I scrubbed myself hard and let my mind wander to work. The Taiwan merger. Employees to hire and fire. A new building I wanted to buy. Anything and everything. I let my mind whirl.

But by the time I was dressed again and about to turn on my laptop, my brain was back on Chastity. I reached for my phone. We hadn't made any rules about our supposedly ended relationship, so a text wasn't off the table.

Hey. What are you up to for Christmas?

I put the phone down and tried to get back to work, but the

device immediately buzzed with her reply. I groaned and closed my laptop, giving up. I walked back into my bedroom, lay down on the bed and opened the phone.

Hey. Mom's for lunch. Dad's for dinner. Small. Casual. What are you up to?

I smiled as I texted.

Not much. My parents are in Europe.

A moment later she responded.

You're an only child too?

I sighed and rolled onto my side. We really hadn't got into a lot of personal stuff. I felt like I knew her well, but we'd missed so many of the pedantic details that made up the person.

Yep.

I closed my eyes as I laid my head on the pillow. I hadn't been sleeping great since I "broke up" with Chastity, which wasn't unusual for me. I rarely got more than four hours sleep most nights anyway. It was the only way I'd managed to get my company off the ground. I did two eight-hour shifts every day, sometimes more.

But thanks to the few nights Chastity had spent in my bed, my body was aching for that feeling of a full six to eight hours of sleep. It had been heaven. I put my phone down next to me, forcing myself to relax. My thumbs had been poised for the next message, anxious for her. I wanted to see her. But I'd been the one to put a stop to everything.

My phone dinged.

I miss you. This is shit.

I chuckled and rolled onto my back. That was the perfect message to receive.

I miss you too. And I agree.

I hit send before I could stop myself. I could safely say I'd never felt this way before— about anyone. Perhaps it was the fact that she was untouchable? I didn't really know. But she hadn't been untouchable a few days ago, and I'd still wanted her more than I've ever wanted any woman before.

I've only got about ten days left until I go back to school full time. Are you sure you don't want to catch up?

When that message came through, every part of me sang out with happiness. She knew that this relationship wasn't going to last, and yet she wanted it anyway. I inhaled sharply and took my time as I messaged her back. After writing the response then re-writing it twice, I was satisfied.

I'd love to catch up with you. Are you sure you'll be okay to just walk away after our two weeks are done?

When I sent it, my gut tightened. I didn't want her to say no, and worrying about losing her was something I thought I'd never feel. It was a really foreign sensation. My phone vibrated straight away.

I'd rather spend two weeks with you than a lifetime without you.

"Fuck," I groaned out loud. "This girl is going to be the death of me." I typed back quickly, before I could change my mind.

My place. Tonight. eight o'clock.

I sat up on the edge of my bed as I waited for her response. When it came, I practically whooped.

See you then. xox

26

CHASTITY

I didn't even bother with underwear this time. I wore a maxi cotton dress that was tight around my boobs, so I didn't need a bra. It was also long enough that no one would ever know I was commando, even though it felt ridiculously naughty to be running through the city with the fresh air blowing between my legs.

I reached Axel's apartment that he owned, shaking my head. Who owned a *whole* building? I went straight up the elevator and stepped into his apartment.

"Hello, beautiful," Axel greeted me, standing in the foyer wearing a basic white t-shirt and a ripped pair of jeans. The soft fabric of his shirt clung enticingly to his muscled chest and biceps. His hair was styled, and his easy smile made him look like he should have been gracing the front of a billboard somewhere.

I dropped my purse and ran straight at him.

He swept me up against his hard body, so I wrapped my arms around his neck and hugged him tight. God, it felt good to be with him again.

When he drew back, I didn't let him speak. I just grabbed his face and kissed him deeply, wanting him to make me feel good again. My chest had felt like it had been clamped in a vise for the past forty-eight hours, and now that I was with him, I could finally breathe again.

He kissed me hard, forcing my lips apart even as his hands roamed my body greedily. He grabbed my ass and squeezed. Then he stopped kissing me and pulled back. "Are you wearing underwear?"

"No." I wore my new, expensive stuff Friday night and everything went to hell, so..." I shrugged.

His smile was too sexy for the health of my fragile heart.

He pulled further back, took my hand, and led me to the bedroom. "So... what? You figured that if you were naked underneath your dress, I could just take you against a wall or something?"

I shrugged. "A girl can only hope." And I'd definitely dreamt of that exact scenario.

He sighed as he drew me closer and cupped my face with both hands. Gently. Carefully. "Not this time, sweetheart."

I put my hands around his waist. "But maybe another time?" I asked, hopeful. I had so many fantasies I wanted to fulfil in the short time we had together. *Sex in the shower. Sex outside. Sex in a car.*

Me on top, him on top. Up against the wall. Maybe on the couch... the kitchen counter...

He chuckled. "What's going on in that amazing brain of yours?"

I smiled. "You don't want to know."

"I doubt that." He smiled. "But for now, I'll let you keep your secrets. I have a feeling they'll destroy what I have planned for tonight, otherwise."

"What do you have planned?" I leaned forward to kiss him softly again. I loved his lips. They were just so soft, full, and lush. I could kiss him all day and never get tired of his taste. His smell.

"The perfect night," he whispered against my mouth. "Where you come on me over and over and over again."

I inhaled deeply, my breath caught in my throat. I wanted that too. "Okay."

He reached down and grabbed my dress, scrunching it up so that the material slid up my legs, over my knees and up my thighs.

I leaned back and held up my arms. I smiled at him, confident and content to let him undress me. He wanted me, I knew that. From what he'd said, he wanted to get me naked from the first moment we'd met.

He lifted the dress to my waist then gave it a couple more tugs to get it over my breasts, my shoulders, then finally I was as naked as the day I was born. Axel was staring at me with ferociously hungry eyes.

"I hope you're going to get naked too." I bit my lip to stop the squeal that rose. For a single moment, I wanted to lift my hands and cover myself up. But I also wanted to drop to my knees and open Axel's jeans and take his cock out. Maybe that's the direction I'd take. I dropped to the plush carpet and reached for his jeans.

"I wasn't planning on getting naked just yet."

I tugged at his belt and flicked open the button, not wanting to give him any reason to try and escape me tonight. "I know I was the one to beg you to go slowly. And I've regretted that move a hundred times since last week." A million times was more like it. If I'd just let him fuck me the first time he'd wanted to, by the time we'd worked out that Axel knew my dad, it would have been too late.

Axel reached down and cupped my chin. "I've actually loved taking it slowly with you. It's been a unique experience."

Well, that was one good thing, I supposed. But tonight

wasn't for slow. I pulled down the zipper on his jeans, slowly. His cock was already rock-hard and thick behind the fly, and as I finally got the last of the zip down and peeled back the denim, he sprang out to meet me. "Oh, hello," I said, laughing a little.

Axel reached over his shoulder and tugged his shirt off. Then he stepped back a little and pushed his jeans from his hips and strolled back to me completely naked now. "Yeah, well you're hot. I'm never *not* hard around you."

I wrapped my hand around his shaft and kissed the head, loving on him just the way he'd taught me.

He sighed and slid his hand around my head, gently guiding me as I took his cock into my mouth and went deeper.

I tasted him and explored him, his moans of pleasure echoing in the fancy bedroom until he grabbed me under the arms and hauled me to my feet.

"That's enough for now."

He reached over and stripped the blankets from the bed, then pointed towards the mattress. "Lie on your back. It's my turn to love on you."

I didn't stop to examine that sentence. Instead, I raced onto the bed, flipped over and lay with my head on the pillow.

He prowled up the mattress until he was hovering above me.

He rocked his hips against me and growled. "Damn, you're divine. I wanna take you so much."

"So, take me," I invited, spreading my legs open and running my hands up his arms.

He shook his head gruffly. "No. Not until you're begging me to."

I smiled at him. "I'll beg you right now."

He shook his head again, then this time he rolled onto his side and slid his fingers between my thighs.

I gasped as he rubbed his fingertip against my clit, startling me. "Oh!" I grabbed his shoulders, and he buried his head in my neck.

"I want you to scream for me."

I closed my eyes to better enjoy the sensations. Axel nibbled on my earlobe, then sucked on the skin of my neck. I didn't care if he gave me a hickey. In fact, I hoped he did. I wanted something to remember this moment, forever.

He moved lower, suckling at my breasts, causing arrows of pleasure to shoot through my belly.

I arched my back and threaded my fingers through his thick hair, holding him close. My eyes were closed, but I forced them open so that I could watch him.

The sight of him kissing my flesh, tugging at my nipple with his teeth was driving me crazy. There was something so erotic about seeing the real-life picture. When he moved lower, I opened my legs willingly, wanting him to do all the magical things he'd done to me the other night, again and again.

He kissed my stomach, then slid down so his head was right between my thighs. He got onto his elbows, teasing my drenched opening with his fingers.

I covered my face with my hands, arching into his caress again, then moaning loudly as he slid his fingers inside of me. "Ahhh!"

"Are you okay?"

I dropped my hands away from my face and nodded. "Yes. It's just... I..."

He moved his fingers in and out of my body, then set his lips to my clit and licked my most sensitive place.

"Holy shit!" I sat bolt upright and grabbed his hair, then collapsed back onto the bed as he began to play me like I was a musical instrument once more.

He flicked my clit with his tongue and lips, making my belly tighten, and strangled screams erupt from my throat. He stretched me with his fingers, making me crave him even more as he slid them inside of me, over and over again.

I panted and grabbed for him, then cried out as he withdrew and crawled back up my body. "Not without me this time."

"No!" I agreed, grabbing onto his brawny arms and pulling him towards me. "Please. I want to feel you inside of me."

I was empty and aching now. I'd been so close to coming, which he must have known.

Axel rolled to the side, grabbed his cock and rubbed himself against my entrance.

I moaned and tilted my hips up to him, wanting to capture his hardness and drag him inside me.

Axel rolled back on top of me and nudged the head inside of me.

I cried out, lifting my legs and wrapping my thighs around his waist. "Please." Begging wasn't beyond me at this point. I dug my heels into his back. "I need more."

He groaned as he settled over me, our lips only a breath apart. He stared into my eyes as he slid into me, an inch at a time.

I gasped at the strangeness of the feeling, then lifted my head and our lips met.

He ground down on my mouth, thrusting his tongue inside as he surged into me fully.

A spike of pain made me gasp against his mouth, but it was nowhere near what I'd expected.

He lifted his head, staring down at me with intense, lust-drugged eyes. "Fuck. You feel amazing. Like a dream."

I ran my hands up and down his arms, feeling a little strange. Awkward. "Is this it?"

He chuckled, a lightness entering his eyes. "We're just getting started, beautiful."

And then he began to move, the true dance beginning.

Every time he withdrew, I dug my nails into his flesh, wanting him closer. Then he'd surge back, and I'd moan, my pleasure ricocheting up a notch. On it went, and with every thrust of his hips, every kiss of his lips, my belly tightened.

My pleasure began to mount, and bit my lip, feeling my pussy squeezing him with every thrust he made. "I'm..." I swallowed hard, "I'm..."

He began to move faster, harder, fucking me into the mattress and making my pleasure climb higher than any peak I'd ever encountered. I went past Everest. I was in the stratosphere.

"Come on, baby," he groaned into my ear, and with that final thrust, my orgasm crested and blew apart.

I screamed, and he fucked me harder, making the wave surge higher and higher until I couldn't hear, couldn't think. I could only feel him shuddering over me, filling me with heat. Then I was falling down, my belly quivering, my pussy clamping down on him and squeezing him over and over again.

And then it was over, and we lay in a mess of arms and legs. Of sweat, and a few tears on my face.

I was a woman.

I was his.

And in this one brief moment in time, everything was perfect.

27

AXEL

I didn't want to move.

Balls deep in the sweetest, hottest woman I'd ever known, I wasn't going anywhere. I didn't want to speak or move or do anything to break the hot, sweaty spell that had us wrapped up.

Everything about that session had been perfect. Her body's reactions to me, her moans of pleasure. Even the way she touched me, kissed me, and the way she tasted. It was officially my sweetest memory of her. And the sexiest.

But as the seconds ticked on and Chastity was no longer panting, the room became still and quiet. Then I realized that despite my comfort and the fact that I didn't want to move, I was probably squashing her. "I should get up." I groaned, pushing up on my hands, my body complaining about the movement in every cell.

She grabbed for me, tightening her legs around my waist, and grabbing onto my arms. "No. Stay. You're not heavy."

I doubted that very much, but I didn't want to leave, either. So, I shifted a little and took some of my weight on my arm, then grabbed her hip and rolled to the side and dragged her with me. "Are you okay?"

She nodded, bliss etched into every crevice on her face. "Oh, yeah. How about you?"

"Yeah... I..." I shifted, and my dick slipped out of her. Damn. "I better clean up." I reached for my cock, searching for the lip of the condom that I always wore. Always. "What the..." I lifted her thigh to search for it, to stare down at her naked, perfect, pink little pussy. Wetness dripped out of her. "Oh my God."

"What's wrong?" Chastity asked, sitting up, then wincing. "Wow, that's kind of sore now."

Guilt hit me from every angle. I'd hurt her. I'd deflowered her. I'd had unprotected sex with a virgin. "Please tell me you're on the pill." Women did that, right? For other reasons other than sex.

"No. I don't need to. Why?" She glanced down at the same spot I'd been staring at. "Did you..."

I nodded and sat up, wanting to punch my own lights out. "I'm so sorry. I didn't even think. I just... you were..."

"I was what?" Chastity asked, her eyes wide and hurt.

I turned back and pulled her close. "No! You were perfect! So perfect! I just... let myself get carried away because you were so sexy." I kissed her forehead, then the tip of her nose. "Damn, you're beautiful. I could just lose myself in you all day."

She stared up at me with eyes that were still filled with tears. "I'm so sorry." She wiped her cheeks. "Should I be worried about anything?"

I shook my head. "Not from me. I get a full work up from the doctor every six months. Last blood test was a few weeks ago. Plus, I'm always careful."

She smiled, a tear slipping down her cheek making her look young and so vulnerable, she made my heart ache. "Not always."

I squeezed her tightly, hauling her closer. "You are a first for me, on so many levels, sweetheart. You're just..." I ran out of words. "Perfect."

She sighed and laid her head on my chest.

I rocked her, because it felt right to hold her like this. I glanced over at the clock on my dresser when I heard her softly yawn. "Hey, how 'bout we have a quick shower, then come back here to sleep?"

She slid off my lap then giggled as she swayed on her feet. "I can barely stand up properly. My legs are all wobbly."

I stood up behind her and slid a hand around her waist. "I'm sorry if I hurt you. I really didn't want to."

She smiled as we staggered into the bathroom. "You didn't hurt me, I'm just achy. I'm sure you know what that's like."

I chuckled. "Hardly. I can't say that my deflowering was very painful."

She rolled her eyes. "I don't want to know about that! What I meant was, I just used muscles I've literally never used before. You know, like when you train at the gym after a long break or something. I'm just achy."

"Okay, then." I agreed with her, she sounded drunk on her happiness. "Come and let's clean up." I turned on the shower, letting the water heat up for a few moments, and tugged her beneath the hot spray. I didn't know how to deal with all the different emotions coming at me. It was all too intense. How did people get any work done when they were in love like this?

I shook my head to get rid of the ridiculous thought. *Shut up! What is wrong with you?* I picked up the bar of soap and started washing her arms and pulled her close, so her back was against my chest. "As long as you're all right." I moved the soapy washcloth down between her legs, gently wiping away the remains of our first encounter.

"I'm more than all right." She sighed. "I'm great."

Waves of happiness flowed over me, and I began to feel like I might drown. I reached for the faucet handle to turn the water off. "Okay, let's get to bed."

"No! My turn." She reached for the soap and began washing my chest. "You're so sexy, I seriously can't believe it sometimes."

I took the soap from her and rinsed off. "Let's go, beautiful." Ushering her from the shower, I grabbed a couple of towels and dried us both quickly. "Let's get to bed." I put my arm around her and led her to my bed once again. "Jump in."

She crawled onto the mattress and lay down on her side, her profile as astounding as every other part of her. From the angle of her knee to the curve of her hip, she was just magnificent.

I crawled onto the mattress and tugged the blankets up over us, then laid my head on my pillow, facing her.

"You okay?" she asked.

I nodded. "Yeah, of course. Are you okay?"

She smiled softly. "I had the most amazing night ever. Of course, I'm all right. But you look worried. Are you regretting what happened?"

I grinned and grabbed for her. "Come here, you." I tugged her and flipped her over so that her spine was against my chest and her ass was pressed into my belly.

When she looked at me, it was like she was staring straight through me. "Are you sure you're okay, Axel? You can tell me."

I sighed and pressed a kiss to her shoulder. Even facing away, she was too in tune with me.

"I am a little worried. I've never risked unprotected sex like that. I..." If she got pregnant, what the hell would we do? Pat would kill me, and her college dreams would be done.

"It's okay. My period's due next week, so the timing isn't right, I don't think. But I'll let you know. Okay?"

"Okay."

What else could I say? It was my fault we were in this mess. It wasn't like the virgin should be the one to worry about contraception.

"Thank you for the most incredible night, Axel. I wouldn't change a thing, seriously. It was perfect."

I squeezed her tightly against me. "Let's get some sleep. I've been looking forward to this for a week."

She giggled softly. "Which part? Just sleeping with me?"

I closed my eyes. "Yeah. You're a good teddy bear."

It was so much more than that, but there was no way I was owning up to everything I was feeling at the moment. I felt too unguarded, too raw. Like someone had torn away all the armor I had carefully constructed around myself over the decades. Laying here with her sated body curled up in my arms, I was totally at peace. My brain wasn't whirling, I wasn't fighting. I was just me. Happy. And it was the most foreign feeling in the world.

"Go to sleep my, perfect girl. I've gotta get up early in the morning, but I'll wake you before I leave."

"Hmmmm." She nestled closer and was soon asleep.

I smiled and pulled the blanket a little higher over her shoulder, then slipped into dreamland alongside her.

When I woke to my cell phone buzzing out my alarm. I groaned. I didn't want to get up. Today was going to be a bitch.

Chastity still slept in front of me, and I still had my arm wrapped around her. We'd barely moved all night.

I lifted my head and stared at the clock. Six a.m., and I didn't remember waking once. *Damn it, this girl is better for sleep than Valium.* I tried to remove my arm without waking her, but as soon as I tried to move away, she rolled onto her back, smiled up at me and blinked sleepily.

"Good morning."

"Good morning," I whispered back, dropping a quick kiss on her soft lips. "You stay asleep. I'll call you later."

She reached up and cupped my cheek softly. "Okay."

I dropped another kiss on her lips because the first one wasn't enough, then got out of the bed quickly before I was tempted to blow off my morning and stay in bed with her.

I raced to the shower, my cock hard and bouncing against my stomach. Damn it, I would have loved to take her again. Just roll on top and slide into her welcoming body. I was pretty sure she would have let me, if it hadn't been her first-time last night. I would have been rather late for work and driven us both into our first orgasm for the day.

And would you have remembered protection this time? Probably not, fucktard! "Damn it! What's wrong with you?"

If we were going to stay together longer-term, I would have asked her to go on the pill for us. Everything with her was so damn natural and easy. If we'd met a few hundred years ago, I'm sure I would have moved her in and had a dozen babies. There's no way I would have kept my hands to myself.

I grabbed my razor and quickly shaved. If I really felt that way about this girl, that in another time I would have happily pumped her full of babies, then what the hell was I doing letting her go in less than two weeks? I shook my head, cleaned up and headed into my walk-in closet. I picked out a custom navy pinstriped suit, a grey tie and my crispest white shirt.

It wasn't 1950. And we weren't Vikings or cavemen. I worked hard. She went to school. We were products of our society and our time, and I needed to be grateful for the moments I had with Chastity.

I glanced in the mirror to make sure I hadn't missed anything. Then I headed through my bedroom and out the door. I didn't look back, though a part of me ached to do so. I had a thousand things to do today, and I needed to get my mind focused, and off the young woman I'd left in my bed.

28

CHASTITY

I stared into the glass of white wine and ran my finger around the rim, softly singing to myself.

"Chastity? Are you okay?"

I glanced up. "Yeah, of course, Mom. Why?"

She shrugged and poured herself another glass of wine. "You just seem distracted that's all. Everything go well with Axel last night?"

I nodded, heat pumping into my cheeks, making my face burn. "Uh, yeah... great."

"Are you seeing him again?"

I stared at my mom, noting the pinched look around her mouth. "Yeah, I will. But don't worry, Mom, I know that there's no future for us. I'm just trying to enjoy it while it lasts." I brushed my hand past the wine glass I'd barely touched and reached for my cell phone. I'd been trying not to text Axel all day. After all, he hadn't reached out, but I'd looked at it so many times, it was embarrassing to admit the number.

"I just don't want you to get hurt, Chastity. You've always been so smart, avoiding boys like the plague. But this one..."

I laughed, "Hardly a boy, Mom."

"Exactly. He's a man. Who knows what he wants—or should."

I could feel my mother was ramping up for another one of her lectures, so I stood up, cell phone in hand. "I think I'm going to go to bed, Mom. See you in the morning?"

She nodded. "I've got to go into the office to pick something up, but then I'll be home in the afternoon."

"Perfect." I smiled. "I want to start baking Christmas cookies and some gingerbread." I kissed her on the cheek and headed to my bedroom. I needed a little space to think, and just be. My mom made it impossible to just be quiet. She always needed to fill the space with music, television or talk, even if it was idle chatter. And while I appreciated that most of the time, today I just needed some space.

I'd woken up around eleven a.m., having slept so well I could barely open my eyes from the sheer exhaustion of it all. But Axel was gone and had been for hours. The expensive penthouse apartment was enormous, cold, and empty without him. So, I'd thrown on my clothes, called an Uber, and raced out of there.

I didn't really like the idea of hanging around his space while he wasn't there. It would be just my luck that he'd have some maid or personal chef, or someone show up. And there I'd be, still wearing the dress I'd come over in last night. The walk of shame, billionaire style. If there was such a thing.

I'd gone home and spent the day with my mom, but now it was bedtime. I hadn't heard from him, and I missed him. I stripped out of my clothes, pulled back the blankets and climbed into bed in my panties and a tank top.

It was still early to go to bed—near ten—but I settled into my tiny mattress and sighed with happiness. Last night had been amazing. Better than any first-time sex story I'd ever heard. And it was all because Axel had been the most patient, perfect, talented lover. And I wanted more.

Hey. How was your day? I miss you.

I hit send, even though I wasn't sure if I should tell him how much I missed him. Would he like that? Hate it? Didn't matter now, it was gone into the ether.

Hey, stranger. I'm still at the office pulling an all-nighter. How was your day?

I frowned.

Seriously? I thought only slacker college students pulled all-nighters before final exams.

He wrote back.

Lol. Hardly.

I wriggled my fingers and tapped my foot against the bed. Should I ask to see him again? Would he want to see me soon? Or more like the weekend? I had no idea of his schedule, but if I had my way, I'd be in his bed again tomorrow. A cheeky thought popped into my head, and I smiled to myself and picked up my phone.

When you finally crash, do you want a teddy bear to sleep with?

I sent it then instantly regretted it. What if he said no? I jumped up and threw my phone on the bed when he didn't instantly respond. *Shit, shit, shit!*

Moving to the bathroom, I brushed my teeth, washed my face, and generally freaked out. I knew I wasn't one of those girls to over-think and over-stress about guys, but Axel was special. I didn't want to muck anything up before it had even begun. We'd agreed to spend time together over the next two weeks, and I wanted *all* those days.

When my nerves got the better of me, and my stomach twisted into knots, I raced back to my bedroom to find I'd missed a call from him. "Shit!" I paced my small bedroom while I rang him back. My heart was pounding and when he finally answered, my stomach lurched.

"Hey, beautiful."

The relief at hearing him talk to me in that tone was instant, and I staggered to my bed before collapsing onto the mattress. "I'm so sorry I missed your call. I was just in the bathroom."

"It's all good. I just thought it might be easier to chat for a minute. I need to get back to work soon."

"Oh." *Well, wasn't that romantic?*

"But I wanted to hear your voice once more. It'll bolster me for the hours ahead."

That's more like it! "Well, I was wondering if we could schedule our next date," I said in a rush. "We've only got two weeks before I head back and I want to see you as many times as I can, if that's okay." Damn, I was a mess.

He chuckled softly on the line. "How about tomorrow? I can't guarantee I'll be any use to you after the night's work I've got planned, but I'd love to see you."

I bit my lip to stop the squeal that rose from escaping. "I'd love that. What time?"

"How about eight?? My place again?"

"I'll be there."

"Great. I've gotta go, but I'll see you tomorrow."

The best words I'd ever heard. "Great. See you then." I hung up and let the squeal out. I was seeing him again! Tomorrow. *Your dad's best friend.* "Oh, shut up, "I told myself. Dad would never find out about our clandestine two weeks, surely. I would never tell him, and Axel certainly wouldn't either. So as long as neither of us went insane and said anything, he would always be none the wiser.

I put a hand to my still tender belly and smiled. Tomorrow would be amazing. More kisses, more sex, more intense, tender, ridiculously dream-like moments with Axel. I climbed into bed and ran my hands over my body, enjoying the tenderness of my nipples, and the sensitivity of my clit. Everything inside of me was buzzing with energy. And I wanted more of it. A lot more of it.

~

The day dragged on so slowly, I was going insane by the time seven p.m. rolled around.

"Are you sure you've had enough to eat?" Mom asked, offering me the Chicken Pad Thai for the tenth time.

"Yeah, I'm fine. I've gotta go pack, then I'll be off."

"You're going to Axel's again?"

I nodded, ignoring the unhappy look on my mom's face and her narrowed eyes. "Yep. Won't be long." I raced to my bedroom, packed a set of clothes for tomorrow and squirted some perfume on my neck. I'd been fantasizing all day about all the things I wanted to do to Axel. Maybe he'd teach me how to ride him? That had to be fun. Being able to look down on him, have him fondling my breasts while I slid up and down his cock. I shivered at the thought as I stuffed some clothes and a toothbrush into my bag.

Mom opened the door as I was pulling out my cell phone. "I'll drive you."

"No, it's okay," I said, waving my phone. "I was just about to—"

"No!" She interrupted, crossing her arms over her chest. "I want to see where you're heading off to every night." From the look on her face and the set of her jaw, this wasn't an argument I was going to win.

"Okay, Mom. That'd be great." Hopefully she wouldn't insist on seeing his actual apartment, though if she did, would she change her mind about him? Money and success generally impressed her, though, it hadn't so far with Axel. But maybe she didn't realize just how rich he actually was. "You ready to go right away?" I asked, glancing at my watch. "I said I'd be there at eight."

Mom nodded and stepped out of my doorway. "Yep, let's go."

We locked up and jumped into her old car.

"You'll need to direct me. I don't know which way I'm going."

"Just head to the city, and I'll show you," I said, pointing down the street. "It's about twenty minutes or so."

Mom nodded, and we took off.

The silence was deafening, so I reached for the radio and flicked on the knob.

"Where does he live?" she asked suddenly. "An apartment?"

"Yeah. The penthouse, in a building in the city," I answered, feeling strangely un-nerved by my mother's behavior. She seemed angry, though I couldn't work out why she would be.

"The penthouse?" she repeated. "Impressive, I suppose."

I laughed then coughed to clear my throat. "No, what's impressive is the fact he built and owns the whole building."

Silence descended again, so this time I just looked out the window and watched the city fly by.

As we got closer, I started directing her along the streets, until finally she pulled up outside the impressive building. "Thanks, Mom. Did you want to walk me up? Or—"

She shook her head emphatically, effectively interrupting me, and I turned away to open the door.

Her hand snaked out and she grabbed my arm. "Please be careful, Chastity."

I turned back. "What do you mean, Mom? What's wrong?"

"I just..." She stopped and swallowed. "You know I've never regretted keeping you."

"I know."

"But you have an opportunity here that I never had. You're

smart. You're amazing. You're heading to graduation, and chiropractic school, and I don't want you throwing any of that away on some guy. I don't care how rich he is."

I smiled and squeezed her hand. "I won't, Mom. Axel is just... fun. He makes me feel special."

"I know, that's what I'm afraid of," she said, then withdrew her hand. "He isn't the marrying kind, sweetheart. So just guard your heart as best you can, okay? You're not the type of girl who has fun and just walks away."

I rolled my eyes and got out of the car. "Thanks for the lift, Mom! I'll see you tomorrow."

I stepped back and waved at her as she pulled into traffic and drove home.

I wrapped my arms around myself and thought about what she'd said. In the past I hadn't been one to date guys casually, and I didn't really think I was now either. But I wanted some fun, and I deserved it after all the time and effort I'd put in to being "good" during my teenage years. It was time to be bad.

29

AXEL

My head throbbed with a migraine, and I was beginning to see stars. The aura had been chasing me all day. Then the light sensitivity had hit, and I had my driver take me home, and I'd climbed into bed. When the doorbell peeled, I groaned. Loudly. "Oh, shit."

I didn't keep a permanent housekeeper like most of my wealthy friends, but at times like this, I wished I did. I rolled out of bed, only opening my eyes enough to see where I was going and felt my way along the walls to the front door. When I opened it and saw my gorgeous little Chastity there, even in my pained state, a sense of happiness washed over me.

Her face was lit up with a huge smile that quickly crashed into a frowning look of worry. "What's wrong? Are you okay?"

I waved her inside then shut the door after her, sagging against the wall for a moment to stop from falling over. "Migraine."

"Then you should be in bed," she said, dropping her bag on the ground, then putting her body next to mine and my arm over her shoulder. "Come on. I'll help you."

I didn't fight her as she walked me back to my room, supporting my wobbly frame.

When I got close to my bed, I pulled my arm off her shoulders, staggered over to the mattress, and climbed beneath the covers again. The room was dark and cool, and I sighed as my head hit the pillow once more. "I'm sorry to screw up our night," I managed to say, though I could barely open my eyes.

She laughed softly. "You're just trying to get out of having sex with me again, aren't you?"

I chuckled as well. "I wish that was the reason." I stifled the groan that rose as a fresh wave of nausea rolled through me.

"What do you need?" she asked quietly. "Water? Painkillers?"

"Just sleep," I told her. I'd already taken everything I had. This was most likely stress induced. I'd had a bitch of a day.

The mattress dipped as Chastity crawled onto the bed, lay down beside me and pulled the covers up over us.

I forced my eyes open to stare at her. "Are you tired too?"

She smiled as she laid her head on the pillow and reached out to run her fingers through my hair.

I moaned at the touch. "God, that feels good."

She pressed harder, massaging my temples in a rhythmic circular motion.

"If you roll onto your back and turn this way a little, I can do both sides at the same time."

"Okay." That sounded like heaven, though I'd never thought that was a place I'd end up. I rolled onto my back and moved so that I was lying at more of a horizontal angle.

Chastity sat up, shuffled into place at the headboard, and gently put my head in her lap.

"I'm sorry," I said again, at a total loss for words with so much pain winging through my usually healthy body. "I don't usually get migraines this bad, but..."

"But what?" she whispered. "Are you okay?"

I nodded while she rubbed her fingers over my temples, then began to slowly trace patterns over my skull and through my hair. "Yeah, I'm okay. Just work shit. That feels really nice." The pain was actually easing a little. Not enough to stand up or try to function, but I might be able to fall asleep if the pressure decreased a little.

"My chiropractor does a lot of cranial work on me, and I know it might help a little."

I sighed again as she worked through my skull, all the way around the back where my neck ached with tension. "Pity you're not trained yet," I joked. "I'd hire you full time to look after me and my staff."

"How many people work for you?" she asked.

"Hmmm... in my building? I don't know. Two hundred, maybe."

She laughed softly. "Two hundred people, check them twice a month, a hundred people a week. Yeah. That sounds like a good plan."

I smiled and relaxed deeper into her touch. I'd said it as a joke, but I knew of CEOs that hired massage therapists to attend their staff. Why not a full-time chiropractor?

"Let's set it up," I said. "You call me when you graduate, and we'll get you an office."

She was silent for a long time until I opened my eyes and looked up at her. "You okay?"

She nodded. "Yeah, that sounds nice. Close your eyes. Try to sleep."

She sounded sad, and I got it. We'd set the terms of this deal already. Two weeks of sex and fun, then we were done. Now I was inviting her to come work for me. That hadn't been part of the plan.

"I didn't mean to—"

"It's okay," she interrupted quietly. "I'm enjoying the time we're having now and not thinking about the future."

I smiled and closed my eyes. "You can't be enjoying this."

"I am," she jumped in to say. "I don't mean the part about you being in pain, that's shit. And I must admit that I'd planned to already be naked with you like this. But my plans included me massaging other parts of your body."

I groaned. "Oh, God... don't torture me. I wish I could. God, I wish I could."

But my cock didn't even stir at the suggestion, which, considering how much I desired the woman in my bed, definitely said something about my current state. All of my blood was pumping into my migraine, and my body was not responding to anything other than the pain.

She giggled. "I'm sorry, I said that all around the wrong way. What I meant was... I'm kind of enjoying looking after you. I didn't think you'd let me."

I couldn't help the sigh that fell from my lips. "Yeah... well..."

"I mean, you don't have full-time staff members cooking and cleaning for you. I doubt you let a lot of people cater to you. You just don't seem like that sort of guy."

I sighed again and didn't open my eyes. I felt vulnerable enough as it was. "How come you seem to know me so well?" I'd never let anyone see me like this before. Not since I was sixteen and living with my parents. Though even then, it was the housekeeper that brought me a barf bucket, not my mother.

It took a lot for me to trust anyone, let alone a woman I was sleeping with. That didn't happen often, and to let them see me in this sort of state... useless, helpless, and vulnerable? She was right. It had never happened. "Come lie down with me." I said, tugging at her arms. "I wanna feel that naked body of yours against me."

"Okay, give me a minute. Just gotta run to the bathroom."

She crawled off the bed and disappeared.

So I took my time shuffling around and lying my head back on the pillow. The pain had eased, and the nausea was only softly clawing at my stomach. I might be able to sleep for a few hours, then I'd feel better. I was sure of it.

The door closed and Chastity crawled back into the bed with me.

"You better be naked," I softly growled at her.

She giggled and shuffled closer, shoving her naked, fleshy, warm ass against my belly.

"Oh, yeah," I said, wrapping my arm around her middle.

"You're not naked though," she whispered.

I pulled her even closer, then kissed her hair. "I couldn't stand up long enough to undress properly. Don't worry. As soon as I can get naked. I will."

She didn't say anything else, she just settled into my arms and was still. And quiet.

Sleep beckoned and yet I fought it, not wanting to lose touch of this moment.

We'd had so many perfect, beautiful times together. And this one, amazingly, was going to be tattooed across my mind for many years to come. The poor girl had come here looking for fun, passion, and orgasms. And here I was, still dressed, cuddling her in bed, totally unable to fulfil any of the fantasies she'd hoped for.

"Thank you for this," I whispered at her before I lost my mind and succumbed to sleep. "I'll make it up to you, I promise." I didn't hear what she said next, if she did respond. Sleep claimed my drug-addled, pained body, and into dream world I fell.

30

CHASTITY

I was in love with Axel. There was no denying it any longer. And due to this fact, I'd concluded that I was an idiot. An absolute imbecile.

I was lying in his bed, horny, hot, and naked, and wiggling against his sleeping body. Well, no, I was lying as still and quiet as I could, because I knew he was asleep. His breathing had changed, and his arms were heavy around me.

But the fact that he was asleep didn't stop me from knowing just how much I wanted him. How much I loved the fact that he'd wanted me close to him while he was sick. He was not the sort of man to let people in unless he trusted them.

And here I was, being held by him, while he slept off a migraine. I felt honored. And dumb at the same time. Dumb because I'd known this guy was trouble from the moment I'd laid eyes on him. From the very second I'd seen him walk through those doors at Dad's gym, I'd known this was the sort of guy who broke the hearts of girls like me. But how was I going to walk away from this with my head, and preferably my heart, still in one piece?

Inside my mind, in that place I didn't want to admit really existed, that part of my brain was already working out how far school was from here, and whether I could get a ride home on weekends to see him. But would he want that? He'd said that we only had two weeks together, but would he want more if I offered it to him?

This cuddle and trust told me he'd jump at the chance to keep his teddy bear. That he'd keep seeing me as long as it worked for the both of us. But then there was the whole Dad thing, the complicating factor. The longer we were together, the more likely it was that my father would find out, and neither of us wanted that.

And there was one other shitty thing to deal with. The fact that I was in love with the guy and wanted to stay with him forever despite my future plans, our deal, and the knowledge inside my brain that said this was not the man to fall for. This was the kind of guy you had fun with. *And I was.* I was having lots of fun.

But as I closed my eyes and willed my body not to clench in anticipation of what he would do next, I wanted to admit to myself finally that he was so much more. He was passionate, and kind, and extremely hardworking. He was a man to admire, to love, to marry. I shook my head and growled at myself.

Stop it! You've got, like, ten days left. Enjoy it, because soon enough you'll be taking the tattered remains of your heart back to college, and the only thing you'll have to hold at night will be the memories of nights like this.

31

AXEL

Waking up without throbbing pain in my head was like sunshine after the storm. My head was clear, but my body ached with an intense hangover-like feeling. I opened my eyes and stared down at Chastity, where she lay sleeping in my arms. Damn, she'd been amazing last night. Compassionate, patient. Behaving so far beyond her years, which she often did.

"Good morning," she said suddenly, her eyes still closed. "Are you feeling better?" She rolled onto her back and the blankets slipped down, revealing her gorgeous breasts and rosy, pink nipples. She opened her eyes and smiled.

A wave of lust washed over me. "Hmmm... much better." I said, tugging the blankets further down to reveal her full nakedness and the surprise she'd obviously wanted to reveal last night. "Did you shave for me?" I asked, admiring her newly bare flesh as I ran my hand up her thigh and over the freshly manicured strip of hair covering her mons.

She giggled and opened her legs, inviting me to touch her.

"You never said anything, but I thought you might like it a little neater. Oh..."

I used my fingertips to circle her clit, then dipped down to where she was already juicy for me. "You feel ready, sweetheart. Have you been thinking about what I should have done to you last night?" Because I certainly was. I couldn't believe a stupid migraine had cost me a whole night with this beautiful woman. And I intended to make up for it now.

I flicked her clit from side to side with my fingers, then bent my head to kiss her mouth. I tasted her tongue with mine as I slid a single finger down between her lips and inside her wet, tight channel.

She groaned against my mouth, then pulled me down on top of her.

I thrust my finger in and out of her sweet, hot opening, loving the way her pussy tightened and clenched around me.

She threw her head back, moaning loudly, which made her breasts arch invitingly into the air.

I moved down and clamped my lips around one tight, plump little nipple and suckled gently.

She threaded her fingers through my hair and held me to her.

My cock was pulsing now, throbbing and hard. But I ignored it, determined to give her the pleasure she craved.

Suddenly she pushed on my chest, and I went with her motions, rolling onto my back. "What are you doing?"

"I want to get on top of you," she insisted, reaching for my sweats and tugging them down over my hips.

I laughed at her display of impatience.

She tugged at my pants, so I lifted my hips and let her undress me. She slid everything down my legs, then threw them to the floor.

When she crawled up to me, I wanted nothing more than to

grab her around the waist and haul her on top of me, but I stopped myself. "Grab a condom from the top drawer."

Her eyes went wide with surprise then she grinned and crawled over to the nightstand where I had a new stash.

I went up on my elbows and stared after her, loving the view her round ass afforded me as she rifled through my drawer. She was sexy and lush, and I couldn't wait to lick her from head to toe.

When she crawled back, she had a "cat that ate the canary" smile as she handed me the rubber and I ripped it open. But before I could slide it on, she was on her belly, grabbing me and wrapping her lips around my cock.

"Fuck!" I cried out, grabbing hold of the sheets beneath me. "Damn, your mouth is perfect."

She moved her hand up and down the shaft while she sucked on the head, tonguing the lip like I'd taught her.

"Come here," I demanded, tugging at her arm until she lifted her head and looked at me.

"What's wrong?"

Nothing! "Come ride me."

I rolled the condom down over my pulsing cock and pulled her up until she was straddling me and rubbing her wet pussy over my belly.

"How do I do this exactly?" she asked.

I groaned at how sweet and innocent yet totally hot she was. I grabbed the shaft and held it up at an angle. "Go up on your knees, tilt your pelvis back, and slide down."

She frowned, the most adorable look of concentration on her face as she moved back and wiggled around, coating my cock with her juices and driving me crazy.

My head fell back on a moan when she finally found the entrance to her body and slid back, wrapping me in tight heat.

"Oh... wow," she moaned as she inched back.

I grabbed her tiny waist and squeezed her, trying to hold onto the slim piece of sanity I still possessed.

"Now I move?" she panted out.

I nodded, opening my eyes even though I hadn't realized I'd closed them, and staring up at her. "Yeah. You move."

She began to roll her hips, and lift up and slide down, slowly driving me crazy with her wet heat.

I groaned and threw my head back, loving the sensations ricocheting through my body while the gorgeous woman on top of me gasped out her own pleasure.

Everything about her was addictive, and I liked her innocence a little bit more than I should have. I loved the fact she was learning with me. That I was her first *everything*. I lifted my head again and forced my drugged eyes to open so that I didn't miss the expression on her face as she learned how much she liked being on top of me. What I saw tugged at my heart. Her eyes were wide, her mouth open in wonder. She leaned down to kiss me, and I reached up, cupping her face, and arching up to meet her lips.

We kissed deeply, weaving our tongues together and meshing our mouths, just as our bodies were entwining. She kept moving on top of me, taking my cock deep into her body, then withdrawing until I couldn't stand the slow pace anymore.

I planted my feet on the mattress and gripped her hips, driving up into her with every downward thrust she made.

"Oh! Axel!" Chastity grabbed onto my wrists, anchoring herself.

"Do you want... me... to... stop?" I asked with every heavy thrust into her tightening pussy.

She closed her eyes and shook her head. "No. Don't stop. Please." She was flushed with heat, her cheeks pink and her chest heaving as she gasped and moaned.

I drove into her harder, faster, fighting back the edges of my own orgasm. Heat tingled at the base of my spine and trickled down the back of my legs, but I fought it off, determined to have Chastity find her pleasure before I did.

"Axel, don't stop. Please, don't stop. Oh, fuckkkk." Chastity bucked against me, coming so hard it felt like she was going to squeeze my dick off. She shuddered over me, her nails digging into my hands.

I had no choice now. I thrust up into her, as hard and high as I could, damning the stupid rubber between us. I roared so loud I probably peeled the paint off the walls. I saw stars. And when I finally fell from the heavens, I had an angel on top of me, cuddling into my chest and sighing with contentment.

32

CHASTITY

It was Christmas Eve morning, and the day could not have started off any better. My body was still tingling from Axel's magical touch, and as I lay here on top of his chest, I didn't want to go anywhere. "What are your plans for today?" I asked, twisting my fingers in his chest hair.

"Um..." He wrapped his arms around my back and kissed the top of my head. "I probably need to finish all that work I didn't manage to get done last night. How about you?"

I smiled against him, wishing I had the guts to lick his skin and taste just how sweet his sweat was. "I'll be baking with my mom, mostly. Wrapping presents. All that stuff." I might catch up with Nicola later too. I hadn't seen my best friend in far too long.

"And tomorrow? You'll be visiting with your parents?" he asked, his throat catching as he said the words.

I turned around and brought my hand up, resting my chin on my fingers that lay on his chest. He looked so adorable. A little red in the cheeks, drowsy-eyed. "You look like you want to go back to sleep."

He chuckled, his chest moving up and down beneath me. "Yeah, well, you'll wear me out at this rate."

I laughed this time too, finally rolling off him and stretching out the slight ache in my legs. "I doubt that very much."

"Can I interest you in a shower?" he asked, running his hand over my ribcage and cupping my breast.

I looked at him with a fake irritation. "Haven't you had enough?"

He mock frowned at me. "Of you? Never! Want me to prove it?"

My breath hitched with excitement at the request. Could I handle more sex this morning? I was feeling pretty good. "Where? In the shower?"

He rolled off the bed, dropped the condom in the wastebasket and beckoned to me. "Yeah. Why? Do you want to be taken in the shower? Have you been thinking about it?"

I got to my feet, swallowing my nerves down. "Yeah, there's something so sexy about being taken against a wall."

Axel reached out and took my hand, pulling me towards him so hard I stumbled into his chest. "I find it so sexy that you have these fantasies about us. Wanna share anymore?"

Heated embarrassment rushed into my face. "Um... Do I have to tell you them all now?"

He chuckled. "Of course not. But once I fulfil this fantasy for you, you've gotta give me another one."

I shivered all over with the promise in his voice. "Okay."

He grinned and dropped a kiss on my lips that made me quiver all over again. "Well, let's get to that shower scene then."

He tugged me into the shower and beneath the hot water, then proceeded to show me that despite being nearly twice my age, his sexual appetite was in no way lacking. In fact, I doubted anyone my age would be able to compete with him. And that made me feel more grateful than anything else.

I had a god of a man. *A sex god.* And he was all mine. For one more week.

I WOKE up Christmas morning with bleary eyes and a soft tension sort of headache that came from being dehydrated. And still tired. I rolled onto my back and stretched my arms above my head, enjoying the loud groan that echoed through the room as I relaxed once again into the warmth of my bed. Christmas day had always been my favorite holiday. Too much food and chocolate. Sleeping late, no study, and time with my parents.

Mom and Dad, being only twenty-one years older than me, had always been fun parents. They had lots of energy and cool friends, and Christmas had always been magical. But as I reached for my cell phone and saw a thoughtful message from Axel, my chest squeezed with pain.

Missing him today would keep me preoccupied. I really was falling head over heels for the guy, and I knew that my most anticipated day of the year was going to be lackluster without him. It was wrong of me to assume that I wouldn't have a good day, but the feeling was there, and it was going to take a lot of effort to shake that mood.

"Good morning!" Mom called, opening the door, carrying in a mug of hot chocolate and the first of my presents. This was a tradition at our house. A present for breakfast, a present before lunch, and a final present before I went to my father's place for dinner.

"Merry Christmas, Mom," I responded, smiling as I dragged myself up to sit in bed. "Thank you."

I took the hot chocolate from her and couldn't help but smile as she handed me a gift, a box the size of a new pair of shoes, wrapped in red paper with a green ribbon. Maybe today wouldn't be too bad after all. I took a sip of my hot chocolate, then the doorbell rang.

Mom's eyes brows furrowed. "Who on earth could that be?"

Shrugging, I set the mug down and began to pull at the ribbon around the box.

Mom got up and tightened the tie around her fluffy housecoat. "I'll go see who that is and grab you some of the gingerbread we made yesterday."

"Perfect breakfast. Thanks, Mom." And it really was. I loved gingerbread so much, especially when it was a little soft and perfect for dunking in hot drinks.

When my mother got back to my room, she had a worried furrow going on between her eyes.

"What's up?" I asked, finally tearing open the paper to reveal exactly what I expected. "Oh, wonderful. Thank you so much, Mom." A new pair of flat leather boots. "These will be perfect for next year."

Mom held in her hands a small box, wrapped in familiar post office paper. "This was delivered for you."

I almost laughed, but that didn't seem appropriate. "On Christmas day? Who delivers Christmas day?"

Mom handed me the box and sat down on my bed once more. "It was a special courier. In a suit."

My heart leapt. *Surely, it couldn't be.* I tore open the paper to reveal a small, black jewelry box with a tiny gift tag attached.

"Were you expecting a gift from Axel?" Mom asked, the words falling into the silence around us.

My heart thudded in my chest. "No, not at all." I flipped over the gift tag, and it read, "To Chastity. Merry Christmas. Love, Axel." My eyes burned with unexpected tears, and I held the box in my hand for a long minute. I didn't want to open it up and break the spell. I wanted to believe just for a moment that he cared for me the way I cared for him.

"Open it, Chastity. The suspense is killing me."

I burst into laughter and wiped away the stray tear that fell. "Okay. Okay." I popped open the lid and gasped. Inside was the most beautiful necklace. There was a thin silver or white gold chain. And hanging at the end of the chain was a floating single diamond the size of a pea. "Uh..."

"That can't be real," Mom said from beside me. She'd moved to stand behind me and was peering over my shoulder.

"I don't know if it is, or if it isn't." I was breathless, taking the necklace out of its velvet bed and holding it up into the air. "Would you put it on me?" The tears were gathering in my eyes once more and my nose was tingling.

Mom clipped the necklace around the back of my neck, and I stood up and rushed over to the mirror.

"It's beautiful," I whispered, loving the way the jewel shimmered and shone in the morning light.

"If that's real, Chastity, do you have any idea how much it would have cost?"

I shook my head. "No. And I don't care." I twisted around and pulled my robe from the back of my chair. "Should we stay in our pajamas all morning before we go to Grandma's? Or do you want to do showers first?"

My mom crossed her arms over her chest, looking thoroughly displeased. "You can't wear that all day, Chastity. It'll raise too many questions."

I forced a smile to my lips, trying to shrug off my mother's mood. "It's freezing today, Mom. I'll wear a sweater, and no one will even see it."

Mom continued to pout at me, so I opened my door. "Let's go get some cookies and start our day right. I have your first present under the tree too, if you'd like to open it?"

That made her smile, but the rest of the day with her was just the same. Stilted. Odd. I didn't want to ask her why she was being so strange, because I knew she'd say something horrible about Axel, then I'd get upset and everything would get thrown out of balance even more.

It was a relief when it was finally five p.m., and I could head over to my dad's house for dinner.

"I love you, Mom. See you tomorrow."

"You're sleeping at your dad's tonight?" she asked, frowning.

"Ah, yeah. I always do Christmas night." That had been the arrangement for longer than I could remember. Mom had always had Christmas Eve, and most of Christmas day.

Dad had gotten dinner and the night of Christmas.

"But I feel like I've barely seen you this week." Mom pouted again. "You've been staying at your dad's and Axel's, and I expected to spend a lot more time with you than I have."

I hugged her tightly. "I love you. I'll see you tomorrow, okay?" When I pulled back, Mom simply nodded, and I grabbed my gifts for Dad and headed off to the Uber waiting outside.

There was a thread of anger I couldn't ignore pulsing through my gut. How dare my mother be so selfish? I'd spent more time with her than *anyone* else. But as she'd pointed out, she was used to unfettered, unlimited time with me. Maybe I'd spoiled her? But I didn't think it was unreasonable to ask for a little time with the guy I was seeing. I was twenty-one already. I should have been dating like this for years.

The Uber drove me to my father's apartment, and I got out of the car juggling my backpack and the presents I'd brought with me. I was still annoyed with my mom. She'd done nothing but pout all day. From the moment I'd received that present from Axel, she'd been uninterested in me.

The gifts I'd given her were greeted with a simple smile, and she'd been silent for most of lunch. I didn't know what her problem was, but if Axel's presence in my life was the issue, I didn't want to fix her problem. I went up to Dad's apartment and was greeted by the sounds of my aunts and uncles and cousins.

"Chastity!" I was pulled into the vortex of hugs, food, and presents.

By the time they all left, I was exhausted, and had collapsed on the armchair, looking at my dad with a silly grin on my face. "That was a fun night. Thank you."

He gestured to the bowls of candies and chocolates that still decorated the coffee table. "Do you want anything else?"

I shook my head and grabbed for my full belly. "God, no. I'm stuffed." I sighed and leaned my head back. I had a headache again. It was so tiring to pretend that everything was okay, when it wasn't.

"Hey, Chastity?"

"Yeah, Dad?" I lifted my head to see his concerned look.

"Are you all right? I mean... you haven't seemed yourself tonight."

"Oh, just had a bit of a fight with Mom," I said, blaming the easiest option, which was mostly true. "I'm sorry if that affected our night. I didn't mean for it to."

"Oh, no," he said, waving his hand to dismiss me. "You've been great. I just can tell that you aren't your normal self."

I missed Axel so much it hurt. That was the main reason for my mood, but I couldn't admit that to my father. "Thanks again for my gift, Dad. The bag for school is just perfect." He had bought me an expensive, black leather satchel that I loved. It would be able to hold my laptop, books, and anything else I needed.

"Glad you liked it," Dad said, then hauled himself to his feet. "I think I'm going to hit the hay. How about you?"

I got to my feet with an exaggerated groan. "I might take a hot shower first, if that's okay."

He came forward and pressed a kiss to my forehead. "Of course, sweetheart."

I hugged him tightly, just for a moment. "Merry Christmas, Daddy."

He held me for another minute, then we drifted apart. "Night!"

I went to my bedroom and pulled out my cell phone. I'd made myself hide it through the day, so I wasn't distracted or focused on Axel. It hadn't worked. I'd ached for my lifeline to him. He'd message again.

Call me when you have a minute.

It was almost eleven p.m. but I called him, anyway, sinking down onto the bed when I heard his voice.

"Hey, sexy. Merry Christmas."

"Merry Christmas," I managed to say back, using my sleeve to wipe my running nose. "Thank you so much for the necklace you sent to my house. It's totally incredible."

Axel's chuckle made my heart squeeze in my chest. "I saw it and thought of you. I had to buy it."

"Well, you shouldn't have."

He laughed again. "Why not?"

"I don't deserve it," I whispered, on the verge of tears now, which annoyed the hell out of me. I'd done such a good job of holding them in all day.

"Are you okay, sweetheart?"

I nodded and swallowed the sob that rose. Damn it. I missed him so much, it hurt.

33

AXEL

I'd been working all day, forcing myself into the CEO frame of mind, Concentrating on the merger, business, financials and growth of my company. Important things for my life, my future. Things that would normally have me focused and enthusiastic. Instead, I was finding it almost impossible to focus. Why? Because I missed her.

I wasn't a romantic, nor a sap. Christmas day hadn't meant much to me since I was a kid. And even then, my parents hadn't exactly made it a warm and fuzzy time for me, like all the other kids I knew. But today I'd ached for the type of Christmas I knew that Chastity was having. Without me. Surrounded by family, presents, food, and cuddles. I felt as lonely as the first snowflake of the season. And as desperate for company.

"Do you want to come over?" I asked, the words leaving my mouth before I thought them over properly.

There was silence on the end of the line. "Ah... I'd love to. But I can't." Her regret seemed genuine, but it was still a stab in the gut. She couldn't be with me—or didn't want to.

"Oh, yeah, I understand," I rushed in to say, standing up from my desk and stretching my legs by walking around my apartment, nervous energy pulsing through my veins. "It's Christmas. I get it. You have to stay with your family."

Another heavy silence filled the other end of the phone.

"I wish I could..."

"Don't worry about it." I said, crossing my arms over my chest. "I get it. I'm not family. It's Christmas. No worries." Now I sounded like a petulant child. I rolled my eyes heavenward and bit the inside of my cheek. *Fuck. Now I'd scared her off.* "Chastity, I..."

"Please don't say any more," she whispered, then a sob echoed into my ears, and my heart broke.

"I'm sorry," I groaned out, clenching my free hand into a fist, and glancing towards the nearest wall. Damn, I'd like to put my fist right into that. "It's just that I miss you too. And I want to see you."

"I want to see you too!" she burst out. "Do you know how hard it's been for me today? To pretend that I was happy to be with my family when all I wanted to do was run over to your place and curl up in your lap? Christmas is my favorite day of the year, Axel. My favorite day. The tree, the presents, the food. My family."

"You had all of that," I bit out. "Then what was the problem?"

"I wasn't with you!" she practically screamed through the phone. "It wasn't supposed to be like this. We were meant to have a casual, no-strings-attached few weeks and I..." She stopped and I heard her gulp.

My heart began to pick up pace, pounding a little harder, and a little louder against my ribcage. "You what?"

"I already told you," She repeated, sighing heavily. "I spent the whole day wishing I was at your place, curled up in your lap rather than where I was, spending Christmas with my family."

She sighed again, and I went and sat down on the sofa, my excess energy now gone.

"It wasn't supposed to be like this," she said again. "I ache when I'm not with you."

"Fuck." I groaned and slid onto my back on the couch. "I want you with me too. Always. Even when I should be working, I want you."

The silence fell between us again, but this time, I could almost hear her smiling down the line.

"So... can I come over tomorrow morning? After breakfast, maybe?"

I grinned. "Definitely. Anything particular you want to do?"

"I want to thank you for my present."

There was so much promise in her voice, my hormones surged in response.

"Are you wearing it?" I asked her. "Or did your mother confiscate it the moment she saw it?" It would be just like that woman.

Chastity giggled on the end of the line. "She tried. But I put it on and hid it beneath my sweater and wore it all day. I'm never going to take it off."

I closed my eyes. Fuck it, I was in too deep here. And I wasn't treading water anymore, I was drowning. *Happily* drowning.

If any other girl of my past had waxed lyrical about how much she missed me, and how attached she'd grown to a gift, I would have cut her off without a second thought. Clingy, emotional females were not my *schtick*. But with Chastity... damn it I wanted to drive to her father's place, pick her up, and bring her home to my bed. *Exactly where she's meant to be.*

I shook myself and sat up. "Do you want me to pick you up in the morning?"

"No, I'll get to your place."

A calmness settled over me as my stomach flipped. "What time?"

She laughed, breaking the tension that had fallen over the phone call. "Are you that desperate to see me?"

My breath whistled through my teeth as I inhaled sharply. "I wouldn't say desperate."

"Okay. How's two p.m.?"

"Uh..." *No!*

"One p.m.?"

This time I heard the amusement in her voice, and I couldn't stop the answering smile that pulled at my lips. "Just get your ass over here as soon as possible, okay?"

She laughed her sweet, luscious ass off at that one. "I will. Good night."

"Sweet dreams," I said, then hung up.

I set my phone down and swung my legs around again to lie back on the couch, staring up at the ceiling. What had that girl done to me? I'd been fighting a strange sort of weariness all day. I didn't want to call it depression, but damn I'd been in a shitty mood. Now? I wanted to laugh and jump around. *Fucking hell*, I was in so much trouble with this girl.

I'd never felt this way before, and I had no idea what to even *do* with all the feelings. I rolled off the couch and went to find my running gear, needing to work through this restlessness somehow. Then, tomorrow, I'd fuck us both into sweet, sweet oblivion.

34

CHASTITY

I tried not to rush through breakfast with my father at a gorgeous little café on the corner, but I was bouncing up and down to go. I inhaled my eggs benedict and hugged him tightly. “Thank you so much for breakfast, and last night, Dad. It was all great.” I grabbed up all my things, including my new bag, and my father’s hand snaked out to grab my arm.

“Hey, sweetheart.”

“Yeah?”

“Are you seeing someone?”

My gut tightened like I’d taken a punch. “What do you mean?”

He threw down some cash on the check and stood up with a grin. “You’ve been distracted, jumpy, and I know you’re rushing off to see someone. Who is it?”

I inhaled sharply and pressed a hand to my stomach. “It’s really new. I haven’t told anyone.”

Dad grinned even brighter. “I knew it! Good for you. I’ve been worried about you at times—all work and no fun. I hope your mom and my choices haven't put you off chasing love, Chastity, because that would make me feel terrible."

I relaxed and smiled at my handsome father. "I've waited for several reasons, and I don't regret a single minute of it. Because now I've found someone I think is really special, and I..." I stopped and shrugged, not sure what else I could say without giving the game away.

"As long as he thinks you're special too. Wait... it's a *he*, right?"

I laughed. "Yes, Dad."

"Not that there's anything wrong with you wanting whoever you want. As long as they take care of you."

My poor father was blushing now, and I rushed him for another hug. "It's all good, Dad. I'll see you on the weekend, yeah?"

He nodded. "Do you want me to drop you off?"

"No. It's not far. Love you."

"Love you too."

I waved as I walked down the street and around the corner. Axel's place was only a few blocks away, but I wasn't walking that far carrying my new bag and all my stuff from last night. I arranged an Uber, which arrived in a few short minutes. Then I was speeding towards Axel's apartment, my heart in my throat. I couldn't believe how excited and happy I was.

When the driver dropped me off, I raced up to the elevator and hopped from foot to foot as I sped up to the penthouse.

When the doors opened, Axel wasn't waiting for me in the living room, he was pacing the foyer, a few feet from the elevator's entrance. "Hey!" His face lit up with a smile I felt like I'd waited my whole life to see.

I dropped my bags to the ground with a clatter and ran for him like I was in a blockbuster rom-com and my life depended on it.

He opened his arms as I jumped at his chest, pressing myself into his powerful body and wrapping my arms around his neck. His lips came down on mine, hot and possessive, and I clung to him, never wanting the kiss to end. And it didn't, for so long.

Axel's hands came up to cup my face, and he slowed his kiss, taking his time to nibble at my lips and taste me. By the time he finally raised his head, I couldn't open my eyes and swayed so badly I knocked into him. "Whoa, there," he said as he tugged me against him.

I grinned up at him, opening my eyes enough to see him through half lids. "What did you do to me? I feel totally drugged."

He chuckled and hugged me again, holding me so close I could feel his heart beating against my chest. "Let's go relax on the couch for a bit."

I didn't want to argue, though I would have preferred he dragged me to bed with him. "Okay." I collapsed onto the couch when we finally reached it, and Axel tugged me into his lap. I turned around so I could face him, half lying across him, and burrowed into his arms. I breathed in his scent that was so uniquely Axel and sighed. "God, this feels good."

He didn't respond, but his answering sigh said it all.

We'd both fallen into this relationship with the best of intentions of parting in a few days, but I already knew that on my end at least, that was going to be one hell of a day.

"Chastity... I..." Axel's phone suddenly went off in his pocket and he groaned. "I'm so sorry, let me just turn that off." He lifted up, pulled out his phone, then stared at the screen. He went deathly still.

"What's wrong?" I asked.

His gaze shifted to me. "It's your dad."

My heart leapt in my throat. "Don't answer it."

"But what if he's planning on coming over here?" he asked. "Pat turned up the other day for a run and didn't even call first."

I swallowed hard, then nodded once. *Fuck!* "Yeah, okay. Answer it."

"Put it on loudspeaker," I hissed just as Axel answered.

"Hey, Pat. Hang on, just putting you on speaker." Axel put the phone down between us and hit the button. "How you doin', man?"

My dad's voice burst into the room. "Good, bud. Good. Merry Christmas."

I clapped my hands over my mouth to stop the scream that rose. I knew they were best friends, but to hear my dad actually talking on the other end of Axel's phone was the weirdest, most surreal thing ever.

Axel shook his head at me and put his finger to his lips to shush me.

I nodded but kept my hands clamped over my mouth.

"Merry Christmas to you, too. How was your day with the family?" Axel asked.

"Oh, it was great, actually. Too much food. Gonna need to train twice as hard this week."

"Is that why you're calling?" Axel asked with grin. "Trying to work off the Christmas cookies?"

"Well, not just the cookies, but yeah. If you're free we can meet at the health club, or I can come to your place if you want to go for a run again."

Panic set it and I slid off the couch and stood up. My heart was pounding, and I couldn't stop shivering. *This was so bad!*

Axel lay back against the couch and fisted his hands on his thighs. But when he answered, his voice was relaxed. His posture definitely wasn't. "Oh, I'd love to buddy, but I've actually got someone here. That woman I told you about."

"The one you're totally into?" Dad asked with a laugh.

"Shut up," Axel growled, his gaze flicking up to me. "I'm not that bad. Can we catch up later, or maybe this weekend?"

"Sure," Dad said. "You go enjoy her. At least one of us is getting some."

"Thanks, Pat." Axel said, his gaze lifting up to meet mine. "See you later."

He hung up, and I screamed, the tension inside my heart too intense to contain. "Oh my God!"

Axel jumped to his feet and grabbed my arms. "It's okay. Calm down."

I twisted out of his grasp and started pacing around the room, throwing my hands up in the air like I was the main act in a pantomime. "What the hell are we going to do?"

Axel was too calm when he asked, "What do you mean?"

"What do you mean, what do I mean? My dad almost caught us together! Imagine if he'd just come over. I would have been here, and he would have—"

"Chastity, relax."

I growled and rolled my eyes but didn't respond. *Relax?* How was I supposed to relax?

"He didn't come over and catch us," Axel said, calm as a cucumber. "We're not doing anything wrong. You don't need to feel so worried. Or guilty."

I stopped pacing and turned around and glared at him. "Not doing anything wrong? Are you kidding me?"

"We're not," Axel said, his gaze burning into mine with an intensity I didn't totally understand. "We're two consenting adults. We're dating. It's no one else's business what we do in our free time."

I put my hands on my hips. "Then what was that stuff about the girl you're seeing? Are you dating someone I don't know about, or did you actually tell my dad about me?" There was no way they'd been talking about me, and I hated the fact my father knew what sort of guy Axel was. One who rolled from one woman to another the same way I went from one good book to the next.

"I'm not seeing anyone else," Axel growled, his hands tightening into fists.

Oh, he was angry, was he? What the hell did he have to be angry about? I inhaled and poured all my frustrations about this situation into words. "Well, how would I know?" I threw back at him. "We aren't exclusive. There haven't been any promises made. In fact, I think the only thing you *have* promised me is that these two weeks will be nothing to you. That you'll walk away and not look back."

Axel stalked towards me, and I found myself backing up until my spine hit the wall behind me.

I gasped as he didn't stop his approach.

Instead, he pressed his body into mine, hard, against the wall. Then put a hand on either side of my head as he stared down at me. "You want promises, Chastity? Fine! I promise that you'll never forget these two weeks or me. I promise that after tonight you'll wake up with bruises all over your body from my teeth. I promise you... that there is no one else for me. Only you."

I gasped at the imagery Axel's words evoked, heat pouring through me and desire whipping my already sensitized nerves into a frenzy. I opened my mouth to say something back, but I didn't get a chance to respond.

HE SLAMMED his mouth down on mine and thrust his tongue into my mouth in the most possessive move I'd ever felt from him, effectively silencing me. But I had *a lot* to say, and so many more effective ways of telling him how I felt.

So, I grabbed his shirt and lifted it up, wanting to feel him. I ran my hands over his hard abs and flat chest, luxuriating in the heat and size of him.

Axel groaned against my mouth, then brought his arms down to cup my face and kiss me harder.

I wanted him, and I wanted him now. I grabbed his jeans, popping the one button with a flick of my wrist, and unzipping him carefully.

He wasn't wearing any boxers or briefs, so instead of encountering another layer to push through, Axel's cock sprang out and bounced against me.

I moaned at the feeling, unable to help it. I loved the feel of his hot, hard shaft in my hand.

Axel pulled back from our kiss and stared down at me, a question clear in his eyes. *Did I really want this?*

In answer, I tugged on his cock, reveling in the gasp and groan he gave me. I'd worn a short skirt and T-shirt and as Axel reached under my skirt to slide his hand into my panties, I wished I'd worn something even more accessible.

He slid his fingers over my clit, making me gasp and fall against him with need. Then he kissed me again and thrust his fingers in and out of me in the same way that I ached for his cock.

"Oh, please," I gasped against his lips.

He pushed me up against the wall and lifted me.

I jumped up higher and wrapped my legs around his waist.

He pushed my underwear aside and set his cock at my entrance.

I shivered, needing him so much.

Then he looked at me and connected our gazes in a way that meant I couldn't look away. I didn't dare.

So, I stared into his dark eyes as he thrust into me.

"Oh. My," I gasped out as he drove into me again and again. I pulled him closer, biting his lip and kissing him hard as his cock filled me up, making me ache—and soothing that ache—all in one fast primitive dance. It was hard. And fast. And hot. And when I came, I screamed and clung to him like a limpet on a rock.

Axel followed me moments later. He groaned and pulled out, holding me tight against him as he came.

Running my hands through his hair, I dug my fingers into his back, never wanting him to leave. I didn't want him to speak and didn't want him to put me down. I just wanted to stay here, enjoying the sound of our panting filling the air and the incredible sense of female satisfaction that came with knowing my man wanted me this much.

"Are you okay?" he whispered.

I nodded and forced my eyes to open. "Oh, yeah."

"Are you sure I didn't hurt you?"

I laughed as I cupped his cheek and stared at him. He was worried about me. Well, time to reassure him that I was more than fine. "Definitely another fantasy fulfilled."

Axel chuckled as he took a step back and I let my legs slide to the floor while he still held me.

My legs were unsteady and wobbled like jelly, so I leaned back against the wall, my belly still tight with after-tremors.

"And which fantasy was that?" he asked, picking up his clothes and arching an eyebrow in question.

"Ah..." I tilted my head, trying to get my messy thoughts into line. "The one about having hot sex against a wall."

He held out his hand and I took it, grateful to have contact again. "Well, how about we get clean, share a shower, then climb into bed for round two?"

"Yes, please," I managed to say, though my usual post-sex drunkenness had hit. I could barely walk, let alone string together a decent sentence.

We staggered to the bathroom and were soon in the hot shower. He washed me while I let pleasure pulse through me.

Axel always made me feel incredible, and I was already dreading the day I didn't have an evening with him to look forward to.

"Let's get you into bed before you fall over."

I nodded in agreement, my eyes at half-mast. I was having real trouble staying awake after that orgasm.

Axel dried me with his big, fluffy towel then patted me on the ass. "Go on. Get under the covers and I'll be there in a minute."

I nodded and staggered towards the door, then the massive bed. The sheets were clean but smelled of Axel too. He definitely hadn't had a woman in this bed since I'd left. Or he'd changed the sheets for me. Either way, I didn't have the energy to care at this point in time. I rolled onto my side and cuddled into the warm blankets, listening to the sounds Axel made from the bathroom as he dried himself, whistling happily as he turned off the lights and slid in behind me.

"Do you want a cat nap before the next round?" Axel whispered into my ear as he dropped a kiss on my hair.

My eyes were already closed. "Yes, please."

Axel settled into the bed behind me and slipped his arm around my waist, holding my breast in a classic male show of possession.

I smiled to myself, loving it probably more than I should.

"Can I ask you... why was me taking you against a wall part of your fantasy list?"

I sighed. It was difficult to explain, but I may as well try. "It wasn't the position so much as the passion. I wanted you to take me without any thought or preparation. It made me feel needed." I relaxed on my pillow and began to spiral down into the darkness of sleep, but I could have sworn that I heard him say something right before I passed out.

Something that sounded very much like, "Oh, you're needed, beautiful. More than you know."

35

AXEL

Chastity and I spent the rest of the day in bed, talking, eating, and having sex. I'd never had such a lazy day. When she left to have dinner with her mother, much to my dismay, I had a dozen missed calls and emails for days. But amazingly, I didn't care. Life was made for the sort of happiness I was feeling at the moment as I floated from one room to the next.

When my phone rang, I didn't even look at who it was, I just picked it up. "Hello."

"Axel, Merry Christmas."

My heart sank, which was not the reaction I should have to my parents calling to wish me happy holidays.

"Hello, Mom. Merry Christmas to you."

"Did you have a good day yesterday? I apologize for being late to call, but with the time difference, it makes it very difficult."

Oh, yes. Christmas morning was thirty-six hours ago, and the time difference of five hours to London made it impossible. "No problem," I told her, because really, why would I have expected any different? "How was your day?" I trudged to the kitchen to put on the coffee maker. I needed a pick-me-up now.

"Oh, lovely. We went to the club and had lunch, then drinks with friends. Dinner out at the hotel."

I ran my hand through my hair and closed my eyes. Trying not to snap at my mother was a constant battle. She was so superficial. So not who I wanted my wife to be. I needed someone loving, smart, and maybe a little soft. Someone I could talk to, be relaxed with. Someone like... "How's Dad?" I asked her, cutting off the inevitable conclusion my sex-drugged brain was about to make.

"He's well," she said but made no attempt to pass the phone to him, nor divulge any extra information.

"Thanks for the phone call, Mom. But I better get going. I have a call from Taiwan in an hour. Better prepare for that."

"I'm glad your business is doing well, Axel."

I inhaled sharply. It wasn't the words so much as the tone. Almost as though she was surprised that I'd succeeded without their help. In a rare moment of weakness I said, "My company turns over a billion dollars a year now, Mom."

Her tutting disapproval down the line was the reason I never told her anything. "You shouldn't talk about money like that, Axel. How... common of you."

I clenched my jaw and held my tongue. Honesty never got anywhere with my mother. "I better go, Mother. Say hello to Dad for me, and thanks for the call."

"Bye, sweetheart."

I almost gagged at the last moment, but quickly hung up. I threw the phone down on the counter and quickly made myself a coffee, weak and sweet. No point ramping myself up if I was going to bed at a normal time.

I glanced down at my phone again. Maybe Chastity would want to come back tonight? More sex? A good night's sleep. Couldn't hurt to ask, could it? I texted her a quick message and got one back within a minute.

I'd love to but I can't. Mom's already shitty at me for not spending enough time with her. But can I come tomorrow night? Maybe stay over again?

I typed back something to say that was fine, and yeah, of course. But my chest was twisted and aching. I didn't really like Chastity's mother. I knew she was a bitch, if Pat's description of her was anything to go by. But she loved Chastity, and that was something I'd never had. A parent to adore me. Which would make Chastity a great mom, I'd expect. She liked the intimacy that came with being close to her parents.

Another tick for her.

"Shut up," I growled at myself, took my coffee and headed off to my computer. After all, what else did I have to do except work? Gym, maybe? Not this late, I'd never sleep. Another woman? My phone was *filled* with booty call numbers.

Hell, no. There was only one woman I wanted in my bed, and her scent was still imprinted on the pillow. I wasn't messing with that. And that was assuming I could even get it up for someone else, which was in question at the moment.

I sat down at my computer and got to work.

Twenty-four hours later, my elevator door opened to reveal Chastity again. I was waiting on the sofa, pretending to read the newspaper. After all, there was no reason she needed to know that I'd been waiting impatiently for her for over an hour.

"Hey, beautiful!" I called out, folding the paper and placing it on my coffee table. "How was your day?" I stood up and stared at her as she walked towards me in a pair of denim shorts and a pink T-shirt. She was delicious, all luscious curves and sun-kissed skin.

"Good." She dropped her bag on the sofa, going up on her tip toes to kiss me.

I didn't let her go, instead gripping her tiny waist and pulling her close for a longer kiss.

She smiled against my mouth, then pressed in closer, opening her mouth to my tongue and moaning in pleasure as I kissed her deeper.

When I finally lifted my head, she was grinning up at me. "I love how you kiss me."

I couldn't stop the answering smile that tugged at my lips. "How do I kiss you, exactly?"

"Like you really want to kiss me."

I laughed. "Of course, I do, or I wouldn't do it."

She shrugged, running her hands up and down my arms. "Well then, all the other guys I've kissed didn't really want to kiss me."

I couldn't contain the envy that clawed at me at her words. "How many guys are we talking about?"

She stared straight at me and raised an eyebrow. "How many women have you kissed?"

Kissed? She had to be kidding me. "A gentleman doesn't kiss and tell."

"And neither does a lady." She gave me a definitive nod and I chuckled again. I loved the fact she wasn't intimidated by me. Chastity always told me what she was thinking and wasn't worried about offending me either.

"Are you hungry?" I asked, taking her hand and tugging her towards the kitchen.

"Not really." She ran her hand along the white marble countertop. "Can I ask you something?"

"Anything," I answered, though if it was another question about my past lovers, I was pretty sure I was going to avoid it like the plague.

"Why don't you have any staff? Don't rich guys have housekeepers? Cleaning ladies? Chefs?"

I pushed my hands into the cold marble and glanced around the stainless-steel kitchen. "Yeah, they do. And I have a cleaner come once a week."

She grinned at me. "But what about other staff? Don't you have a cook at least?"

I shrugged. "I don't really need one. I live here alone. I'm pretty neat and self-sufficient." To an anal level, if my ex-girlfriends were to be believed. I tilted my head at her. "Why? Do you think I should?"

She shook her head. "Not at all. I was just wondering, that's all."

I went to the fridge. "Want a beer? Or a wine, or something?"

I kept everything pretty stocked. Or my assistant at work did. I had several, and I suppose in a way, they doubled as personal staff. They ordered groceries and organized restaurant reservations.

"No, thank you."

I turned to stare at her. "Anything you'd like do then?"

She grinned at me. "Yeah. I want to make love to you."

I put the beer back in the fridge and picked her up. "Well, why didn't you just say so?" I carried her to bed and made love to her the way she wanted me to. Slowly. Thoroughly. As though we had all the time in the world. And tonight, we did.

36

CHASTITY

I woke up to the feeling of Axel's hard cock pressing into my butt crack and his hands tweaking my nipples. I giggled and bumped my ass back into him. "You want some more?"

"Hmmm... always."

I was so warm, but I was also really wanting to complete my bucket list. "Could we have sex on the kitchen counter?"

He stopped tweaking my nipples and froze. "Uh... what?"

I twisted onto my back and stared up at him. "You know I have my fantasy list, and I want to get through everything before I go back to school."

Axel groaned. "Don't talk like that."

"Like what?"

"Like you're leaving tomorrow."

I bit my lip and stared up at him. He didn't want me to go, that was damn certain. But would he consider continuing this relationship once I returned to school? Two hours was a decent drive, but not insurmountable. And long-distance had a bad reputation for never working, but if he was extremely busy with work and was okay with me coming back for weekends, surely we could try?

He sighed. "I'm sorry. You're right. Let's do it."

He slid out of bed, and I sat up. "I killed the mood, didn't I?"

"No... It's not your fault. I'm just... not looking forward to you leaving."

I threw back the covers and got to my feet. "Neither am I."

He smiled wickedly and held out his hand. "Well, let's go make some memories."

I hurried over to him and took his hand. Making memories with him was the only thing that was keeping me from bursting into tears at the prospect of not seeing him again.

We walked over to the kitchen and Axel grabbed a hand towel and popped it onto the counter. "Can't let that gorgeous ass get cold."

He grabbed me around the waist and hoisted me onto the counter. "Oh! It *is* cold."

He grinned as he pushed my knees apart and stepped between them. "You won't be cold for long."

Happiness surged through me as he leaned closer to kiss me.

His lips touched mine and I sighed, running my hands over his shoulders, loving the sturdy muscles beneath my palms.

Vaguely, I heard a sound, then footsteps penetrated the bubble around me.

"*Chastity*? What the hell are you doing here?"

I gasped and pulled back, covering my bare breasts with my arms. "Dad!"

Axel twisted his body to cover mine, putting his back to my father. "Pat, go wait in the living room."

"Axel. What the fuck?"

"Just go. We'll be there in a minute."

Dad stomped away and I stared up at Axel's face, panic-stricken. My stomach was lurching, ready to vomit. And my heart was pounding with a sickening thud. "Oh my God. What are we going to do?"

Axel stepped away, and all signs of the passionate man I'd known only moments before were gone. "We're going to face the music," he answered. "Though, I think we better get dressed first."

37

CHASTITY

I was shaking. Literally shaking like a leaf in the wind. *Like a girl whose father just caught her having sex with his best friend. Thank God we'd only just started! It could have been so much worse.*

"It's okay," Axel said, pulling on a sweatshirt and some pants.

"It's not going to be okay," I managed to say, though my throat ached, and my chest hurt. "It's not. He's never going to forgive me."

Axel growled, in frustration I assumed. "We've just gotta tell him the truth. That we met way before we knew how we were connected. And by then, it was too late."

"Yeah, I suppose."

I clipped up my bra and pulled on a sweater to cover myself. I felt naked and alone. My father had seen me naked! And having sex with Axel. Surely that was too much for any father to handle. I tidied myself up the best I could, and Axel waited for me. "Thanks for covering me when he walked in," I said, crossing my arms over my chest.

"What do you mean?"

I frowned at him. Hadn't he even noticed that he'd instinctively protected me? "You turned your back and blocked my father's view of me. Didn't you do it on purpose?" I was sure he had.

"Uh, yeah. I suppose." Axel said, lifting his chin a notch.

Why was he acting defensively? I ran my hands through my hair and sighed. "Shall we go?"

He nodded, and together but separately we walked out of the bedroom, around the kitchen and into the living room where my dad sat in the armchair facing us. His cheeks were slashed with angry red, and when I looked at him, he glanced away as though he couldn't even bring himself to look at me.

I sank onto the sofa to the left, and Axel stood over near the sofa on the right. We hadn't worked out a strategy of what we were going to tell him other than the truth, so I had no idea how this was actually going to go. I put my hand to my mouth. I was going to be sick.

"So," my dad said, running his hands up and down his thighs in an agitated move I'd only seen on him once before. "How long has this been going on? Since my birthday?"

"No!" I said, immediately jumping in. "We met at the gym, and we had no idea who each other was. We went on a few dates and then found out that you two knew each other."

Dad sat up straighter and slid to the edge of the recliner chair. "And when you found out Axel was my best friend, what did you do, Chastity?"

I felt as small as a child sitting at the feet of a giant.

"We, ah..." I swallowed hard. "We broke up."

Dad jumped to his feet, throwing his arms out wide. "Then what the fuck is going on here?"

I sobbed and caught the sound by covering my mouth with my hand again. *Dad, I'm so sorry.* My stomach was clenched so tightly now, it felt twisted.

Axel gripped the back of the chair, and my traitorous gaze swept over his magnificence.

Even as terrified as I was for my relationship with my dad, I still couldn't stop myself from admiring how good Axel looked standing there, tall and handsome.

"Pat, look. I'm sorry you had to find out this way. Not ideal in any way."

"Not ideal?" Dad repeated, his gaze narrowing on Axel. "You were up here *fucking* my daughter, Axel."

Axel put his hands up in surrender. "I'm sorry, Pat."

"You're not sorry." Dad groaned, then put up his hand to stop Axel from speaking. "And you have no idea how I feel, Axel. No idea!"

"No, I don't," Axel said, his tone calm.

I curled up tighter on the couch, bringing my knees up and wrapping my arms around my legs.

"No, you don't. Because you don't have any kids," My dad hissed. "And why don't you?"

"I'm sure you're going to tell me," Axel muttered, glancing down at the carpet at his feet.

"Because you're a selfish, narcissistic asshole."

Oh, no, you don't! "Dad!" I unfurled and jumped to my feet. "You can't talk to him like that."

My dad whirled on me. "I've known Axel since you were in elementary school, sweetheart. You don't get to tell me how I speak to him."

Tears blurred my vision, and I fought back the cry that lodged in my throat. "But, Dad—"

"No!" My father growled at me. "I'm disgusted with you. Disgusted with you both."

Then he turned his gaze on Axel. "You're twenty years older than her, for fuck's sake."

"We know that," I managed to say, coughing to clear my

throat. "This was only meant to be a holiday fling. Nothing serious."

Dad pushed Axel in the chest. "You bastard. You take my daughter... MY DAUGHTER, and convince her to have some slutty affair? She's better than that, Axel, and you know it!"

"It wasn't his fault, Dad," I said, my face bursting into a hot flush. I had to tell him the truth. He couldn't blame all this on Axel. "I was the one who begged him to date me for the couple of weeks I was here. He didn't want to go on after we found out the connection, but I—"

Dad grunted at me and dismissed me with a flick of a hand. "You're a child, Chastity. You don't know anything about this guy."

My tears dried up and my mouth dropped open. I was a child? "Excuse me?"

Dad glared at Axel, who was standing placidly despite being pushed back a few feet. "You and I are done, you got it? Come on, Chastity. We're going home."

I tried not to see the hurt on Axel's face, but it was impossible to ignore. I tried again. "Dad, please stop. I know this is a shock, but I'm almost twenty-two. And I like Axel. He's been great for me."

My father finally turned towards me and gave me his full attention. "You have no idea how I'm feeling, Chastity. Shock doesn't even come close to covering it. And as for Axel, I fail to see how some rich player who's slept with half the women in the city can be good for you. You've got your whole life ahead of you."

"Dad, stop!" I gasped. "You have no idea about our relationship, or how amazing Axel has been to me."

"Yeah," My father said, rolling his eyes with an exaggerated groan. "I'm sure he turned on the charm to get in your pants,

Chastity. But don't expect him to stick around. He created the saying, '*hit it and quit it*'."

Anger boiled inside of me. I knew that Axel was experienced, he had to be. He was twenty years older than me, gorgeous, single, and rich. It would be sad if it didn't have a little black book stashed somewhere.

"Stop!" I yelled, not willing to take the character assassination any longer. Axel wasn't saying a thing, but I couldn't stay quiet. "I love him, Dad. I love him! He's amazing. And even if this fling lasts only two weeks, I'm happy. How can you not see that?" Where the words came from, I had no idea.

And when both men stopped and turned to stare at me, I realized I may have overstepped the mark.

"What?" I asked, flicking my hair back over my shoulder.

"Did you just say you love him?" my father asked, his eyes wide with shock.

"Uh..." I swallowed hard. *Shit.* had I said that? "Yeah... I..."

Dad swung around to glare at Axel. "Now she loves you? Fucking hell, man! Why'd you have to go and screw with my daughter, of all people!"

Axel turned to stare at me, his mouth hard and pressed into a thin line. "That wasn't the deal, Chastity."

It was my turn to be shocked speechless.

Dad shoved Axel again. "What did you just say? She says she loves you and you say that wasn't the deal?"

Axel's eyes blazed with anger. "It wasn't! I told her what was on offer, and she was happy with it."

Dad's hand tightened into a fist, and he swung his arm in a lightning-fast move. *Cr-aaack.* Dad's fist connected with Axel's face and sent him spiraling into the sofa. "You're a smug bastard," Dad grunted, then grabbed my arm. "Let's go."

"Axel..." I didn't want to go.

Axel wiped at the blood dripping from his lip. "Go."

"But—"

His gaze flashed up at me. "Chastity. *Go.* There's nothing more to say."

I disagreed. I had so much more to tell him, share with him.

But from the hard set of Dad's jaw and Axel's equally stubborn set, I had no choice in the matter.

"Let me grab my bag," I told my father, pulling my arm out of his grip.

"Where is it?" he asked.

"The bedroom."

Dad huffed out half a laugh. "How was it sleeping in that bed by yourself all night? Bit lonely?"

I frowned at my father. "What do you mean?"

Dad crossed his arms over his chest, a malicious smile on his lips. "Everyone knows Axel won't sleep with his women. He spends more time in the guest room than his own bedroom."

I inhaled sharply, wishing I could pull my dad to the room and show him the indentation of Axel's head.

"Well, that shows just how much you don't know him, Dad. Axel's slept with me, all night, *every* night we've been together."

My father's face changed into a twisted amount of disgust and shock.

But I didn't wait for his response, I stormed to the bedroom, grabbed my bag, and marched back. "You ready?"

My dad nodded, but his demeanor had changed, and I wasn't sure what I'd said, or Axel had said to change it. It didn't matter. Axel wanted me gone, so I was going.

"We going?" I repeated as I threw my bag over my shoulder and glared at my father.

"Uh, yeah."

The wind had definitely been taken out of his sails, but I was anxious to go now.

Axel was staring towards the fireplace, his back to me.

I didn't say goodbye, instead walking straight to the elevator and pushing the button.

Dad stepped up beside me a minute later, and together we went down the lift, out the door and into his car.

I don't know how I managed to keep it all together until I was safely inside my bedroom at my mom's place, but I did. And only then did I allow the tears to fall. And after that, they didn't stop.

~

Continue Axel and Chastity's journey with book 2 - '***Pregnant to my Dad's Billionaire Best*** Friend.'

Download: HERE!

PREGNANT TO MY DAD'S BEST FRIEND

1

AXEL

When Pat and Chastity left, the whole room fell silent. I shuddered with the oppression of it. I was alone.

I hauled myself up off the sofa and walked to the fridge, got an icepack, and put it to my lip. I was going to be swollen and bruised tomorrow, which was going to look great for those new investors I'd lined up. They'd think I was some sort of thug. Or even worse, a guy who couldn't defend myself. *Maybe I better reschedule.*

I'd seen Patrick's punch coming, but I let him hit me. How could I not? He was furious and needed his pound of flesh. Better my face than his relationship with Chastity. I could take a hit, though it had been a long time since anyone had landed one.

My jaw throbbed, my lip was still bleeding, and yet that wasn't the most painful part of my body. My heart *ached* like someone held it in a vise and was squeezing. Hard. I shook myself. *Pull yourself together.* It was nowhere near noon, but I poured myself a whiskey anyway. *It's five o'clock. somewhere.* And it wasn't like it mattered, anyway. My best friend had just pointed out that I had no morals, so really, a drink at ten in the morning should be the norm for me.

I took a sip, wincing from the pain in my mouth, then held the cold glass to my lip and sighed. *What a colossal fuck-up.* I ran a hand through my hair and groaned. "Fucking hell." I shook my head and tipped back the glass, finishing my drink and pouring another. The amber liquid sloshed into the glass, and I gulped it down as well. I'd never imagined losing my best friend and my girlfriend on the same day.

Not that she'd been my girlfriend, technically, but Chastity definitely fit the role. And she said she'd loved me... *holy shit.* What a thing to say at that point in time. It was the last thing I'd expected her to say, and the last thing Pat had wanted to hear.

My legs weren't feeling all too stable any longer, so I stumbled over to the dining table and sat down on a chair. The words from our brief fight kept going round and round in my head. But the last encounter had been the most hard-hitting. When Chastity had announced to her father that I'd slept with her every night, then left the room in a huff, Patrick had walked over to me and demanded an answer.

"Is she telling the truth, Axel?"

"Yeah." I'd returned, then lifted my gaze to his bewildered expression. "So what?"

"So what?" Patrick had repeated, his eyebrows flickering up. "So that means– Oh my God. You love her too." Then he'd walked away, collected his daughter, and left my life forever.

Now, what was I supposed to do with that information? Go after them? Call Chastity? Fight to keep her for what... another few days? There wasn't room in my life for her, and it was obvious she didn't have any space for me either. Not when she was going back to college. And certainly not once she headed off to chiropractic school in another state.

I groaned and pushed myself to stand. I needed a shower,

maybe a nap, then it was time to get back to work. I'd neglected my business a lot this week in favor of time with Chastity. It was time to get my life back on track, and my priorities straightened out.

I headed to the shower in an attempt to clean myself up for work, but the plan backfired. I got a pounding headache and ended up in bed for most of the afternoon. It never developed into a migraine, which was lucky because Chastity wasn't going to come over and massage away the pain. Not tonight. Not ever again.

2

CHASTITY

There was a knock at my door that I'd been waiting for. I'd been home almost an hour, so I was kind of amazed mom had left me alone this long.

I hugged my pillow tight to my chest and squeezed my eyes shut. "Come in."

The door squeaked open then a moment later mom sat down on my bed behind me, the mattress dipping to accommodate her weight. "Your dad told me what happened. I'm so sorry, Chastity."

I rolled onto my back and looked up at her. "You and Dad actually talked?"

She nodded, a small smile lifting the corners of her lips. "Yeah. I even made him coffee and he sat at the kitchen table."

I wiped at the tears still covering my cheeks and pulled myself up to sit against the headboard. "No way."

She chuckled. "Yeah, well, what can I say? It's a Christmas miracle."

My stomach churned as I recognized the truth. "More like you two finally had a reason to talk about your troublesome, delinquent daughter. I've never really given you a reason to get together before, have I?"

Mom ran her hand over my arm. "No, you haven't."

My eyes burned and more tears slid down my cheeks. I swiped them away, and my mother sighed.

"Chastity, I'm so sorry. I knew I recognized Axel from somewhere but couldn't work out where. It must have been when I'd been around your father's place."

"Or on his Facebook profile," I teased Mom, sending her a sideways waggle of my eyebrows. Like most women, my mom occasionally stalked her ex's FB profile. Why, I didn't know, but she did.

Mom shook her head and withdrew her hand. "I'm still sorry I didn't realize sooner."

I sighed, glancing down at the blankets with a heavy heart. "We broke up when we found out about the connection to Dad, but we couldn't stay away from each other. We didn't want to. So, it's my fault as much as Axel's. We knew what we were doing, but we just hoped—"

"You'd get away with it," Mom finished with a sigh. "What was the plan? Just have a Christmas fling, then forget about him?"

My throat closed up as a wave of depressing emotions pushed over me.

I nodded and swallowed hard. "Yeah, I thought I could."

Mom inhaled sharply, going still. "I knew you wouldn't."

"What do you mean?"

She pushed her hair back off her face. "Oh, honey, you've been head over heels in love with him since your first date. Axel isn't the sort of guy you just see a few times then get over."

"What sort of guy is he?" I asked, though my spidey senses told me not to inquire.

Mom tilted her head at me. "The sort that breaks your heart.

Then you have to spend the next ten years trying to get over him."

I pressed my lips together, considering her words. "Was that who Dad was for you?"

She stared at me, her eyes wide and searching. Then she nodded. "Yeah, he was."

"And now?" I asked. "What is he?"

She shrugged. "It's too late for him to be anything to me now, Chastity. I made some mistakes, and so did he. And in the end, we didn't find our way back to each other. Even though, I'd kind of hoped we would."

I reached for my mother's hand and squeezed it with my own. "I'm sorry, Mom."

"And I'm sorry for you, sweetheart. I wish I could have saved you the heartache."

I picked at the corner of the pillow I held in my hands. "I don't regret it. Being with Axel was the happiest I've been ever, I think."

"And what happened with your dad?"

I laughed, but not with humor. "Yeah, I could have done without that part."

"I bet." Mom got to her feet and started backing towards the door. "How about I make us some pasta for lunch, put on a movie, and veg out on the couch?"

I lifted my chin and nodded. "Thanks, Mom. Be there in a minute."

"Okay." She left my room and shut the door behind her, leaving me alone with my broken heart.

I put my hand to my throat, touching the solitary floating diamond Axel had bought me for Christmas. Such a beautiful gift. I still couldn't believe he'd spoiled me so much when supposedly I meant nothing to him. *Well, he is a billionaire, after all.* Something I kept forgetting. Sure, he had a nice car and a flashy apartment, but he didn't really live the way I thought a billionaire would live. A fact I kind of loved about him.

I rolled onto my side and squeezed my eyes shut to stop myself from crying again. It wasn't fair. None of it. I stayed that way until Mom called me from the living room. When she called, I managed to get up, walk through the apartment, and eat lunch. Everything felt numb now. And all I wanted to do was go back to school and pretend nothing had happened.

Maybe I could? If I went back to campus I could try and forget I'd ever met Axel and fallen in love for the first time, only to be told that falling in love "wasn't the deal," like I was some sort of business merger. I closed my eyes and fell asleep while a rom com played on the TV. No room in my life for fake romance today. Real-life romance had already broken me, and there was nothing left to feel.

3

AXEL

It was New Year's Eve, and I'd been invited to a dozen parties. And where was I on the most party-centric night of the year? Home. By myself, drowning my sorrows in my second bottle of red wine. To be fair to my liver, the bottles cost over a thousand dollars each, so hopefully the hangover tomorrow wouldn't be as vicious as a cheap one. "To me," I announced to the room, holding my glass up in the air. "And a prosperous new year." I chuckled to myself as I took a gulp of wine. It had been a prosperous new year for twenty years now. Was I due for a bad year? I felt like I certainly deserved one. I'd broken Chastity's heart and ruined my oldest friendship.

Yep. Definitely got a kick in the ass from Karma this year. I took another sip and sighed as I pushed my cell phone around on the counter. Neither Patrick nor Chasity had called me since the event. I hadn't even received an angry text. *Nothing.*

I flicked open my phone and pulled up Pat's number. Would he answer if I called? Surely, he had to be over our fight by now. A small part of my brain told me to stop. But the larger, drunk part of my brain forged forward, dialing his number with a single press of my finger. I put the phone to my ear and within a few rings, he answered.

"What do you want?"

I laughed, though I didn't mean to. "You picked up! Didn't think you would."

"Are you drunk?"

I nodded to myself, then realized he wouldn't be able to see me. "Yep. Are you?"

"No, but I'm at a party, so I can't talk long. What do you want, Axel?"

"I want some advice."

"Advice?" Pat asked, scoffing. "From me?"

"Yeah. You know me better than anyone else, apparently." I let the barb sit there, stuck in his gut.

"Ask. And make it quick."

I wanted to ask him if Chastity was with him but bit my tongue. "Okay... so. You know how you told me to go for that girl I was into?"

"I didn't mean—"

"You said that if I was finally interested in someone for more than a quick fuck, then I should pursue her, did you not?"

Patrick huffed and puffed on the other end of the line, and I got off my bar stool and staggered around the living room, needing to move.

"Yes," he begrudgingly admitted. "I did. But I didn't know—"

"I know you didn't know it was your daughter, but the facts of the case haven't changed, so can I ask your advice again? Even though it didn't work out so well last time."

There was an exaggerated groan on the other end of the line, and I took that for acquiescence.

"Okay. Well, the girl, the one I've been seeing for the last couple of weeks... we broke up. Again. And I cannot stop thinking about her." I paused to see if Pat hadn't hung up on me, but when I checked the screen, the timer was still ticking away, so I knew he was still there.

"She's so different, Patrick, from anyone else I've ever met." I eased myself down onto the sofa and threw my head back. "She's sweet. But so fucking strong. She doesn't let me get away with anything, and we talk about everything. She's smart. And funny. And..." I swallowed against the memory of her helping me the other night.

"And what?" Pat bit out.

I sighed, not really wanting to admit this to a friend, but if there was anything that was going to win Patrick over, it was the truth.

"And compassionate and honest. I had a migraine the other night and didn't cancel our date. And you know what she did? She just sat on my bed and did this head massage thing until I fell asleep. I've never had anyone look after me before. Not my mother, not anyone. How does someone so young have such a big fucking heart?"

There were tears in my eyes now and I tightened my fingers into a fist and pressed my hand against my mouth. "You still there?" I asked him.

"Yeah," he answered, his voice soft. "I'm still here."

I put my head up. "So, what do I do, Pat? I think I really hurt her when I didn't say I loved her back, and her dad fucking hates me."

Patrick sighed on the other end of the line. "You're an old man, Axel. She's at the beginning of her life. What are you going to offer her to make up for the twenty years of life she missed out on with you?"

I inhaled sharply. Was he really asking what I had to offer his daughter? As, in this lifetime? Forever? I put my head up and opened my eyes, grabbing what little courage I had left by the balls, and speaking from the heart. "I'll give her everything, Pat.

Marriage. Babies. Houses all over the world. Whatever she wants."

Patrick groaned. "Axel, don't fucking promise things you don't mean!"

"But I do!" I practically yelled into the phone. "Don't you get it? She's the one I want! She's everything, and I'll wait for her. To finish college. Go to chiropractor school. Everything, if she wants that. She doesn't have to work."

"She'll want to work," Pat ground out.

I laughed. "Yeah, I know. I can give her the world, and she'll still want to earn it herself. Kind of poetic, isn't it? The only woman who doesn't want me for my money."

There was a long, drawn-out silence. Then Pat spoke. "I don't forgive you."

"I know."

"And you have to convince Chasity of all that shit you just said, not me."

I closed my eyes, relief washing over me like a cold, cleansing rain. "I know."

There was another long silence. "And if you ever, and I mean ever, lie to me again—"

"I won't," I promised, though I knew there would be instances in the future where Chastity would want to tell her dad a thing, and I had to lie about it. I hoped Patty would forgive the trespasses. Because I knew what he really meant.

"Okay, then," he finally huffed out.

"Okay, then... I can call her? Try and win her back?" My heart leapt in ecstasy at the idea.

"You can try," Pat said, his tone now turning sad. "But I'm not sure she's here anymore."

"What do you mean?" I asked. "She wasn't heading back to school until next week, was she?" That was the original plan, anyway.

He sighed. "Yeah, well, her mom said that she wasn't coping and wanted to head back early. So, I'm not sure if you wanna brave an on-campus declaration of love, but you might have to, if you want her back."

"Her mom?" I asked, hearing the unusual tone he used "Are you two seeing each other again?"

My old friend sighed. "We had lunch the other day. I don't know, man. Maybe too much water has gone under that bridge to start again."

"You're wrong," I managed to say, though my drunken brain was beginning to lose the fight to stay clear and conscious. "You two never really had your chance. The odds were stacked against you from the start."

There was a pause, then Pat said, "So you think I should, you know... give it another go?"

"Yeah, I do," I managed to say, though Katherine and I weren't exactly the best of friends. "After all, any woman who brought up someone like Chastity can't be all bad. Right?"

Pat groaned at me. "I've gotta go. Let me know how the groveling goes down."

I laughed as I navigated the island counter and headed towards my bedroom. "You'll probably see it on YouTube. It's gonna be epic." I hung up the phone to the sound of my best friend laughing his ass off and fell into the middle of my bed. The room was spinning, but it wasn't all bad. All the nasty emotions and feelings of the week were gone. They'd drowned in alcohol, and Pat's reassurances would make sure they wouldn't come back.

I had to apologize to him again. Properly. When I wasn't soaked in aged alcohol. And I would. I didn't regret what Chastity and I had shared. But I did regret lying to Patrick. We shouldn't have done it, though would we have had the chance to get to know one another like we had if we'd been honest from the start? We'd never know.

I crawled up to the pillows and closed my eyes. Below me, I could hear people cheering and music continued to pound. I forced my eyes open and stared at the clock on the other side of the room. Midnight. "Happy New Year."

I smiled as I closed my eyes again and pulled the blanket over me. This year was going to be different. I needed to scale back at work. I wanted more of a life. More vacations, more time off. More hours and days and nights with Chastity.

I just had to win her back. *But how?* She wasn't a typical woman. She wouldn't be won over by flowers or chocolates, or a standard apology. Pat was right, I'd need to go big. And I'd work it all out in the morning, when the alcohol was cleared from my system, and I could think straight. But for now, I would celebrate getting Patrick back on my side, at least a little, and tomorrow I'd start to build the road back to Chastity's side.

4

CHASTITY

The day after everything went to hell with Dad and Axel, I got my period. I was so devastated, I packed up to go back to school, and talked my mom into driving me. Not that I'd wanted to get pregnant at almost twenty-two. But in that moment, it felt like I'd lost all connection to Axel, and it had broken my heart all over again.

It was stupid, I know, but that was how I'd felt. And in some ways, it had been a learning experience for me about my mom as well. I'd finally understood how she may have felt back when she'd become pregnant with me. Had she adored my dad the way I absolutely loved Axel? Was she totally terrified, but so excited about the idea of having a piece of him inside her? Probably? Maybe? I wasn't sure because I'd been too scared to ask her.

Instead, I'd gone back to school, had a sad, mediocre New Year's surrounded by drunken college freshmen, and studied. What else did I have in my life? My college friends weren't back yet, and I didn't have a life. That was obvious.

"Hey, Chastity," Naomi said, the librarian who I was on a first name basis with. "There's someone here to see you."

I turned towards the front desk and couldn't see anyone. What was she talking about?

"Uh, what do you mean, someone's here to see me?" This wasn't a hotel. People didn't visit.

"I mean—" Naomi leaned forward and got closer to me, whispering the way all people did in libraries. "There is a very handsome, older man, asking for you. He went to the front office and your dorm. Then he came here and finally found you. Here."

I glanced around again, but still couldn't see anyone I knew, though my stomach was tight, and my heart was beginning to thud. It had to be Axel, though people had described my father in a similar way. I'd left without saying a proper goodbye to my dad, so it was possible he'd driven all this way to see me. Again. We did need to sort a few things out.

"Where is he?" I asked, standing up and looking around.

Naomi smiled at me. "I wouldn't let him in to come and find you, of course. So, I told him you'd meet him outside, if you wanted to."

I gathered my books up and slid them into my new leather bag. My heart was really pounding in my chest now. "You wouldn't let him in?"

Naomi grinned at me. "Well, he didn't have an ID badge. We don't allow strangers in campus buildings, you know that."

I laughed at how protective she was being and shook my head. "Thanks, Naomi. You're awesome."

If it was my dad, Naomi would feel silly for making a big deal out of this, I was sure. But from the look on her excited face, she didn't think it was my father. So, with shaking hands, I pulled the heavy bag over my shoulder and headed for the exit, which was also the entrance to the library. *It's probably just Dad,* I kept telling myself.

Because I desperately wanted it to be Axel, and if it wasn't the man I wished for, then I didn't want to be too disappointed when I saw my father out the front of the library. *Just breathe.* I walked up to the glass doors at the front of the large library and peered through. I didn't see anyone there that I knew. My stomach twisted. What was the bet Naomi had been mistaken? *That's unlikely.*

I frowned and placed my hand on the glass door. Moment of truth. I pushed the door open and stepped out into the fresh air. "Hello?" I still couldn't see anyone.

"Chastity?" I heard him call, and my heart leapt.

That wasn't my dad.

I crept forward to the edge of the steps. The library was massive and built on a huge foundation. There were at least twenty steps to the bottom. I stood at the top and stared down, every part of me aching to run down to him. Because there he was, all six feet two inches of muscled billionaire. My dad's best friend. *My love.*

"Axel," I whispered, and he grinned, though I was sure he couldn't hear me from where I stood.

He thrust his hand into his pockets and just stared up at me. He wore faded blue jeans and a black, chest hugging T-shirt that made him look about thirty. *A very hot thirty.*

A girl with long curly hair walked past him, then stopped and turned, craning her neck to stare at him.

I sighed and shook my head. "Did you have to wear that?" I muttered to myself as I began the slow decline towards him, grabbing hold of the handrail in case I fell in my haste. My legs didn't feel steady, and my heart was bursting with happiness.

Axel wandered towards me and met me at the bottom of the steps. He didn't reach for me, so I clung to the rail and stayed where I was.

"Hey," he said, smiling at me like we'd never been apart. With too much warmth and familiarity considering how we'd broken up. Then hadn't spoken since. So, what the?

"Hey, yourself," I managed, trying not to smile back. "What are you doing here?"

"I wanted to talk to you."

My eyebrows flickered up. I felt them practically climb to the top of my forehead. "And you didn't think to use the phone?"

I'd been clinging to my cell like a lifeline for the past week, hoping and praying that he would come to his senses and call. I'd dreamt about it, and despite how real this felt, part of me wanted to pinch my leg and make sure this was real. But I also didn't want to look like an idiot, so I just swayed on my unsteady legs and focused on standing.

"I did think about it," he said with an even bigger grin. "And I did, about an hour ago when I arrived. But you had your phone off."

I frowned, then realized where I'd gone wrong. "Oh, yeah. I turn it off in the library when I'm studying. It's too distracting."

"Too many guys trying to contact you?" Axel asked with a smile, though there was a strange pain hidden deep in his eyes.

I snorted and flicked my hair back over my shoulder. "What do you want, Axel?"

"I want to apologize. I'm here to apologize."

I gestured with my hand, "Okay, then do it." Because that was not an apology.

He barked out a laugh, then shook his head. "God, I've missed you."

Hmmmm, okay.

His face sobered. "Do you want to go somewhere else?"

I shook my head. "No. This is fine." If we went somewhere else, I'd be lost. He'd touch me or kiss me, and I'd fall into his arms with a sob of relief and beg him never to leave me again. I couldn't do that yet. Not until all the shit between us was sorted out. I crossed my arms over my chest and lifted my chin. "Go for it."

He nodded and straightened, standing tall. "I'm so sorry about what I said in front of your father. It was wrong of me, and it was a lie."

I grimaced at him. "Really? Which part?"

"The part where I told you that it wasn't part of the deal for you to fall in love with me."

Oh, yeah. That part.

"Uh..."

He rushed to continue, "It was wrong and cowardly, and I'm so sorry I hurt you."

Oh, wow.

I dropped my gaze to the ground in front of his feet. That was a pretty perfect apology, but his words brought a huge lump to my throat. All the feelings I'd been suppressing suddenly rose to the surface. I swallowed hard, trying to dislodge the lump so I could speak again. "Um, well, yeah. You hurt me. But it's okay now." I lifted my head to look at him again. "Is that all you wanted to do? Come and apologize? Because I'm a big girl. I can handle a little rejection." I didn't like it. Hell, I'd *hated* it. But what other option did I have?

"No." Axel shook his head. "I came here to tell you that I want to keep seeing you, if you'll allow it. I know you've got your last semester here, then chiropractor school, and you have your whole life ahead of you but if you'll let me, I want to be a part of it. All of it."

My mouth dropped open. "Seriously?

He laughed, breaking the tension surrounding us. "Yes. Seriously."

"But what about my father?"

Axel sobered. "We had a chat."

"You did?" I was shocked. "What happened? What did he say?" I couldn't believe Dad had actually spoken to Axel. Last time I'd spoken to my father, he was still furious.

"We talked and I apologized. I told him that I love you, and I think we're all good now."

"You what?" I took a step closer, sure my ears were deceiving me. "Did you just say that you told my dad..." I couldn't repeat it out loud. If I'd heard him wrong, I'd look like an idiot.

Axel grinned, thrusting his hands into his pockets again and flexing his shoulders so that his arms rippled with tight muscles.

"That I loved you. Yeah, I did."

"Uh..." What on earth was I gonna say to that? *It would have been nice if you'd told me.*

Axel took a step closer so that he was now within touching distance. His gaze was intense, his eyes boring into mine. "Can we go back to your dorm room? Or somewhere we could talk a bit more privately?"

I swallowed hard. "Yeah, okay."

He took my hand and interlaced our fingers, and my heart leapt in my chest as love for this incredible man wove through me.

Damn it... I thought I was over you. A little, anyway. "My dorms on the other side of campus," I managed to say, though my voice wobbled, and I suddenly felt totally out of my depth. However, that wasn't a new sensation around Axel.

He smiled down at me. "Lead the way."

So, I did. With my heart in my throat and a billionaire on my arm, I wove through my beautiful school grounds and took Axel all the way to my dorm room.

5

AXEL

Who would have known that the biggest deal of my life wouldn't be an international billion-dollar deal? It was convincing Chastity to give me a second chance.

She tugged me through the campus like I was on some sort of tour, then down a corridor in her dorm that looked far too similar to the one I'd stayed in when I was at Yale.

"These places all look the same." I laughed, glancing around, and soaking in the surroundings.

Chastity opened the door to her left. "Did you enjoy college?"

I nodded. "Yeah, it was great. I got away from my parents and really partied." I shook my head at the memories. "I definitely didn't study as much as I should have, but I think I've made up for it, with time."

She gestured for me to follow her inside and I walked into the blessedly empty dorm room. There were two beds, two desks, and a whole lot of girly paraphernalia. Clothes, books, pink cushions and a whole lot of neatness that I hadn't expected.

"Is your roommate around?" I asked.

"Hope? No, she'll be back next week."

I couldn't stop the laugh that bubbled up on my lips. "Hope and Chastity? Someone in Admissions has a sense of humor."

She nodded but didn't smile, then sat down on what I had to assume was her bed.

I glanced around. "Can I sit? Or..."

"Yeah. You can sit on Hope's bed if you want, or there's two desk chairs behind you. Whatever suits."

I grabbed the black desk chair closest to me in the end because it seemed more likely to hold my weight. The two flimsy beds looked a little fragile for my liking.

"So..." Chastity began, "What were you saying out there? You want us to keep seeing each other? Even though I'm here and you're in the city? How would that work?"

I sat up straighter on the chair. I'd prepared for this, and I hoped I had all the answers. Chastity was smart, and she had a quick mind that put together patterns and information quickly.

"Well, you know I have an insane amount of work to do during the week, so I hoped that if I could rearrange my schedule to take off most weekends, I could come here or you could come home, and we could spend time together then."

She frowned. More questions were coming, I could feel it. And happily, I had a lot of answers and two sets of keys in my pocket.

"But how?" she repeated. We're hours apart, and I don't have a car."

"Ah!" I grabbed the first set of keys out of my left pocket. "Catch." I tossed the keys to her.

She caught them easily and held them up, "What are these?"

"Keys to your new car. I asked you mom for a bit of help on something you'd like—that she approved of—so if you don't like it, we can trade it."

Chastity's eyes went wide. "But I was going to get a car when I went to Sherman."

I nodded. "I know. And you can sell this one if you want to after you graduate. But it's there so you can easily drive home on weekends, and I'm hoping it will make it easier for us to see each other."

She stared at the keys, looking dumbfounded. "You bought me a car."

"Yeah," I said. Had I made a mistake there?

"It's too much," she whispered.

I sighed, got up, and moved over to her bed to be closer to her.

I sat down next to her, though the bed creaked, and I was pretty sure I was going to break it. "It's not. A car is just a car. I want you to be happy, and for us to work. I was hoping the car would help, but if you'd rather a plane, I can get you one of those too." With a full-time pilot to fly her around. But I was pretty sure that wasn't what she wanted.

She shoved me in the side as if I'd been joking. "Be serious! But what about the weekends. I have to study, and you can't stay on campus, so where are we going to go? It'll get too complicated."

I pulled the second set of keys out of my pocket. "That's why I bought an apartment about ten minutes from here." I lifted the keys up and showed her the silver jingling in my palm.

Chastity's gaze flicked from my hand to the keys, then back again. "You did? Why?"

I laughed and leaned forward so that I could place the keys on her bedside table. "Because I knew you'd have a hundred questions, and I wanted answers for you. I want to see you, love you, be with you. I don't care where. And when you go to Sherman, we'll work out something then too."

She was staring at me now, with suspiciously shiny eyes. "But I'll be in another state."

I shrugged. "So?"

"So, this is my dream, and I can't give it up. I..."

I grabbed both of her hands and twisted around so I could look straight at her. "Sweetheart, you don't have to give up anything. My business is moveable, and in the end, saleable. I'll go where you go, if you want me to. We can make it work. I promise."

Those suspiciously shiny eyes suddenly glossed over, and a single tear slipped down her cheek. "You really want me that much?"

"I do. I've never met anyone like you. You're an incredible woman." I reached up and cupped her cheek. "And I haven't slept more than a few hours since you left."

She sniffed and wiped her cheek. "I didn't really get that part. Why was Dad so shocked that you slept next to me?"

I loved the fact that she didn't really understand that, and she thought it was completely normal to share the intimacy we did.

"Because I don't sleep next to anyone. I never have. I don't feel safe or relaxed." I blew out a long breath when I'd finished. I'd never admitted it aloud, but what I'd just said was true.

"But with me, you slept all night," she said, sniffing again. "Right next to me."

I grinned at her rosy face. "I did. And that's because I am totally and utterly in love with you."

She stared at me. "You are?"

I nodded, my heart pounding like a hammer in my chest. "I am, but you need to tell me... am I too late? Or will you give me a second chance?"

She burst out with a strange laugh and threw herself at me, her arms around my neck as she hugged me tightly and cuddled into my lap.

I laughed as I held her to me, loving the heat of her against me. "Is that a yes?"

She nodded. "Yes, of course. I missed you *so* much." She moved back from our tight hug then threw her leg over my thighs to straddle me.

I grinned at her. "Do you want to come see the new apartment? Maybe we can christen the shower there?" It had incredible amenities. A double rainfall shower. A huge tub. A bedroom big enough to do gymnastics routines in.

She cupped my face and smiled with a cheekiness I'd missed. "Could we maybe stay here? I've never had sex in this bed."

I glanced down at the single, narrow bed. "Of course, we can. I suppose if we break it, I'll just buy another one."

She nodded. "Yeah, you do that." Then she came forward to kiss me.

I surged up to meet her lips, moaning when her flavor came through. "Damn, I've missed you." She smiled and moved forward again, but I pulled back. "There's one more thing that I've been worried about." I swallowed hard, the tightness of uncertainty returning. "That first time we didn't use protection. Did you ever get your monthly cycle? Or?"

Her lips curved downwards. "Yeah, I did. Last week."

I gripped her waist a little tighter. "You sound disappointed."

She sighed and bit her lip. "Oh, I was a little bit. I mean… it was stupid. Having a baby now would be insane. And I'd have to give up my place in chiropractic school, but…"

A surge of something I'd never felt before came bursting up inside of me. "You wanted to have my baby?" Damn… why did I find that so hot? The image of her big belly, swollen with my child made me grip her even tighter.

She nodded but glanced down at the space between us as though she was embarrassed. "Well, yes. It sounds crazy, but I mean… I love you."

I grabbed her chin and lifted her face to meet mine. "If you want a baby, I'll give you a baby. This month, next. Whenever you're ready."

Her eyes went wide, and her mouth dropped open. "Really? You mean it?"

I growled at her, sounding like the caveman I felt like. "Yes! I want you in every way there is. I'm committed to us. You'd be an amazing mother, and I would love to fill you and make you pregnant one day."

She moaned softly and kissed me again, her eyes sliding closed.

There were no more words now. I tugged her clothes off and she was soon jumping up so I could get out of mine.

When she moved onto the bed, on her back, I stared down at her and sighed. "I am one lucky bastard."

She reached out for me, and I slid down on top of her, moaning with pleasure when her soft, naked body pressed against mine.

I whispered into her ear, "God, I love you."

And she gasped and clung to me.

I set my cock to her entrance and slid into her easily, her body welcoming me as I joined us together. Over and over again.

She moaned louder and kissed me deeper, her fingers clinging to my shoulders, and grabbing at my ass, forcing me into her again, and again. And when she came on me, the ripples of her body sent me over the edge, into a place I'd never been before.

For the first time in my life, I wouldn't be venturing into the future alone. From now on, it was Chastity and me.

6

CHASTITY

After a post-coital nap, Axel convinced me to abandon my studies and go and see the apartment he'd purchased in the area.

"I can't believe you actually bought an apartment here," I said, shaking my head as I climbed into his car. "That's so extreme."

He turned the key and started the engine on his ridiculously expensive sports car. "I wanted to be close to you."

I crossed my arms over my chest and stared at him. "Stalker."

He laughed, and the sound filled the cabin of the car, the most incredible sound on the planet.

I couldn't help but smile, happiness pouring through me.

"So, it was a bit much, huh?" he asked, driving through the streets towards town.

I glanced out the window. "Well, it was kind of a grand gesture. I can't fault you there."

I looked back at him, my chest tightening. "But what if I'd said no?"

"You mean to us getting back together?"

I nodded. "Yeah. What would you have done?"

He shrugged. "Signed the place over to you, dropped off the keys, and taken my broken ass home again."

My mouth dropped open. "You would have given me an apartment? Just like that?"

Axel turned down another street then glanced at me. "Yeah, of course."

I didn't believe it. How could anyone just give away something so valuable? My own mother had worked her fingers to the bone to provide a roof over my head. I stared out the window, a swirl of emotions clogging up my chest and throat.

"Hey, hey... what's going on inside your head?" Axel asked, sliding a hand over my thigh.

I looked down at my leg and stared at the way he possessively caressed the skin there. I'd missed his touch. So much. Taking a deep breath, I tried to calm the panic. "Nothing. I just can't really comprehend having that much money. My parents, my mom in particular, struggled to pay the mortgage. The utilities. Food. And you would just... give me an apartment." Axel pulled into a parking lot just off the street and shut off the engine.

"Why'd you stop?" I asked.

He turned in the seat and grinned at me. "Because we're here."

"Whoa, that really was just five minutes." I glanced around. It was a nice neighborhood, but I didn't really recognize it.

"Hey, listen to me for a sec, okay?" he soothed, squeezing my thigh a little.

I turned around to face him, his tone telling me he was about to get all serious on me.

"Okay. I'm listening."

"I say this without vanity, but I have a lot of money."

I laughed at him. "Oh, yeah, you sound incredibly modest."

He sighed. "I have a point, so listen to me, okay?"

I crossed my arms over my chest, uncomfortable with the topic of the conversation but nodded, nonetheless. "I'm listening, go on."

He took a deep breath then exhaled slowly. "I grew up wealthy. My parents sent me to the best schools, got me everything I wanted, then ignored the fact that I existed."

I reached across the car and squeezed his hand, hating that he'd had such a loveless childhood.

"It's okay, though, because after they'd paid for me to go to college, they basically cut me off to prove that I couldn't survive without them."

I grinned at him, already knowing where this story was going. "But you did."

"Of course, I did. I made sure of it. I got a good job, then started my own company and have been pushing hard ever since."

"It makes sense," I agreed, smiling at him. "You wanted to prove you could do it on your own."

"I did, and I still was—until I met you. Now I'm looking into taking on some partners, downsizing maybe. Selling off the business or just delegating some of my roles. I'm not sure yet, but you've inspired me to change my life."

I huffed out a laugh. "Ah... I don't understand. I've made you want to stop working?" *Was that a compliment?*

He sighed. "I'm not explaining this right. I don't want to just accumulate wealth for the sake of it anymore, Chastity. I want it to mean something more. I want the money to give us a better life. That's the point of money, right?"

I nodded, still not seeing the big picture yet. "Sure," I said, though it came out more like a question.

He ran a hand through his hair and sighed. "Look, all I meant by this is that is..." He groaned then looked me straight in the eye. "Money means nothing to me if I can't have you. So... if you didn't want me, then the apartment, the money I had to buy it, and the car, all mean nothing."

I leaned over and kissed him. He was going around in a circle, and instead of listening to the words, I heard the intent behind them. Pulling back, I looked into his eyes. "I love you too."

He smiled at me. "How are you already smarter than me?"

I laughed. "Hardly! But it's nice that you think I'm smart. So, are you going to show me this apartment?"

"Let's go," he said, and jumped out of the car.

I followed suit and looked around. "Nice area."

There were a few cafés and restaurants, as well as random shops along the opposite side of the street, facing the modern-looking apartment building that was apparently our destination.

"I thought it would be good to be close to some amenities. The place has a gym for me, a laundry service if we both just want to chill." He took my hand and led me into a huge building that was far flashier on the inside than it looked on the outside.

It had marble floors and a concierge waiting at the desk. "Can I help you, sir?"

Axel nodded. "Yes and no. I'm Axel Patterson and I purchased a penthouse here last week. The closing was a few days ago and I have the keys, so I'd like to take a look now. Do you have any access cards that I need?"

The concierge's eyes widened. "It's nice to meet you, sir. I'm Tony. Let me get the building forms out for you and I'll set you up with everything you need."

"Chastity's name needs to be on everything as well," Axel said, indicating to me. "She goes to school nearby and will probably use this place more than I do."

"Of course, sir," Tony said. "I'll just get your daughter to sign the papers too."

I laughed out loud, then looked at the guy behind the desk. "I'm not his daughter, Tony."

The guy stared at me, frozen with shock.

I put my hand on the desk and grinned at him. I couldn't believe he'd actually said it, and a streak of cheekiness took over. "I mean... I understand your confusion and technically, he could be. The age gap between us is twenty years. But nope. Not us."

Axel glared at the concierge, steam practically rising from his ears. "She's my girlfriend, and I suggest you give her the respect that deserves."

Tony sputtered out an apology and I turned away, so he didn't see me grin and struggle not to laugh again. It was the first time someone had assumed I was Axel's daughter, and I was pretty sure it wouldn't be the last. We had to keep a sense of humor about it, surely?

Within ten minutes we'd both signed all the relevant paperwork and were being personally escorted up the elevator by the concierge.

"If you need anything from me at all, please don't hesitate to call."

"You can go, Tony," Axel said, flicking his hand to dismiss the poor guy.

I smiled at him as he shut the door, then raced over to the windows that faced the ocean, only a few blocks away. "Oh my God, Axel, this view is incredible." I pressed a hand to the cool glass and stared out. *Wow.*

Axel dropped the keys on the kitchen counter behind me and I whirled around, still sensing his displeasure.

"What's the matter, Daddy?" I asked him, grinning as wide as I could. "Don't you want people to think I'm your little girl?"

He thrust his hands into his jean pockets and glowered at me. He looked as sexy as sin, and I marveled at the fact the concierge had mistaken him for anything more than my boyfriend. He looked thirty, thirty-five, tops.

"No. I don't want that," he growled.

I pouted and dropped to my knees, crawling over the plush carpet and staring up at him. I wanted him again, and I had to assume that the best way to get him out of this mood was to prove to him how young and virile he really was.

He stared down at me as I approached, then got up on my knees right in front of him.

"This carpet is incredible," I said as I reached for the button on his jeans. "You'll have to give me the grand tour. In a moment."

"In a moment, huh?" he asked, sliding his hand around the back of my head, his eyes darkening with desire.

"Yeah..." I nodded, opening the zipper and taking out his cock. "Later."

I took the head into my mouth, loving the way his groan filled the air around me. I was so much more confident doing this now. I moved my hand on the shaft, enjoying the way his flesh got larger and hotter against my palm. His taste was so special. Like macadamia nut oil, but hot and sexy. It was so distinctly him, and I loved it. All of it.

Then he was tugging me to my feet and grabbing me up in his arms. He twirled me around, set me on the kitchen counter and kissed me hungrily. He lifted my skirt, found my underwear, and tore our mouths apart so he could drag my undies off and down my legs.

When he came back, I opened my thighs willingly.

He was grunting and moving with quick, jerky motions. He wanted me, and he didn't care about finesse and concern. This was about passion and need. And imprinting himself all over me. He grabbed my ass and dragged me to the edge of the counter.

I gasped at the move as the cold marble pressed into my behind. But then he was there, hot and insistent against me. I lifted my chin, and he kissed me, his tongue piercing my lips as his cock pressed into my softness. The hard, mushroomed head of his opened me, and I threw my head back, gasping at the pressure. It was so fast, so powerful. A sob rose in my throat at how right it felt to be with this man in my arms.

He set his teeth to my neck and sucked the skin there, marking me. Again. Then he thrust all the way to the hilt.

I moaned at the feeling of fullness.

"You okay?" he whispered.

I closed my eyes as the wave of his love flowed over me. "Yes," I reassured him, not wanting to break the spell cast over us. "Don't stop."

And he didn't. He pulled back, then thrust forward into me, again and again.

I gasped and moaned, clinging to him as he relentlessly fucked me into the kitchen counter hot and fast, the sounds of our slapping flesh and groans filled the white kitchen.

Suddenly he groaned and pulled out, spilling his heat all over me while he plundered my mouth for a final kiss. When he pulled back from the kiss, he was panting and pressed his forehead against mine.

I closed my eyes and held him tightly against me, reveling in the feeling that came from bringing him to such a state of pleasure.

"I'm sorry." He panted, smiling up at me. "I couldn't control it."

I laughed and lifted my head. "Never apologize for fucking me. Never."

Axel bent his head and kissed my lips. "We've gotta get you on the pill."

I groaned and glanced down at my new top, now covered in cum. "Yeah... or invest in a new wardrobe."

We laughed as we raced to the new shower to clean up. He'd remembered to pull out of me this time, but before at the dorm? He hadn't.

7

AXEL

I tugged my jeans back on and grimaced at the feel of them against my clean skin. "We need some new clothes."

Chastity chuckled as she stood wearing only her underwear, staring down at the soiled top and skirt on the floor. "Well, I certainly do."

Heat flushed up my cheeks. "Ah... yeah. Sorry about that. Let me make a phone call and I'll get you some new things. What size are you? A six?"

"Ha!" she said, crossing her arms over her ample breasts. "More like an eight or ten."

I kissed her lips and stepped away, grabbing for my phone. "Give me a sec."

A cheery Tony picked up when I called the front desk. "Concierge speaking."

"Tony, it's Axel from the penthouse."

"Oh, sir! I wanted to apologize again for my blunder."

"You can make it up to us by sending someone out to do some

shopping. We both need some new clothes. Jeans, and a couple of tops. Put it on my bill."

"Of course, sir. I'll get someone to watch the desk, then go myself. Can you give me your sizes and some color options?"

I did, then hung up the phone.

Chastity came up next to me, sliding her small hand into mine. "Are you going to show me the apartment now?"

I looked down at her, loving the soft look of contentment in her eyes. "Sure. But it'll be the first time for me too, so I'm not sure I can give you much of a tour."

Her eyebrows climbed up her forehead. "What do you mean?"

I shrugged. "Exactly what I said. I bought this place, sight unseen. So, let's go see it together."

"You—"

I grabbed Chastity's hand and dragged her to the front door. Buying a penthouse apartment in a great area wasn't a financial risk as far as I was concerned. It was furnished and had been styled by an interior decorator. It would be an easy piece of real estate to sell once we were done with it.

"Let's start at the front door," I said, dragging her back to the front door, then turning her around to face the apartment. "So, this is the apartment I bought." I waved my hand around, and she giggled. She was standing in her underwear, looking utterly gorgeous.

"It's very nice," she said. "Where's the bedroom?"

I groaned and tapped her gently on her round ass. "Let's go see, shall we?"

We turned left, down the hall and stepped into the first room. The master suite.

"I think we found it."

"Oh... I like it!" she said, running her hand over the blue and black patterned comforter, then sticking her head in the ensuite bathroom. "It has a bathtub and the biggest shower. Come see!"

I grinned as I walked after her, loving her enthusiasm. "Next time, we'll look at apartments together and choose one we both like."

She twisted around and wrapped her arms around my neck. "I love this one. The view is amazing. The bedroom is huge, and I'm going to love soaking in that tub."

Tick, tick, tick. I do know her! "I'm glad you like it," I said, kissing her soft lips and sliding my hands around her tiny waist. "Once we get some clothes, how about we go out for some early dinner then come back and I give you that orgasm I owe you?"

Her eyes widened as her eyebrows shot up again. "You don't owe me anything."

"Oh, but I do," I said. "And I will love giving it to you."

She bit her lip, her cheeks coloring a beautiful shade of rose. "Dinner sounds great, but how long are you staying? Should I go back to school to pick up some stuff? Or are you heading home soon?"

It was Saturday afternoon, and I had several important meetings on Monday. "I'll stay until tomorrow afternoon, but then I'll really need to head back to the city."

She kissed me again. "Okay, perfect. So, we can just chill together tonight and tomorrow. Then you'll drop me back?"

I nodded. "Of course. I have to introduce you to your car, too."

"Ooohhh." She grinned.

I held her hand as we walked around the rest of the apartment. There were three bedrooms, a huge kitchen and living area, and two bathrooms.

"Can I invite my parents to stay here one weekend?" She asked when we'd finished the tour as she looked through the kitchen cabinets for a glass to get some water.

"Ah... yeah. Of course," I responded, though I hadn't really thought about anyone using it except us. "Or if you have any friends you want to come stay, that would be fine too. It's three bedrooms. We can still make a whole lot of racket at one end if they're sleeping down the other end of the apartment."

Chastity slapped her hand over her mouth, her eyes bulging. "I still can't believe Dad walked in on us. He hasn't really spoken to me since that day."

I inhaled sharply. "It would have been a bit of a shock." And one I really couldn't empathize with. I didn't have kids. Speaking of which... "How do you feel about going on the pill?"

She drank a sip of water, then tilted her head. "Is that what you normally do with your girlfriends?"

I laughed out loud at that one. "Uh... no. I don't have girlfriends, and normally a woman's choices regarding her body are totally up to her."

Chastity pressed her lips together and squinted at me. "Normally? I'm really not understanding."

I pressed my hands into the marble countertop and groaned. "I can't control myself with you. In my past, those women were experienced. They carried protection, and so did I. The encounters were calculated. But with you, I can't stop myself. I want to feel your naked pussy wrapped around my cock. It's just..."

I growled because I couldn't quite put into words how little control I had around her. She was so sweet, and yet as seductive as Helen of Troy. I didn't want latex between us. I didn't want anything between us. I wanted to be able to take her anywhere, any time.

She slapped her hands to her cheeks and closed her eyes. "Oh my God," she whispered. "I can't believe you talk like that." I stared at her, noticing the way her chest rose and fell as though she were excited.

"Unless you want to get pregnant?" I asked her. "Because

that would change everything." And I would not complain. A baby with the woman I loved? What better way to enjoy our new life?

Chastity dropped her hands down and smiled at me. "I love the fact you want that. It's amazing. But I have so many things I want to do first. I've never even left the state. I haven't traveled..."

"Oh, then we need to do that." I said, ideas flooding my mind. "Paris. Spain. London."

She laughed at me. "Disneyworld. Canada. Vegas!"

"When's your birthday?" I asked, realizing I didn't know, which was sad considering I'd just offered her a baby.

"It's next week, actually. January the tenth."

"Perfect! Let's go to Vegas."

Her eyes went wide and suspiciously shiny. "Seriously? Just like that?"

"Yes, Let's go and do Vegas properly. Lots of gambling, shows, and drinking."

She walked over to me and slid her hands up my torso. "Axel, that would be amazing. Thank you."

I bent my head to kiss her, then heard the knock at the door.

I groaned. "Fucking interruptions."

She giggled. "That's probably Tony with our clothes."

I glanced down at her cleavage pushed up by her white bra. "I prefer you undressed."

She raised an eyebrow. "And the people in the restaurant at dinner?"

I pulled out of her arms. "No. They don't get to see you like this."

She waved her hand at me and flounced away. "Then go grab the clothes, and I'll meet you in the bedroom."

I watched her luscious ass flex as she moved. *Grrr... I could take her right now.* Another knock at the door sounded. "Coming!" I stomped toward the entry wearing only jeans and wrenched open the door.

"Oh. Sir. I brought..."

I extended my arm to Tony, who was standing at the door laden with suit bags and retail bags. "Come on in."

Tony hurried forward. "May I put these in the bedroom?"

"No. Chastity is in there. Just set everything on the sofa."

He'd bought a lot from what I could tell. He was carrying at least eight shopping bags, and long suit bags obviously containing something for me.

"There you go, sir," he said, heading towards the door.

"Thanks, Tony." I waved him out. "Just lock the door behind you. Thanks."

As soon as the door had shut, Chastity walked out, all gorgeous suntanned flesh on display. "When are you going to forgive him?"

I shrugged. "No idea. Maybe next year." I lifted up a bright pink bag. "I think some of these are for you."

"Oohhh." Chastity dropped to her knees, and I watched her go through the bags with gasps of delight and squeals of glee. "This is better than Christmas."

I sat on the sofa and watched her as she unpacked everything and began to try the clothes on. This was how Christmas should have been. Us nearly naked, having just had sex. Presents everywhere, and Chastity as happy as a clam.

Next Christmas I'd make sure we were together for the whole day, whether she wanted to do her normal lunch and dinner routine with her parents, or I whisked her off to Paris for the week. Either way worked for me. Now that I had this delightful girl back in my life, I was never letting her go again.

8

CHASTITY

I grabbed Axel's face for one final kiss and hugged him tightly to me. We'd had an amazing night together. I'd worn my new black dress Tony the concierge purchased for me, and we'd had a lovely dinner. Afterwards, we'd gone for a walk, eaten ice cream, and made love all through the night. This morning he'd taken me out for a late brunch, and we'd laughed and chatted like we'd been together forever.

Axel hadn't stopped touching me or kissing me, and no one who was looking at us would ever have mistaken us for father and daughter. But the weekend was almost over, and Axel had a two-hour drive ahead of him.

"I don't want you to go." I pouted, clinging tightly to his hands. He was dropping me off at the front gate, and I didn't want to go back to school without him.

He chuckled, raised my hands up and kissed my knuckles. "Trust me, beautiful. If I could stay, I would."

I sighed. "Yeah, and I suppose I have to get back too. Classes. Studying. Stuff." Everything my life had been before I'd met him.

He pulled back and grinned down at me. "Don't forget to

check out your car. I had it put in the dorm's parking lot, out the back. Keys are in your room."

"Which one is it?" I asked. "There's hundreds of cars out there."

He winked. "You'll know which one it is, trust me. And if you can't work it out, just call me and I'll tell you what to look for."

Ooooh... a mystery! And a surprise! "Axel, you spoil me too much." And I really didn't feel like I deserved it.

"Hardly," he said, walking back to his car. "Wait until you've been with me for a year or two. By then I should have spoiled you sufficiently."

He opened the door to his car and turned back to grin at me.

"Two years?" I asked, staring at him in awe. "What do you mean?"

"Well, I need to fly you all over the world first, make love to you in every major city on the planet. Buy you clothes, and jewelry, and anything else your heart desires."

A lump of emotion caught in my throat. "You've already bought me jewelry and clothes, and you are everything my heart desires."

Axel ran back to me and swept me up in his arms, groaning as he hugged me tightly. "*That* is why I love you. You really don't want me for my money, do you?"

I pulled back and glared up at him. "Are you honestly asking me that? Of course not! Look... I love that you're successful and smart and work so hard. That makes me admire you. But I grew up with very little money, and I intend to make my own. So, no, I'm not with you for your money."

He kissed me hard and fast on the lips, then pulled away. "Thank you."

"Now," I said, giving his broad chest a shove. "Go make more millions, Daddy Warbucks."

He mock scowled at me.

I laughed, wrapping my arms around my body. "Bye." I watched him drive away, my heart beating to a dance tempo in my chest.

When he'd driven away and I could no longer see him, I squealed, unable to keep it in any longer. We were back together! And my dad approved of us. I wasn't really sure how Axel had pulled that off, but he had. My cell phone rang and I pulled it out of my pocket. A huge grin split my face as I answered, "Miss me already?"

Axel chuckled. "Oh, yeah. Definitely. But I wanted to ask you one more thing."

"Yeah?"

"Can you call your dad? I think he wants to talk to you."

I laughed. "That is seriously freaky mind reading. I was just thinking about you and Dad, and wondering how you really convinced him we were okay."

"I just told him the truth, beautiful. About how much I love you, and he knows me well enough to know that's never been me before, which makes you special."

I gulped. I wasn't sure I'd ever get sick of hearing him say things like that. "Um... thank you for telling me that again. I kinda love hearing it."

"Good. Because it's the truth. But I think Pat misses you."

My breath hitched in my throat. "Yeah, I didn't really say goodbye to him."

And considering that Dad was one of the main factors of why I was looking forward to going home this holiday season, that said a lot about how much our relationship had deteriorated.

"Well, the apartment's there if your parents need a place to stay, and you have your car too, whenever you want to drive back to see us."

I closed my eyes for a brief moment and sent a prayer of

thanks up to the sky. "Thank you, Axel. Really. That sort of freedom is mind blowing to me."

"Go see your car and send me a photo of you in it."

I laughed, turning on the ball of my foot to walk in the direction of my dorm room. "Going to get the keys now."

"Okay, beautiful. Chat soon."

He hung up and I slid my cell phone into my pocket and ran all the way back to my room. The keys were still sitting where I'd left them, and I snatched them up.

"What sort of car are you?" I asked the silver key, staring down at the fob attached to it. I froze. "No way." I raced out of my room, down the hallway, and almost knocked over another girl in my haste. "Sorry!" I yelled as I kept running. "Oh my God!" I passed through the door that led into the parking lot and glanced around. Left. Right. "Oh my God."

There it was. A bright blue VW Beetle. And from the looks of it, brand new. I slapped my hands over my mouth to stop the scream that rose in my throat. I crept closer, staring and gaping. There was a huge red bow stuck to the hood and I had to gulp back the tears that threatened my composure. "It's beautiful."

My phone dinged, and I lifted it up.

Do you like it?

I twisted around, set my phone to selfie mode, and took a pic of me grinning, tears in my eyes and the car in the background.

I sent him the photo and added text.

You made me cry. I'm so overwhelmed. Thank you.

I lifted the keys and pressed the button, part of me expecting it to not work. There was no way this was my car. But the lights flashed and when I walked over, the door was unlocked.

I got a message straight back.

One of many gifts you'll be getting, so prepare to be spoiled.

I squealed, sounding juvenile when I did, then I hopped in the driver's seat, with nowhere to go. It was beautiful. So new, it smelled amazing, but strange at the same time. I ran my hand over the leather steering wheel and stared down at all the buttons on the dashboard. I had no idea how to work any of this, but I was sure I could figure it out.

Picking up my phone, I took a few more photos then flicked to my address book. Time to call Dad.

He picked up on the second ring. "Chastity."

"Hey, Dad."

My gut was tight with tension, wondering what he would say next.

"I missed not having you here for New Year's."

I smiled. I didn't usually spend New Year's Eve with my dad, but I got his meaning.

"Yeah... I wish I'd been there too. I hope you understood why I left."

"I did. Breaking up is hard."

I nodded, though he couldn't see me. "Yeah, it was. My first break-up, actually."

"Have you heard from Axel since then?" he asked, the tone of his voice higher than normal, like he was anxious.

"Yeah, he came by school yesterday actually."

"He came by?" Dad repeated. "How?"

I laughed. "What do you mean, how? He drove. Came into the college grounds and found me at the library. But the librarian refused to let him in, so he had to wait outside."

My dad laughed. "Axel was refused entry into a library? Oh, I would have liked to have been there to see that."

I grinned. "Yeah, it was sort of awesome."

There was a long beat of silence, then he asked, "So... what happened?"

My chest squeezed tight, and my breath caught in my throat. "Well… we got back together."

Silence.

"Dad?"

"I'm here. Did you two sort everything out?"

"Yeah, we did. As much as we could. I was worried about you and how you felt about everything. But Axel said you gave him permission to come and apologize."

I bit my lip, inhaling deeply through my nose. I hadn't realized talking to my father about this stuff would be so difficult.

"I did. And I'm glad he apologized for being a dick. Tell me… how does a billionaire say I'm sorry? I've never heard those words cross Axel's lips."

"Well," I smiled at the memory. "He did say he was sorry, multiple times. And he bought me some things to make dating each other easier. You know, with the whole long-distance thing."

"What kind of things did he buy you?"

"Well, he got me a car."

"A car! What kind?"

"A Beetle."

I could almost hear my dad's teeth gnashing together.

"What else?"

"Well, the second thing isn't for me, so to speak…" Though he would have given it to me if we'd broken up. Something I still found to be an utterly ridiculous concept. "But he bought an apartment about five minutes from here, so he can stay when he comes for weekends. And he said you or Mom, can come stay too. It's three bedrooms."

More silence, with a little bit of teeth cracking on the other end of the line.

"Dad? You okay?"

"Just be careful, baby, okay? I love Axel, but his track record with dating is shit. He's not good boyfriend material, and I want only good things for you."

My stomach dropped. "I know, Dad. Thank you. And I'm really sorry about everything."

"You mean about dating my best friend behind my back and lying to me?"

Gulp. Fuck.

"Yeah. All of that, Dad. I'm so sorry."

God, it took a lot for me to say it. I wasn't sorry for dating Axel, but I was extremely sorry for hurting my father. So, I was sucking it up and being accountable.

"I know, baby. Okay." He took a big breath, then blew it out in a sigh. "Thank you for telling me you two are back together."

"No problem."

My stomach churned and I put a hand on my belly to stop the feelings from rising too high.

"I better go, Chastity. We'll talk during the week, okay?"

"Sure! Thanks, Dad."

He hung up and I closed my eyes as a wave of pain washed over me. I'd known this moment was coming. Debt collection, for all the sneaking around I'd done.

I opened my eyes, got out of my new car, and locked it. I'd send Mom a few pics and show her my new gift, though just like my dad, I was pretty sure she wouldn't be happy to hear about it.

9

CHASTITY

And guess what? I was right. My mother wasn't happy at all about the photos I sent her. She was actually pretty pissed off that I'd gotten a new car, while she still drove around in something nearly twenty years old.

I tried to backtrack and apologize, for what, I wasn't sure. Having a rich boyfriend, maybe? Either way, I went into my final semester with a heavy heart and a mix of emotions.

Schoolwork was difficult and my life seemed lackluster without Axel's presence. But he messaged me all the time and we chatted every night. When Friday finally rolled around, I couldn't wait to get out of the place.

"Hey, I was thinking of coming back home this weekend," I said to him on Friday around lunchtime. He'd called me on one of his rare breaks. "Are you going to be around?"

"Of course, I'll be around," he said, sounding extremely enthusiastic. Then he hissed, "Shit. I've got a ton work to do on Sunday, and a business dinner Saturday night."

I bit my lip, sadness welling up inside of me. "Can I come to the dinner? Or would I be totally out of place?" I hated inviting myself. *Talk about rude*. But I wanted him to know that I'd fit into his life however I could.

"You'd like to do that?" he asked quietly. "Come with me to one of my boring work dinners?"

"Yes! Of course, I would. But only if that would suit you. I don't want to sit there all alone because you're talking to some foreign guy I've never met."

Axel laughed. "No, actually, these business dinners are social events. My board of directors bring their wives. I just... I've never had one to take."

I inhaled sharply, those words twanging at my heart strings. "Well, we're not married, but I'd love to go if you're okay with that."

"I would love it," he said.

"Then it's a date." I grinned, feeling excited for the first time all week. "I can drive home tonight, maybe catch up with Mom for a bit, then come over?"

"I've gotta work late tonight," he said. I could hear the regret in his voice. "But how about I pick you up for lunch on Saturday and we spend the day together? Then do dinner, sleep together, then Sunday, I'll need to get working again."

Lunch, dinner, a night, and most of Saturday? I'd take it. "Sounds perfect. And I'm sure my parents will want to see me."

There was a beat of silence. "Did you call Patrick?"

"Yeah, I did." And his opinion of Axel still worried me.

"Good. So, you're both okay?"

I bit my lip and mulled it over for a moment. "Yeah, I think so. Although, if you need to work on Sunday, maybe I'll invite him for lunch or something. It might be good to see him. Clear the air."

"Great idea, beautiful. Now, I've gotta go. But I'll see you tomorrow, yeah?"

"Yes!" I repeated, jumping up from my chair and grabbing my

bag. "I've got one more class, then I'll hit the road. My first trip in the new car."

He chuckled. "Enjoy. I'll see you soon."

"Bye."

He hung up, and I jumped a little. I was going home in my new car, and I was going to see Axel again. There couldn't be a better way to spend a weekend.

With my last class finished, I raced back to my room to pack. I had some clothes at my mom's house, but I still needed a few things.

"Where you going?" Hope, my roommate, asked as I hurried in. "I thought you were sticking around this weekend."

I grinned at her. She just wanted a study partner. "Not anymore. My boyfriend wants me to go to a business dinner with him, and I thought I could take my new car for a spin."

Hope glowed green with envy. "Yeah, I get that. It's so nice in those first few months of a relationship, isn't it? The honeymoon phase is the best."

I grabbed my suitcase and began packing clothes. Panties and bras, leggings and jeans. Which dress was I going to wear tomorrow night? The black one the concierge purchased or was there a better choice? If this was going to become a regular thing, I was definitely going to need some new clothes. Some dressier ones. "Honeymoon phase?" I repeated, reaching for some text-books I could read in any down time.

"Yeah," Hope said, sitting on her bed and pulling her legs up so she could sit cross-legged. "You know—the first three months are when everything's awesome. Your partner's perfect. He says all the right things, the sex is amazing. Then after that, things start to annoy you. The sex goes downhill, and you start to fight." Hope pouted as though she were remembering so many fights, and break-ups, it tugged at my heart.

"Well, this is my first relationship," I said, closing the zipper on my suitcase. "He's twice my age and has dated more women than I can count. So, hopefully between us, we can find our way through the jungle together."

I'd been really worried about the long-distance thing, but if this was how it was going to be—weekends together, and planning trips like Vegas next week—then we'd make it. *No problem.*

"Is he really twice your age?" Hope asked, her eyebrows flicking up on her forehead. "Like... actually, double?"

I shrugged. "Pretty much." I was twenty-one, almost twenty-two. And Axel was forty-one.

Hope's mouth dropped open, and she stared at me like I was crazy. "Then he's old! Why would you want to date someone like that? Unless he's rich and you're with him for his money or something?"

I glared at her. "Excuse me?"

"I'm just saying—"

"You're saying I've either got Daddy issues or I'm a gold digger." I shoved the suitcase onto the ground and snatched up my phone. "Axel is sweet and sexy and successful. And if you want a concrete reason for why I'm with him..."

I flipped to the few photos I had of him, then found the one of him standing in nothing but a towel. His hair was still wet from the shower, and he had a smile on his face that melted my heart. But the reason I chose it was because every muscle in his arms and chest was so clearly defined. He was fucking delicious. I turned the phone around and walked it over to her bed.

"That's him?" she asked, taking the phone.

"Yes," I ground out, my temper getting the better of me. "And just so you know, he's got money. He bought me my new car. But that's not why I'm with him. It's because he's *seriously* amazing in bed."

I snatched my phone back from the jealous chick that I used to consider a friend and grabbed my bag. "See you on Monday." Then I walked out the door, muttering to myself.

"What is wrong with everyone?" I groaned, taking my keys out and swinging them around my fingers while I walked to the car. "Mom's shitty at me, Dad thinks Axel's an asshole. Now, Hope is making me feel like crap, too."

I walked out into the parking lot and found my new little car. The happiness I felt in seeing it was gone. If I went to visit either of my parents, they'd grump about the car or Axel, and I really wasn't up for that. So, what were my options this weekend? The apartment? Did I really want to be alone? My mom's? I groaned at the possibility of dealing with her.

Getting in the car after tossing my suitcase in the backseat, I started the engine and pulled out of the lot. My mind in a jumble, I just started driving, mulling over each of the places I should go. Mom would be happy to see me, but would she turn my newly ignited relationship against me? Probably. Did I want to deal with that tonight? Nope.

Dad? He might have plans this weekend. After all, he was a young, single guy, much like Axel had been. He'd have plans up the wazoo. But then again, I would love to see his face when I told him I was going to a work thing with Axel.

A lightness filled my heart as I drove past the apartment Axel had bought for us to spend time together and kept on driving home. I glanced at the fuel gauge, making sure I had enough gas to get all the way to my dad's place, assuming he wanted me to stay with him last minute. Otherwise, I'd have to just ask Axel if I could crash at his condo two nights in a row. That would probably test our relationship since he'd said he couldn't do tonight.

I clicked my cell phone onto Bluetooth speaker mode and called my dad.

He picked up right away. "Hey, sweetheart. This is a surprise."

"Hey, Dad! Yeah... well, I have another surprise. I'm driving down this weekend and was wondering if I could crash at your place tonight? No stress if you have plans to go out, I'll just study and get an early night."

"Ah... yeah. Okay, sure!"

"It's okay if you can't, Dad. I'll figure something out."

"No!" He said, a little more forcefully than I'd expected. "I want to see you, and you can come. I already have dinner plans, so if you're okay for me to go out for a couple of hours..."

"Yeah, of course I am. I have a ton of studying to do."

"Then, if you don't mind me asking, how come the surprise trip if you have a lot of work to do?"

I inhaled sharply, guarding my heart against the possible backlash I was about to receive. "Axel has a work dinner tomorrow night and asked me to join him. And since we didn't really get to say goodbye properly last week, I thought we could spend tonight together and go out for breakfast, maybe?" I held my breath and waited.

When my father spoke, his voice was a little higher and quieter than I expected. "A work dinner? You're going to a-a work dinner with him?"

I grinned and tried not to laugh out loud. "Yeah. Why? Is that bad?"

"Oh, no," Dad reassured me. "It's not that. Just... don't worry about it. I'll see you when you get here. You've got your key, right?"

"I do."

"Well, I'll see you at home. There's food in the fridge and some cash in the fruit bowl if you want to order something in."

Love filled my heart. "Thanks, Dad."

"See you soon."

He hung up and I let the giggle escape. "Well, that was a step in the right direction."

Glancing at the dashboard, I realized I wasn't going to get to Dad's until about six pm, and that was assuming the traffic wasn't terrible. I might have missed seeing him before he went out, but that was okay. There was plenty of time to catch up with him before tomorrow.

10

CHASTITY

As it happened, the traffic was terrible.

I got to Dad's closer to seven pm, than six. Something I made a note of for future travel. Friday traffic was shit! I parked on the street, grabbed my bags, and carried everything up to my dad's apartment. The place was clean and quiet, and exactly what I needed after a stressful week of school.

I heated up some leftover chicken I found in the fridge, made a salad, and sat down in front of the TV to watch some Netflix. When my phone went off, I picked it up with my mouth full. "Hmm... h'lllo."

"Hey, beautiful. Did you make it down okay?" Axel's deep voice vibrated down the phone line and happiness filled my heart.

"Hey!" I said, putting my plate down and swallowing what was still in my mouth. "Yeah, I did. But for future reference, Friday night traffic sucks."

He chuckled. "Yeah, it does. Probably not something you've had to deal with before."

"Especially not as the driver," I agreed. As a passenger, I

rarely noticed traffic patterns, but that was about to change. "Next time, unless we have something happening, I think I'll come down on Saturday morning."

"Sounds good," he said, and his voice was all soft and warm Like honey.

"You seem happy," I said, grinning down the phone line. "Have a good day?"

"Yeah, sort of. But I'm much more excited about tomorrow than what happened today."

"What's happening tomorrow?" I asked.

He laughed loudly. "I get to see you! Feel you. Take you to bed. God, I've missed you."

I leaned back in the couch cushions, enfolding myself in his warmth. "You sure you don't wanna see me tonight?"

He groaned. "Gah, I'd love to, sweetheart. But I'm going to pull an all-nighter to get everything done so we can have most of the day together tomorrow. I'm sorry."

I sighed. "Sounds like a fair compromise."

"It is. Don't worry. My aim it to have a lot less work long-term, but while you're in college and I'm running off my feet, I may as well make hay while the sun shines, yeah?"

I nodded. "Yeah. True."

Though, my education was still another three years. Did that mean it would be like this the whole time? With me begging for one night with him?

"You okay?" he asked, concern coloring his tone.

I brushed away the feelings of disappointment. I'd been the one to push to come up this weekend. He had plans and yet he'd still accommodated me, so I shouldn't complain.

"Yeah. I'm fine," I said. "Just tired."

"Whose house are you staying at tonight?" he asked. "Or I should really ask where I'm picking you up tomorrow?"

"I'm at my dad's." I said, then suddenly realized the stupidity of that choice. "Is that okay? I can meet you at the beach or somewhere else."

"No. It's fine," he hurried to say. "I'll come up and say hello to Pat. May as well get all the awkwardness out of the way."

I giggled nervously. That would be fun. *Not.* "Okay. What time?"

"Noonish?"

"Perfect," I said and got up off the couch. Nervous energy pulsed straight through me, and I couldn't sit still.

"See you then, beautiful."

"Don't work too hard. Bye."

We hung up and I needed to do something constructive with my energy, so I went and took a shower and washed my hair. But my mind wouldn't stop throwing up scenarios about how tomorrow's meeting between my father and his best friend would go. How was my dad going to handle Axel coming here to pick me up for a date? I wasn't sure, but I was going to find out soon enough.

I got out of the shower, into my pajamas, and was just sitting down on the couch with a book when Dad came home.

The door opened and he sang out, "Hey, sweetheart! I'm home."

"Hey, Dad!"

He walked down the hallway and into the living space, a bright smile on his face. "How was your night?"

"Quiet but good. How was yours?"

He put his keys down on the counter and ran a hand through his hair. "Yeah... good."

"Hot date?" I asked as a joke more than anything else.

But then his face went all startled and worried. "Yeah. Sort of."

I frowned. "You look really nervous. What's wrong?"

"Nothing. Just not ready to talk about it, that's all. Too new."

I tilted my head. "I never really understood that expression. Do you mean it's too early to tell if it's going to last?"

"Yeah, pretty much."

I sighed. "I think that's a bit of a cop-out."

"Oh, yeah? You're an expert now?"

I laughed. "Hardly. But I always figured that you could tell within an hour or two with most people whether you're going to be friends or not. And the same with romantic relationships. So? Do you like her?"

He nodded, "Yeah, I do. So, I suppose I'm just nervous."

"I get that." My father hadn't been in a serious relationship since my mother. Well, not serious enough for me to have met a girlfriend, anyway. "Dad... did you ever want to get married? Have more kids?"

"Huh?" He bent his head and ran a hand through his hair again. "What's with the third degree, Chastity?"

"Sorry!" I rushed to reassure him, jumping up from the couch. "I didn't mean to interrogate you. It's just that since being with Axel, it's made me think more about life and relationships—and you and Mom."

"What about us?" he asked, crossing his arms over his chest in a defensive way.

I slapped my hand into my forehead. "Shit. This conversation isn't going well at all. Let's start again. Dad, how was your day?"

"No," he said, dropping his arms down. "It's okay. Continue the conversation. Why are you worried about your mom and me now?"

I shrugged. "Because I've just realized that I'm almost twenty-two, and neither of my parents ever re-married. And I suppose I'm just worried that it's my fault that you missed out on having more kids or getting married. I don't know."

The sadness rose up inside me, then I covered my face with my hands. "I'm sorry."

Dad came over and grabbed my arms, squeezing my biceps. "Hey. Look at me."

I dropped my arms. "What?"

"I never regretted the choice we made to have you, sweetheart. Yes, perhaps I would have gotten married and had other children, maybe... I'll never know. But I love you. Okay?"

I nodded. "Okay, Dad, but don't you ever—"

"No, I don't. I have a great life, and a daughter I'm proud of."

I smiled, though my chin trembled. I didn't like to think of how much my parents had missed out on because of me. Of the choice they'd made in keeping me. I took a deep, trembling breath, and wiped my eyes. "Okay."

"Good girl," he said, then walked away towards the kitchen. "Let's break out the chocolate stash I kept from Christmas."

I laughed at him. My health-nut father had a chocolate stash. *Awesome!* "Sounds great."

We ate and chatted about nothing in particular, and when I went to bed, I was happy.

THE NEXT MORNING, I slept in and staggered to brunch around eleven am.

"What are your plans for today?" my father asked over Eggs Benedict at a local diner.

"Well, Axel's coming over soon to pick me up," I said, staring down into my iced hot chocolate, then flicking my gaze up to his frozen face.

"Oh, yeah. That's right. He's taking you out for dinner."

I nodded, sucking the milk through the straw. "Yep."

"And what time's he coming to get you?" Dad asked.

"About noon."

He glanced at his phone. "Shit. That's soon."

"Yeah."

We kept eating, and the conversation stopped.

"We've still got an hour," I said. "And I can tell him to come later, if you want?"

"No. No... it's fine. Where's he meeting you?"

Oh, crap. "He's coming to the apartment to pick me up. He thought he should come say hello."

My dad froze with his eggs halfway to his mouth. I watched as a golden drop of yolk gathered then slid down onto the plate once more.

"Is that okay?" I asked him.

Dad put his fork down and straightened up. "Okay, honey. You need to be straight with me. How serious are you guys?"

"You really want to talk about it?" I asked. Because I wasn't sure my father wanted to know.

His head jerked in a version of a nod. "Yes. I think I have to know, or this isn't going to work."

I put my hands down into my lap and stared at him. I was pretty sure I was going break my dad if I told him the truth, so maybe I should just ease him into it slowly. "We're serious."

He narrowed his eyes at me. "What sort of serious? You guys have only known each other for a couple of weeks."

"Well..." How did I say this without telling him Axel had offered to make me pregnant and look after me financially for the rest of our lives together? "He's taking me to Vegas for my birthday next weekend, and he bought me a car, and got an apartment around the corner from my school."

Dad put his hand down on the table and began to drum his fingers along the tabletop—a classic nervous tick of his.

"Vegas is cool. You'll have a great time. But none of that is unusual for Axel. He throws his money around to impress girls all the time. Always has."

Ouch! I glanced down to take a moment to remove the dagger he'd thrown at my heart. I looked up again. "Dad, can you trust me when I say that we're serious? That we have no intention of breaking up."

"Has Axel told you as much?"

I nodded, inhaling deeply through my nose. I didn't want to tell my father all the things Axel had told me. Partly because they were private, but also because if we broke up in six months because of a fight or we just weren't working out, I didn't want my father to have anything to hold over me.

He sighed. "Okay... I'm going to take your word for it, but I want to tell you one more time that I don't think he's the relationship type, sweetheart. He's just too old to learn new tricks."

I pushed my half-eaten breakfast away, my appetite gone. "So... what? Why are you telling me that? Again?"

"Because I don't want you to say in six months that I didn't warn you." He threw some cash down onto the check.

I sighed. "Consider me forewarned Dad."

Standing, he hoisted his jeans up from low on his hips. "Then let's go. You need to introduce me to your boyfriend for the first time ever."

A shot of happiness pierced the sadness and I jumped to my feet, grateful that he seemed willing to give us a chance. "Brilliant, Dad. Let's go."

11

AXEL

I was running late, which I hated, but it couldn't be helped this morning. Fucking business meeting ran an hour overtime, so now I was racing to get ready. I had a quick shower and threw on some black jeans and a light pink t-shirt. Something young and fun for the day that was significantly different from corporate attire.

I glanced at the clock. Noon. "Shit." I was supposed to be there already. I shot off a message to Chastity to let her know that I was running late and jumped in the car. My gut was tight with nerves and anger. Patrick hated it when I was late for our stuff, so I was gonna cop shit from him too about being late today.

By the time I pulled up outside Pat's house, my gut was a twisted knot. I got out of the car and pocketed my keys and headed up to the apartment I'd been to a hundred times. But this time it would be for a totally different reason. I was going to my best friend's place to introduce myself as his daughter's boyfriend.

I shook my head as I jogged up the steps, running a ragged hand through my hair. "Fucking hell." This was such a dumb idea. I entered Patrick's level and walked over to his door, my heart pounding from the exercise and the stress. I lifted my hand to knock on the door and caught myself hesitating. I shook my head at myself, again, and knocked hard.

WE'D ALREADY BEEN through the worst. Pat had seen me naked with Chastity already. He'd walked in on us, seconds away from actually fucking. Today would be awkward, but nowhere near as horrifying as that day had been. For all of us.

The door opened and Chastity stood on the other side, beaming smile and golden skin tempting me.

"Hey, beautiful," I greeted, reaching out for her and dragging her into my arms for a kiss. That first press of her lips on mine had me moaning and sighing into her. God, it had been a rough week. But as I held her and kissed her, everything else floated away—the stress, the exhaustion—leaving only the need to love her. I pulled back and smiled down at her. "I missed you."

She wrapped her arms around my neck and smiled up at me. "I missed you too."

I glanced towards the kitchen. "Should we go say goodbye to your dad, then head off?"

"Sure," she said, pulling away. "What are we doing this afternoon?"

I lifted my eyebrows up in a suggestive way. "Well, I thought we could get re-acquainted, then maybe go to beach?"

"Re-acquainted?" Pat repeated as we stepped into the living room. "You're showing your age there, Axel."

I turned and looked at Chastity's dad, a guy I'd known for over ten years. A man whom I'd gotten drunk with, and even scored chicks with. And now I was here, presenting myself as his daughter's partner. Weirdest feeling ever. I tugged Chastity into my side and wrapped my left arm around her. Then I extended my right arm and held out my hand. "Hey, Pat. Happy New Year."

He stared down at my hand and I waited, my heart thudding a little bit too hard. He reached out and shook my hand, his face solemn. "Nice to meet you."

I grinned. "This is a bit fucked up, huh?"

His face cracked into a smile. "Hell, yeah."

I glanced down at Chastity, then eased my grip on her. "Do you mind if your dad and I have a quick chat?"

She pulled out of my arms, worry clear in her eyes. "Yeah, of course. I didn't have a shower this morning before breakfast, so I might take a quick one now." She backed away, then turned and fled.

Pat sighed heavily, deflating like a balloon. "Shit, man... my head is completely fucked up." He ran both hands through his hair. "Trying to talk to you like my friend, but having to treat you like the guy sleeping with my daughter." He turned away and went straight to the fridge. "I think I need a drink."

I followed him into the kitchen and pulled out a stool to sit on. "Go for it. It's past noon."

Patrick took down a bottle of whiskey from above the fridge and turned to me. "You want one?"

I shook my head. "Nah, gotta drive." And having sex with a twenty-one-year-old takes concentration.

Pat splashed some whiskey into a tumbler and downed it.

Whoa.

Then he poured himself another.

"Look, man," I said, guilt beginning to ride me. "I promise you... neither of us wanted this."

Patty leveled me with his gaze. "Then why, Axel? Seriously."

I sighed. "Because she makes me happy, man. Like seriously, nothing else matters when I'm with her happy. And I've never felt that before."

I heard the shower start and looked straight at him. "Look, I'm serious about this relationship. I'm already in talks to sell part of the company so I can back off on the hours I work."

Pat's eyebrows climbed his forehead. "Bullshit. You wouldn't do that."

I shrugged. "Already doing it."

Patrick shook his head. "I never thought I'd see the day you'd settle down."

I huffed out a laugh. "And I'm sure you never thought it would be for your daughter."

His head shot up and he stared straight at me. "No..." he began slowly. "I definitely never thought that."

I licked my dry lips and stood up from the stool. "Can I grab a bottle of water?"

"Yeah. Sure." Pat turned and grabbed one out of the fridge behind him and slid it over the counter. "You have to understand why I'm concerned, Axel. I mean, you don't have relationships. Never have. And Chastity is so young, and she's got so many plans. You've gotta make sure you don't get in the way of any of it."

"I won't," I declared, grabbing the water bottle and taking a swig. "I want to support her in whatever she chooses to do."

"Yeah, but you're rich," Pat said, crossing his arms over his chest.

I groaned. "And I can't even pretend I'm not, can I?"

He chuckled. "Nope. I'd say I know all of your faults and virtues."

Fucking hell. This was worse than any job interview I'd ever been to. "So, you know I work hard, and I haven't committed before. But I love her, Pat, and if she'd let me, I'd just take care of her for the rest of her life."

"But her education—"

"I said, if she'd let me," I said, butting in. "But she won't. She's independent and wants to make it on her own. And I respect that."

"Good!" Pat said, his arms still crossed and defensive.

I sighed. "Look, bud. The only way I'm going to prove to you how serious I am is with time. When I'm still around in three months, three years, thirty years."

"Thirty years?" Patrick grinned, finally lowering his arms. "You really expect to live that long, old man?"

"Hey!" I exclaimed. "You're older than me."

He laughed, and the serious tension in the atmosphere broke. "Okay, Axel. I'm going to give you the benefit of the doubt. But if you break her heart, just know I'll make sure a weight bar falls on you at the gym when you least expect it."

I grinned and nodded. "Deal."

The door to one of the bedrooms opened and Chastity popped out, wearing a flowery long dress with thin straps and a hesitant smile. She looked spectacular. "You two okay out here?"

"Yeah, we're fine, beautiful." I put out a hand and gestured for her to come closer.

She came straight to me, wrapping her arms around my waist and glancing up. "You ready to go then? I packed my bag."

I nodded, smiled at Pat and held out my hand. "Thanks for the talk."

"Likewise." He shook my hand and showed us out.

I sighed. That had been surprisingly awkward, but better than expected.

When the apartment door shut, Chastity turned to me with her eyes wide and her mouth grinning in a huge, wide smile. "What just happened?"

I shrugged, tugging her towards the stairs. "I think we have an understanding." I opened the door to the stairs and together we began to jog down the stairwell.

"Yeah, I'm sure you do," Chastity said with a laugh. "He thinks we won't make it through the first month."

I followed her down to the ground floor then grabbed her hand and led her towards my car, which I'd parked out the front. "You're right. He doesn't." And I didn't blame him. If I was in his shoes, I'd be worried too. We jumped in the car, and I turned to her. "So, gorgeous girl, where to?"

She turned her head and stared straight at me, her gaze alight with desire. "To your apartment, and to bed. Please."

I groaned out a growl and started the car. "I was hoping you'd say that. You don't want lunch first?"

"Nope. Home, please."

I raced through the streets and found myself laughing with happiness as we wove around the other cars.

When we got to my parking garage, I zoomed into my spot, jumped out of the car and went to open the door for her, but she'd already gotten out herself, so I grabbed her as soon as she walked around the hood.

"Can't wait till we get upstairs, huh?" Chastity asked, going up on her toes to put her arms around my neck.

"No way," I told her, grabbing hold of her luscious ass with both hands and hauling her against me.

I couldn't wait a minute longer. I dropped my head and kissed her, loving the moan she immediately made as she curled her fingers into my hair and held me tightly to her. I swept my tongue into her mouth, loving the way she wiggled against me, aroused and hot. I pulled back and grabbed her hand, guiding her towards the elevator doors. "Come on, I want to take you somewhere clean."

We got into the lift and the doors closed, then Chastity turned to me, her cheeks flushed with heat. "There's just something totally hot about the idea of having sex in your car... or on the hood or something. We might get caught!"

I dragged her to my side, glancing up at the security camera in the corner of the elevator. "This place's security is tighter than Fort Knox, so we'd definitely get caught. But if you're set on it, I could order the guys to turn off all the cameras in the parking garage on the day you choose, but I don't want anyone watching us. Or you."

"How come?" she asked as the doors to the penthouse dinged open.

Cupping her gorgeous face, I told her the truth. "Because you're mine. Now let's go inside and I'll show you how much I love you." Swinging her up into my arms, I walked into the apartment, the door shutting loudly behind us.

12

CHASTITY

Being back with Axel in his apartment, with his lips against mine, was a dream come true—quite literally. When we'd broken up after Christmas, I'd been afraid I'd never see him again, let alone feel his body against mine. But now look at us... I was back!

He carried me into the main bedroom and I sighed as lust coursed through my body. This was exactly where I wanted to be, and who I wanted to be with.

Axel set me on my feet and cupped my face to kiss me tenderly.

I groaned with frustration, not wanting soft and tender. I wanted him. *Now.* I grabbed his shirt and tugged it up, placing my hands against his hot skin beneath.

He moaned against my lips and although he sounded surprised, he didn't stop my hands.

I grabbed for his belt, making short work of the buckle, then the button and zipper of his jeans.

He pulled back and grinned at me as he tugged his shirt over his head.

Yes! That's what I'm talking about. I pushed my spaghetti straps down over my shoulders and shimmied until my dress pooled around my ankles. I hadn't worn a bra because I didn't need to, so I stood before him in only my sandals and a pair of black lace panties.

"God, you're beautiful," he said, cupping my breasts with his big, warm hands.

I jumped at him, wrapping my arms around his neck and pressing my naked breasts against his chest. I groaned, loving the feeling of him.

He grabbed my ass and lifted me up against him, then walked the few feet to the bed and threw me backwards.

I landed with a bounce and moved up the mattress to lie down.

"Panties. Off. Now."

I scrabbled to push the black lace down my thighs and lay back on the bed, completely naked.

He pushed his jeans down his legs and stepped out of his socks and shoes. He stood looking down on me for a minute, his hungry gaze roaming over every part of my body as I wiggled and ached for him.

I didn't close my eyes. Quite the opposite, I stared back at him. He looked even more cut than last time I'd seen him naked. His stomach was washboard flat, with abs that stood out against his skin in defined rectangular slabs. And that v-thing that ran down either side of his waist, over his hips and beyond. *Damn, that is just so sexy.* I bit my lip, contemplating running my tongue along that indentation and making him moan for me. I held my arms out and arched my back, thrusting my breasts into the air. "Come down to me."He grinned and knelt on the bed, prowling over me like some big, dangerous cat.

When he was right over me, I looked up at him, loving the

way he covered me completely. I also admired his strength as he held himself above me, his arms bulging with muscles.

"Please," I begged, reaching up and dragging him down.

When he pressed against me, the heat of his skin made me gasp. "God, I love that."

He grinned then he kissed me, making heat unfurl inside my belly.

Then he moved down, pressing his lips to my neck, my throat, before working his way down to my nipples, where he stopped and loved on me for too long.

"Please," I begged, tugging at him, needing him inside me, reassuring me that we were back together, and that everything was okay.

"Hang on a minute." He rolled away, going to the side drawer and grabbing a rubber. He sat up, ripped it open, and expertly rolled it on over his thickness.

I pressed my lips together in frustration, not liking the look of that, or the feel of it. But he was doing the right thing by both of us, so I needed to focus on the *why*, and it was because I'd asked him to.

When he crawled back over to me, I opened my thighs and welcomed him into my body with a sigh.

"I love you," he whispered into my ear as he nudged my legs further apart and slowly sank into me.

I gasped at the feeling as he thrust all the way in, filling me up and making my belly tighten with pleasure. "I love you too," I whispered, clinging to his back and wrapping my legs around his hips, wanting him deeper.

He moved faster and harder, stoking the flames of my arousal higher until the only sounds in the room were moans and groans, and the slapping of flesh against flesh.

Heat trickled down the backs of my thighs, my core heating and tightening until I couldn't control it any longer. I let go, my orgasm cresting over the mountain of pleasure and for a single moment, everything was frozen in time. Then the spell broke, and I was sliding down the other side and into sensation. I cried out, shuddering in his arms as my pussy contracted around him.

He fucked me harder, making the pleasure last longer and longer, until ripples spread out everywhere, drugging my mind and sating my body. Then he thrust deeply and froze, groaning over me.

I grabbed his ass cheeks and held him tightly into me, then he collapsed on top of me, panting hard. I stroked his hair and dug my fingers into his back, never wanting him to leave me. But he began to stir, reached between us, then pulled out of me. It was a strange and shocking feeling. I felt empty now. "Aw, I wanted you to stay."

He chuckled as he rolled over and stood up. "Gotta get rid of this. Give me a minute." Pulling the condom off his cock, he disappeared into the bathroom for a minute then returned.

I shivered, cold now. So, I slid beneath the covers then threw back the blanket for him. "Coming back?"

"Definitely." He jumped into bed, lay on his back, and pulled me into his arms.

I put my head on his chest, into the crook of his shoulder, and rested my hand over his heart. He was still breathing hard, and his heart thundered under my palm.

"Bit of a workout, huh?" I asked.

Axel laughed, picking up my hand to kiss my fingers, then placed it back on his pec. "You, woman, are the hottest thing around."

I giggled against him, loving the compliment. "I doubt that but thank you for saying it."

"You okay?" he asked.

I nodded, then tilted my head back to look up at him. "Yeah. I just... I don't like the condom thing. It feels weird, then you leave so quickly afterwards. I think I'll get to the doctor this week and organize some birth control."

"Sounds great," he said with a sigh, wrapping his arms around me. "I prefer having nothing between us, too."

I closed my eyes and let the exhaustion of the session settle over me. Every part of me felt so good. So happy, warm, and relaxed.

"You wanna sleep for a bit?" he asked.

"Yeah." I sighed. "Are you up for a nap too?"

He kissed the top of my head. "Hardly. You've got me buzzing with energy. So how about I tuck you in and come back when you're awake? I don't want to wreck your bliss with me jumping around." He sat up and removed his arms from around me.

"Hey—I don't want you to leave." I reached out my hand for him and struggled to open my eyes.

He pulled the blankets up over me and kissed my cheek. "Sweetheart, I'll just be in the living room. You sleep and come out when you're ready. But I want you well rested, because I'll be making love to you all night tonight."

"Oh, okay." That sounded like a plan, I suppose. I closed my eyes and cuddled into the pillow. A little rest wouldn't be a bad thing. Every part of me felt heavy and totally satisfied. I needed energy for tonight.

He woke me a few hours later by climbing back into bed with me. He lifted the blanket, which wafted cooler air over my hot skin, and he reached for me.

I crawled closer and cuddled into his bare flesh. "Hmmm... have you come back to sleep too?"

He chuckled and kissed the top of my head. "Well, we have to be at dinner in an hour and a half, and it'll take about thirty minutes to get there, so I figured you might want to wake up soon."

My eyes popped open. "Shit! I totally forgot about the dinner!"

He laughed. "Yeah, I figured. And you know, I could always cancel."

"No," I said, sitting up in bed and yawning loudly. "I brought my new dress that Tony picked for me. And, oh God, I need to wash my hair!"

I threw the covers back and ran for the bathroom. I could hear him laughing from the bedroom as I turned the shower knobs and got the water going.

"I thought you were a girl who could get ready in ten minutes?"

I stuck my head out the doorway and playfully glared at him. "I can! For anything except a fancy dinner. I've got to try a bit harder for tonight, and at least wash the sex off me."

He just grinned at me and crossed his arms behind his head, lying on the bed and not moving. *Freaking men!* All they had to do was throw on a suit. No makeup or hair straightening for them!

I glanced at the clock. *Five-thirty. Shit!* I'd slept half the afternoon away.

I jumped into the shower, washed my hair and the stickiness from my body, then the race was on. Dry hair—then straighten—makeup, clothes, shoes.

I was rushing around, and it built up a sweat that messed with my foundation, but I was almost ready before him. I was slipping my feet into my high heels just as he was pulling on his suit coat.

"You look amazing," he said, his appreciative gaze sweeping over my body.

I grinned and flipped my hair over my shoulder. "So, what's the deal with tonight? Will it be all business? Social? Will the wives like me?"

He laughed and held out his arm. "It's mostly business, but the women will be there to keep the conversation flowing."

We walked towards the elevator doors. "And the women?"

He snorted. "They're going to hate how young and beautiful you are."

I straightened my shoulders, "I've dealt with women like that my whole life." Namely my mother. "Let's do it."

And we headed down the elevator and into the car, off to my first dinner as Axel's official girlfriend.

13

AXEL

Walking into the restaurant with Chastity on my arm was an exhilarating moment. She was fucking gorgeous, so everyone looked at us. With her long blonde hair and curves for days, I was hard pressed not to stare, myself. She clung to me like she would never leave my side, which also felt fantastic. But when I got to the table and my two colleagues' wives looked at her, I knew we were in for a rough night.

The claws came out as their eyebrows lowered, their gazes narrowing over Chastity like she was a gnat they needed to squash.

Shit. I knew it. Why did I bring her to this thing? I was considering turning her around when Max stood up and walked around the table to shake my hand.

"Axel. How are you doing?"

"I'm great, Max, Thanks for asking. This is Chastity." I indicated to the gorgeous young woman on my arm, and tried not to wince as the wicked witch of the east rounded the table and glared at my date.

"Axel." Margaret nodded at me, her tone so frosty I would have shivered, except I knew her too well to worry.

I smiled broadly at Max's wife and squeezed Chastity's arm to reassure her. "Margaret, this is Chastity. Sweetheart, this is Max and his wife. Max and I have been in business for—"

"Longer than you've been alive," Margaret snapped, then chuckled softly as though she were joking.

She wasn't.

Chastity didn't miss a beat. "Oh, I doubt that. I know he looks young, but Axel isn't that old." She extended her hand to Max, who was looking at my girlfriend like he wanted to give her a tongue bath. "It's nice to meet you."

Max shook her hand, then I pulled her away to meet the other pair.

"Brian. Nice to see you," I greeted my friend, whose wife was also about twenty years younger than him. The difference was Brian was about seventy now, which made Sharon the oldest of the three women.

"Chastity, this is Brian and his wife, Sharon."

Brian coughed and spluttered, then held out his hand to her.

"Very nice to meet you both," Chastity said, shaking Brian's wrinkled hand, then nodding at the stony face of his wife.

I held in the groan. I was proud of my girl so far, but we had a long way to go to get through the night. "Shall we sit down and order?" I asked, pointing to the large, round table dressed in a thick white tablecloth and expensive silver place settings.

"Of course," Brian said, leading his wife back to the table.

I glanced over at Sharon while I sat down next to Chastity. She looked different than the last time I'd seen her. Thinner, more aged. Hopefully Brian and she were well. I often worried about Brian's health but was in general too afraid to ask personal questions of the old dragon. He was an incredible financial administrator and I figured he'd tell me when he wanted to slow down.

A waiter came around and placed our napkins in our laps, and Chastity picked up the menu, which was all in French.

She laughed suddenly. "It's not translated. How do we know what we're ordering?"

I grinned and took the menu from her. "We order the five-course banquet and eat whatever they put in front of us."

"Five courses?" Chastity repeated, holding her stomach as though she was going to have trouble putting that away. "That sounds like a lot of food."

I was just about to tell her the courses were tiny, and she'd probably be hungry later, but Margaret got in first.

"You don't have to eat anything that goes against your diet. I know how you young girls are about your weight."

She's in bitch mode tonight. "Margaret—"

Chastity placed her hand on my arm, signaling for me to stop talking.

I did, at her request, and sat back to watch.

"Is there something about me that offends you?" Chastity asked, narrowing her eyes at the other woman.

"No. Why would you think that?" Margaret asked, crossing her arms over her ample chest.

"Because you're snipping at me like I'm some evil witch that's come to steal your husband or something. And no offense or anything, but I'm happy with Axel."

Margaret dropped her arms and sat up straighter, her eyes flashing fire. "Of course, you're happy with yourself. You've tied down one of the wealthiest men in the city, and you're what? Twenty years old?"

Chastity tilted her head as though examining her rival. "You don't need to be jealous. I'm sure you were hot when you were my age too."

"You bet your sweet ass I was!"

Chastity laughed, turning the tables on the other woman. "Well, thanks for the compliment, but my mom always tells me I need to lose at least ten pounds. I just can't. I'd rather enjoy my food." And to prove the point, she snatched up a warm, white roll and broke it apart, taking a bite and smiling sweetly.

The air went out of Margaret, and she reached for her glass of red wine. "Tell your mother she doesn't know what she's talking about."

Chastity smiled softly. "Thanks."

I stared at the two other men at the table, who looked equally as perplexed as I felt. Had Chastity just won that round? I hoped so, though it was hard to tell with women.

The waiter came around and we ordered our usual, as well as more drinks and bread. I had the feeling we might be calling an Uber tonight, because I was getting the distinct feeling I was going to drink too much.

"So, Chastity, are you working? Or are you still in school?" Margaret asked.

Chastity didn't flinch. Deadpan, she said, "Oh, I don't do anything, really. Axel wants me to just stay home and have babies. Oh, and play with his money, of course."

I groaned and tipped my wine down my throat. None of the others spoke and I was the one to glare at her. "Don't put it like that." I supposed, technically, I'd asked her to do something similar. But offering to look after her surely shouldn't sound like that.

"She's not serious?" Margaret asked me, staring at me like I was the devil.

Chastity picked up her glass of white wine and dipped her head to cover her smile, but she couldn't stop her laugh and pressed a hand to her mouth when it burst out between her fingers.

The whole table seemed to relax at hearing proof that she was joking, which made me even more defensive.

"To be fair, I offered Chastity a life of luxury. She never has to work or worry about money, or anything. Ever again." And any woman of my past would have jumped at the offer, but not my girl. She wanted to earn her own way in this world.

Sharon turned to Chastity with a puzzled expression on her face. "And what did you say to that?"

Chastity placed her glass of wine down and grinned at the other woman. "I said thank you, but I've got college, then chiropractic school to finish before I can even contemplate babies. And the money..." She shrugged. "That's a whatever type of thing."

"Whatever?" Brian repeated, his eye twitching like she'd hit a nerve. Hit it square on.

Chastity shrugged. "Yeah. I mean, I can make my own money, right?"

"Not like Axel's money, you can't," Brian reminded her, and I cringed. He didn't need to say that. It wasn't necessary.

She shrugged again. "True."

I wanted to laugh at the beautiful way she just accepted their words, but I didn't like the way everyone was looking at her. Margaret's eyes had shifted to catty once more, and whatever truce had been won initially seemed to be forgotten.

The waiter came and served the first course, then the conversation shifted to work—business and economics. The women became silent, as they usually did when the men took over.

Chastity didn't speak much until the very end of the night, when dessert came, and she ate the whole thing in about three moans. "God, that's amazing."

Brian finally turned around to her and asked her about school. She waxed poetic about getting into her chosen field, and I was proud of her, but when we were ready to leave, I could feel the sadness behind her smile.

"You okay?" I whispered as we stood up from the table.

She nodded but didn't respond, which I knew wasn't a good sign.

I paid for the table's dinner as I always did, and the six of us walked out of the restaurant together.

"I wish you the best of luck in the future," Brian said politely, though there was a stiffness to his posture that made him seem uncomfortable.

Chastity smiled back at him. "You, too."

"Yes. Good luck, dear," Margaret said, shrugging into her jacket and sticking her nose in the air. "I assume we won't be seeing you again?"

Chastity's gaze narrowed and my stomach tightened. "Why's that?"

"Well, a night like this can hardly be interesting for a woman like you."

"A woman like me?"

Margaret nodded. "Yes. You seem sweet, but you have so much going on in your life that I'm sure a business dinner with us was boring for you."

Chastity glared at Margaret. "That's not the reason you don't think you'll see me again. It's because you assume Axel will dump me and he won't bring me to any of these stupidly expensive dinners again. Am I right?"

Margaret didn't answer but she stuck her nose in the air even higher, if that were possible.

Chastity took a step closer to the women. "Listen up, okay? I don't give a shit what you think of me. I don't care if Axel's my father's age. And I bet you don't care if I'm a good person or not, which FYI—I am. I'm sure Axel has never brought a girlfriend to one of these dinners before, so I would have thought you'd give me a little more credit than that. But, no, all you care about is making me feel like crap because you're insecure in your marriages and yourselves."

She took a step back and flicked her gorgeous hair over her shoulder. "You won't see me again, Margaret, don't worry. And it's not because Axel and I will break up, but because I won't encourage Axel to work with your husbands, or see you, ever again. So, go home and chew on that, you stuck-up bitch."

She grabbed my hand and stared up at me. "Can we go home to bed now? Please?"

I wished so badly that I had a camera right at that moment. Then I would be able to keep forever that picture of Margaret's face, just as she looked at that moment. But I didn't, so I etched it into my memory, nodded at my two business partners and walked Chastity out of the restaurant.

I'd take my beautiful girl home and make this up to her. I'd make love to her all night, and through the day tomorrow. If she wanted to come with me to these events, I'd have to work out a way that she was treated better. Otherwise, I'd be going to a lot of these nights alone, just like I always had. And that was fine by me.

14

CHASTITY

Saturday night had been truly enlightening to me. It became seriously obvious to me that I was going to be judged badly by Axel's work colleagues. They wouldn't look at me and see a girl who loved Axel. Or someone who worked hard and had potential for her own life. No, they'd see blonde hair and youth, no brain, and gold-digging tendencies.

So, after Axel whisked me home and we had sex on the floor because I couldn't even make it to the bed before I jumped him, I told him I'd skip the business dinners for a while. He'd happily agreed, and we'd had a great Sunday together.

We slept in, went out for breakfast, then had a long, hot, shower session before I headed back to school mid-afternoon. The traffic was a lot better, but God, I was tired. Driving was exhausting, and I was looking forward to getting an early night.

The other thing that had become crystal clear to me over the weekend was the fact that I'd hated the way Axel used condoms every time we had sex. Having to pull them out of a drawer, or something similar, interrupted the flow and didn't feel right at all. Not physically or emotionally for me.

So, after I'd had a great night's sleep, I woke up Monday morning and made an appointment to see the on-site campus doctor. She was great. She explained to me about my birth control options and gave me a script for the pill. I had to wait for my period to come, then I could start taking them and we'd be safe to do whatever we wanted, whenever we wanted. I couldn't wait.

The pill taking process sounded simple enough, and my period was due on Wednesday, so although that meant that my weekend in Vegas with Axel might not be as sex-filled as I'd first hoped, at least I'd have better control over my body in future months.

Classes were hectic but enjoyable, and I fell back into a normal routine with studies. Only a few more months and I'd be done, and although I couldn't wait for the rest of my life to begin, there was a certain bittersweetness to finishing.

Wednesday came and went, and... nothing. *Thursday. Friday.* And my period still hadn't arrived. I was beginning to worry. I couldn't be pregnant. Not after... what had it been? Once? Twice without protection this month. Last month we'd gotten away with it.

By the time the black town car that Axel had organized for me arrived to take me to the airport, I was a bundle of nerves. *Maybe I should have bought a test from the pharmacy along the way so that I knew for sure?* "Calm down. It'll be fine. It'll be fine." I sat with my hands clenched tightly in my lap almost the whole way.

Axel had sent me a message during the day to say we were flying to Vegas for my birthday, just as he'd promised me. I'd hardly gotten any work done after that. I'd washed my hair and packed and spent extra time getting ready, so I looked as pretty as possible for our trip.

But as the car pulled off the highway before we hit the city I called out to my driver, Reggie. "Aren't we going to the airport?"

"Yes, ma'am."

"But this isn't the right way, is it? Unless I'm confused." Which I wasn't. I knew my way around the city.

Reggie smiled and glanced up into the rearview mirror. "We're driving to a private airstrip. I believe you're taking a plane from there."

I shook my head and giggled to myself. Of course, Axel had a private airplane. He was rich. Why did I keep forgetting that? *Probably because you'd still like him if he had no money at all.*

I stared out the window as we pulled onto the runway. Happiness bubbled inside me when I saw Axel ahead of us, standing next to the plane like he was casually waiting for a bus or something. Seriously, the man looked just as confident in an elegant French restaurant as he did buck naked walking around his apartment. How did he do it?

"Just a moment, ma'am," Reggie said to me as he opened his car door, so I waited, only to have him hurry around and open my door.

I smiled at him as he offered me his hand and I took it, standing up in the cool breeze that ruffled my dress around my legs. "You didn't need to do that."

"I certainly did," he said, and nodded his head. "I'll get your bag."

Axel walked towards me, looking far too sexy in a pair of grey trousers and a crisp, white, casual shirt. The top buttons were undone, and his sleeves were rolled up. As always, he took my breath away.

"You're spoiling me already," I said as he stepped up. I put my hands on his chest then tilted my head up for his kiss.

His warm hands slid around my waist and pulled me close. "I'm only getting started."

He certainly was. The plane ride was all decadence, with imported chocolates, foot spas, and champagne. When we flew over Vegas, my mouth gaped open. The lights that illuminated hotels and casinos were just as incredible as they looked in the movies. We landed not far out, and a car was waiting for us to take us straight to a hotel.

Axel held my hand as we drove down the Vegas strip. Tears blurred my vision at seeing the people, the fashions, the sights. It was all so beautiful. Fantastical, really.

"Hey. Are you okay?" Axel asked, squeezing my hand.

I nodded and wiped my eyes with my free hand. "Yes. It's like a movie. I can't believe I'm here."

He chuckled.

I turned to look at him. "What's so funny?"

"You are," he said with a grin. "I love spoiling you with things like this. Your joy is infectious. Happy Birthday."

The car was still moving but very slowly, so I unbuckled my belt and crawled across the huge backseat and into his arms. "Thank you." I wrapped my arms around his neck and kissed him, his lips moving on mine with a hunger so strong it made me gasp.

The car slowed down, and the driver said, "We're here, sir. I'll get your luggage and meet you inside."

The driver excused himself and I was left inside the car with Axel for a moment. I pressed my forehead against his and sighed with happiness. "I'm so lucky to have you."

He pulled back and stared down at me. "Funny... that's exactly how I feel about you." He glanced outside, where a waterfall sparkled in the dim evening light. "Shall we go inside? I want to show you this hotel. It's fantastic. Everything that's great about Vegas is here, all in one hotel."

"Oh, yeah? What's the best part?"

"I'll let you decide," he said, and pushed open the car door.

I squashed the urge to sigh. I didn't want to get out. I wanted to stay inside this little heaven and kiss him until we both couldn't breathe.

"Come on," he urged, then waggled his eyebrows at me. "I'll show you the bedroom first if you like?"

"Okay." I grinned and hopped out of the car, staring up at the glamorous posters hanging above the entrance. "Can we go to a show while we're here?"

"Absolutely. We can drink and play blackjack. See shows and lounge around the penthouse or pool. It's your weekend. Whatever you want to do."

I grabbed hold of his hand and let him drag me inside. I didn't care that all the girls that walked past us stared at Axel like they wanted to devour him. And I tried not to care about the fact the women were all sexy, and made me feel grossly inadequate, because Axel tugged me tightly into his side and barely glanced at them.

He checked us in and whisked me up to the penthouse, where the space was ginormous and so plush it almost seemed surreal.

I picked up a sparkly silver couch cushion and hugged it to my chest. "I can't believe we're really here."

"Why?" he asked, grabbing my arm and twirling me around to face him. "Did you think I'd cancel last minute or something?"

I laughed and ran my hands up his thick, solid arms. "Oh, no. I just... this feels like a dream." I went up on my tip toes and kissed him then pulled back. "Though, how did you get away? I know you usually have meetings and things on the weekends."

He shrugged. "I hired a new manager this week. I'm teaching him the ropes and gave him some of my responsibilities for this weekend. I'll see how he did when I get back on Monday."

"Ohh, I'm impressed. I wasn't sure you'd be able to delegate much of your role. I know you built your company from the ground up."

He shrugged. "I have more important things in my life now. It's worth making some sacrifices."

I grinned at him. "Like what?"

"Like having time for you. I think it's about time I had a life. A *real* life. And that means cutting back on the eighty-hour, and sometimes more, work weeks."

I ran my hands down his shirt front, popping the buttons as I went. "That's a great idea. But since we're in Vegas and I am absolutely starving, how about we get dressed and go out for dinner?"

I tugged the shirt tails out of his waist band and ran my hands over his hot skin. "Can I touch you?"

"Only if I can touch you too."

That could get messy. "Shower, then?" Screw my hair. I could dry it again later.

"Definitely."

He turned me around and whacked me on the ass. "The shower's that way. Go."

I squealed as I raced into the main bedroom and began to strip out of my dress. "This place is amazing!"

The master bedroom was bigger than my mom's house. With a king-size or bigger bed at one end, and a wall of glass windows showing off an incredible view at the other end of the room.

When I got naked, I had a twinge of conscience. "Axel... ah..." Should I tell him I was late? That there was a small yet distinct possibility that I could be pregnant?

"What, beautiful?" He groaned into my ear as he pressed in behind me, one hand going around my waist and up my ribcage to cup my breast as he bit softly into my neck.

My eyes slid closed as the fingers of his other hand found my clit, pressing into my flesh and arousing me even more. "Let's get to the shower before we make a mess out here." I grabbed his hand and pulled him to the shower, letting the heat and steam surround us before I wrapped my hand around his shaft and kissed him.

He groaned against my mouth and gasped as I tugged on him. "Oh, you want it like that, do you?" he asked.

I nodded. "Yeah, I do. Something different."

He dropped his head and kissed me as he slid his fingers between my legs, torturing me with sweet touches and intimate caresses. We moaned and gasped our way to mutual orgasms, his cock wrapped tightly by my hand, my pussy squeezing his fingers. And as he held me against his chest, hot water cascading over my back, I knew life after this was never going to be the same again.

15

AXEL

After our hot shower session where I came so hard that I saw stars, I grabbed Chastity and dragged her downstairs to show her the sights that can only be seen in Vegas. The buffet-style never-ending food, the flashing, colored lights and the bells and whistles coming from the casino.

My beautiful girl clung to my arm and squealed happily with every new experience, and I loved every minute of my time by her side. There was no pretense with her. No false sophistication.

Every other woman I'd ever been with had been deliberately disgruntled most of the time. I assumed it was their aim to make me try harder, so they were happier. Although, it could have been because they were constantly hungry, too.

Instead, Chastity ate everything in front of her, and she was lit up from the inside with a happiness I'd rarely seen in my life. She had a huge smile firmly in place on her face at every moment.

A hand caught my eye, and I glanced up to see Ralph, one of the pit bosses, gesturing at me with a grin. He was inviting me up to the next floor to play at my normal table.

But I wasn't sure it would be Chastity's scene, so I held up my hand to him and nodded my head, indicating I'd be up soon. *Maybe.*

Ralph went back to his patrons, and I turned to the woman standing beside me with a water bottle held tightly in her hand.

"Do you want to play cards?" I asked, indicating towards the high roller tables. "We've just been invited up."

She frowned as she stared at the elevated tables set in the darkness. "Not really. They look way too serious."

I chuckled to myself more than to her. But when she quirked an eyebrow at me in question, I wondered if she knew what they were. "Do you know what those tables are?"

Chastity shook her head, "No idea. But I *can* tell you that those ladies over there look like they're having a much better time." She pointed to a group of women in their sixties, with matching pink satin jackets and squeals of delight as they played the slot machines.

I laughed, enjoying her sense of humor. "Yes. But those ladies are playing with dimes." I turned and pointed towards the tables where I would play when I came to Vegas, especially if I'd brought a woman who wanted to be impressed by how much money I made. And could lose without blinking an eye. I shuddered at the thought of my past life. What superficial crap I used to think was normal.

"And those?" Chastity asked, pointing to the tables behind me. "What are they playing with?"

I shrugged. "Millions."

"*Millions?*" she repeated, her mouth dropping open. Then she shrugged. "Now I'm super glad I didn't agree to go up there with you."

"Why not?"

"I can't afford to lose twenty dollars, let alone more. And my dad always says that you shouldn't gamble with more than you're able to lose."

I inhaled sharply, pain kicking me in the gut. "You can't afford to lose twenty dollars?"

Chastity and I didn't talk much about money, and I knew Pat did well enough, but was she really so strapped for cash that she would worry about twenty dollars? Maybe I should take out some credit cards in her name or set up a bank account for her. I didn't want her worrying about a paltry thing like money since I had more than enough for both of us.

She sighed and rolled her eyes dramatically at me. "It's just a turn of phrase. Jeeze, relax."

A tightness squeezed my chest. "I can afford for you to lose some money here, Chastity. Think of it as part of your birthday present and we can go gamble wherever you want. Slot machines, cards, roulette." I'd never made such a suggestion to anyone before, but it was liberating.

"Oh, the one with the ball?" Her face lit up.

"Yes."

"Oh, yes, please!" She tucked her hand back into the crook of my arm and we went straight to the roulette table.

Well, there went the rest of the night. She wouldn't bet more than a couple of dollars at a time and pouted when she lost. Which was only superseded by how beautifully she celebrated when she won.

I hardly did anything all night, just sat back and watched her. She barely drank anything, though she was offered every cocktail under the sun by the waitresses who came past. When the clock ticked over to midnight, I moved in behind her and wrapped my arms around her waist. "Happy Birthday."

She turned to me and grinned. "Is it Saturday already?"

"Yes. Do you want to stay here? Or should we move the party back to the suite?"

She pressed her ass back into my groin. "Definitely bed." She put her hand up to stifle a yawn. "I'm getting tired, anyway."

"I hope not too tired," I whispered into her ear and heard her giggle. "Grab your winnings and let's go."

Chastity scooped up the few chips she still had and tucked them into her purse. "That was such an awesome night. Thank you so much."

"For forty dollars' worth of chips?" I asked, pulling her away from the flashing lights and sparkly sounds of the casino floor. "I'm not sure that qualifies as awesome."

"No, not the money." She shook her head. "For all of it. The whole weekend. The plane flight and the hotel room made me feel spoiled enough. But this," she gestured around us, "is amazing. You wanting me to have a good time. Spoiling me. Even if we went home right now, it would still be the best birthday I ever had."

I swiped our room key to take us up to the penthouse, and as the doors closed on the elevator, I pressed her up against the mirrored wall and kissed her.

Chastity didn't hold back. She kissed me hard, running her hands over my shirt and pressing into my ass, hauling me harder against her body.

When the doors dinged open, I pulled back and stared down at her flushed face. Her red lips. "God you're beautiful."

She grabbed my hand and hauled me into the room. "Show me. Please."

My girl didn't want gentleness, which was obvious. So, I reached over my head and pulled my shirt off. I needed to be naked, and so did she.

She gazed at my chest for a moment, then launched herself at me, kissing me hard.

I picked her up and her legs went around my waist, clinging to me tightly. I held her ass and kissed her, spearing my tongue into her mouth again and again, just as I wanted to do to her body. I walked us into the bedroom and tossed her down on the bed where she scrabbled back, her chest heaving with excitement.

She gasped as she kicked off her heels. "More. Please."

I groaned as I unbuckled my belt, then unzipped and pushed my trousers off my legs, my skin hot and tingling already. I kicked away my socks and shoes, then once I was naked, I reached for her where she sat on the bed.

She squealed as I grabbed her thighs and pulled her to the edge of the mattress.

I pushed her black dress up her creamy, perfect thighs, and grabbed the sides of her panties, dragging them down her bare legs and tossing them over my shoulder. *That's better.* I wasn't going to get that dress off as easily, so I peeled the straps down her arms and exposed her breasts. "Fuck, Chastity. You're sexy."

She got her arms out of the straps and left her dress bunched around her middle. Then she reached up for me.

I crawled onto the bed with her, andI dipped my head to suckle her tight, hard nipples, savoring the flavor of her skin. But it wasn't long before she was groaning and tugging on my hair.

"Please. Now. I can't wait."

Damn. Forgot protection. "I need to get—" I went to move off her to find a condom, but she tugged me back.

"No. It's fine. The timing... please. It's fine. I need to feel you inside of me."

Yes... I slid between her thighs, and she wrapped her legs around my waist. Then she pressed her wet pussy against me, and I couldn't help my reaction. I powered into her in one long, strong thrust.

She gasped when I buried myself to the hilt, and I stilled, worried I'd hurt her. "You okay?" I whispered into her ear, pressing her down into the mattress with my weight. She was so tight, so wet, so hot, it was difficult not to come even now.

She nodded, her nails digging into my back. "Don't stop. Please, don't stop."

Fucking hell. I didn't. I pulled back and thrust up into her again. She screamed and arched her back, gripping me so tightly it was obvious what she wanted. *More.* I pushed up on my hands so I could stare down at her lust-drugged eyes, and I rode her hard, like I'd never ridden anyone before.

She moaned and gasped and cried out with every roll of my hips.

I fucked her forcefully and fast until she was coming on me, squeezing my cock and forcing my orgasm to the forefront of my tingling body. But I fought the wave back, wanting this night to be as good for her as possible. She lifted her hips with me, wanting more, so I thrust into her again and again, until she came so hard tears leaked down the sides of her face.

The look of wonder in her eyes was my undoing.

I thrust home one final time and came inside her. Hot, wet, torrents of pleasure pulsed through me, and her pussy squeezed me hard, milking my cock until there was nothing left to do but collapse on top of her and thank God, or whoever had sent me this precious woman.

She was the best gift of my life.

16

CHASTITY

After the best sex of my life, I slept like a log then woke early the next morning, nervous butterflies flapping their wings inside my belly. I had to find out if I was pregnant. It was time. For my sanity. *What will Axel say?* I managed to roll away from Axel without waking him, which was always difficult because he clung to me in sleep.

After I got away, I grabbed some casual clothes and raced to the elevator. It took me down to the lobby, where I met one of the many staff members, a blonde woman in her twenties.

"Could you help me, please?" I asked her.

"Of course, ma'am. What do you need?"

I dropped my voice to a whisper. "I need a pregnancy test. Do you have any drugstores around here?"

The woman nodded and her fake smile disappeared. "Yes, of course. There's one on the next level down. How about I walk you there?"

"Oh, not if that's too much trouble."

The girl smiled at me, and this time there was a lot more

genuine warmth in her face. "Not at all. Happy to help. Come this way."

I followed her down, chose the pink box with three tests because I assumed I'd need more than one, and bought it. The girl was still waiting for me as I came out of the shop with my brown paper bag.

"Are you okay?" she asked, biting her lip.

I nodded. "Yeah, I am." Terrified, but kind of excited too.

"So, this will be a good thing?" she asked, nodding towards the bag.

I sighed. "Not exactly planned, or on my schedule at the moment, but..."

"The father?"

I smiled. "He will be ecstatic."

The girl, whose name was Daisy if her name tag could be believed, laughed. "That's unusual for the woman to be worried and the man to be the happy one."

"Yeah, well, we're not your average couple. Thank you again for your help."

Daisy nodded at me. "No problem. Good luck!"

She headed off and I went to find an elevator that would take me back to Axel, and the next great decision of my life.

I assumed Axel would be happy, but what about my parents?

What on earth were they going to say when they found out I may have, possibly, made the same mistake they had so many years ago?

Don't get ahead of yourself. I chastised myself. *Gotta do the test first.*

17

CHASTITY

After walking around in confused circles for too long, I finally asked someone how to get back to my room. Everywhere looked the same, and I seriously had no idea how to find our elevator again. But once again, I was found and escorted to my destination by one of the staff.

"Thanks so much," I said to the second blonde girl to help me today and rode the elevator up to the penthouse. My stomach was in knots as I gripped the paper bag holding my tests. The doors dinged open, and I walked into the apartment.

"Hey, birthday girl! Is that you?" Axel called out, strolling into the living area where I now stood, wearing nothing but his birthday suit.

On my birthday. So that was kinda funny.

I found myself giggling at my own joke, and he grinned as he lifted his chin. "Everything okay?"

"Yeah. Of course. But what would you have done if I'd been housekeeping?"

He shrugged. "Tell them I was waiting for you to come back

to bed. Then I would have gotten them to send out a search party."

I walked over to him and ran a hand over his warm skin, loving the feel of his huge muscles beneath my palms.

"Are you coming back to bed?" he asked, reaching out to grab my waist and haul me against his naked body. "Or did you go searching for food because you worked up such an appetite last night?"

My stomach wavered with nerves. "Ah... I've gotta go to the toilet actually."

I hadn't gone this morning because I'd been so anxious to get out the door as soon as possible. Now, I was busting.

Axel stepped back and stopped squeezing me. "Oh. Sure. Then what? Bed first? Or breakfast buffet or both?"

With my brown paper parcel held tight in my hot little hand, I knew it was time to reveal all.

With my heart in my throat, I ripped the paper off, opened the box and took one of the long sticks out. "Should I assume this is pretty self-explanatory? Or do you think I should read the instructions?"

Axel's jaw dropped.

Anxiety pulsed through me. My chest squeezed tightly, and my bladder ached to go to the bathroom. Not a great combination.

"Is that what I think it is?" he asked.

I pressed my lips together. "Hmmm. Well, depends on what you think it is."

"Are you pregnant?" he asked, taking a step towards me, the joy in his face hard to miss. His eyes were sparkling, and his mouth turned up in a grin.

"I don't know yet," I said, taking a few steps towards the bathroom. "I have to go pee first."

"Then go pee!" he practically yelled, with a happy grin on his face.

I ran, laughing with hysteria the whole way to the bedroom ensuite. I shut the door to the bathroom and raced over to the toilet. Ripping off the foil wrapping, I stared at the strange piece of white plastic. "Definitely should have read the instructions."

It was too late now though. My bladder had decided it was time to go, and urgency overtook my movements. I pulled the cap off the end, sat down and peed on the stick like they said to do in the movies. It was strange and not exactly clean, but in the end, I had a wet pregnancy test, and my bladder was empty.

"Thank God for that." I put the plastic cap tip back on and set it down on the vanity to wash my hands at the sink.

"Anything yet?" Axel called out from the other side of the door.

I shook my head. He was too much. "You can come in, you know."

The door swung open, and Axel stood in the doorway, wearing his jeans this time.

I raised an eyebrow at him. "Thought you should get at least partially dressed, did you?"

"With news like this I was debating making a cocktail."

My heart fell and I glanced down, unable to meet his eyes. "That bad, huh?"

"Hey, hey... I was joking." He crossed the huge bathroom to cup my face. "I love you. I want to spend forever with you. A baby would be—"

"Unwanted? Too early? Totally unplanned?" I threw at him, just the first few words my brain came up with.

He stared straight into my eyes. "It would be amazing."

He bent his head to kiss me, and I lifted my chin, needing the contact. The reassurance.

I reached for him, grabbing onto his waistband, wishing I

could strip him of the jeans and climb on top of him right there. But before I could do anything of the sort, he pulled back again and tilted his head as he looked at me. "You know, if you really don't want this, we don't have to do it. It's your body, Chastity, and your choice."

A lump rose in my throat as my eyes burned with tears. "No, I couldn't."

Get rid of my baby? Axel's baby? I just couldn't. Not for the sake of going to chiropractic school. Not for my parents. No.

He pulled right back this time and grabbed my hands tightly. "Moment of truth then?"

I nodded. "Yep. I'll grab it. I hope I can decipher the results. Maybe I should have brought the box in with me."

"I'll go get it," Axel said, and turned to leave the bathroom.

I picked up the piece of plastic, a strangely excited feeling hitting my stomach as a hysterical laugh bubbled up. "I don't think I need the box." It wasn't one line, or two, a cross or a plus sign. Nothing vague or hard to decipher with this one.

Axel turned back. "How come?"

I handed it to him. "Because it spells it out for you."

Axel lifted the pregnancy test and stared at it. I knew what he could see. The same thing I had. One word.

PREGNANT.

His gaze flicked up to me, and he was un-naturally still as he asked. "You're pregnant?"

My hand went unconsciously to my flat stomach and pressed hard. "Ah..."

"You're pregnant!"

Hot tears rose into my eyes then fell down my cheeks, a wave of unexpected emotion crashing into me. I sobbed as he hugged me tightly, and I let more tears fall.

"It's okay. It's going to be okay," he said, cuddling me tightly, and laughing softly. "I hope this doesn't mean you're as devastated by this news as you sound?"

I pulled back and shook my head. "No." I gulped and turned away to grab the tissues in the box by the sink. "I'm just... I don't know. It's a lot." Blowing my nose, I then took some deep breaths to calm myself. I'd been feeling overly emotional this week. Now I knew why. I splashed some water on my face and patted my cheeks dry with a nearby towel. "Are you happy about the result?"

I had to ask him, even though I knew the answer. Suddenly there was intense need to surround myself in positivity. It felt like I was going to need him to get through this choice in one piece.

"Me?" he repeated. "I'm *very* happy. To have a baby with your heart and soul, your eyes... that's the dream, Chastity. But if this is the wrong timing for you. If you'd rather wait until you've finished your degree, it's your choice. I won't be the one to push you to keep it if you don't want to."

"Oh, I do want to!" I rushed to reassure him. He was extra sweet to offer me the out, but it wasn't an option for me. Not now.

"You do?" The hope and love in his eyes were almost heartbreaking. I'd never thought anyone would love me this much.

I nodded. "Of course, I want this baby. It's your baby. But... all my plans. My parents." I shook my head sadly as the tears gathered again, making my heart ache.

"Come on. Let's go sit down." He took my hand and walked me out of the bathroom and back towards the bed.

We sat down facing each other, and there was a comfortable silence that stretched around us like a soft cloud.

"You know," I began, wanting to change the topic for a moment. "I love being with you. Even just like this, holding hands in the quiet. It's really nice. I've never been this comfortable or happy with anyone before."

And there was so much more to it. I wanted only good things

for him. Happiness, health. And I wanted to be there for him. And not for the parties, and the fun, and the glamor. I wanted to be there through all the dark moments. If this was love, then let me have it forever.

"I feel the same way as you," he said, suddenly serious. "Honestly, Chastity, whatever you want, we'll do it."

I swallowed the tightness in my throat. "This isn't just about me. What do you want Axel?"

"What do I want?" he repeated, like he was surprised I'd asked.

I nodded.

He sighed. "I want to work a week on, a week off, so I can enjoy you and not miss out on so much. I want to travel. I want to buy you the perfect family home where we can let our kids run. Not some high-rise apartment without a tree in sight."

"Really?" I asked, a lump in my throat making me swallow awkwardly.

"Really."

There was a long silence.

"So," he began, "are we heading down to breakfast? Your birthday is only just beginning. I have lots of ways to spoil you today."

I nodded, feeling the tightness in my chest ease for a moment, and my hand finding its way naturally back to the flatness of my belly. "Okay, let's do my birthday. Then we can talk about this more later."

He stood up and held out his hand. "Definitely. I have a feeling it's all we'll want to talk about for a long time to come."

I got to my feet, a sick feeling in my stomach. "I know. It's hard to think about anything else." Like how the hell I was going to tell my mom. My dad... my professors. *Shit.* They were all going to be so disappointed in me.

He smiled and I melted a little. "That's because it's exciting. And amazing. And going to change our lives in the best way."

I took a wavering breath, trying to will some courage into my heart. "You're really excited by this?" I quirked an eyebrow at him. "When are your lawyers gonna come running at me with a pre-nup?"

He grinned at me as he reached for a blue shirt and pulled it on. "That's for a marriage."

"Oh." Now I was embarrassed. "I didn't mean it like that. I just meant aren't people going to worry that I did this to get your money or something?" I didn't know what I was saying. But I did know I was going to get a lot of flak from everyone I knew. My family, my friends. There would be no way to go on to chiropractic school now.

"I don't give a flying fuck what anyone else thinks," he said, and there was a conviction in his tone I envied. "All I care about is what you think, and what we choose together. But as we said, let's leave that conversation for later today. We've got breakfast to devour. Then a show later tonight."

"Give me one sec." I quickly changed into a light summer dress and sighed. This was the start of a new chapter for me and for Axel, and I honestly had no idea how it was going to end.

18

AXEL

Taking my newly pregnant girlfriend to breakfast was an entirely different experience. I watched her like a hawk, a million questions rolling around in my mind. Was she supposed to eat fried bacon? And wasn't there a rule about cheeses that she was to avoid now? I had no idea and felt stupid opening my mouth to ask her. She probably wouldn't know either. Surely, she wasn't far enough along to worry about those things yet? We needed to get her into a specialist as soon as possible. I was sure one of my friends would know a good obstetrician.

We sat down in one of the many restaurants the hotel boasted. I watched her take a sip of water and a memory of last night's casino fun tugged at me.

"Hey, sweetheart. Did you know you were pregnant last night? Is that why you barely drank anything?"

Chastity put her glass down and shrugged. "Yes, kind of. I had my suspicions, but I didn't actually *know* yet."

"But that's why you weren't drinking?" I asked to clarify. I loved the fact that she was protecting our baby already, even though to her last night, it had only been an idea. A possibility.

She nodded. "Yeah, I know it's bad for the baby, and the last thing I wanted to do was take a risk."

"Even though you didn't know if you were going to keep it?"

She nodded and a small smile quivered on her lips. "Let's be honest here. I was always going to keep it. The idea of losing that connection to you when I love you so much is, well... I can't even fathom it."

"Then tell me what's still worrying you." Because it was obvious by her slightly somber mood that something was playing on her mind this morning. Her smiles weren't the usual wattage.

A waiter walked up to our table, and we turned to give him our attention, ordering food and hot drinks off the menu, then turning back to one another.

"Go on," I urged her. "Tell me what's bothering you."

She glanced down at the table and ran her fingers over the silver spoon in front of her. "I think it's just the whole pregnant at twenty-one thing. Well, twenty-two, anyway. But I haven't even finished college yet. Just like my mom," she said, her voice cracking as she said "mom," then she picked up her glass to take another sip of water.

Her eyes were looking suspiciously shiny, and I wondered how much had been said to her over the years about her parents' "mistake" in getting pregnant so young.

I had to tread carefully here, because this was it. The crux of the issue. I could see that Chastity had other hurdles to overcome, and her education was one of them. But this admission that she was going to be seen the same way her mother had been—young, and stupid—was the real problem.

I thanked the waiter as he delivered my coffee and Chastity's hot chocolate and picked my mug up. "I think our situation is quite different, sweetheart."

Chastity rolled her eyes, then took a sip of the hot chocolate, a milk moustache imprinting on her top lip for a moment before she licked it clean.

My gut tightened with desire. The things that woman had done with her tongue had been utterly amazing. And I couldn't wait to get her back into bed so I could love her more.

"Yeah, we are different. But my parents had been together for almost three years before they had me. We've been together a month!"

I chuckled. "So? What's the timeline got to do with it? Your parents obviously weren't meant to be together, or they still would be."

A nagging voice at the back of my head said that I should say something to Chastity about Pat hinting he was getting back together with his ex. After twenty years apart, it seemed ridiculous that they would want to be together now, but what did I know?

Chastity picked up her knife and fork and began cutting up the buttermilk pancakes and syrup that she'd ordered. "Timing means a lot, actually. Everyone will know that we didn't plan this, they'll call you stupid and me slutty, and it'll be a whole ridiculous thing."

She forked a piece of pancake and ate the bite, her moans of delight making me smile.

"Good?"

"Oh, yeah."

I sipped my coffee and watched her eat, loving the way she dug into the food. "Sweetheart, look. Like with everything in my life, I'm not going to give anyone the time of day who disagrees with how I run my life. I stopped giving a shit about other people's opinions a long time ago."

She raised an eyebrow, and in between bites, asked, "so, you're not going to care that your friends and probably your family are going to think that I'm trying to trap you? That I got pregnant on purpose?"

I grinned at her. "God, no. I'm going to tell them all that I was the one who got YOU pregnant on purpose and I had to hurry, before you ruined my plans to trap you and went on the pill."

Her hand froze mid-air, her mouth hanging open. "Seriously?"

"Yep. I'd much rather them think I wanted to trap you, than the other way around." Which wasn't too far from the truth in regard to the fact that I wanted Chastity however I could get her. For the first time in my life, I felt lucky to have a woman. This woman. And I wasn't letting her go.

She took a bit of pancake, chewing thoughtfully, then said, "Is that true?"

"That I *planned* to impregnate you?" I laughed at the thought. "Of course not. I've heard from various friends that have gone through years of IVF that it can actually be difficult to get pregnant. But we did have unprotected sex multiple times, and I admit that I didn't mind the idea of having a baby with you right from the start. And now that we are? I'm elated."

She picked up her glass of water and sighed. "You know, I feel really sorry for those couples who have to spend tens of thousands of dollars to have one baby."

"Try hundreds of thousands," I corrected her, finally picking up my cutlery to eat.

Her eyes bugged open. "Are you serious?"

"Very," I said, cutting into my eggs. "I know at least three couple that have spent six figures to get one child."

Chastity's hand slipped down to her belly. "So, we've already saved a hundred thousand dollars by getting pregnant naturally?"

I laughed. "That's one way to look at it, yes. And as far as the timing goes, sweetheart, I don't want to wait five years to be with you and hold our child just because society thinks you should date for years before committing to someone. I knew the moment I saw you that you were the woman I wanted in my bed, then when you spoke with that quick wit and smiled at me..." I shivered. "I was done for."

She laughed and pushed her plate away, sighing again. "I really hope my parents aren't disappointed in me."

I stifled the groan that rose. "Sweetheart, there is absolutely nothing for them to be disappointed in. You've found a man who loves you, can easily financially support you and our child, and who desperately wants this baby. What else is there?"

She wrapped her hands around her mug of hot chocolate once more and pressed her lips together. She wasn't convinced.

I sat up straighter in the high-backed chair. "Look, how long before you have to tell people? I'm sure we can wait a few months. Just until you are feeling secure, and safe enough to share." Surely by then she'd want to tell everyone.

Chastity met my gaze, and I could finally see a sparkle of happiness there. "You're right. I have months to decide how to tell people, and I'm sure I can still finish my college degree while pregnant. I'm not due until... hang on a second." She grabbed her cell phone and began tapping away.

I waited, having no idea what she was actually doing.

"Ah, October fourth. Approximately. Oh, yeah, that's a lot of time."

October fourth sounded like a perfect day to me.

She was looking happier now, and I wanted to take advantage of that and make sure she stayed that way. "Perfect. Now, I have a lot planned for you today. I've booked you in for a facial and a massage with the hotel's spa, and we have tickets for tonight's show."

"Really?" she asked. "You've gone all out for my birthday!"

I grinned at her. "That's only the beginning. I want to take you shopping for a real present, of course, and get you a ring to go with that necklace of yours." I waggled my eyebrows at her, then dropped my gaze to the single diamond nestled above her cleavage.

"You want to buy me a ring?"

I nodded. "Yes, I do." I'd propose marriage right here and now if I thought she'd say yes, but she was reacting like a deer in the headlights during every new conversation, and I didn't want to scare her off. She already thought I was crazy because I wanted this baby so much. "But just as a birthday present. Maybe we can call it a promise ring?"

"A promise ring?" she repeated, her fingers going to clutch the floating diamond at her throat.

I nodded. "Yes, it was all the rage in my parents' era. A promise ring was the first sign of commitment. Then the engagement ring, wedding ring, and eternity ring, of course."

I watched her throat work as she swallowed hard. "And you... are thinking about all of those steps?"

"Of course, I am," I said, reaching across the table and squeezing her hand with mine. "You're the woman I want to spend the rest of my life with, and you're carrying what I hope is the first of our children."

Her eyes were all shadows and doubts, so instead of forging on with the awkward proposal, I just smiled. "But one step at a time, yeah? A tradition must be kept. So first, a promise ring. My only question is, would you like me to choose something that goes with your necklace and present it to you at dinner? Or would you prefer to go shopping with me and choose something yourself?"

Her eyes lit up this time as she smiled at me. "That's such a thoughtful question."

I shrugged. "What can I say? You bring out the best in me." Which was such a stark contrast to any of my exes, who'd definitely brought out the worst.

"Why are you asking though?" she questioned, grinning cheekily at me. "Afraid you'll choose wrong?"

I barked out a laugh. "No. But this is something I want you to wear every day, so you have to love it. It only makes sense to ask you to choose it. Although... if you'd rather a surprise."

"No! I'd actually love to come shopping with you."

"Done," I said, glancing at the time on my cell phone. "We probably have enough time to hit the slot machines before your pamper package and I'll arrange a viewing at a jeweler for the afternoon."

I'd need to go to Tiffany's. They didn't advertise their prices, which I knew would affect her choices. I didn't want her choosing a piece based on the price, and knowing her, she'd pick one of the cheapest rings they had.

I wanted her to love it. Price wasn't a factor, or a limiter.

"Axel, thank you."

"You're welcome, birthday girl," I said with a grin, then pushed my plate away. "Where to first? The slot machines or roulette again?"

"Actually," she said, "I'd love a quick shower before the day spa. Wanna join me?"

Abso-fucking-lutely.

She stood up with a sultry smile and I grabbed her hand. We had an hour.

Oh, all the things I could do to her perfect body in an hour.

19

CHASTITY

I'd never been so pampered in all my life. I had a luxurious facial with an older woman named Trixie, then a massage with another woman called Celine.

The day spa was quiet and serene, with music playing gently in every room and water flowing over rocks in the foyer. It was nothing like being in Vegas in the movies, and yet it was only here that I felt totally relaxed about being waited on hand and foot. At home I would never have been able to justify such luxury.

"You're all done, so take your time getting up and I'll see you out front," Celine whispered in the quiet of the room, squeezing my shoulders one final time.

"Thank you so much," I told her, barely able to open my eyes.

That massage had been incredible, and I was so sleepy and relaxed I didn't want to move.

But Axel would be waiting for me, and he'd said he was taking me shopping. What an idea, *me*, choosing a diamond ring for my birthday present. It was just an insane!

It felt like I was living some sort of fairy tale at the moment, because this wasn't my life. It couldn't be. I forced myself off the table and got dressed again, a lethargy that was bone-deep making my arms drag as I pulled on my clothes.

My hand strayed once again to my stomach, and I pressed my palm firmly against my flesh. My tiny, tiny baby was inside me growing, safe and sound. But what if something bad happened? What if I lost it? How would I feel then? Relief? No. My stomach plummeted and I had to swallow hard to stop the bile that rose. Miscarriage was common, wasn't it?

I needed to look it up. I didn't want to lose this baby. Even if the timing meant that school was going to need to be postponed and all my friends and family would think I was nuts. I wanted this—with Axel. We would be a family. And for me, there was nothing more important.

I grabbed my cell phone and headed for the door of the massage room. I stepped out into the foyer and grinned as Axel walked towards me. His hair was damp, and he'd changed clothes.

"Hey, gorgeous. How was your massage?" he asked, reaching for me.

"Amazing." I loved the way he stepped up and slid his arm around me in that possessive habit he had. I reached for his face, which was clean shaven and still slightly damp. "Did you have a shower again?"

"Yeah. I went to the gym for an hour and needed another."

I smirked at him. "Only *you* would feel the need to train on vacation."

He leaned forward and whispered in my ear, "Gotta keep fit for you."

I slapped his chest playfully. "Hardly."

He pulled back and grinned. "Shopping time? Or are you ready for lunch?"

I was a little hungry, but I could definitely wait. "Shopping, please."

He slid his hand around my waist and pressed his palm to the base of my spine. "This way."

He led me out of the day spa and into the brightness of the casino levels once more. We wove through the assortment of people, and I found myself grinning like a loon.

There was a happiness bubbling up inside of me that made me feel a little ashamed. I loved my cheap clothes and costume jewelry, but there was something ridiculously exciting about being spoiled by the man I loved. And the intent behind where he was taking me, shopping to buy me a ring... was just the best.

A *promise ring*, he'd called it. A universal sign of commitment. Something I could wear and rely on, which said to anyone who dared question us that he loved me, and wanted us to be together for a very long time.

"In here, sweetheart," he said as we reached one of the most well-known and expensive jewelers of all time.

"Oh, no," I said, slamming on the brakes and stopping us in the middle of the walkway. "They'll be way too expensive."

He slid his fingers from my waist once more and gripped my hand instead. "No, it's not. And how about we make a deal that until you're my wife, you let me worry about how much money I spend, and how?"

"Your w-wife?" I repeated, suddenly feeling more anxious than excited.

My mother would *kill* me if I married someone after knowing him for two months. Was that why we were in Vegas? *Oh God!*

He laughed loudly, a sparkle twinkling in his eye. "Don't worry, I won't ask until I'm sure the answer will be yes. So how about you just let me worry about my money, and I'll let you worry about yours."

"Okay." It probably wasn't fair to tell him how he could spend his money, but surely there were cheaper options. "But—"

"If you won't come and pick which one you want, I'll just choose myself," he said with a sigh and what looked like a reluctant shrug.

I narrowed my gaze at him. "You're baiting me."

He put a hand to his chest. "Me? Why, I'd never."

I glared at him this time. *Smart ass.* "Fine. Let's go." It was my turn this time to drag him into the shop, and I was blinded by the brilliance of the lighting. "Whoa." I put my hand up to shield my eyes, part of me wishing I was back in the tranquil setting of the day spa.

"Can I help you, sir?" a woman in front of us asked, and Axel slid up to the counter and spoke softly to her.

I raced forward to try and catch the last of their conversation, but she was already moving around the shop and opening all the cabinetry.

"What did you say to her?" I asked as I watched the woman look in and under every glass box.

"That we were looking for a birthday present."

I waited but he didn't say anything else, although I was pretty sure he'd said a hell of a lot more to the woman, but what hope did I have of finding out? And why was I fighting this anyway? Axel had more money than he knew what to do with. He'd already bought me a diamond necklace, a car, and an apartment. Surely, a simple little ring could be added to the list of his gifts.

"I've taken out a selection of our newest, most modern rings. Were you interested in only white diamonds, or perhaps you wanted something with color?"

"Color?" I repeated, stepping closer to the display she was arranging before me. *Wow.*

"Yes, we have canary diamonds, pink diamonds, and of

course, this three-stone ring that has two brilliant cut sapphires on each side." She picked up a ring and held it out to me.

It was white gold or platinum and had three large stones across the top. One diamond, with a blue sapphire on each side. "Um..." I reached out for it and held it in my fingertips.

"Do you want to try it on?" Axel asked.

I wasn't sure. I didn't like blue or classic rings like this as much as the intricately designed, ornate pieces. "I would prefer something less classic." I set the ring down and peered at the display of massive stones in front of me. "These are beautiful, really. But they all look like engagement rings, and I was hoping for something simpler."

Axel and the saleswoman exchanged a look, then she flurried off once more.

I turned to him. "What was that about?"

"Nothing."

"It wasn't nothing. What did you tell her?"

He sighed heavily, obviously not wanting to tell me the truth. "I told her that you deserved the best and that money was no object." He looked crestfallen, and guilt hit me hard in the chest. There was nothing worse than someone throwing your gift in your face.

I slid towards him, wrapping my arms around his waist and staring up at him with all the adoration I was feeling for him hopefully clear in my eyes. "I love you for this. How about I make you a deal this time? I won't think about the money if you don't either. I'll choose something I love, we go with that one, no matter what. If it has a hundred diamonds on it or none at all."

"Deal. But you've gotta try on at least ten different rings. That's my only rule."

"Done!"

The saleswoman hurried back with a grin on her face. "I have scoured the store for our most unusual rings, and I hope you don't mind, sir, but I also found a few pieces in our antique collection."

I almost groaned. Of course, she did. And they were probably the most expensive rings in the store.

I threw my hands up, noticing straight away that absolutely nothing had a price tag attached to it. Like my mom always said, *"If you have to ask how much it costs, you can't afford it."* I sighed. "I'm very adverse to him spending this sort of money," I explained to the saleswoman, "but I have been overruled, so let's do this."

I tried on more than ten rings, probably closer to thirty. Rings with flat bands, and intricate designs. Rings with massive stones, and ones with pink, yellow and white diamonds. In the end, I chose a ring I wouldn't have thought would be the one. It was rose gold with two vines of leaves on either side. It had white diamonds and pink sapphires and sat so beautifully on my finger that I didn't want to take it off.

"I, um, think this is the one," I said, through a throat clogged with emotion. I kept extending my arm out to stare at it and felt a strange type of intense emotion sweeping through me every time I looked at it.

"Do you want to put it in the box?" the woman asked, offering me a classic Tiffany-blue square shaped ring box.

I pulled my hand back and curled my fingers into a tight ball to stop her from taking it away from me. "No, I'll wear it."

Axel chuckled and picked up my hand, pressing a kiss to my fingers. "It's perfect. Happy Birthday."

Tears filled my eyes as I went up on my toes to kiss his lips. "Thank you."

Axel went with the woman to pay for my gift, and I wandered to the other end of the store because I didn't want to know how much it cost.

I wanted to focus on the intent behind the gift and the love I had for my family that was growing by the day. We had a whole day ahead of us, and most of tomorrow too. And I for one was going to enjoy every minute of this, and maybe consider it our first babymoon!

20

AXEL

The rest of the weekend went by too quickly. We ate rich food that had me aching to return to the gym. We gambled some money away and went to a show.

Chastity was perfect company the entire time. During the day she was fun, and cute, and stuck to my side like glue. During the night, she made love to me with a single-minded focus that made me want to tuck her into my body and never let her go. But according to her, she *had* to return to school, and that stuck in my craw something fierce.

"Are you sure you need to go back?" I asked her once more as we descended the stairs off the plane at the private air strip I owned.

I took her hand and glanced over at the two cars in front of us. I had to get back to the city, and my car waited for me.

She was determined to return to college, and her driver waited for her in the black town car. She bit her lip and ran her hands up and down my arms, not answering.

I gave it another shot. "You know, you don't actually have to finish the last six months, sweetheart. I can buy you a business or whatever you'd like to manage. You don't need a degree to work with me. I'll teach you everything I know." And that was something I'd never offered anyone before.

She frowned at me this time. "And what? Tell our baby that I'm officially a college drop-out, and that I never finished because I got pregnant? I don't think so."

I inhaled sharply at her tone. I wasn't going to win that argument. It was obvious she wasn't really talking about us, but from her own personal experience growing up.

"I understand, but I'll miss you," I said, touching my forehead to hers and drinking in the last of her warmth.

"It's only five months," she reassured me. "Not even, really. Then I'll be finished, and we can focus on us and our family."

I smiled as she stepped away and went to pick up her bag. "You'll have a nice bump by then, I hope," I said, letting my gaze linger around her still tiny waist.

Her hand came up and pressed against her belly button. "You're right! Thank goodness those graduation gowns are roomy, yeah?"

I nodded, a lump coming to my throat. She would look so beautiful heavily pregnant with her large belly and swollen breasts. I couldn't wait until I had her next to me in bed with all her womanly curves on display once more.

"I love you," I told her, unable to stop myself.

She grinned and launched herself at me once more. She kissed me hard, and I gave back twice as much, pressing her lips apart and tasting her tongue, wanting to get as close to her as I possibly could. But too soon she was pulling away. "I love you too," she whispered. "And hopefully I'll see you next weekend. Maybe down at the apartment near school if you can drag yourself away from work?"

"I'd love to," I said, though I had a sinking suspicion I'd have a lot of work to do this week to make up for the weekend I'd just taken off.

"Drive safely," I called out, then looked away. Damn I was turning into a soft cock. *What the hell?*

She got in the car and the driver drove away, and I stomped over to my sports car and jumped in. She'd turned me into some mushy, half-wit. And it needed to stop. *Now.* Sure, I'd miss her this week, but she had studying to do, and I had a company to run. Surely, that would keep me busy enough not to worry about her too much.

I turned on the ignition and got on the phone to make some calls. I'd hired a new manager this week, and I was hoping he'd done at least half the work I'd assigned him. If he had, I'd at least be able to sleep tonight. If he hadn't, well, I wouldn't.

As my shit luck would have it, he'd done *a lot less* than half the work I'd assigned. In fact, he'd royally fucked up two deals, and had knocked off at noon on Saturday and taken the rest of the weekend off because to quote the pompous dickhead, "I deserve days off to rest." Not when I trusted him with my company, he didn't. So, I fired him on the spot, then went home and got to work.

I worked all night, making multiple international calls and video chats trying to right the wrongs my ex-manager had accomplished in my absence. I got about twenty minutes sleep around six am, then kept going through the rest of the day.

It was disheartening to say the least. Not the fact that things had gone so wrong. That happened all the time in business. I'd learned to roll with the punches and take the hits when necessary. Afterall, the long game was the only game worth playing.

No, the true problem lay in the fact that I now knew for certain that I couldn't trust anyone to do my job. I simply couldn't step away from my business the way I wanted to. It was too risky —unless I took the time to groom someone to be me—but that would take months. Years, even. If it were even at all possible. Without a stake in the business, there was no driving force that would compel anyone else to work the way that I did.

But it wasn't just me anymore. I couldn't just run my life from dawn to dusk and back again, around my business. I had Chastity and the baby, now. How was I going to be a company CEO, a partner, and a father? And all of them well?

I didn't think Chastity would appreciate the little amount of time I would have for her once she was through college and lived with me full time, which I assumed was the plan though we hadn't talked about it yet. But that was a puzzle for another day, because I had no answers tonight.

Monday night came, and although my eyes felt like they were being held up by matchsticks, I reached for my cell phone and called my woman.

"Hey! I was just thinking about you."

I instantly smiled and for a moment, my exhaustion seemed further away. "All good things, I hope."

"Oh, yeah. Definitely," she said, a smile evident in her voice. "How was your day?"

"Ah... good, overall."

"You sound tired," she said just as I was closing my eyes and running a hand through my hair.

I laughed. "Yeah, I am."

"You should sleep. I'm sure you stayed up all night working. Can you get an early night?"

The question hung in the air. *Could I?* "I've got a lot of work to do."

"But you could probably do it tomorrow." she urged, interpreting my tone and words correctly.

I shook my head. "How do you read me so well?"

She laughed. "I don't know. Maybe because I care about you."

"Just care?" I asked, teasing her for her word choice. I hoped she did a hell of a lot more than just care about me. I was besotted with her and was hoping the feelings were mutual. I stood up and stretched my back, then walked over to the kitchen to make a quick protein shake. Once I got some food into me, I could probably go to bed. She was right.

She sighed softly. "I don't mean I don't love you, because I do. But I mean, I actually care if you're well and healthy. If you're happy or working yourself into the ground. To me, caring about your welfare is more important."

I smiled as I shook the protein shaker and headed to my bedroom to strip off. "I don't think anyone—and I'm counting my parents in this as well—has actually cared about me before."

"Seriously?" she asked. "Well, then I'm not looking forward to meeting them. What horrible people."

I grinned. "Yeah, well, they'll want to meet their grandchild for a minute, then they'll be off traveling the world again, so don't worry. You won't have to put up with them for long."

"Hmm... I'm not sure if I should be happy about that, or sad."

I shrugged. "It is what it is." I'd come to terms with how shit my parents were years ago. I kicked off my shoes and sat on the bed.

"Are you getting ready to go to sleep?" she asked.

"Yeah, I'm just getting ready now." I tugged off my shirt then lay down on the bed. "How are you feeling today, sweetheart?"

"Oh, I'm good. No nausea or anything yet, but I made another appointment with the doctor to tell her why I can't go on the pill anymore."

I grinned. "Yep. That ship has sailed." And for me, happily so. "Hey," I began, closing my eyes because they were too heavy to hold open any longer. "After graduation, will you move in here with me? Or we can buy something else if you want. A house with a back yard maybe?" We'd need to move further out of the city and away from my building, but what was an extra ten-minute drive?

"Are you asking me to move in with you?" she questioned, her voice breathy and light.

"Of course, I am," I told her, though my enthusiasm was probably lacking in my voice due to exhaustion. "I'd have you move in this week if you could. But I know you need to graduate first."

"I'd love to move in with you in May," she said. "And I adore your apartment, but I'd much prefer a house if we could get one."

I snorted. *If we could?* "Anything you want, sweetheart. It's yours. Just look at what's for sale online, and as long as it's not too far away from my work, it's yours."

She inhaled sharply. "Easy as that?"

"Yep," I said, feeling a wave of tiredness washing over me. "I want you and the baby to be happy." And if she wanted suburbia, with its large backyards and flowerpots, then we'd get that. Though, I didn't want her running herself into the ground either, so maybe it was finally time to hire a housekeeper.

I yawned loudly. "I'm sorry, sweetheart, but the sandman has come. I'm not going to be able to stay awake much longer." In fact, I could feel my brain spiraling into the darkness even as I said the words.

She chuckled softly. "I love you. Talk to you tomorrow?"

"Definitely." I didn't remember hanging up the phone, but I must have at some point, because the next time I woke up it was almost ten hours later, and Chastity's sweet voice was still ringing in my mind.

21

CHASTITY

I stared at the doctor in disbelief. "Did you just offer me a chemical abortion?"

The woman before me blinked at my tone. "It is my obligation as your doctor to give you all the options available to you. Going ahead with the pregnancy is not the only one."

I stood up and grabbed my backpack. "I came here for help, not for... whatever this is. I'll see a private doctor from now on." Who the hell did she think she was? Just because she was working in a college setting didn't give her any right to try to alter my choice. I turned towards the door and reached for the handle. What sort of backwards thinking was this?

"Those are expensive if you don't have insurance, and I really think..."

I whirled around and glared at her. "The baby's father is a billionaire. Yes, you heard right. A *billionaire*! So, don't tell me I don't have access to the right care. You know nothing about my situation."

The doctor's eyes widened, and she blinked quickly. "Oh, I'm sorry. Your file indicated that you were on a financial scholarship."

I slammed both hands onto my hips and glared at the woman. "I'm on a scholarship because I worked my *ass off* in high school and got the grades to qualify for one!" The fact that my parents didn't have the thousands of dollars to pay full tuition was none of her business.

I growled in frustration and stormed out of the office, grabbing my bag tightly to me and leaving the medical building.

I couldn't believe she'd said such a thing! I hurried to my dorm and ran down the hall. Hot tears filled my eyes, and I didn't stop running until I reached my room. I threw myself on my bed and cried until I felt sick. What a horrible woman!

Was this seriously how I was going to be treated by everyone who knew my news? It wasn't like I was extremely young and single. I was twenty-two and had the love and support of a man who loved me. What else did I freaking need?

I sat up and dashed the tears from my face, anger surging through me now. How dare that doctor—or anyone—assume I couldn't look after my baby. My parents had done it without the financial support of anyone, and they'd done a good job. I tapped on my phone and called Axel, swallowing hard to try to disguise the sound of the tears I knew he'd still be able to hear in my voice.

"Hey, sweetheart, I'm just two seconds away from stepping into a meeting. Can I call you back?"

I inhaled sharply, tears still blurring my vision. "Yes. But I need you to answer one question first."

"What's happened? What's wrong?"

"You want this baby, right?" I managed to ask, wiping away the tears on my cheeks.

"Yes! Absolutely."

"And you'll help me get a good doctor and buy a crib and diapers?"

"Hang on, I'm just telling the guys I need a minute." He put the phone on mute because I heard nothing for a minute, then came straight back to me. "Sweetheart, what happened?"

I shook my head. "Nothing."

"This isn't nothing. Did you tell your mom?"

"Oh, God no." I shuddered. That was going to be a conversation and a half. "I just spoke to the doctor here and she gave me my options."

There was a heavy beat of silence. "Uh… I'm not sure I'm following."

I wanted to roll my eyes, but while I was frustrated, I was impressed that he'd admitted he didn't know what I was talking about.

"The doctor told me how to have a chemical abortion and was of the opinion that was the best course of action."

"They fucking… *what*?"

His anger paralleled mine, and I instantly felt bad for the doctor. She was gonna get it.

"So, I just wanted to make sure you've got my back with the doctors and the hospital and all that stuff."

"Sweetheart, I'll—" He coughed and took a breath. "I'm sorry. Give me a second."

I waited, because it was reassuring to hear that he was as mad as me.

"Okay. I think I can speak now."

I grinned on the other end of the line, my heart light and happy. This was why it was a good idea to be with Axel. Not for his money, but for his heart. His sense of humor, and the sex. Who could forget how good the sex was?

"Chastity, your health is everything to me. So, number one, I will call my insurance guy today and purchase you the top level of coverage. Number two, I will transfer one of my properties into your name, today. You can choose whichever one you want. That will be financial surety for you, no matter what happens. And, number three, I will have that doctor gone from campus by the end of the day."

"Oh." My stomach dropped. "You don't have to—"

"I do. And it will be done. Give me a couple of hours, and I'll get my assistant to send you a list of properties you can choose from."

"Axel, my love. Calm down. I don't need property. I just needed your support, and you've given that. Thank you. I feel better." And that was the truth. I could breathe now.

"Oh, I haven't even begun to show my support, sweetheart. I need to go, but you'll receive a message soon from Cheryl. Okay? You met her the other day when you came to the office."

"The dragon at the front desk?" I asked.

He chuckled. "Yeah, that's her."

"Great! I liked her."

He laughed. "You would. Okay. Talk later. Love you."

He hung up and I sat on the bed in shock. Now, that was a man! When presented with a problem, not only did he solve it, but he also tied everything up in a pretty bow and gave a bonus set of steak knives too.

I got off the bed and reached for the box of tissues to blow my nose. If this was how emotional and unstable I felt this early in my pregnancy, I could only imagine how bad I'd be later on.

My phone rang and I picked it up, not recognizing the number but it was a local area code. "Hello? Chastity speaking."

"Chastity! It's Cheryl here, Axel's office manager."

"Oh, hi, Cheryl. Axel said you would call but I wasn't expecting you right away."

"Are you busy? Should I call back later?"

I dropped back on the bed with a sigh. "No. Not busy at all. Go for it."

"Mr. Patterson asked me to call you with a list of his properties without mortgages attached. Unfortunately, that list is the shortest one, but there are still a few to choose from."

I sighed heavily and ached to talk to someone with a maternal view on things. "I really don't want one of his properties, Cheryl. He's being over-protective."

"It's not any of my business."

I rubbed my fingers into my forehead, hoping to relieve some of the tension from my head. "Cheryl, I need someone to talk to and get advice from, and as I've told you before, my mom isn't exactly an Axel fan, so could you help me?"

There was beat of silence, then, "What do you need?"

"Okay, my problem is this... Axel wants me to choose a property of his to transfer over into my name, but he doesn't get it. I don't want his money."

"Then why is he doing this?"

My stomach twisted. "How much can I trust you, Cheryl?"

She laughed softly on the other end of the line. "I've worked for Mr. Patterson for almost fifteen years, Chastity. I'll take his secrets to the grave."

Perfect.

"I'm pregnant."

Silence.

"Hello?"

"Ah, yes. I'm here. That's a first."

I huffed out a laugh. "Well, I'm glad to hear that. But Axel's trying to compensate for our lack of time together, and he wants to reassure me that he's not going anywhere and that the baby and I will be taken care of. Which believe me, I appreciate, but I never want him or anyone else to think I'm with him for his money. And I don't need a house or a business. Or anything else like that. So, what should I do?"

"Well, I'll preface my thoughts with the knowledge that you really don't have a lot of say in whether you get this asset transferred over to you or not. Mr. Patterson will do what he likes. But that being said, I don't see a negative in choosing something that could be an asset for you or your child in the future. If you two break up in a year, legally you will be entitled to a settlement and an annuity that will set you both up forever."

I sighed. "Again, not what I want."

"But, if you two are still together in twenty years' time, then that property can be transferred to your baby's name, which will be a nice nest egg. The question of why you're together only comes about if you break up, and if that isn't your intention then you should have no qualms about doing this, because you know you'll never have to cash in on it anyway."

And the penny dropped, so to speak. "You're right, Cheryl. If we're together forever, it's not going to matter."

"No. It won't."

I sighed. Okay. So once again I had to accept this ridiculously expensive gift and hope I never needed it.

"Cheryl, you've convinced me to relax a bit, thank you. So, of the places on the list, which do you recommend?"

"The most expensive one, of course."

I laughed. "No, really."

"Hmmm... Well, for myself, I'd choose the apartment in New York, but if you really want something that will be for pure asset value, then I'd go with the small apartment block in Phoenix. It has great returns and was recently renovated."

"But won't I have to deal with leases and people, and all that?"

"Yes. Would you prefer something here in town? Perhaps for one of your parents to live in, or—"

"Oh, my mother would die!" I shook my head, but then again, it would be a great way to pay her back for everything she'd sacrificed for me. "What did you have in mind?"

In the end I chose a large house near the beach that was

currently on long-term lease. I hoped never to need to use it and would instead invite my mom in to live in it once she'd come to terms with me and Axel being together. But like most people, I had no idea what the future held, so I thanked Cheryl for her help and lay back on the bed, my head whirling. I was still falling down the rabbit hole and was dizzy from all the spinning.

22

AXEL

When I'd learned that Chastity had chosen one of the least valuable houses I owned, it didn't surprise me. In fact, I laughed out loud when I heard the result. But at least she'd chosen one, and somehow had gotten Cheryl on her side. I wasn't sure how she charmed people the way she did, but I was convinced Chastity was part witch. She was magic to me.

I made a few phone calls, got the paperwork moving on the house and called the school to make a formal complaint. Happily for me—and not so happily for the doctor Chastity had seen this morning—I knew several members on the board at her school. They assured me that a different physician would be in place within the week.

I called a friend whose wife had twins and got the name of their obstetric specialist. Chastity would have the best care money could buy. I hadn't worked this hard and this long for nothing. This was when my money mattered. Not expensive homes and weekends away, though those were nice. It was being able to give those I loved the life they wanted. And for Chastity, at least for the moment, all she was concerned about was caring for her pregnancy.

And I adored that about her.

When I got in my car to drive home, I put my cell on speaker and called to tell her everything that had happened during the afternoon. I wanted her to know how proud I was that she'd chosen a house so close to the beach and good schools, so that if she wanted to live there long-term, it would be perfect for us.

But she didn't pick up. So, I left a long voicemail and ended up driving home, eating dinner, and getting more work done. Why she wasn't answering her cell, I didn't know, and a knot twisted in my gut worrying about her. Maybe she'd been in an accident? Or maybe she'd just fallen asleep early? Pregnant women did that, right?

I was considering calling her mom to see if she'd had any contact with Chastity tonight, when there was a knock at the door. Glancing at the time, I saw it was ten pm. A bit late for anyone to drop by on a Monday night. I walked over to the door and opened it, happiness flashing through me when I saw who stood on the other side of the door. "Hey, Pat."

"Hey," he said, looking nervous and not attempting to walk inside like he normally would.

"Didn't use your key this time?" I joked, raising an eyebrow in question.

He huffed. "Never using it again."

I laughed because really, what other choice was there? Then I held open the door to my friend. "I was just catching up on some work. You want to come in?"

"Yeah, if that's okay."

"Of course." I stepped back to allow him to enter, something I hadn't needed to do for a very long time.

The guy who was my best friend or had been for a decade before I fell in love with his daughter, walked in the door.

"You want a drink?" I asked, pretty sure he needed one if the look on his face was anything to go by.

"Only if you're joining me."

How could I say no to that request? If Patrick was here to talk, I might need the fortification. "I suppose I could stop work for a while. It's been a rough day."

"Oh, yeah? How come?"

We walked together towards the kitchen where I grabbed a couple of beers out of the fridge for us and cracked their tops. "I hired a new manager thinking he could take a load off me so I could get a bit more of a work/life balance, and all he did was fuck up some meetings and make things more difficult. Not exactly what I'd been looking for."

"You're doing... what?" Pat asked, his eyes goggling. "Work/life balance? Who are you and what have you done with my friend?"

I laughed as I handed him the drink. "Yeah, well. I'm getting old." I gestured for him to follow, and we wandered over to the couch and sat. I groaned as I relaxed into the cushions. "Shit... it's nice to sit down." I'd been going all day.

Patty grinned at me. "You *are* getting old."

I took a swig of beer and shrugged. "It's time to slow down. I don't want to keep working at the pace I have been. It'll kill me eventually." Of course, before Chastity I'd been quite happy to work myself into an early grave. *Live hard, die young. All that crap.*

Patrick leaned forward and rested his elbows on his knees as he cradled his beer with both hands. "What's the real reason, Axel?" His tone was slow and careful as he asked the question.

I sighed and took another sip of the beer, not sure I wanted to go down that path. "You sure you want me to say it?"

Pat nodded. "Yeah. Gotta hear it, I'm afraid." He glanced up and met my eyes, and he was deadly serious.

This time I sighed even heavier. My best friend didn't want to know how much I cared about his daughter, he really didn't. But then again, shouldn't a father know how treasured his only child was? I shook myself and prepared to tell the truth. "It's Chastity. She's the difference," I said. And though my stomach felt like I'd just been punched, I pushed on. "She deserves a good life, and I don't mean an easy life with money and diamonds everywhere. That's not what she wants."

One side of Pat's mouth tilted up. "But I'm sure you've showered her in both. Kaiti told me you took Chastity to Vegas for her birthday."

"Yeah, I did." I swallowed hard, busting to tell my best friend the news I was going to be a father. But it was both too soon in the pregnancy, and not my secret to tell. "I bought her a diamond ring, got the most expensive suite in the place. But I think her favorite part of the trip was spending a total of eighteen dollars over six hours in the casino. Seriously, you should have seen her." I shook my head. She'd been adorable.

"Sorry. You bought her a what?" My friend was staring at me like I'd grown a second head.

"Oh, it's not what you think," I said once I'd cottoned on to what he was flabbergasted about. "When I propose it'll be with your full consent. Don't worry." I wasn't going to make that mistake.

Patrick sat bolt upright. "*When* you propose? Are you fucking kidding me, Axel?"

I swallowed hard and faced off against the man who obviously still didn't think I was good enough for his daughter. "Yeah, I said when. What's wrong with that?"

"But you're—"

"What? Forty-one? A hardened bachelor? A workaholic?"

"Yes!" he exploded. "All of the above!"

I slid to the edge of my chair, anger biting into my jaw. "So what? What's that got to do with the fact that I love her? And I'll make her happy! And just so we're on the same page, I'd propose tomorrow if she'd say yes. But she won't because she wants to finish college first and I fucking love that about her." I shook my head, biting the inside of my cheek. "She's so fierce. And smart. And loyal." I glared at my best friend—her dad. "I love her, okay? More than you obviously realize."

Pat's mouth dropped open, but no words came out. Then he tilted his beer back and drank most of it in a couple of long swallows. He put the empty bottle down on the coffee table in front of him and wiped his mouth with the back of his hand. "Wow. I mean, I know you've said you love her and all that, but I thought you meant as a passing fancy. Someone to enjoy for a while, then you'd both move on. But you're talking—"

"Forever. Yeah, I am." And it was obvious that Pat needed to hear the truth, because he was living in Lala Land if he thought I was playing around. I crossed my arms over my chest and glared at him. Sure, I'd been out with a lot of women over the years, but I'd never bought any of them apartments or rings, or anything overly personal. God, most of them I couldn't even stand to sleep beside for a few hours.

"Is that why you came over here?" I demanded. "To learn my intentions? Because I was pretty sure I'd made it clear how I felt about her last time we spoke."

"Well, yeah. I mean, it's obvious from what Kaiti said that you two are getting along, but I didn't think you actually saw a long-term future together."

I sat up and glared at my friend. "Why not?"

"Because, well... you're you, Axel. There's no way you'll find the time she needs around your work. And yeah, she's at college for another four months, but what's going to happen when she moves away to study chiropractic? Surely, you're not going to do the long-distance thing. That never works."

I swallowed hard and picked up my beer to take a drink, mostly to give myself time to think about what I was about to say next. I didn't want to lie to my friend but announcing that Chastity wouldn't be able to attend chiropractic school wouldn't go down well either.

"Look, Pat, I want to make it work. I've been looking for the right woman for twenty years, so if it comes down to it, I'll sell the company, move to wherever she is. None of this bullshit matters." I gestured to the expensive apartment around me. "Not if I don't have her."

Patrick stared at me, his dark eyes full of intense emotion. "She really means that much to you?"

"Yeah, she does. She means everything."

He inhaled deeply and stood up. "Then, I think I got what I needed."

I stood too.

He extended his hand to me. "Okay. Then I'll back off. And for what's it worth? You have my blessing."

I extended my hand and shook his. "Thank you." We walked towards the door and as he went to leave, I called out, "So, how are we going to do this?"

"What this?" he called back.

"Us. Are we friends still? Or are you officially my girlfriend's dad, and nothing more?"

Patrick inhaled deeply, then sighed. "I'd like to go back to being friends. I miss training with you. My fitness level has dropped the past few weeks."

I laughed. "I'd like that. So, what? We just talk football and work and shit?"

"Avoid personal talk? Sounds like a plan to me."

I laughed as I shut the door, then sighed. He was so going to kill me when he found out about the baby. I shrugged. Oh well, he'd punched me before. I'd wear his anger again if I needed to, because I wouldn't change a thing.

23

CHASTITY

I'd only meant to put my head down on the pillow after my last class for a moment, just to shut my eyes for a second. Then I'd woken up the next morning feeling like utter crap. My head hurt, my body ached, and my stomach squeezed tightly with hunger. I'd missed dinner. Damn it.

"Oh, God." I groaned as I rolled over and reached for my phone. No one said I'd feel exhausted from doing nothing. I really needed to download some pregnancy apps or get some books. I knew next to nothing about what was happening to me. I stared at the screen on my phone.

"Oh, Axel." Gah. He'd called multiple times and messaged as well. Poor thing thought something was wrong, which would be the normal assumption to make if I hadn't answered my phone for twelve hours. But in this case, I was okay. Sort of. *Except that your baby is draining the life out of me!*

I sent a quick text to assure him I was still alive, then rolled out of bed to stagger to the bathroom. I wasn't sure if he'd get my message right away or not but sent it anyway, just in case. It was still early, not even six am, and technically he should be asleep. Maybe, but not likely.

I went to the bathroom, then crawled back into bed. No nausea or anything I'd expect from typical morning sickness, but I just felt sick. Like I had flu or something. Even my sinuses felt clogged.

You okay? Can I call? Axel messaged straight away.

I sighed. I couldn't do it. Not yet. Plus, Hope was fast asleep across the other side of the room. She wouldn't appreciate being woken up while I tried to talk to my boyfriend.

I managed to text him.

Can I call later? Feeling like crap and needing a little more sleep. Love you. xox

Then I passed out again.

I woke up much later and had to bolt to get to my classes. I hated being tardy and having the lecturer glare at me as I tried to sneak in. But I got through the morning's lessons sipping on water, and anxious to get something to eat. I went straight to the cafeteria to grab sandwiches and some fruit, then I called Axel.

"Hey, sorry about stressing you out last night," I told him, biting into a crunchy apple. "I meant to just have a nap before dinner, then call you after. I didn't think I'd end up sleeping straight through."

He chuckled. "It's fine, as long as you're okay."

"I'm okay," I reassured him. "Though I'm not sure what to expect next. Maybe I need to see that doctor sooner rather than later."

"I got the name of a great specialist, and my insurance broker has found you an individual plan. You just need to contact him and give him some information, and it's done. If I send you the numbers, can you make an appointment with the doctor and deal with my insurance guy? Shouldn't take too long."

"Of course," I said, grinning from ear to ear. He really was looking after me. "Send it over."

"Great. I have to go, but we'll chat tonight, yeah?"

I nodded even though he couldn't see me. "Thanks, Axel."

"Anytime, sweetheart. Love you."

"I love you too! Thank you! Bye."

I called the specialist immediately and answered the questions the best I could. The receptionist seemed nice enough, though lacking the warmth I was expecting from people dealing with pregnancy and babies.

I texted Axel soon after to tell him that we had an appointment within the next two weeks. Then I set about downloading all the apps and books to get myself up to date on what was happening with me, what would happen in the next few months and years. All that information was overwhelming in lots of ways, but some apps were hilarious, and I focused on those.

And that was how the rest of my week went, reading and studying for exams. Napping when I needed to, and flicking through a dozen pregnancy apps to work out which ones I liked best. When the weekend came, Axel had to work.

"I'm so sorry, sweetheart, but there's no way I can take another weekend off. Do you want to come here and relax at my place?"

Relax after a two-hour drive and not spend any time with him? Probably not.

"To be honest, I'd be happy to just chill here. I'm behind on my own work because of all the tiredness, and if that's gonna continue through the semester—" And all the books pointed to the fact that tiredness was a major side effect of pregnancy. "—then I should probably try to keep on top of things too."

"Oh, yeah that makes sense," Axel said, though I could hear the disappointment in his voice.

I sighed. "I miss you, too. Don't worry. But it's only like... four and a half months until I graduate now." I'd worked it out almost to the day. "Then we can spend as much time together as possible." Hopefully, assuming he had learned by then to step back and work less.

"That's true." His sigh mirrored my own.

"Hey, have you hired anyone new to help you run your business?"

He chuckled. "Hardly worth it at this point. I've spent the whole week trying to undo the damage the last one caused. I'm not sure I'm cut out to let someone else be me."

I laughed at that. Of course, he thought that way. "Well, they can't be you, that's impossible. But all leaders delegate. And I'd hoped that you wanted to find someone soon, because I'm going to need you when the baby comes."

My mom would pitch in to help, I was sure. When the time came to tell her, and she'd got over the shock of becoming a grandma, that is. But I didn't want Axel to be one of those dads who just popped in for five minutes to say hello, then worked the rest of the time. That wasn't what I wanted for me or my baby.

"I'll be there," he said firmly.

"How?" I asked, sitting up in bed and crossing my legs.

"I haven't figured that out yet."

I rolled my eyes. It wasn't going to work itself out. "Have you talked to my dad? He might know someone that would fit."

Axel sighed. "He popped by last night, actually. I told him I wanted to scale back, and he laughed in my face."

I giggled. "Yeah, I could imagine that. He thinks you're married to your work."

"Well, I have been for a long time. But things are different now."

Horror struck me and I squeaked. "You didn't tell him, did you?"

"No. I thought that you'd want to do it together or by yourself. Either way, it's your call."

Relief swamped me. "Thank you for that. I'm reading all this stuff on the baby and the pregnancy, and it's scary. So many women miscarry, especially their first. I think I want to wait until we're sure everything's okay before we tell anyone." From what I'd read, some people waited until twelve weeks, some longer.

"Even your mom?" Axel asked.

"Especially my mom," I said, twirling my finger around the pink blanket scrunched up on the bed beneath me. "She's gonna be freaked out enough as it is. But I don't think I could deal with all her emotions as well if I lost it." The very idea had me tearing up.

"We can do this however you want, sweetheart," Axel said, his voice deep and sexy, yet reassuring at the same time. "Can you send me all the details for the doctor appointment, and I'll make sure I'm there."

"Yes, I'll text you now."

I put him on loudspeaker and tapped in the details. As soon as I was done, Hope walked in the door, so I took him off speaker to put him to my ear again.

"Thanks again for organizing someone. I feel a lot better now."

"No problem. Well, I better get some work done, but I'll call you tomorrow, okay?"

I nodded and stood up, reaching for the covers on my bed. "Sure. I think I'll get an early night again. Love you."

"I love you."

And we hung up.

I reached for my pajamas and began to get changed. My nipples were sensitive, and I was getting teary again, which was bloody annoying.

"Hey, you okay?" Hope called out suddenly.

I glanced up at her, blinking rapidly to dispel the tears. "Yeah, fine. Why?" I still hadn't forgiven her for her juvenile, rude comments about Axel.

"You just look really pale, and you're sleeping all the time at the moment."

I shrugged. "Just run down, I think. It's been a tough couple of weeks, and this last semester is gonna be rough."

She nodded. "Yeah. Okay."

I didn't want her to be the first person to find out about my pregnancy, though if I started throwing up every day, it was going be hard to hide it.

I walked over to our bathroom and closed the door. Time to wash my face, brush my teeth, and go to bed. I glanced at the scale. It wasn't mine; it was Hope's. I'd never been one to worry about my weight. If I fit in my clothes and felt healthy and full of energy, all was well. But the pregnancy apps said I could gain between twenty and fifty pounds. Did I even want to see that happen on the scale?

I shook my head and brushed my teeth, focusing on the only thing I could control at the moment, and that was what I was going to do next. *Sleep. Eat. Study.* That was my weekend. When I walked back into the bedroom and climbed into bed, I found Hope still hovering around.

"Are you going to bed already?" she asked.

I gestured at my pajamas as though it should be obvious. "Yeah, why?"

"Oh, it's just that there's a party out on the quad, and I thought you might want to come."

I rolled onto my side and faced her. "Look, Hope, I have a boyfriend, and it's serious. So, I don't think I'll be going to any mixers this term."

"Why not? It's just being social."

I groaned and hauled myself up to sitting. "I just wanna get through this last semester, okay? Balancing study and Axel is going to be hard enough." Not to mention the physical demands of a pregnancy. "I just don't need any other pressures, okay?"

"Okay." Hope scurried to the door, then glanced back. "I know you're kind of pissed at me still, so I'm sorry for what I said. I didn't realize you guys were serious."

I sighed as I resettled into bed, my body aching with exhaustion. "I don't think that's much of an excuse, but okay. Thanks for the apology."

Hope opened the door, but still hung around. "Can we go back to how things were? I don't want to fight."

And neither did I. I didn't have the strength. "Okay. But I don't want you making any cracks about Axel's money or his age, or anything like that."

Hope pretended to zip up her mouth.

"Okay, cool," I said, waving at her. "See you in the morning."

"Night." She slipped out and closed the door behind her.

I sighed heavily, my body already relaxing into sleep. Why did everyone give us so much grief about being together? We weren't hurting anyone, and it was nobody else's business. It shouldn't be this difficult all the time.

24

CHASTITY

The weekend was uneventful, as was the next week. I studied, attended classes and talked to Axel every day. He was busy, but so was I, so I tried not to think about how absent he might be in the future.

I read in one of my pregnancy books that women became mothers when they became pregnant. Men became fathers when the baby was born. I took that to mean because I felt pregnant, exhausted, and slightly queasy most of the time, the bond with my little one had already begun. For a man, until he could hold his child in his arms and look upon its face, it kind of made sense that the bond wouldn't be the same.

A large part of me was hoping that Axel would check in a lot earlier than after the birth, but hey, I was getting way ahead of myself. I was only six weeks along.

The day of the specialist appointment arrived. I let my professors know I had a medical appointment so I wouldn't be in class, and Axel sent a car to pick me up to drive me down to the city. Initially, I'd said I'd drive my car, of course. It made sense.

But when Axel had insisted and I'd woken up that day feeling truly sick, I was grateful for his protectiveness.

I sat in the car with a bottle of water in one hand and a dry cracker to chew on in the other. Why did something so wonderful like growing another human being have to be so torturous on the body? It didn't make sense. I sighed and put my head back on the head rest, drifting in and out of sleep while we drove into the city. As we pulled up in front of a huge, white building, I woke up.

The driver cleared his throat. "We're here."

I glanced out the window. "Is this a hospital?"

"Yes. Mr. Patterson will be here shortly."

I pulled out my phone and there was a text from Axel.

Running 5 mins. behind but will meet you in the office. Dr. Martinez. Second Floor.

I sighed. "He sent me all the details. I think I'll go in."

"All right, ma'am. I'll park around the corner and be back to pick you up and drive you home." He got out of the car and came around to open my door.

I picked up my bag and got out.

The driver handed me his card. "My cell number, so you can call me when you're done."

I grinned at him. "Thanks."

"Good luck," he said, then walked back to the driver's seat.

I sighed and stared up at the huge white building. I wasn't sure this was the sort of place I wanted to come every month. It looked super impersonal and clinical. But I shouldn't judge a book by the cover, so to speak. Even though literally, everyone did. Otherwise, why bother with pretty cover art?

"I'll see you in a bit. Hopefully won't be more than an hour." I took a deep breath and trudged inside. I had no idea what to expect. A scan? Blood tests? Or just a chat about what was coming? I walked inside, found the stairs and walked up to the level that the supposedly legendary Dr. Martinez practiced on.

The office wasn't difficult to find, so when I pushed open the door, I walked up to the reception desk.

"Chastity Lennox for a twelve o'clock appointment."

The receptionist looked through her huge, dark-rimmed reading glasses at me, then towards the computer. "Oh, yes, the new patient. Dr. Martinez doesn't usually accept new patients. You must have a connection to our current patient list." She pushed an iPad across the desk at me and I took it. "Just fill in the forms and I'll upload them for the doctor."

I didn't have my normal level of energy or sunshine but tried a smile at her. "My partner got me the appointment, so I'll make sure to thank him. Thanks for your help."

The woman nodded at me, but I didn't see much defrosting of the outer layer of her cold professional crust.

I made my way over to the chairs and sat down, then filled in the forms the best I could. They wanted to know everything from my last period to my insurance, to my weight, and goals for the pregnancy.

When the door to the office opened and Axel stepped in, the whole room seemed to turn to look at him. He stood tall and gorgeous, with an expensive suit and his hair all slicked back. He spoke to the woman at the front desk, who practically melted when Axel spoke.

I grinned as she pointed at me, looking surprised as hell. *Ha! Yep, he's mine.* I waved and smiled at him as he hurried over.

"Sorry I'm late, sweetheart."

"All good," I told him as he bent down to kiss me on the lips. "I haven't been called in yet."

"Chastity?" was suddenly by a nurse holding a door open.

I grinned at him. "Saved by the bell." I stood up next to him and took his hand, tucking the iPad under my arm. "That's me."

The person I assumed was the doctor, who was a woman in

her forties, smiled at me and I had an instant sense of relief. "Come this way," she said.

"I'll just take that from you," the receptionist said, rushing forward to take the iPad from me.

"Oh, yeah. Thanks." Okay, so if this was the doctor I was getting, I would be happier to come to a place like this.

She gestured to the first room. "Right in here. I'm Dr. Martinez."

"Nice to meet you," I said, shaking her hand.

Axel and she exchanged pleasantries, and we were soon sitting in the small office, with brightly colored pictures on the walls and a bookcase behind the desk like I'd always pictured I'd have in my dream home.

"What a great room," I said, glancing around. "I love it."

The doctor smiled at me. "Thanks. I love it too. So, tell me, how I can help you today."

Axel reached out for my hand and squeezed it, which I assumed was the signal for me to talk.

"Oh, okay. Well basically, I'm pregnant, which was a bit of a surprise. I have no idea what to do next or what to expect, so Axel said he'd find the best obstetrician for us, and here we are."

The doctor's grin was genuine. "Well, I appreciate the vote of confidence." She glanced down at the paperwork. "So, you'll be about six weeks according to your dates, but we can confirm that with a dating scan today. How are you feeling at the moment?"

"Terrible." I huffed out a laugh. "Nauseous. Exhausted."

"Any vomiting?

"No," I said, "Not yet, anyway."

"That's good. Though you'll need to stay on top of your water consumption. Dehydration in early pregnancy is the main reason for hospitalization."

I picked up my bottle of water and took a big sip. "Thanks for the tip."

"I'll get you some pamphlets and information for your first trimester, then let's move into the next room to do your first scan."

We all stood up and the doctor opened a door into the exam room.

"Now this part looks like a hospital," I said, glancing around at the sterile white walls, the electronic monitors and equipment.

"Yes." She laughed. "This part is. Would you please wait in my office while we get ready, Axel?"

Axel glanced at me, and I nodded. "Sure." He stepped out and she shut the door.

"This first scan is a little invasive. This wand goes inside the vagina, and then we can see the fetus and check for position and a heartbeat." She picked up a large metal rod, with a thick end and rounded cap, and applied a condom to it.

"Are you serious?" I asked. "You wanna put that thing inside me?"

She nodded. "Yes, it's the only way to see the fetus today. Unless you want to wait until twelve weeks for the First Trimester scan. We'll order blood tests today to check your iron, vitamin D, pregnancy hormones, etcetera."

I stared at the thing she called a wand. "Is it going to hurt?"

"No. Just a little cold and uncomfortable."

I sighed. "Okay. I want to try it. I want to see the baby."

"Well, it's technically only a fetus, but I do find a lot of expectant mothers enjoy seeing this scan in particular."

"What do I do?"

She got me up on the table with no underwear on but draped a sheet over me, then went and got Axel.

"Everything okay?" he asked when he walked back in.

I nodded. "Yeah, she'd going to do a scan to see the baby, then do blood tests and stuff. Do you have to get back?"

He shook his head. "No, I'm here as long as you need me."

I wasn't sure I believed him, since he seemed a little jumpy and had glanced at his phone three times already. But for the moment we were together, and this was important for him to be here for. I reached out my hand and he grabbed me. "Thanks for coming," I said, smiling up at him.

He ducked his head and kissed my lips, then pressed his forehead to mine. "Of course."

I closed my eyes, shutting out the bright lights and focusing on Axel's energy for the moment. Yes, this was the reason I was here, and in this position. My love for this man. It had been far too long since I'd felt his skin against mine.

"Okay, Chastity," the doctor instructed, getting my attention again. "Just put your feet on these little metal stirrups. It'll be a little cold and you'll feel some pressure."

"Oops!" I squeaked as she pressed a very wet, lubricated, cold rod into me.

"You okay?" Axel asked, looking concerned.

I shifted a little, trying to find a comfortable spot. "Yeah. Just a bit of a shock, really."

"Here we go. Just looking at this screen over here," Dr. Martinez said, adjusting a large screen to our left.

I stared at it, only making out weird black and white swirls.

"I can't see anything," I said, my stomach lurching with fear. What if I wasn't really pregnant? And I was just... I don't know, sick?

"There it is," the doctor said suddenly, moving the rod a little deeper and pressing harder.

"Where?"

She lifted her hand and pointed at the screen. "There. Now, I'll just measure it, and see where the heart is."

I watched her clicking on a mouse, amazed at the dexterity it took to do such a thing. Meanwhile, Axel was squeezing my hand tightly. I glanced up at him. "You okay?"

He nodded, his eyes trained on the screen, not looking at me. "Yeah. Just can't believe this is really happening."

I laughed. "That's because you're not the one with a metal wand up inside you."

He glanced down at me then and pressed his lips together like he was trying not to laugh.

"Measuring six weeks and two days. Perfectly in line with your dates. And there—there's the heartbeat. Measuring at 160 beats per minute. Very healthy."

I stared at the screen and could suddenly see what she was talking about. A tiny little blob with a fluttering pulse that flickered on the screen. "Wow." My eyes filled with tears. "That's our baby." I glanced up at Axel, who was staring at the screen with wonder in his eyes that was mirrored in the love in my heart.

He kissed me again, this time harder. "I love you."

"I love you too."

The doctor took some images, organized the rest of the tests, and gave me enough info to weigh me down for the next month. Despite the nausea and having some stranger stick a metal wand in very private places, I was having the best day of my life.

25

AXEL

The next month flew by. I was buried in work but managed to get down to the apartment for a weekend in the middle of February. Chastity was constantly studying and feeling sick, so she was hard to get hold of sometimes, but we made do. *Just.*

We were both focused on the end goal. She had to get to her graduation, and I had to find a way to reduce my hours. Unfortunately, though, I wasn't holding up my end of the bargain so much.

I was sitting at my desk in the office late on a Friday night when Chastity rang. "Hey, beautiful," I said, smiling for the first time today. "How are you feeling?"

"Ugh. Almost ten weeks today, and..." She groaned. "Wanna vomit every minute of every day. How are you?"

I frowned at the phone. "Are you drinking enough water?"

"Yeah, I am. Got a bottle next to me all day long. One good thing about feeling sick all the time though is I've lost five pounds. Worst diet ever."

"That doesn't sound good," I told her, worried at why she was weighing herself while pregnant. That didn't sound like a healthy thing to do. "Should we see Dr. Martinez a little earlier than planned?" We had an appointment at twelve weeks, but I'm sure she'd get us in sooner if something was wrong.

"No, don't worry about it. It's totally normal, according to my app."

"If you say so." Maybe I should have been doing my own research, but I'd been buried in paperwork the last couple of weeks.

"Hey, how's the manager hunt going? Still, no one you like?"

This was a question she asked once a week and unfortunately, I answered the same every time. "Not great. I interviewed a few people yesterday—"

"But they all sucked?"

I laughed, enjoying her quick wit and sense of humor. "Yeah, they all sucked. God, I miss you." And I did.

"Well, you could come down for the weekend. Have a night off?"

I glanced around at my desk filled with everything I needed to have done by Monday morning. "I'm still at the office."

She sighed heavily. "So, you'll be working all weekend again."

My heart squeezed tightly. We could both use some time together and mentally, I needed a night off.

"How about I come down tomorrow night? I'll get a driver so I can use the time to work there and back, then take off the night and we can chill, have dinner. Whatever you want."

She gasped. "Really? Oh my God, I'd love that."

I laughed. "You're sounding better now."

"Oh, yeah. The nausea's even gone for the moment, I'm so excited. Thank you! What time?"

We discussed the details and said goodnight.

When I hung up, despite the extra burden I'd just laid on myself, I felt much happier. I'd never really understood those new-age hippy sayings about re-filling the well, and looking after yourself so you could look after others. I'd always trained hard, eaten well, and run off my desire to succeed. But it wasn't enough anymore.

I had another reason to work now—to breathe—and that was Chastity and the baby coming. Without seeing her, all the stress and demands of work were becoming overwhelming. I texted her a quick message as I smiled to myself.

Can't wait to see you and our secret little bump. Been too long. I love you.

Then I got back to work with renewed enthusiasm. I worked all night, got four hours' sleep, then went to the gym in the morning.

When the driver came to pick me up, I was ready, packed and with laptop in hand, prepared to work during the drive down. I hadn't thought about it before, as I liked driving my car and felt like a rich dickhead if I had a driver everywhere I went.

But this way, I didn't lose two hours of work time and could easily justify taking the night off. In fact, it meant that taking every Saturday night off was now possible. I could go down to the apartment, spend one night a week with my girl, and keep running my company. The plan was in place. Now just to make sure it all went smoothly.

When the driver pulled up, Chastity's car was already parked out front, but she was nowhere in sight.

"Thanks, Harry," I told the driver. "See you tomorrow around noon."

"See you then, Mr. Patterson."

I zipped up my briefcase, grabbed my bag and headed up to the apartment. My heart was light, and excitement buzzed through me.

When I opened the door, I called out, "Honey! I'm home." I

sounded like some stupid sitcom character, but it still made me happy.

Chastity called back, "Hi! Are you alone?"

I shut the door behind me and dropped my bags. "Of course. Why?"

Chastity walked out of the bedroom naked as the day she was born. "Just because," she said, shrugging like this was any other day.

I couldn't help it. I ran for her, picking her up and spinning her around, which she responded to by squealing and laughing. When I set her down, I didn't let her go, instead wrapping my arms around her warmth and tugging her close. "This is a nice surprise."

I glanced down at her glowing face, leaning back so I could cup her breasts and run my thumbs over her nipples. "These are darker than before." Her areolas, once a dark pink, were now browner in color.

She nodded. "Yeah, according to my app, it's a breast-feeding thing. They go darker so the baby can see them."

"Hmmm..." I loved that she knew everything about it, but it wasn't the focus for my sex-starved body at the moment. "So... does this mean I can take you to bed?"

She smiled coyly up at me. "Yes. I'm feeling better in the afternoons now, so I'd love to go back to bed for a bit."

"Oh, best news I've heard all day." I cupped her gorgeous face and kissed her, moaning when the pleasure of her lips against mine hit me. Damn, I'd missed her. Her taste, her smell, her touch. I swept my tongue into her mouth, kissing her deep, and long, and hard.

She grabbed me around the waist then started pulling at my shirt, getting her hands underneath and on my skin.

I groaned and pulled away, wanting to get as naked as she was. "Let's go." I grabbed her hand and pulled her into the bedroom, tugging at my clothes and throwing them to the floor. "Anything I need to know?" I asked quickly, my hungry gaze roaming over her curvy figure. "Anything sore or sensitive?"

She bit her lip, her gaze running up and down my body. "Well, um... my nipples are a little sensitive, but everything else is good."

I fucking hoped so. My hormones were pumping now, and the weeks of missing her were adding up. "Then get on that bed, missy."

Chastity turned and ran towards the bed, and I chased her, swatting at her round backside as she ran.

She jumped on the mattress and turned around, going down on her belly to face me.

"Uh?" Not sure what she was trying to achieve from that angle.

"Come here," she said, grabbing my thighs and hauling me closer.

When her wet, hot mouth closed around my cock, understanding clicked into place. "Oh, fuck." A wave of sensation washed over me as she sucked on me, tonguing the tip, and nibbling on the flesh that was so desperate to fuck her. I grabbed at her hair and tugged her back gently. "Enough, or you'll make me blow right here." Her mouth was divine, but her pussy was heaven. And I'd missed the feeling of her wrapped around me.

She grinned up at me. "That wouldn't be a bad thing."

"Oh, yes it would. I want to make you come too."

I tugged her arm and gently pushed her toward the mattress, so she rolled onto her back. I slid over her luscious body, licking her nipples as I crawled up.

She wrapped her legs around my waist and whispered in my ear, "I'm so wet already. Please."

How was I going to say no to that? Groaning, I shifted to line myself up with her. I rolled onto the side and took my cock in hand, dragging the head through her wetness and painting her pussy with her juices.

She gasped out her impatience, squeezing my arms. "Please hurry."

I met her gaze with my own and stared into her eyes as I rolled on top of her beautiful body. "I love you."

"Oh, I love you too." She wrapped her legs around me and tightened, urging me closer.

I felt her opening with my cock and thrust forward slowly, entering her heat and moaning as pleasure pulsed through me.

"Yesssss," Chastity groaned, throwing her head back into the pillows, her eyes closing as she experienced her own wave of pleasure.

I went slowly, even though it almost killed me. But I wanted her body to accept me, need me. Even get a little desperate for me. So instead of fucking her into oblivion, hard and fast like my cock was demanding, I took it slow. For both of our sakes. I rocked my hips, slowly going deeper and deeper. Penetrating her flesh again and again until Chastity dug her nails into my arms and tilted her hips up in greeting.

"Axel! Please! Stop torturing me."

That's all I needed to hear. I drove into the hilt, and we both cried out. It felt so good to be together. Deep inside of her, I froze, needing the moment to get hold of my control once more.

She dug her teeth into my shoulder, biting me softly. "Please don't stop."

"Oh, I won't," I ground out, finally ready to make us both fly to the stars. I began to ride her harder and faster, chasing away the loneliness and time apart. Pounding into her wet, welcoming flesh until she was screaming my name. Until the room was filled with the sounds of the creaking bed frame and our sounds of pleasure.

When we reached our peak together, I thrust balls deep into

her body and released my seed into her tight pussy. She rippled around me, squeezing my cock like a vise as her body shuddered beneath me.

I'd never felt anything like it. The pure, physical pleasure came through, then I was awash in love, in hope, in more feelings than I'd ever had to cope with before. I rolled off her, so I didn't squash her and pulled her into my arms, holding her tight. I never wanted to leave this woman, which for me, was the scariest feeling of all.

26

CHASTITY

When Axel rolled off me and tugged me onto his chest, I went willingly. My body was totally satisfied and a little sore, so I closed my eyes to rest and enjoy the utter bliss that wrapped my body up in a cloud. There was nothing like the post-orgasmic satiation feeling. Axel was an amazing lover.

I must have fallen asleep, because the next thing I knew, Axel was walking into the room fully dressed and I had my head on the pillow. I blinked, wiping at drool falling out the side of my mouth. "Oh... Ah..." I tried to speak, still exhausted and struggling to think. *Shit,* I felt terrible. Sick. Weak. I swallowed hard and forced myself to focus on talking. "Did I fall asleep?" I managed to ask, sitting up slowly, still naked, my stomach lurching.

"Yep. Sound asleep." He grinned. "Been an hour or so now, and I thought you might want some dinner."

My head was a little weird, but I attempted a smile. "Yeah, sure."

"What's wrong?"

"Oh, I'm just a little dizzy. Probably hungry." Though the idea of food was making my stomach dip. "Actually, I might lie down again." I put my head back on the pillow and pulled the sheet over my nakedness.

He sat down on the bed next to me and rested a hand on my hip. "How about I order in? Or I can go down the street and pick us up something?"

I smiled at Axel, so grateful that he was just so... him. "That sounds great. Hey, is it normal for billionaires to be so... well, amazing? And kind of normal at the same time?"

He cackled this time, then sobered quickly. "Ah, not really. Most of the men in my circle of business have yachts and helicopters. Full-time drivers and chefs."

Sounded like the perfect life... for some.

"Not you, though," I said, reaching for his leg and holding on to him. I really loved that part about him.

"Not yet," he said with a wink, then stood up and walked towards the door. "I'm starving so I'll go now and give you time to shower or rest, or whatever you need to do. You're looking a bit pale."

I swallowed hard. "Yeah. I get a few hours off in the afternoon where I feel okay, but the evenings can be rough." I'd been so glad when Axel had recommended catching up around four pm. It was the only time of day I felt any good and we hadn't had sex in so long, I felt like a terrible girlfriend. My body had missed it too. *Wow!* I'd come so much it had been amazing.

"I'll hurry. Back soon, beautiful." Then he disappeared.

I groaned, nausea rolling through me. The sickness had hit a real peak lately and I was hoping it wouldn't get much worse. I could barely think half the time and I'd almost failed a quiz recently. People at school were beginning to notice I wasn't myself, and I wasn't sure how much longer I could keep my pregnancy a secret. "Shower time." I hauled myself to my feet and pressed a hand to my still flat stomach. "A couple more weeks and I get to see you on the screen again."

Everything I read told me that the sickness correlated with high pregnancy hormones and a healthy fetus, as a general rule. If that was true, then I had to hope and assume our little one was doing well. He or she had certainly taken a lot out of me recently.

I staggered to the bathroom, still feeling dizzy, and managed to have a quick shower before crawling back into bed. Nope. I wasn't going to be able to stay up much more tonight.

When Axel came back with food, I groaned a bit and he laughed. Which didn't make me feel great but lightened the mood considerably.

I ate what I could and fell asleep on him again while watching a movie. The next morning at breakfast, I managed to get up and go down to a cafe at street level, but I ordered a peppermint tea and nothing else.

"Are you sure you don't want anything to eat? You are looking a bit skinny," Axel said.

I would have laughed at the skinny comment if I wasn't feeling so sick. I inhaled sharply, my nose practically twitching at the stench of cooked eggs and bacon around me. "Oh, no, I'm fine. The smell of the meat... it's just." I shook my head and swallowed the bile that rose. I took a calming sip of my tea, then tried talking again. "The morning sickness is pretty bad at the moment, but it'll pass."

"When? Do you know?" he asked.

I sighed. "The books all say different things. Some women feel this sick all nine months, and if that happens, please shoot me."

Axel grinned but didn't say anything.

And I was only joking... sort of. "Anyway, the general consensus seems to be that after twelve or thirteen weeks, it should get better."

He nodded and ate his Eggs Benedict, which seemed to be his

breakfast of choice. "How are you coping with classes, feeling so ill?"

"I'm not coping well," I told him, a little ashamed. "I'm trying my best, but I know people are noticing. My roommate, in particular."

"Does she know?"

I shook my head. "I haven't told her, but she's remarked on how pale I am. How much I sleep. Once we get the twelve-week scan done and I can tell everyone. I think I'll have to." It was only a matter of time until my professors said something. "But I'm hoping I feel better by the end of the semester. I need to be okay for my final exams."

He reached over the table and squeezed my hand. "I'm sorry about the timing for you."

"Are you?" I asked, raising an eyebrow at him.

He grinned his gorgeous, flashy smile at me. "I'm not sorry you're pregnant. That's amazing and I can't wait to tell everyone I know that I'm going to be a father finally."

I squeezed his fingers, the excitement in his voice warming me all over. "I hadn't really thought about that. Have you always wanted kids but just didn't get around to it?"

He smiled and took his hand back so he could use both to eat. "Yes and no. I always said I wouldn't mind having kids with the right person, but to be honest, I wasn't sure that was ever going to happen."

"Which part? The kids part or the right person part?"

He laughed then took another bite of his eggs. "Well... both, I guess. I wasn't sure I'd ever find someone like you. And if I didn't, then I'd just work until I died, I guess."

He said it so matter-of-factly, I wasn't sure how to respond. "Um... well, I'm glad you did find me, and I'm glad you get to be a daddy."

His eyes flared at the mention of the word "daddy," but I

didn't think he was thinking about the baby anymore. "Is that an invitation to go back upstairs?" he asked.

Heat flushed my cheeks, and I buried my embarrassment by drinking some more tea. "Uh, sorry. No, I don't think I can." Not unless he wanted me to vomit all over him. I could barely move at the moment without feeling sick. I couldn't imagine all the jostling that would take place if we were in bed.

He nodded, but I noticed the wave of disappointment crossing his features.

"I'm sorry."

He shook his head. "Don't be. I just miss you. That's all."

"I miss you, too. And if it wasn't for this—" I waved in the general region of my stomach. "—I'd be keeping you in bed all day and night like we used to."

He smiled, but the heat of his excitement was gone.

"I hadn't really thought about how difficult this must be for you," I said. "You've sort of lost your girlfriend, haven't you?" I'd been so sick and focused on me, I hadn't really thought about how his life had changed.

"It's okay." He grinned. "You're doing an amazing job of growing our baby. That's all that's important."

"Thanks." I thought I was failing in lots of ways, especially at school. But his compliment was appreciated, nonetheless. I took a few more sips of tea and sighed. "Tell me more about why you're having so much trouble finding a manager." When he looked away, I tried again. "I know you don't like to talk about it, but don't you think it's important that you take time off when the baby's born?"

"Of course, I do. I wouldn't miss it."

Wouldn't miss which part? The birth? The first few days, weeks? What about feeding? Nights? Was he going to help me at all? "But who's going to run your company for you?" I asked, feeling a bit like a pushy wife. But this was important. "I want you around in those first few months, not just days. I'm going to need your help." And surely, he'd *want* to be there for me.

"I'll find someone, Chastity," he said, his tone changing so that he was a little cold now. "And we can always hire a night nurse or a nanny. You'll have as much help as you want."

"I don't want a nanny," I said, though a voice in the back of my head said there might be a night I wanted the help. "I want you."

A muscle tightened in his jaw as he straightened up. "We have over six months until I need to take time off. So, please, stop harassing me about it. I'll find someone."

I gaped at him. "Harassing you? Excuse me? I'm just asking a question that you don't have an answer for."

He tugged on his shirt and frowned at me. "Leave it. My business has nothing to do with you. I said I'd sort it out, and I will."

Oh my God. Seriously? "Fine." I finished my tea, and decided it was time to go back to school.

We said a frosty goodbye and Axel stayed in the apartment to do more work, waiting for his driver to arrive.

I drove the whole fifteen minutes home, seething the whole time. "Wouldn't want to miss a minute's work. After all, that is the most important thing in the world, isn't it?"

Maybe my dad had been right, and Axel was a workaholic who would never change. There were worse things, of course. He wasn't into drugs or alcohol. He could provide for me and the baby, and if I never wanted to work, I didn't have to. But I wasn't an ice queen. I didn't want money—and no love or time.

It was probably unfair to want everything, but I did. I'd rather have to work and have a husband that was present than be one of those women who never saw her man. I loved Axel too much to endure in silence, and I was going to fight for more.

27

AXEL

I'd thought after our little spat at breakfast Chastity would withdraw from me like so many other women had before her. The cold shoulder was a common game they liked to play. But she surprised me.

She called more often, messaged every day. It was almost like we were living together already. Almost. She'd ask about my day at work, then FaceTime me every night. She was completely in my life, and it was great. It was like having a full-time girlfriend, but because she was still in college, and I didn't need to carve out time for dates, I didn't stop. Instead, I worked non-stop.

Two weeks flew by and what felt like only days later, we were back at the hospital. I'd arrived early and met her there, and now we waited in a huge white room for the twelve-week scan.

Chastity's hand was on my thigh, and I sighed as I glanced at my watch. *How much longer?* I'd had to cancel two meetings and a lunch appointment for this time slot.

"The sonographer is running an hour or so behind, but she'll be as fast as she can," the receptionist told us.

"An hour?" I repeated. They had to be kidding me.

The receptionist nodded, giving me an apologetic smile, and dashing away to the desk again.

Shit! I ran a hand through my hair, frazzled. I better get on the phone to Cheryl and rearrange some more meetings.

"Do you want to go?" Chastity asked me from the chair to my left.

I twisted around. "Go? And miss it?" After she'd asked me to come and reminded me of the scheduled time three times?

She nodded. "Yeah. I know you have a ton to do. And an hour for you is what... another million dollars?" She winked comically to show she was joking, but she wasn't far off the mark with that one.

I'd never worked out a monetary value to my time, as every hour we made money. I also paid hundreds of employees per hour, so it was possible some days I'd be in the red. But she wasn't wrong in her calculations.

"No. It's okay. I'll sit here with you and chat," I said, though my cell phone vibrated in my pocket, drawing my attention away from her.

Chastity sighed. "I have to get some bloodwork done, too. How about I ask if I can do that now? You can take your phone calls outside, and we can meet back here in an hour?"

Gratitude for my beautiful woman swept over me. "You're amazing. Thank you for understanding. I'll just be at the entrance to the hospital, so if you need me, just call, okay?"

She nodded and stood up. "Okay. And we're doing lunch after this?"

"Definitely." I couldn't lose too much more of the day, but we both needed to eat. "How's your stomach? Are you okay?"

Her smile was bright this time as she ran both hands over her still flat stomach. "It's a little queasy, but it's better."

"Fantastic." I dropped a quick kiss on her lips. "Thanks for this." And I thanked the universe for sending me such an understanding woman. I raced out the door to work.

It was lucky I did go out to take the next call, because one of my deals was close to collapsing, and the insurance company I'd hired to cover me on a new build was balking at my additions to the contract.

I juggled three different calls and was still on the phone when someone tapped me on the shoulder. I twirled around to see Chastity's furious face, her mouth pinched, and her cheeks slashed with red. "Ah... Michael. I need to go. I'll call you back when I can." I hung up on my real estate agent and slid my cell into my pocket. "Are you okay, sweetheart?" What had I missed?

She crossed her arms over her chest in an exaggerated move and glared at me. "No, actually, I'm not okay. My bloodwork made me vomit. I fucking hate needles."

"I didn't know that." I wasn't sure what I could have done to help her even if I had been there.

"And you've been gone almost two hours and wouldn't answer your phone."

Two hours? *No way.* That would mean I'd missed everything. "What?" I pulled my cell out and glanced down at the time. "Oh, no."

"So, you missed the sonogram. Congratulations. You've proven my dad right. You only care about your work, and even a baby isn't going to change that."

That wasn't fair. Not in the slightest. "Chastity, be reasonable."

She picked up her bag, rummaged through it and came out with some small pieces of paper. "Here," she said as she slammed her hand into my chest.

I caught the soft paper that she pushed at me and stared down at the little black and white pictures. "Uh..."

"That's the baby," she said, crossing her arms once more.

"Which you missed out on seeing with me, even though you promised me I wouldn't have to do this alone. That you'd be there for me."

I couldn't really see much except circles and smudges. I knew Chastity was connected to this more than me, but I really couldn't get excited the same way she was.

"Uh..." I looked back at Chastity. "I'm so sorry sweetheart. I didn't realize—"

"What? What didn't you realize? That this was important to me? I thought it was important to you too." She was really angry. Her face had gone white now.

I wasn't sure how to handle her. "No. I didn't realize so much time had gone by. Why didn't you call me?"

"I did!" she screamed, her arms straightening as she tightened her hands into fists. "I called you three times and sent you like *ten messages*!" Then she turned and stormed off down the street.

Oh. Fuck. I ran after her, my Italian leather shoes really not made for hustling. "Wait! Sweetheart, please wait." I grabbed onto her arm and tugged her a little.

She stopped and whirled on me. "What do you want?"

Ah, whoa. I hadn't seen this side of her before. "I thought we were going out to lunch afterwards. Please, let me make it up to you."

"You *can't* make this up to me, and I don't *want* to have lunch with you," she all but hissed at me. "I'm going back to school. My plan was to tell my parents about the pregnancy after the scan, but now that I'm not sure about you and me, and what we're going to do. I'll wait."

I froze, like someone had thrown a bucket of ice water down the back of my shirt. "Uh... sorry. Repeat that. I don't understand what you mean." She couldn't be saying what it sounded like she was saying. Who broke up with the father of their baby over *one* missed doctor's appointment?

"I meeeeean," she said with exaggerated, teenager-like attitude, "that I don't know what sort of relationship we have, Axel. And I'm not going to tell my parents that I'm pregnant until I know how you and I are going to function as a family in the future."

My jaw dropped open. "You're not sure about us? All because I missed one appointment? You have to be kidding me." She was joking, right? She had to be.

"I'm not kidding, Axel. I've tried to ignore your workaholic tendencies and the fact that you don't have room in your life for me. I convinced myself that you'd make space for me—and for us—in your life when the time came. But I'm not sure I can wait six months to see what sort of partner and father you'll be."

I stared at her, shocked. "Chastity, that is not fair. I give you every spare moment I have, every day."

"Exactly!" She exploded again. "You have two minutes here, and five minutes there. That's not a life, Axel."

"But I—"

"Have you hired a new manager yet? Or two or three or four? Because to make up for even half the hours you work, you're gonna need half a dozen guys, I'd say."

I straightened up, a wave of annoyance washing over me. "Chastity, I've spent fifteen years building my company. I can't just suddenly step back and hand off my roles and responsibilities to someone else. It doesn't work that way."

Her eyes filled with tears this time, and my heart all but broke. "Goodbye, Axel. Enjoy your billions." She pushed past me and walked away.

I stared after her, totally conflicted as to what to do. So, instead of acting on the impulse to chase after her once more, I just stood there like an idiot and watched her get into the car I gave her and drive away.

I was still standing there on the sidewalk, when my phone

began to ring again. I grabbed for it, hoping and assuming it was Chastity. Had she changed her mind? Did she want to yell at me some more? I didn't care as long as she wanted to contact me again. But it wasn't Chastity. It was Neil from the office. "Ah, yeah," I responded to whatever he said. "I'm heading back now. I'll be there in fifteen minutes."

I wandered to where I'd parked the car and got in. That's when I remembered the pictures, and pulled them out of the pocket I'd shoved them in. Most of them were blurry and hard to decipher, but the last one was totally different. Some sort of 3D technology where I could actually see the baby's head and face, nose and mouth.

"Wow." It looked like a real baby already. Probably as small as an apricot, or something silly like that. Chastity had sent me a picture this morning describing how big it was. I groaned and threw the pictures on the passenger seat, started the car and took off.

Just because I made a mistake, did not mean I was going to be a bad father. I knew a bunch of men who missed every appointment their wives made, and some of them missed the births too. That didn't mean they didn't love their wives or their children. Although once I thought about it, half of them were divorced now. Surely, their work ethic wasn't a factor in that? It was simple statistics of marriage and divorce, that was all.

I shook my head, a stack of heavy emotions squeezing inside my chest. I had to work through this problem so that I could find the best path forward. Chastity was very important to me, but she was being unreasonable. Perhaps it was the hormones? Or stress and lack of sleep? I had to talk to her again. Surely, she'd see sense when she calmed down again.

28

CHASTITY

I'd never been so angry in my entire life.

"That stupid... fucking... *jackass*!" I screamed to the inside of my new car. The car he'd bought me. "Fuck. Him."

The college was on the right of me as I drove, so I slowed down and pulled into the dorm's parking lot, then parked into the nearest spot on an angle and couldn't be bothered reversing to fix it. I turned the engine off with a flick of my wrist, still shaking with fury, then slammed both hands into the steering wheel. "Fuuuccck!"

What an asshole. What sort of guy promises to attend the most important moment of our life, then walks outside to work on his phone for two hours? And worst of all, he didn't even notice how much time had passed! I got out of the car, slammed the door, and stomped all the way back to my dorm.

Something could have been wrong with the baby. Did he even think about that when he left me? Abandoned me to my fate? Our fate, supposedly? Together.

Luckily or possibly unluckily—I wasn't sure yet—my roommate Hope was in our dorm room when I got back. She was studying quietly, her reading glasses on while she sat at her desk in the corner of the room. I stormed in, slammed the door behind me and threw my bag on the bed with a scream of frustration.

Hope whirled around on her swivel chair and pulled off her glasses. "Hey! What happened?"

"That... that..." I put my hands on my hips and faced my roommate. "I'm pregnant, and you may as well know, because the whole world is going to find out soon enough." I'd start popping soon and there was no way I was going to be able to hide my belly, even in my graduation gown. *Who had I been kidding when I made that joke?*

Hope nodded slowly and bit her lip. "Yeah, I assumed so."

I gaped at her. "You already knew?" *Wow.* And I thought I'd done a good job of hiding it.

"Yeah, well... I guessed anyway. You're always feeling sick, you've lost weight, you barely eat." She shrugged. "I figured you were either pregnant or something really bad was happening to you. But it's been months, and I know you and Axel are pretty serious. So..."

I collapsed down and sat on the bed opposite her. "Why didn't you say anything?"

"Because it wasn't my business. And I knew you'd tell me when you were ready."

Love swelled in my heart for the girl I shared my room with. "Thank you for that." After the day I'd had it was nice to be pleasantly surprised about a person.

She grabbed her bottle of water and took a swig. "It's okay. I still feel bad about being a bitch about Axel. And I'm still really sorry about how I was at the start."

I sighed. "It's okay. You were probably right about him."

Hope got up and walked over to her bed, sitting on the mattress so she could face me. "Why? What's happened?"

I sighed. "How long have you got?"

"All day," she answered, staring at me with patience and understanding.

"O-kay." I took a deep breath and began, telling her about the appointment and what had happened. "I feel bad in a way," I said, snorting at my own stupidity.

"Why would you feel bad?"

"Because I kinda set this up as a test." Full well knowing that he'd choose his work over me, and desperately hoping I'd be wrong. But I wasn't, and it was my own stupid fault for thinking he might have changed.

Hope frowned at me as though she didn't understand, and of course she didn't. She couldn't read minds and knew nothing about Axel.

I sighed, deciding to reveal all. "Axel is a workaholic, and it's one of the reasons my dad doesn't think we should be together. For me, I've always thought it was a good thing. He has a great work ethic and has massive success because of it. But that was only until I realized that the baby and I are going to come in second to his work if something doesn't change."

And even though he'd said things would change and that he *wanted* things to change, today had shown that if anything, he was busier than ever.

"Does he have managers or someone who can step up and take the reins?" Hope asked.

"That's exactly what he suggested initially. That he could step back and hire someone to take over, or at least help him. But anyone he's tried out hasn't worked and I think he's just too used to being in control. He's not going to be able to delegate and step away. And I don't know..." I shrugged.

I felt totally lost in this regard. If he couldn't trust anyone to help him, we would have no hope of having a life together.

"So, hang on. Back it up a step. So, how was this day a test?" Hope asked, moving to the edge of her bed.

"Well, I've tried to be extremely supportive and a good girlfriend over the last few weeks, but I made it super clear that for me, this was one of the most important scans of the whole pregnancy. This would tell us if the baby was alive and well, and afterwards, I could start telling people—including my parents." Which I still hadn't done, and felt sick to my stomach about doing, especially now.

Hope snorted. "And he missed the appointment? How?"

"Well, they were running late so I gave him the out. I let him go outside to work, which was something I didn't want him to do... but again, I was trying to show him how supportive I was. When they came to get me, I rang him three times, and then texted him a dozen times. All of which he ignored and just kept working."

I still couldn't believe he'd missed all my messages. He was literally *on* his phone.

Hope lifted her legs and crossed them, now sitting on the bed like a genie. "Well, if he was on the phone, your calls probably went to voicemail."

That wasn't the point. The receptionist gave him a time, and he never once noticed he'd blown an hour past it. "But he knew I was inside, waiting for him. This was our moment to see the baby. To check everything was okay with her."

"Her?" Hope asked, sitting up suddenly. "You're having a girl?"

I clapped my hand over my mouth. *Oh, shit.* "I didn't mean to say that! Axel doesn't even know."

"Oh, that's so awesome!" Hope said, grinning from ear to ear.

Sadness swept over me, pushing away the last of the anger. "Yeah, I think so too. It's not certain. I got a blood test that can determine the sex and checks for abnormalities, and I'll get those results in a few weeks. But the sonographer said that if they had to guess, they'd say eighty percent chance it's a girl."

Hope sighed. "So cool."

It was! A baby girl to adore. Pink walls and blankets, hair ribbons and beautiful dresses! Tears gathered in my eyes, and I blinked them away. "Yeah, it is. And he missed it. The whole appointment. We hadn't even decided if we wanted to know what it was and I was so angry with him for not being there for me, I just said yes I wanted to know."

And despite being angry about Axel missing the appointment, I still felt a little guilty about going ahead with the question without asking him what he wanted to do.

Hope tucked her hair behind her ear and sighed. "Well, look. He's definitely a workaholic asshole, I'm totally with you on that one. But he loves you—you know he does. *I* know he does. Everything he's done for you so far has been amazing."

She had a point. The sex. The Vegas trip. The car. The phone calls. The jewelry. I lifted my hand and stared down at the vintage-style Tiffany ring on my hand and sighed. "Yeah, but if he isn't there for me when I need him, what's the point of being together?"

Hope put both hands up as though saying "stop." "Um, hang on a minute. You're considering breaking up with him?"

"Um, well..." Was I? *Maybe?* I was certainly angry enough to do so!

"Despite all the love, money, and sex? Just because he missed one appointment?"

I jumped to my feet and glared at her. "It's not about the appointment! It's about the fact that his company is always more important than me, and I can't have that be our lives. Is he going to miss the birth because work calls? Or the baby's first birthday? No!" I shook my head and pressed both hands to my belly, "No. We deserve to be loved, and for me, that means quality time."

"Then I think you need to talk to him," Hope said, standing

up and going over to her stash of candy and grabbing a bag of jellybeans. "Want some?"

I nodded and held out my hand. "Yeah, we do need to talk." But what would I say? *"Hey hon, how about you pull your head out of your ass and focus on what's important in life?"* My phone began to ring, and I picked it up, staring at the screen for too long. "It's him."

Rage filled me and I rejected the call with one push of the button. Then, for good measure, I blocked his number in the settings. "See how he likes it."

Hope laughed and I twisted around to stare at her. "What?"

"Um, no offense, but are you sure you're not overreacting? I mean... you're usually the nice one, always giving people a second chance."

I shook my head. "Not this time. I need some space to think." And work out what the hell I was going to do now.

"Well, I suppose you have six months," Hope said, stuffing more candy in her mouth.

I stared at Hope, absorbing her words. I did have six months. That was a long time. Longer than we'd even been together. "You're right. I'm going to have a shower. I feel totally dirty after those tests. I swear they're always shoving something in me or taking something out of me. It's gross. Then I'm going to eat and study. Gotta catch up where I've been falling behind."

And that's exactly what I did. I ate a late lunch, went to the library, and ignored all the good news I'd had today. And the bad. For the rest of the night, I just wanted to be a college student with nothing to worry about except exams.

I'd think about Axel in the morning. Maybe.

29

AXEL

When I got back to the office, I scrolled through my cell phone while I was got off the elevator and walked in the door. There it was, the evidence of what Chastity had been complaining about. Multiple voicemails she'd left for me, several missed calls, and lots of texts that I really didn't want to read.

"Shit." I went to walk down the hallway to my office but instead stopped, looking for advice since I was in foreign territory. I ran my hand through my hair, brushing it off my face and behind my ear. I needed a haircut. "Hey, Cheryl, I don't know if you know the answer, but is there a reason I wouldn't get these calls or notifications if I'm on the phone?"

I handed her my cell, and she took it. Her face was calm as she clicked and scrolled through. I wouldn't trust anyone else with such a personal object, but Cheryl had been with me since day one of my business. I owed her for part of its success. She ran the staff like the captain of a ship.

Cheryl glanced up at me after thirty seconds or so. "Can I walk you to your office, sir?"

Oh, it was that bad, was it? Another thing I appreciated about her was her tact. "Yes, of course."

I followed my bustling hen of a manager, who just looked at the staff that were loitering and they jumped back to work. When we got to my office, she opened the door and went inside.

I shook my head. *Uh-oh. She never comes inside.* I shut the door to my office and walked over to my desk. "What is it, Cheryl?"

"I..." She swallowed hard, tears in her eyes.

Now panic was setting in. "Seriously. What's wrong?"

She walked at me slowly, arms raised. I went on instinct and moved towards her too. Her arms went around me, and she hugged me tight. I closed my eyes and let her hug me, squeezing her back.

When she pulled away, I let her go quickly. Our very first hug in fifteen years. I was shocked. She pulled a tissue out of the box on my desk I kept there for clients and dabbed at her eyes.

Feeling slightly uncomfortable, but also surprisingly happy, I finally sat down in my chair and looked at her. "Are you going to explain?"

She nodded and straightened her spine, back in professional mode. "The hug was to say congratulations—you're going to be a father. I'm so proud of you, Axel. It's wonderful."

It was my turn to fight back the emotions. This woman was the closest thing to a maternal influence I had in my life. My own mother was little more than a stranger. And despite the fact I'd never acknowledged Cheryl's role in my life, her approval meant more than I could say. "Thank you, Cheryl. That means a lot."

She smiled for a moment, then stepped forward and sat down in the chair opposite me. "That said, what the hell happened today that you missed the twelve-week sonogram? You know how important that one is, don't you?"

I wasn't sure that I did, but from the look on Cheryl's face, I'd fucked up by missing it. "Ah... I know it's important."

Cheryl snorted. "But you don't know why. Okay. It's the scan that shows embryo viability. If Chastity had miscarried, or there was something wrong, this is the scan that would have told her, and she would have needed your support."

I shifted in my chair. "But nothing is wrong. Right?"

She ignored my question and kept plowing on. "And what the hell were you doing outside the hospital working while Chastity needed you?"

Well, that was easy to explain. "The doctor was running an hour late and Chastity told me to go outside and work for an hour."

"And did you?"

I frowned. "Did I what?"

"Go outside and work for an hour?"

Um... "I did go outside, but I lost track of time. I was juggling three phone calls and must have missed the time."

Cheryl pursed her lips and gave me a sour expression. "From the looks of those messages, you missed it by a long shot."

"Well, I..." *Didn't mean it. Not at all.*

And of all the people in the world, Cheryl should know that about me. I couldn't count the number of times she had to order dinner in for me or call me from her house to tell me to finish up and go home. Time flew by when I was busy.

She cut me off though, not allowing me to explain. "And to answer your original question, if you have two phone lines going on a cell phone, a third person can't get through. So, if you were juggling that many phone calls, poor Chastity had no hope of getting you. And as for the messages, you probably ignored all the notifications, because they would have buzzed like normal."

I glanced down, unable to look at Cheryl at the moment. I felt her disapproval radiating off her like lava.

"I was on the street, the traffic was loud, and—"

"Your excuses are not going to fly with that poor girl."

I flicked my gaze back up to Cheryl, who now sat cross-legged with her arms crossed in my chair. Yeah, she was mad.

"Poor girl?" I repeated. "I've given her an apartment, a car, a house! Trips, jewelry, insurance, and everything else I can think of to spoil her. So, I missed one appointment. *One!* How does that make me a bad person?"

Chastity was overreacting and Cheryl was too.

Cheryl stood up and put her hands on my desk, so she was staring straight at me. "Axel, you know I admire you. As a boss, you're the best. But there's a reason you've never kept a girlfriend around for more than a few months."

"Yeah, because none of them were the one."

"No. Because you're already married."

I blinked at her. "I'm what?"

She stood up again and gestured to the room around us. "You're married to this company. To your success. And I'm not sure you can have both."

I tidied up some papers on my desk that didn't need tidying and grabbed a fountain pen so my hands had something to do. "You're gonna have to speak a bit plainer, Cheryl. I'm feeling dumb today."

She clasped her hands together in front of her. "Axel."

Even the sound of my first name on her lips sounded weird. Up until ten minutes ago, she'd never used it before.

"This girl is the right one for you. I knew it the first time I met her. She is honest and down to earth, and if you sold everything tomorrow and ended up with next to nothing, she'd still want to be with you."

I swallowed hard. "How do you know?"

"Because I know women, and I can tell you've got a good one there. Better than I thought you'd ever find, to be honest."

I couldn't help but laugh at that one. "Really? You thought I'd end up married to... who?"

Cheryl flicked a piece of lint off her blazer. "Oh, well, a gold digger for sure. But the level of bitchiness and narcissism was still up for debate."

My jaw dropped open. "Wow. I didn't know you thought so little of me."

She actually rolled her eyes this time. "I think very highly of you. But as a wealthy man who envelopes himself in luxury, you were always surrounded by women attracted to you *for your wealth*." She tilted her head suddenly. "Where did you meet little Miss Sunshine, anyway?"

I smiled at the new nickname. It suited Chastity down to a 't'. "At the health club, actually. She was waiting in the foyer having a hot chocolate and I was just leaving."

Cheryl's eyes lit up with entertainment. "That kind of makes sense. She wouldn't have known how wealthy you were, and you would have seen a beautiful young woman who didn't fit in at your club. And that piqued your interest." She nodded once as though her curiosity had been satisfied.

I pinched the bridge of my nose. "Okay... so, can I get back to work now?" Back to the one thing in my life that made sense.

Cheryl stared at me like I was stupid, her eyebrows jumping up her forehead. "Have you got a plan for getting her back?"

"What do you mean, getting her back?" I hadn't lost her.

Cheryl sighed and turned to walk out the door. "Okay, but don't come crying to me when she breaks up with you."

I threw my hands up in the air and groaned loudly. "Fine! Come back."

She sauntered back to the chair and sat down.

Okay, I'd play the game. I took a deep breath and forced myself to stay calm. "Why do you think she's going to break up with me?" No one else had ever broken up with me, ever. "I mean..."

Cheryl stared at me with wide eyes again. "You haven't read any of your messages, have you?"

"I didn't see them." And had been avoiding looking.

"Well, I think you'll find that she's pretty furious, and with all her pregnancy hormones, she'll be jumping to the worst-case scenario."

I groaned. "I knew her hormones were making her overreact."

Cheryl pressed her lips into a thin line. "Please tell me you didn't say anything to her."

"Uh..."

Cheryl shook her head. "You are such a man sometimes."

"I don't see how that's an insult." Although it sure as hell sounded like one.

"I'm going to move along because I've got a list a mile long today." She clapped her hands together and looked me in the eye. "Do you want this girl?"

I didn't like being treated like a child, and it pushed up against my pride. But I chomped down on my ego and said, "Yes. Of course, I do."

"Then apologize until you're sick of apologizing, then start sending flowers."

That sounded tedious but doable. "You think she's that mad?"

"Have you called her yet?"

I nodded. "I did in the car, but I think her phone's switched off." Which was the only reason my calls would go straight to voicemail.

Cheryl stood up. "Or she's blocked you. So, in that case, start apologizing, don't stop apologizing, and I'll call the talent recruiter today."

She walked towards the door and has got as far as opening it before I called out. "Hang on. What talent recruiter?"

She twisted to look at me, already half out the door. "You know the only way you're getting Chastity back is if you prove that you can be a good partner, and a good father—and that means working less."

It didn't sound like a question, but I nodded, nonetheless.

"Then I'm getting you some managers. It's time you stepped back, Axel, and let the twenty-five-year-olds take over. You were a hot head back then, and I'll find you another just like it. Three, if I have to."

I opened my mouth to respond, then slammed it shut again. "Thank you, Cheryl."

"You're welcome, Mr. Patterson," she said, assuming her assistant role once more. "You deserve to have a life. You've worked hard enough to be where you are. Time to enjoy more time outside of these four walls."

I nodded. "You're right. Thanks."

Cheryl left and I was filled with the intense need to get in my car and find Chastity. Track her down at school and beg her to come back. I'd pay for another sonogram, and we could re-do the day properly.

But I didn't. I swiveled around in my chair and stared out the window, my office allowing me a one-hundred-and-eighty-degree view of the city and the buildings surrounding me.

Cheryl was right. I could apologize, yes, but the only way of actually showing Chastity that I intended to change my life was to truly change it. I'd told her that I wished to work forty hours a week, but did I really want to pull it back that much?

Maybe I could start taking weekends off unless there was an emergency or a deadline. That would change a lot of my lifestyle.

"Argh... I don't know." I lay back in my chair and sighed. This wasn't how it was supposed to be. And the worst part was, I wanted to call Patrick and tell him. He'd give me good advice and lament on how different women and men could be. But I couldn't do anything more than call him for a run.

Oh, yeah, I definitely wanted a run. But first, I turned the chair back around and picked up my phone. I listened to the two voicemails Chastity had left and read the messages she sent.

Her calls were frantic and became increasingly angry. Her texts were the same. And beneath it all was an overwhelming disappointment that choked me. She really needed me today. Was the multi-million-dollar deal that I'd saved with an hour's worth of phone calls worth it? Probably was, since it was her future I was building too.

I had to tell her. I had to explain. But how did I do that when she was so angry? I'd do what Cheryl suggested. Apologize for disappointing her, then start working towards my goal of reducing my hours, as soon as I worked out what that goal was. How far could I step back before the deck of cards collapsed?

30

CHASTITY

I hated to admit it, but at first I'd loved ignoring Axel. I blocked him on my phone, so I didn't get any phone calls or texts, and it was bliss. I got a ton of work done and stood on the moral high ground long enough to feel too content in my heightened level of happiness.

That feeling lasted about twenty-four hours. Then I started to miss him. Like, really miss him. Which sucked, because he was in the wrong, and I should be mad at him for a hell of a lot longer than one day.

But the doubt had started to creep in, and the guilt at how I'd acted. After all, I'd been the one to send him outside. I should have told him to stay, made him hold my hand through the blood tests. Maybe communicated better how much I actually needed him.

I shook my head to try and clear the thoughts from my mind. I couldn't study while my brain whirled, and second-guessing myself in regard to Axel was absolutely doing my head in.

It was Friday night, another week done, another step closer to graduation.

"You hanging around here for the weekend?" Hope asked from her side of the room as she packed her bags for a rare trip home to see her parents for the weekend.

"Yeah. I don't have any plans." And I was feeling so much better now. A lot of my fatigue and sickness had gone. Not completely, but it was better enough that I could actually catch up on the studying I'd been missing out on.

"Axel still hasn't called?" she asked.

I grinned at her. "I still have him blocked, so I have no idea."

"If his calls are blocked, he can still leave voicemails."

I'd never blocked anyone before, so I didn't know the rules exactly. When I unblocked him eventually, would a flood of messages come rushing into my phone?

I inhaled deeply through my nose and rolled onto my side on my bed to face Hope. "Yeah. There's a few on there. I've been avoiding listening to them."

Hope laughed while zipping up her suitcase. "Why would you do that?"

"Because I know he'll be saying he's sorry, and I'm not ready to hear it." I sat up and reached for my cell, staring down at its blank screen. I didn't want to admit to Hope or anyone else that I missed seeing his missed calls and messages there.

"Well, I'm off. But if you need me, I'm only a couple of hours away."

I smiled at her. We'd become closer than ever in the last few days. "I know. And thanks."

I'd considered going to see my parents this weekend, but since I didn't know what I was going to tell them, I just gave them my normal excuse about needing to study. I hadn't seen them for a few months, and although I was keenly aware of it, my parents didn't seem to have noticed the lack of visits.

There was a knock on the door and Hope walked over to open it.

"A delivery for Chastity," an unfamiliar male voice said from behind the door.

"Thank you," Hope said, then turned around with a massive bunch of roses in her arms and an insane grin on her face. "Look who got flowers."

I rolled my eyes. "What a typical thing to do." But I couldn't stop myself from sitting up on the bed and reaching for them. "Is there a card?"

"Yeah, on top."

The flowers weren't just flowers. They were perfect, long stemmed, red roses. My favorites. "Thanks." I took the vase and stared down at the roses for a moment, absorbing their perfection before I set them down on my nightstand and reached for the card.

It was a hand-written card. "Interesting. It actually looks like he wrote this himself." This wasn't typed card done by the lady at the florist, but then again it could have been written by Cheryl for all I knew. I didn't actually know what his writing looked like.

I stared at the card and read it aloud. "Dear sweetheart, I am so sorry I disappointed you. I will make it up to you. Love, Axel."

I sighed as my chest squeezed tight, my heart cracking open a little. "How does he think he can make it up to me? It's impossible." Tears that I'd been fighting all week swam into my eyes and I blinked angrily, rubbing them away. "No. I'm not going to cry. I promised myself I wouldn't."

I was going to be strong, for me and my little girl.

"Are you okay?" Hope asked, hovering around my bed.

"Oh, yeah, of course. You go. See you on Sunday night."

Hope reached down and hugged me quickly. "Call me if you need someone to talk to."

I hiccupped up a laugh. "I might need to, since you're the only one that knows about everything."

I hadn't dared to tell my mom or dad about the fallout

between Axel and me, which sucked. I needed advice and someone to vent to, and yet the two people I trusted most in this world didn't know about my pregnancy and didn't want me to be with Axel.

They'd tell me to break up with him or get rid of the baby, or a hundred wrong things I didn't want to hear. So, help wasn't going to be found in that corner.

I waved to Hope as she left and focused on the card. He was going to make it up to me, was he? Did he have a time machine?

I fell back onto the bed and sighed, still clinging to the card. Maybe I should listen to his voicemails? Or unblock him? I didn't have to answer, but at least I could see what he was messaging me.

That sounded sensible enough, so I reached for my cell phone and unblocked him. There wasn't a flood of texts or anything that came in, so I had to assume that if he'd sent anything, it was now lost in the ether.

I pushed my phone away and closed my eyes. This wasn't fair. It wasn't meant to be like this.

Get up. Stop being so pathetic.

I forced myself to stand up and stretch. It was time to get some dinner, and maybe have an early night. I hadn't been sleeping very well despite being totally exhausted.

I did exactly as I'd planned, and fell fast asleep before ten pm, the aroma of my roses filling my nose and giving me sweet dreams.

THE NEXT DAY I woke up to a text on my phone.

I'm not sure if you're getting these messages but I wanted you to know how much I miss you. Your voice. Your kisses. Everything.

I clapped a hand over my mouth to stop the sob from rising.

He wasn't playing fair sending messages like that. I missed him too much to even think about the fact that he missed me too. But what was the point of a relationship if I didn't trust him and couldn't count on him?

I thrust my cell phone away and went and took a shower, marveling at how much better I was feeling. I put my hand down on my belly, noticing the slight swell going on. "Good morning, baby."

Happiness filled me to the brim. A baby with Axel's gorgeous eyes, fitness and brains would be a handful. I'd be super busy when he or she was older, that was for certain.

I sighed, got out of the shower, dried myself and got dressed.

A wave of nausea flowed over me, but this time it felt more like hunger than anything else. "Hmmm... breakfast today."

I hadn't eaten a proper breakfast in months, so this would be interesting.

I managed a piece of toast and some apple juice. A win for me.

Then I went back to my room to study rather than the library. I wanted to stare at my roses a little longer.

When there was a knock at the dorm room door, I jumped. "Come in," I called out, though my heart had begun to pound like I was running a marathon. Was it him?

"Hi, sweetie!" my mom called out as she stuck her head around the door.

"Mom!" I cried, jumping to my feet and racing for her.

She wrapped her arms around me, laughing as she hugged me tightly.

I couldn't let go of her once I had my arms around her. The tears rose and I sobbed, burying my head in her neck.

"Hey, hey, hey. What's going on?" Mom asked me, brushing back my hair off my face.

"I'm just so glad to see you," I sobbed, rushing for the tissue box to mop up the tears on my face and blow my nose.

"Oh, sweetie, I'm so sorry it's been so long."

Mom walked across the room and sat down on my bed. Then she grabbed my hand and tugged on me to sit down. "Come. Sit."

I blew my nose, tossed the tissue in the wastebasket beside my bed then grabbed another tissue in case I needed it. "What are you doing here?" I asked her. "Not that I'm not glad to see you. I am, obviously, but I wasn't expecting you."

Though I had the apartment to use if Mom wanted to stay overnight, which would be great.

"I know you weren't, but I just woke up this morning and felt like I had to come and see you. So, I grabbed a takeout coffee, and here I am."

I smiled at my mother, her instincts insanely on point. "Are you going to stay until tomorrow? We can go sleep at Axel's apartment tonight if you want. It's got three bedrooms."

Mom's cheeks colored as she blushed bright red. "Um... thanks, sweetie, but I have a date tonight, actually. Dinner at eight. I can stay most of the day, but should try to head off around four, so I've got time to get ready."

My jaw dropped open. "Really, Mom? Wow! That's great."

'You think so?" she asked, her tone so hopeful it broke my heart.

"Yes! Of course! You deserve to be happy." And she was so young still. Barely forty-three. She still had forty to fifty years of life ahead of her, And I wanted her to find someone to spend those years with.

"Who is it?" I asked. "Where'd you meet him?"

"Oh... well, maybe I should take you to brunch and tell you," She stood abruptly.

That didn't sound very good. "I just had breakfast, Mom." And there was no way I could eat any more without worrying about my morning sickness. "You can tell me. Hope's gone for the weekend, so you can relax."

But my mother was doing the complete opposite of relaxing. She was wringing her hands and pacing back and forth across my room.

I slid to the edge of my bed and narrowed my eyes at her. "Why are you acting so strangely, Mom?"

She ran her hands through her hair, looking the very picture of worried. "I came all this way to tell you the truth, but now that I'm here, I'm terrified."

I pushed myself up to my feet. "What is it, Mom? Quick, tell me before I think it's something terrible, or you're dating someone younger than me or something."

That would serve me right, wouldn't it? After all, Axel was the same age as my parents. Would it be the same if my mom was dating a twenty-year-old guy? I wasn't sure I could deal with it.

Mom stopped and twisted around to look at me. "It's your dad," she all but squeaked.

I crossed my arms over my breasts and leaned forward. I mustn't have heard her properly. "Uh... come again?"

"It's Patrick. We uh... went out for coffee a few months ago, just to, you know... talk about you. And it was nice. We had a good time. So, we had dinner, and another dinner. And then—"

I raised both hands into the air and pushed them out at her as though to say stop. "Hang on a second. Let me get this straight. You're dating my father? After twenty years of being broken up, you two are together again?"

She nodded quickly, jerking her head up and down in too fast movement. "And there's something else."

She looked terrified now. Her face was pale and there were tears in her eyes.

I rushed over to her and took her hands in mine, totally blown away but wanting to push those feelings aside to help my mother through whatever this was. "What is it, Mom? Did you find him with someone else?"

She shook her head animatedly. "Oh, no, it's nothing like that."

I squeezed her hands. "Tell me. It's okay. I'll help you if I can."

She laughed and rolled her eyes heavenward, blinking quickly as if to stop the tears from flowing. It was a move I knew well. "No, it's not like that, I just..." She stopped again, and it was my turn to sigh.

What on earth could it be?

31

CHASTITY

I stared at my mom, waiting impatiently for her to tell me whatever she'd come to say. When she didn't start speaking, I moved my hand in a circular motion to tell her to get a move on and groaned in impatience. "Go on, Mom, I'm dying here. So, you and Dad are dating again. That's good, right?"

She seemed happy about it. I was still processing it myself. They'd always been at odds, about pretty much *everything.* And I could feel an undercurrent of annoyance at the fact that they'd decided to make it work when I finally didn't need them to. It would have been nice for them to have sorted this out twenty years ago, but still. *Stop being so selfish.*

Mom nodded, then bit her lip, still not speaking. She was obviously stressed so it had to be something totally crazy.

An idea occurred to me, and I grinned at her. "You two aren't getting married again?" I laughed. "Because that would be kind of weird."

They'd gotten married when Mom was four months pregnant with me and were divorced before I was even two years old. I wasn't sure how I felt about the idea of either of them marrying again, let alone marrying each other. *Weird* didn't even begin to cover it.

Mom gave a nervous giggle. "No, it's not that. Oh my God, I wish it was that."

It was worse than them getting married. "Now you have to tell me. Spill!"

Mom tugged her hands out of mine and walked a few feet away, then twisted around to look at me. "I'm pregnant."

"You're... what?" I whispered. *No.* "You can't be." It was impossible, she was old! And I was... no, no, no.

"I know, right?" my mother said, pressing her hands to her belly in a protective gesture I knew too well. "It's crazy, but I am." She was grinning like a loon, like she was happy about it!

"How far along are you?" I whispered, wrapping my arms around my waist. *Oh God. Oh God. Oh God.*

"Only about nine weeks, but I had to tell you!" Mom exclaimed, her face lighting up like she was announcing that money was falling from the clouds instead of rain. "Even though I know it's a little early to get my hopes up. I've been feeling so sick, and my doctor said my hormone levels are good." Then she bit her lip and stared at me, worry clear in her eyes. "Are you really upset?"

"Well... uh..." I had no idea what to say. "I think I need to sit down." I staggered back toward my bed and sat down on the mattress once more. "Shit... uh..."

"I know what you're thinking," she said, beginning to pace once more.

I doubt that very much. There was no way my mom knew I was thinking about the Father of the Bride: Part 2 plot we were re-enacting. My mom couldn't be pregnant at the same time as me. She couldn't.

"You're thinking I'm way too old to be doing this," she said, throwing her hands around in that flamboyant, animated way she had. "I had to stop drinking, which was not fun, I can tell you. And going back to the start, when I'd just finished raising you. It's crazy. I know, I'm crazy."

You definitely are.

Mom practically bounced across the room and jumped onto the bed with me. "But I've always wanted you to have a baby brother or sister."

"Oh, well—"

"And I know you won't be around the same way you would have been when you were little, but I hope you'd still want to be a part of this baby's life. Because I want it, Chastity, I really do. And your dad—"

I jumped in, interrupting her for once. "How does he feel about it?"

"I only told him a few days ago. He's..." Mom shook her head but was smiling at the same time. "He's really happy, actually. Worried about me, but he can't wait. We both can't. This time will be different."

Famous last words. I pushed the tornado of feelings down and focused on my mother. "What are you two gonna do? Move in together?"

What would they do? They both owned their places, but I wasn't sure who'd relinquish their home first. *Dad, maybe?* Mom's house would probably be better for the baby. More space.

"I think we will, probably," she answered, sounding uncertain. "We haven't decided how or where, but we've got time. Seven months, give or take."

Seven months. She had seven months to plan her future, and I had six months to plan mine. The avalanche of emotions that I'd been pushing down began to leak out between the cracks. Tears blurred my vision and pain crushed my chest until I couldn't breathe.

"Oh, no. You're really upset! I'm so sorry, my darling girl." Mom hauled me in for a massive hug.

I tried to hold back, but I couldn't. Three days of holding it all in and I couldn't stop the tears any longer. I curled into my mom and cried hard.

"I'm so sorry," she kept repeating.

I was too overwhelmed to tell her it wasn't her fault. So, I just let the emotions flow, crying and sobbing and clinging to my mom until the storm had subsided. When I finally pulled away, I grabbed for my tissue box, grateful there were a few left so I could mop up the mess on my face. "Don't go anywhere," I told her, though my throat sounded rusty, and the words cracked. "I need to wash my face."

I raced to the ensuite and splashed some cold water on my cheeks and around my eyes. I looked horrible now, red, blotchy and terrible. But I had to get back in there. Mom needed to know that I wasn't crying because she was pregnant. I probably would have cried with her here, anyway. Her timing in lots of ways was kind of perfect. I needed to talk to her.

So, once I felt a little more human, I straightened up and patted my face dry, then took some deep, calming breaths. I couldn't hide my news now, not anymore. She deserved to know the truth.

"I'm so sorry, Mom," I told her as I walked back into the room, grabbed my swivel chair from my desk and sat on it. "That wasn't about you. I have a lot going on at the moment, and I think your news was just the straw that broke the camel's back. So, thank you for letting me cry. I needed it." I took another slow breath, feeling the emotion rise within me once more. *Shit*, I wasn't going to get through this conversation without crying again.

"So, you're not upset?" she asked, her tone hopeful.

"No... not at all. I'm, surprised, of course. But if you're happy, Mom, how can I be anything but happy for you?"

"Oh, thank you, sweetheart!" Mom jumped up and moved to hug me again.

I put my hands up to stop her. "Wait, don't hug me just yet."

Mom stopped, midway, arms outstretched, and recoiled back to sit on the bed once again. "Well, okay. How come?"

"Because I have news for you too, and you might not be happy with me, so let's try and keep all the hugs for the end." Hopefully there would be hugs at the end. I had a terrible feeling there wouldn't be.

"What's happened?" she asked, her eyes wide and wary now.

I stood up and wandered over to the roses by my bed. "Well, shit... I'm not even sure where to begin. Let's start with the shit news. Axel and I had a fight." I wasn't looking at her. I couldn't, so I just stared into the endless perfection of his gift.

"Have you two broken up?"

I shook my head and spun around to look at her. "No, I don't think so. He keeps messaging to apologize, and he sent flowers. But I'm not ready to talk to him yet."

"What happened? Did he cheat on you?"

I gaped at her. "Oh my God, no! Why would you think that?"

"Oh, sorry. It's just Patrick said that Axel's always been kind of a player, and with you two doing the long-distance thing, I sort of assumed..."

I leaned back against the wall behind me and crossed my arms over my chest. "You assumed that because you don't know him, Mom. He wouldn't cheat on me. He's got more integrity than that." If he wanted another woman, he'd just tell me. He wasn't the sort of man to lie and sneak around. I would put money on it.

"Is that the ring he got you?" Mom asked, pointing to my hand.

I put my arm out and wiggled my fingers to show her. "Yeah, that's it."

Mom took my hand and stared down at the rose gold creation nestled around my ring finger on my right hand.

She didn't say anything, so I explained, "He called it a promise ring."

Mom nodded. "Yes. That's beautiful, Chastity."

I could see she was totally overwhelmed by the size of the ring and chose to ignore her discomfort. I didn't want her to make some comment about his money that I couldn't cope with right now.

"So, what happened?" Mom asked.

I sighed. "Basically, I wanted him to go with me somewhere important, he missed it because of work, and I'm mad at him for prioritizing his company over me."

Mom screwed up her face as though she wasn't impressed with my answer. "That's a bit unfair, Chastity."

Uh... excuse me? "You don't even know what he missed."

She narrowed her gaze at me. "You didn't tell me. But from what you've said so far, Axel works his ass off, buys you expensive gifts and trips, and calls every night and would never cheat on you. All in all, a perfect guy."

"But—"

"His success hasn't come from sitting around doing nothing all day, Chastity."

I rolled my eyes. "I know that, Mom."

"Would you prefer him to be unemployed? Or a student like you?"

"Yes, I think I would prefer it if he was a student," I told her, being a smart-ass out of spite.

Mom stood up and glared at me. "Then you need to break up with him, and go find yourself a nice, dumb, twenty-year-old. Because when you date someone twice your age, they have responsibilities you don't understand, Chastity."

"That's a bit much, Mom." How was she taking his side in this? She didn't even like him!

"You've never paid your own bills, sweetheart. So please don't tell me you know what it's like in the real world, because you don't."

I dropped my gaze, my cheeks burning with shame. "Gee, thanks."

"Look, sweetie, you know I'm not a real Axel fan. I think he's too old for you. But I don't think being mad at him because he missed a date or whatever due to work is a good enough reason to break up. If he was playing golf or drinking with his friends, that's a different story."

I wiped at the tears that had fallen from my eyes. "No. He was working."

She shrugged. "Then you're gonna have to choose. Do you want Axel, with all his workaholic tendencies? And the money that comes with it, I might add. Rings like that don't grow on trees. Or do you want a guy your age, who doesn't come with any of the money but none of the responsibilities, either. Because people don't change, Chastity."

I slammed my mouth shut and bit my tongue, figuratively, not literally. I personally thought people could change, and my mom telling me to just get over it wasn't good enough.

She suddenly put a hand to her belly and staggered sideways a little. "Whoa, head rush. I think I need something to eat."

"Hang on. I've got something." I rushed to my nightstand and grabbed out my emergency supply of dry crackers and a bottle of water. I handed both to my mom, and she took them, munching on a cracker right away.

"Thanks," she said, sighing heavily. "You never made me this sick."

"So, you think it might be a boy this time?" I asked, pushing the conversation away from Axel and me for a minute.

"I don't know," Mom said. "But we'll find out soon enough. Because of my age, they're giving me every test under the sun."

"I can imagine." I glanced down at the ground. I knew a lot more about pregnancies than she was aware. How was I going to tell my mom that we were going to have babies at the same time? I'd been worried that she wouldn't approve of me being so young or of Axel being the father, or me putting off chiropractic school, but this... wow, this was a whole new level of crazy.

Mom walked over to my headboard and stared down into my drawer. Then she scooped something up, more food I assumed, and turned around with a strange look on her face. "Chastity, what's this?"

I froze. There was my mother holding up the sonogram of her grandchild.

32

CHASTITY

"Uh..." *Oh shit.* That was not the way I'd planned for my mother to find out about her grandchild.

"Chastity," my mother repeated, her voice harsh and clipped. "Is this yours?"

I nodded. "Yes. It's from the sonogram I had on Wednesday that Axel missed. That's why I'm still mad at him."

My mom groaned and threw the picture on the bed, placing one hand on her hip. "Well, shit, Chastity. This wasn't supposed to happen."

I gasped at her tone, so stark and harsh, almost cruel. And the way she'd disregarded the sonogram was just nasty. I'm sure she wouldn't have done such a thing to photos of her own baby.

Mom *tsked* again, shaking her head in disapproval like she used to when I was a child, and she was scolding me. Like I'd come home late or failed a test.

I couldn't do anything but stop and stare at her. Her mouth was pinched like she'd sucked on a lemon, and it was obvious she was mad as hell.

Any other time I would have been falling over myself to apologize and fix whatever was wrong. I couldn't stand it when my mom was mad at me. But today, after everything she'd just revealed to me, all I could do was think about how different her reaction to my pregnancy was in comparison to how I'd reacted to hers.

I bit my lip and tilted my head to the side. "Um... Hang on a minute, Mom. I don't think you're being very fair here."

"Fair?" Mom repeated, gaping at me. "You've known this guy, what? Four months? Five, maybe? And you haven't even graduated yet, let alone—" She gasped loudly. "Chiropractic school." She slapped herself in the forehead with her palm, making a loud *thwacking* noise for effect. "You're going to have to defer. Oh, fucking hell, Chastity. This will really screw up your future if you go ahead with it."

"Go ahead with it?" I repeated, glaring at her. "I'm more than twelve weeks and my baby is healthy. I'm healthy! Why the hell would I choose not to continue with it?"

Mom put both hands on her hips. "Because it will ruin your future! Don't you see? You're just repeating my mistakes."

"Your mistakes?" I threw my hands up in the air. "Why am I always referred to as your mistake?"

I'd heard it since before I could remember. The guilt trips about everything she'd missed out on. And when I got to my teenage years, Mom would torment me with stories of how she got pregnant and all the reasons why teenagers having sex was a bad idea.

She was the real reason I'd still been a virgin at twenty-one. She'd terrified me from childhood. And despite all that, I was now in the exact position she'd always said she didn't want for me. Her position—her life. But I had one key difference. Axel.

Mom's eyes dimmed as she realized what she'd said and how I'd taken it. "I didn't mean it like that," she defended.

My temper exploded. "Oh, yes you did!" I bellowed at her,

walking across to the other side of the room so I could put some distance between us. "You always fall back on that excuse. Blaming me because you didn't finish college, and have struggled with your life. But it wasn't my fault that you got pregnant so early."

"I know that."

"And it wasn't my fault that you made Dad drop out of college to take care of you. That you two broke up."

She crossed her arms over her chest and pouted. "I know that too. But—"

"But nothing, Mom. This is different. I love Axel and he can take care of me financially, which is something you never had. I'll graduate from college even though I'll be twenty-five weeks pregnant. And if I never go on to the next level, then so be it. Axel said I never have to work again if I don't want to, and that's certainly not the life that you ever had." I clenched my hands into fists at my sides, hot anger pouring through me.

"Chastity," Mom said, her eyebrows lowering into an angry frown. "You need to really think about this. A baby will tie you to Axel for the rest of your life. You don't know him well enough for that, and you're too young to realize what you're throwing away by having a baby this early."

"What are you talking about?" I screamed at her. "I know exactly what I'll be missing out on, because you've reminded me of it every day of my life. You didn't get to travel or graduate. Remarry. Well, I'm not going to have any of those problems because Axel is rich. And he'll make sure we travel and enjoy the world. My life will be different than yours, and I can't believe you can't see it."

She didn't want to see it, I knew that. My mother was jealous as hell that I'd found such a wealthy boyfriend, for my first relationship. She probably wanted me to struggle along like she did.

She said she wanted better for me, but I wasn't sure she really did.

"You're the one that can't see it," Mom hissed at me like a snake. "You're a baby yourself. You can't look after a child. You can't even cope with Axel missing one appointment because he was off making more money. You two will never make it and then you'll be stuck with a baby all by yourself." She had that super smug look on her face that I hated. She always thought she knew better, and in this case, she couldn't be more wrong.

I took a breath, my anger exploding. "You came here to tell me you have a completely unplanned pregnancy at the age of forty-three, with your ex-husband whom you've barely spoken to in twenty years, and you have the gall to tell me it'll never work?"

Who the hell was she kidding? Was my dad kidding? They were never going to last. They didn't last time, and what had changed in twenty years? Nothing.

"Chastity," Mom said, turning her head slightly, giving me the side eye.

"No." I stomped to my bedroom door. She was not in the right here and I would not be talked down to today. Not over this. "You need to leave. But thank you for doing the one thing I needed you to do—put my relationship with Axel into perspective."

Mom rushed over to me and grabbed my hands, but I shook her off. "You need to leave."

"But—"

"No buts. It's pretty obvious who needs a reality check around here, Mom. I have always supported you with whatever you needed to be happy. And today, when you needed me to support your life and your choices, I did. But you find out the exact same thing about me, that I'm pregnant to a man I love, and you fly off the handle and want me to get rid of it?"

Her bottom lip quivered a little. "That's not what I said."

No, she couldn't have said exactly that, could she? But I knew exactly what she'd been thinking, and it made me sick. "Well, you said enough," I said to her. "Thanks for nothing."

Mom opened her mouth to argue again, and I groaned. "Fine. I'll leave then. Because I'm not hanging around here, waiting for you to go." She could drag this out for hours. According to my father, she'd been the queen of drama. I'd never really seen her in full flight, and I didn't intend to.

I stomped over to my cell phone, grabbed it, and ran out of the room. Then I dropped to a jog but kept moving down the hallway and out into the fresh air. "Gahhh!" I screamed out. *Shit*, I didn't grab my keys, which meant that I was stuck on campus. It would have been great to be able to jump in the car and just go. Put some distance between my mom and me.

I shook myself. No matter. There were a lot of places I could hide where she couldn't find me. I twisted on the ball of my feet and marched off in the direction of the library cafe. I needed a coffee. Oops. Shit. I couldn't. No caffeine for me. So, I just kept walking and stomping my feet until I found myself running out of steam.

Then a thought occurred to me. Who was the first person Mom was going call and bitch about me to? "Oh, shit. Dad!"

I didn't want my mom telling him about my pregnancy before I did. We'd always had a deal, Dad and me. That I wouldn't let him be blindsided by Mom about anything related to me. I'd had to text him under the cover of darkness multiple times just to give him a heads up on something she had planned.

And despite their relationship changing, I still felt like I needed to be the one to tell him if she hadn't done so already. I took out my cell and pushed the button to call him. Three rings in and with my stomach in knots, he picked up.

"Hey, Chastity! Long time, no talk."

Oh, good, she hasn't got to him yet. "Hey, Dad! I need to talk to you for a minute, can you spare the time?"

He grunted as though getting up from his chair. "Ah yeah, give me a minute. I'm just going to walk somewhere quiet."

I waited, impatiently tapping my foot against the concrete and looking around. I half expected my mom to just jump out of nowhere and sabotage the phone call. Where would she be, anyway?

"Okay. What's up?"

Which one should I start with? His news or mine? "Uh, Mom visited me this morning and gave me your good news."

Dad was silent for a minute then he said, "I didn't know she was going to see you, otherwise I would have come too."

"It's okay, Dad. I know you always try and do the right thing. That's why I'm calling you. I'm happy for you and Mom, I really am. You both deserve a second chance to be happy, and if this is it, then I couldn't be happier for the both of you."

"Thanks, Chastity. I wanted to tell you, but it seemed too early to say anything."

I nodded, tears welling in my eyes. "That's how I've been feeling lately too."

"What do you mean?"

"I have news for you as well. I thought it was too early to say anything up until this week, then I chickened out on telling you. But Mom knows now that she surprised me on campus, and she's angry at me, so I have to tell you now." *Even if you get angry at me too.*

"What is it?" he asked. "Are you okay?"

I laughed, swallowing the tears in my throat. "Um, not really. But that's just because Mom and I had a fight. Overall, yeah, I'm good." Except for the argument with Axel, but I was very quickly putting that in perspective. Funny how a fight with my mother could make me realize I was being too harsh with Axel.

"Well, tell me," Dad urged.

I took a deep breath. *Shit.* I was going to have to call Axel and let him know that both my parents knew. After all, my father was practically in shooting distance of Axel in the city.

"I'm pregnant too," I said quickly. "Over twelve weeks. I had my scan on Wednesday, and everything is good. I've been wanting to tell you guys but didn't know how to say it because I knew you'd be disappointed in me. But I'm going to graduate, and Axel is going to take care of us. So, you don't have to worry about anything."

I finished the words all in a rush, and despite the fact Axel and I hadn't worked out our issues, I knew he'd look after us financially no matter what. He'd already given me a house, for cripes sake!

"Wow... I don't know what to say."

My heart sank and I staggered over to a park bench. "You can ask me how I'm feeling or what Axel thinks. Anything, Dad." *Just please don't tell me I'm throwing my life away.* I didn't think I could handle going through that conversation with both of my parents on the same day.

"I don't know what to say," he said again, in the same bewildered, shocked tone.

I blinked and hot tears coursed down my cheeks.

"Okay, Dad. Bye."

"Chastity, wait—"

I hung up on him, my heart breaking. I'd known my parents weren't going to take this news well, but a small part of me had hoped—*really hoped*—I was wrong. That they'd be happy for me, or at least ask if I was happy. Surely that was important. Wasn't it?

Dad tried to call back, but I just let it go to voicemail. I needed to call Axel now and let him know that both of my parents might be coming to berate him. My mom would have trouble with a two-hour drive ahead of her, but Dad, well, his work wasn't far from Axel's.

I picked up my cell phone, tears blurring my vision. I couldn't call him because I'd just burst into tears, and no one wanted that. Instead, I sent him my first text in three days.

Hey. Thank you for the roses. They're beautiful. We need to talk, but I can't at the moment. Sorry. Just told my parents about the baby and they were as supportive as anticipated. Just warning you. Talk soon. xox.

The air shuddered in my chest as I tried to breathe. How had this day turned this badly so quickly?

My phone began to ring, and I stared down at the screen. Axel was trying to call me, but I'd just told him I couldn't talk. And I *really couldn't*. My throat felt swollen and sore.

I closed my eyes and shook my head. No. I couldn't talk to him. Not now. I was going to walk back to my room and go back to bed. Maybe if I woke up a second time all of this would just go away.

33

AXEL

I stared down at my cell phone. She'd rejected my call. Again. I shouldn't be surprised, but I was. I sighed loudly and pushed it across my desk. I was a bit tired of the games, but what could I do? I was in the wrong this time and had to suck it up and wait for her to come to me.

My office phone rang, and I picked it up. It was a Saturday, so I was only doing a half day.

"Yes?"

"Mr. Patterson, I have my lead candidate here to meet you."

"Send him in, Cheryl."

My office manager didn't work Saturdays much anymore, but she'd sworn not to stop working until we'd found a team of managers for me to start to train. I wasn't ready to step down or slow down drastically, but Cheryl had convinced me that it was necessary for the benefit of the company and my relationship.

And I was sure once I was able to enjoy my weekends again, and slotted in a vacation or two, I might welcome the pull back. But for the minute, the fact I was being forced to change my work habits ate at me like a stomach ulcer.

The door opened and a woman walked in. First surprise. Not that I should be surprised by anything Cheryl did nowadays, she was a wonder, but I hadn't expected a female.

I stood up and walked around my desk to shake her hand. "Axel Patterson."

She shook my hand, meeting my gaze head on. "I'm Taylor. Taylor Maze."

"Nice to meet you, Miss Maze. Please take a seat."

She moved over to the chair opposite my desk and sat down, crossing her legs and placing her small black bag on the floor next to her chair.

"Please, call me Taylor."

"Then you can call me Axel. We're not very formal around here. Well, except for Cheryl, of course."

Taylor's eyes lit up as I mentioned Cheryl. "She's wonderful. You're really lucky to have such a brilliant office manager."

"Yes, I am."

Okay, so the girl before me obviously had the credentials I needed, or her resume wouldn't have made it past the first round of Cheryl's inspection. Now, I knew that Cheryl liked her, and the sentiment was mutual. That was rare, because Cheryl was tough. And she looked through you to your soul and judged you on it. Which was why I trusted her, and why it made me happy that she liked Chastity.

"So, Taylor, tell me why you want to work sixty-to-eighty-hour weeks."

The money was always the allure for people, but that didn't mean they had the drive to do the job and be successful.

She smiled at me. "Because that's what you need to do to succeed. To buy a home in this city."

She was right, but I wanted a more in-depth answer. "True. So, may I be frank?" I was starting to feel like this interview was redundant. She was a young, enthusiastic, qualified woman.

Giving her a go at the job seemed like the right thing to do, and she couldn't do any worse than the last idiot I'd hired.

"Of course," she said, and sat poised, waiting for me.

I took a deep breath, getting ready to be more honest with a stranger than I was prepared to be with my own parents. "The reason I'm slowing down, or at least trying to get more help around here at the executive level—" at my level, "—is because I've finally met a woman I want to spend my nights and weekends with. Go on vacation with. I've been working non-stop for two decades, and it's been pointed out to me that I deserve a life."

"You obviously do," Taylor agreed as she glanced around the room. "Look at all you've accomplished."

I'd hit all my financial targets, plus more. But the problem was the maintenance of such a huge company. All the moving parts needed constant attention, which was why a managerial team was the answer. Cheryl and Chastity were right.

The team could do the tasks I didn't enjoy, which would free me up to focus on new acquisitions, and the clients who were too temperamental for anyone else to handle.

"So, tell me how you think you'll do being me—" I urged her, "—having your whole life revolve around work, because I have to warn you, you'll be here weekends, nights, early mornings. Not every day, but often." I had to know if she knew what she was getting herself into. She was young, about twenty-four, maybe twenty-five. She deserved a life too.

"I'm ready for that."

"Well, the last manager I hired told me the same thing, but the very first week I hired him, he took most of the weekend off even though there were meetings and deadlines to be met."

And he'd been motivated, according to him. Forty-five, and wanting to retire by fifty. I'd thought he was the perfect candidate. But no, I'd been wrong.

Taylor shuffled forward on her chair. "May I be frank also?"

"Please," I said, gesturing openly to her. "It would be a welcome change." The corporate world wasn't the place to find genuine, open people.

"I don't talk about my personal life generally with potential employers, but you seem to want to know the true reason I'm driven to work the way I do, so I'll tell you the full truth. I've been with my girlfriend for three years. She's a corporate lawyer and we live in a tiny apartment about two blocks from here."

I nodded. "It's good when you have a partner who has a similar drive." Which I didn't have in Chastity, unfortunately. She didn't understand why I needed to work the hours I did.

"Yes, it is. But we sat down a few months ago and decided that we would put aside ten years to work our absolute butts off. To buy a house. Travel. Get ahead. And then, if we wanted to, we would start a family. But I am absolutely committed to making our future a reality, so if you hire me, Mr. Patterson, I promise you will not regret it."

I stared at her and absorbed her passion. Many leaders talked about the "why" you need to keep working, keep doing whatever it is you're doing. For me, it had always been my parents that had driven me. I didn't want to rely on them for money, I wanted to impress them with my success. It had never worked, but during the path to success, I'd found my true love for what I did.

Now, my "why" had changed, and yet I empathized with Taylor's position. And I found myself liking her also. "You can start today," I told her. "With the caveat that you pass the drug screening and background checks. Of course."

She jumped to her feet. "Seriously? You don't want to know how many languages I speak? Or which college I went to?"

"Well, languages may be an advantage." I had several interpreters, but they weren't always available when I needed them.

"I'm fluent in French and can get by in most conversations in German and Italian."

She was perfect. "I'll get Cheryl to bring in a laptop and you can work in here with me for the first few weeks, then we'll find you an office. Assuming, of course, that you don't quit before then."

"Oh, I won't, Mr. Patterson. Thank you." She reached over the desk and enthusiastically shook my hand.

"Axel," I reminded her.

She grinned. "Yes, sir."

"Well, let's get you started." I got my new manager a computer and off she went. I ended up pulling a full day, ordering takeout for dinner around ten pm and working until midnight. When I woke up the next morning, I had hope that finding a proper management team was possible. And I had to tell Chastity.

I picked up my phone and it was only seven am. To text, or not to text? That was the question. Screw it. I had to let her know.

Hey, beautiful. I'm hoping you want to chat today. I hired a new manager yesterday and she started work immediately. Call me when you can.

I sent off the text and I hadn't even gotten up from my bed before she'd called.

"Good morning," I greeted her.

"Your new manager is a woman?"

I laughed at the obvious jealousy I heard in her tone. "Yeah, she's Cheryl's pick."

"Um... okay."

She sounded terrible. Depressed and lonely. I had to pull her out of the mood somehow. "She's only worked for me for one day, but I think you'll like her."

Chastity sighed. "I probably will. What's she like?"

"She's brilliant with numbers and convinced me she's driven enough to succeed, but we'll see. I've been fooled before."

"Is she married?" Chastity asked quietly.

I grinned. This was the cruncher. "She has a female partner. They've been together three years."

Silence.

"Oh, that's great." Chastity beamed now. "Can't wait to meet her."

Yeah, I thought that might change everything. "How are you doing, sweetheart? You've had a tough week, haven't you?"

She sniffed and didn't say anything.

My heart clenched. "I'm not sure how many of my messages you got, sweetheart, but please know that I'm sorry I missed the sonogram."

"It's okay," she said. "I shouldn't have over-reacted the way I did. I'm sorry too."

Whoa, that's a bit of a fast turnaround. "Um, although I appreciate what you're saying, what's happened to change your mind?" She sounded defeated. Not like my girl at all.

"I just... my mom pointed out that you weren't off drinking or gambling or golfing... can't remember. Anyway, she pointed out that you were working. And that's important, especially since I used the fact that you're successful against her when she was comparing our two situations."

"What situations?"

"The whole—oh my God. You don't know, do you? Can we FaceTime?"

Happiness exploded inside me. "Yes."

She hit some buttons and I sat back down on the bed and got comfortable.

Suddenly there she was. My girl. Looking a little pale, but better than I'd expected.

"I've missed you."

"I've missed you too," I told her. "Very much. So, what do you need to tell me?"

Her eyes went all wide and her mouth dropped open like a shocked cartoon character. "Guess what?"

"What?"

"Mom and Dad are pregnant again."

It was my turn to be stupefied. "Uh… excuse me?"

"Mom surprised me yesterday by driving up to school. She wanted to tell me she and dad have been seeing each other for a while, and that she's nine weeks pregnant."

"But… but" I stammered.

"I know, right?" she exclaimed. "I told her I was happy for them, but when she found my sonogram picture, she went off about me ruining my life and all this other crap that I'm so sick of hearing."

I shook my head. "That's insane."

"It is! Mom's forty-three."

"Yeah, God, I've gotta call Pat now." Would he be excited or angry that he'd accidentally impregnated the same woman twice?

She laughed then covered her mouth suddenly. "I talked to Dad yesterday and he wasn't very happy about our baby, so I hung up on him. I think I probably owe him an apology."

I jumped up off the mattress, struck with an idea. "How about I drive down for the day? I'll call the driver and be there around lunchtime. Do you have time this afternoon to catch up? I've missed you and that way I can apologize in person."

Her whole face lit up in a smile. "I'd love that. Meet you at the apartment? Or at one of the cafés?"

"How about we meet at Jenni's?" That was the breakfast café we liked the best. "I'll text you when I'm on my way, so you know what time to leave school."

"Sounds like a plan. Thank you."

"I'll call your dad on the way, find out if he hates me again."

Her eyes were big and watery as she nodded. "Yeah, give it ten minutes before you call. I need to go apologize."

"It'll take me that long to line up a car and pack up. See you soon, beautiful." I hung up the phone and raced to the bathroom, my heart thumping in my chest. I was excited to see her, more than I'd even imagined I would be.

And Pat was going to have a baby too! Of all the crazy timings in the world. My best friend and I were having kids together. And his son or daughter would be my son or daughter's aunt or uncle. *Freaky.*

34

AXEL

I went to the bathroom and took a shower, just to fill in the time until I could call Patrick. Then I got dressed and put in an order for a car. I could work there and back and spend time with Chastity in the same day. We had so much to talk about. But for now, Pat. I glanced at the time. It had been twenty minutes since I spoke to Chastity. Surely, that was long enough for them to talk. *Hmmm... maybe not.*

I made a quick protein shake with four eggs and kale, then packed for the day. When the driver arrived, I jumped in with my laptop and cell. I sent off a text to Chastity to let her know I was on my way, then it was time to call Pat and find out how he felt about the burgeoning pregnancies.

The phone only rang once before Pat picked up. "I was just about to call you."

I grinned as the car wove through the city and relaxed back into my seat. "Chastity asked me to give her some time to speak to you. Did she call?"

"Uh, yeah. She did."

I rolled my eyes and scrubbed my fingers through my hair. "So, is everything okay with you two?"

There was a long silence, then Pat said, "Yeah, she and I are fine. You and me, on the other hand..."

I stifled the groan that rose. "I wanted to tell you weeks ago, but Chastity asked me not to. She said she wanted to be the one to tell you."

More silence.

I pushed on. "I love her, Pat. And I'm really excited about the baby. I hope you can be happy for us too."

"You're gonna need to give me some time, Axel."

"For what?" I demanded, angry at my friend for being such an ass about everything. "I told you I love her, that I'll take care of her. I'd marry her if she wanted. If this was any other woman, you'd be happy for me. In fact, you'd probably say something like, "Shit, this woman must be pretty amazing if you wanna commit like that. Wow. You a dad. I never thought I'd see the day!" Wouldn't you?" I pressed.

Patty chuckled softly. "You're an asshole."

"Come on, man. Can you separate the two for a minute?"

There was a big sigh. "I can try."

"Fine," I huffed, then injected some happiness into my voice and pretended this was the first time my friend had heard the news. "Hey, Pat, guess what? I'm gonna be a father!"

"Congrats, buddy," Pat managed to say, though it was strained. "When's she due?"

"Early October."

There was silence again.

I cleared my throat. "Any news on your end?" I asked. "You know, with that woman you started seeing, and I didn't tell Chastity about?" I coughed again to make the point. I hadn't told Chastity that her parents had started seeing each other again, which I hadn't liked doing, but did it for Patrick.

“Yeah, actually. I didn’t think it would last past the first few dates, but it ended up being good.”

“With your ex? That’s surprising.”

He huffed out a laugh. “Yeah, it has been. We... well, both of us have changed and grown a lot. But anyway, I have news too.”

“Tell me.” Like I didn’t already know.

Pat sighed. “Kaiti’s pregnant. I’m going to be a father again.”

“I want to say congratulations,” I told him. “But you don’t sound very happy about it.”

He groaned. “Well, I—well... look. I am happy. It’s just unexpected.”

I laughed. “Is it too early to make a joke about the fact you’ve only knocked up a woman twice, and it was the same woman twenty-two years apart?” I waited, holding my breath. But happily, part of my best friend was still inside my future father-in-law.

“Yeah, go for it. I’ve thought it a few times.”

“You two obviously have good chemistry. What were the odds of her getting pregnant again?”

“At forty-three?” Pat asked. “The doctor said about one or two percent.”

“Whoa. Sounds like fate.”

Patty groaned. “You sound like Chastity. Stop it.”

I grinned. “Hey, listen. I’m on my way to see Chastity now. I need to suck up for a mistake I made on Wednesday. Can we catch up tomorrow maybe? Dinner on me?”

“Do I even wanna know what you did wrong?” my buddy asked.

“I missed her sonogram because I took some work calls.”

Pat laughed. “I knew it. Your job is going to get in the way with you two.”

“Shut up. I’m fixing it, okay?”

"Yeah, right. But okay, dinner tomorrow. I'll meet you at Jack's at eight?"

Jacks was our favorite steak place. "Yeah. Perfect. See you then." I hung up feeling lighter and happier than I'd felt in months. Pat knew about our baby, Chastity wanted me down at the apartment to spend time together, and Cheryl was on the warpath to find me the best managers around. Life was good.

Almost two hours later, we pulled up outside Jenni's. I closed my laptop and opened the door. "Hey, Terry, I should be ready to go by six pm."

"No problem, sir," the driver said. "I'll be here."

I got out and walked over to the café. I stopped outside and stared into the window. Chastity was sitting in a booth at the back, a cup of tea in hand. Happiness filled my chest, and I pushed open the front door.

She glanced up and her face lit up with a smile.

I waved and forced myself to walk calmly across the room.

She didn't get up and jump at me like I was hoping, but she was smiling and moved slightly to the left so I could slide into the booth alongside her.

"Hey," I said, moving in and reaching for her.

She leaned forward and I kissed her lips, but she pulled back way before I wanted her to.

"Have you ordered?" I asked.

She shook her head. "No. Just the tea. It helps my stomach."

"How is the nausea?"

"Oh, so much better." She beamed. "The last few days I've been feeling much better."

"That's great."

The waitress came by, and we ordered drinks and food, then I turned back to my girl. “What can I do to make it up to you?”

She looked down at the table, gripping her mug tightly. “You can’t.”

“I’m very sorry, sweetheart. I didn’t think about how my actions would affect you.”

“It wasn’t about the day. That appointment. Not really.”

“What was it, then?” I asked, then thanked the waitress for my coffee, and went back to focusing on Chastity.

“It was what the appointment represented.”

I sighed. Cheryl was right. “You think that I’ll always prioritize work over you.”

“Well, yeah. And I get it. I do. You’ve worked really hard to get where you are with your company. And I admire your work ethic and devotion. But when it comes to the baby, I don’t want an absent father.” Her eyes were welling up with tears as she spoke, but she didn’t let on, simply blinking them away.

Sadness swept over me. “I wouldn’t be absent.”

She looked up and met my gaze and I could see the uncertainty swimming in her eyes.

“I wouldn’t.”

She sighed. “I suppose I need to just wait and see, but I need to say that if we stay together, I need a real partner. Not one that just earns money, throws a nanny at me, and pops his head into the kitchen once a week.”

My jaw dropped open. “That’s not what it would be like.”

“I know, but—”

“Think about how much time we’ve spent together since we met. We’ve been on a weekend away, had a bunch of dinners and nights together. Hours on the phone almost every day.” I’d really tried with Chastity to have a normal relationship.

"That's true, but we're not living together yet."

"I'd move you in today if I could, but you want to finish college first."

She sighed. "Only ten weeks to go."

"How's it going?"

She brushed her hand through the air. "I don't want to talk about school. Can we talk about what happens after I move in with you? How's it going to work?"

"What do you mean?" I asked. "Do you want to look at houses to move into together right away? I assumed we'd move into my apartment first, but you might have a point. We don't want to move too close to the birth."

She laughed. "That's, ah... not what I meant, although you're probably right. The apartment isn't the best place for a baby, but lots of people do it. I just... can we table that for later?"

I grinned at her, loving the terminology. "Okay. What did you mean then?"

"I mean, have you made any changes at work that will mean we can spend more time together? Or have you hired a housekeeper and a cook?"

The waitress brought our food, and I stared down at my Southwestern omelet, suddenly ravenous. I picked up my knife and fork and began to cut. "Well, I haven't looked into getting full time staff at home yet, but that's on the list." It hadn't been on mine of course, but surely Cheryl would have it on hers, and that counted.

"Then what?" Chastity asked, picking up her fork and picking at her fruit salad.

"You've lost more weight," I told her.

She shrugged. "My appetite isn't great."

I made a mental note to talk to the obstetrician about that and continued on, "I've started making changes at work."

"Tell me," she said, looking excited.

"Well, the main thing, of course, is hiring my first manager, Taylor. But if Cheryl has her way, I'll have a team of them by the end of the quarter."

"Well, that's great," Chastity said. "But are you okay with that?"

"I'm worried about the company, it's true. But the way I was working isn't sustainable. So, I'll start with one, then see how she does."

"I think it's great," Chastity said.

I thought about it for a moment, then realized I felt the same way. "Me, too."

We both ate for a little while, then she asked, "So, I don't think you answered my question. What's going to happen next?"

"Well," I said, pushing my plate away. "If you'll let me, I'll take you upstairs and make love to you."

She glanced down. "Ah, maybe we can do that another time."

"Okay. Well, then how about a movie? A nap? What do you want to do?"

She chewed on her lip. "I just wanna talk for the moment."

"Sure. Should we get an ice cream or a hot drink or something, and walk down the street?"

She nodded. "Yes, please. Some fresh air would be good too."

I paid the bill, grabbed her hand and tugged her into the street. I knew it would take time for her to wrap her head around everything and forgive me for disappointing her. "Hey, you know I can't promise I'm always going to be perfect." I squeezed her hand as we walked along the street to the ice cream shop.

She turned to me. "Of course, I know that."

"But please understand that I'm going to try to be the best father I can possibly be." I wanted more for my kids than I had. Siblings, a proper home. Love and affection. All the things that had been missing from my own childhood.

This time she beamed up at me with her huge smile. "I know. And I can't wait to see it."

35

CHASTITY

I couldn't believe how nice it was to be back in Axel's company again. He was happy, and relaxed, and seemed totally ready to change things in his life for me and the baby. I keep wanting to pinch myself in case I was dreaming. But were those changes even possible for a guy like him?

"Hey, can I ask you something?" I questioned after we'd gotten ice cream and were back walking along the sidewalk again. This strip of shops was quiet on a Sunday, and it was nice to just be out in the fresh air, enjoying the sunshine.

"Of course."

"My mom and lots of other people have told me that a leopard can't change its spots."

He licked his own chocolate mint double scoop in a waffle cone and tilted his head. "Still waiting for the question."

Right. "Well, your company is your whole life, right? How is it possible to change your priorities overnight?"

He grinned down at me. "Are you asking if I'm cured of my workaholic-ism?"

"I don't think that's a word." It didn't sound right, but I could be wrong.

He laughed. "Look, honestly, I don't know. I've worked my company up from just Cheryl and me in one office, to a building with more than a hundred staff. It's going to be hard to let go of a lot of the control. But if I want a life, then something's got to give."

Guilt hit me hard. Even though he'd done exactly as I asked, putting into place some steps that would make it easier for him to be a good father, I knew he'd done it under duress.

"I'm sorry," I said, glancing down at the ground. Was I really *that* girlfriend? The one who made her boyfriend give up everything he loved to be with her? That wasn't me. That *couldn't* be me.

"No need to be sorry," he reassured me, still walking casually along the street. "Hey, there's a nice little park right there. How about we sit and relax for a bit?"

"Yeah. Perfect," I said, stepping onto the grass and walking over to the little park bench. "Oh, that's better. Thanks." My legs ached now, and I read online that I needed to increase my magnesium or something. I had to get to a drugstore and buy some stuff when I had a minute.

Axel put his arm along the back of the seat, not around me directly, but it felt like he was hugging me in a strange way.

"I'm still sorry," I managed to say, because my appetite was gone and for the first time, I was beginning to see the situation from his perspective. "I didn't really think about how much you'd need to give up and change for this baby." I'd been way more focused on what I was giving up.

"Hey, I told you that you don't need to be sorry. You are the woman I've dreamed of for so long. Someone I can truly love, and with a baby on the way, things couldn't be better. But it's true, I hadn't really thought about the other changes that would come with the dream."

I grimaced. "Yeah, me either."

"Are you coping with school? Is there anything I can do?"

I smiled. His offer warmed my heart. "Thank you for saying that, but it's okay. I just have to put my head down and power through for a few months, then I'll be done, and we can concentrate on the baby."

Axel grinned at me. "Do you want to talk about where we're going to live?"

I inhaled quickly, excitement filling me up. "Yes! What about the house that you gave me?" It still sounded ridiculous to say it out loud. He *gave* me a house, mortgage free. It was just an insane gift. Like winning the lottery.

"Oh, no, that's for you. For the baby."

"But I really liked it!" I continued. "Great location. Huge yard. Not too far from work for you." Not to mention the fact that the master bedroom had a jacuzzi in the ensuite!"

He grinned at me. "If you like it that much, we can go see it on a free weekend. But that means you'll have to choose another house off the list because I want you to have something that earns money so you can invest it or save it for the baby."

I stared up at him, too much love in my heart. "You're incredible. Do you know that?"

He huffed and looked the other way, obviously not used to such a compliment.

I twisted on the seat and reached for his right hand, holding it with both of mine. "I'm sorry I was so upset over the sonogram. Next time, I'll be more honest about how important it is to me. Or I'll get my mom to come or something." *Maybe.*

He stared down at our entwined fingers, then up at me. "How is your mom doing?"

I sighed. "Not really sure. I haven't spoken to her since we had our fight yesterday." She hadn't messaged once or tried to call, which was unusual for her.

"What happened exactly?"

I gave him a quick rundown on our fight, ending with me running off on her. Childish, I knew. But, God, had my temper been up yesterday! Then, as soon as she'd gone, I'd crashed, climbing into bed and not surfacing until the next day when Axel had messaged me. I knew pregnancy messed with your emotions, but I wasn't used to the roller coaster of it all. Flaming furious one minute, in tears the next.

"What happened when you went back to your room?" he asked.

That had been a little strange. "She was gone. But the baby's picture was back in my drawer, and it was shut. So, she went to the trouble to clean up the room."

"Or she wanted to look at the sonogram again. I know I have been."

"You did? The ones I threw at you?" I asked him, tears blurring my vision. I sniffed and blinked to force them back. "Sorry."

He grinned at me, reached into his wallet and pulled out my favorite sonogram photo. "I take it everywhere with me now. I'm not quite sure what I'm looking at, so I definitely can't miss the next appointment. I need a professional to show me what is what."

I laughed at him. "Yeah, it looks like a bit of a blur, doesn't it? Well, this is the head." I pointed to the large, round object in the picture. "This is the nose, and the little hand."

The tears were coming at me again. "I love looking at these pictures. I can't wait to see them in real life." I so wanted to tell Axel about the baby's sex, but since it wasn't a hundred percent yet and he'd missed the sonogram, I decided to wait. "I get my blood test results next week."

"What are they for?" he asked, putting his photo and his wallet away.

"They check my health stats like iron levels and vitamin D. But they also did a chromosome screening to test for abnormalities, and it will give us the sex of the baby."

His face went from interested to shocked, his mouth dropping open. "They can tell already. Isn't it a bit early?"

I laughed. "Yeah, I thought so too. But the new technology lets us find out relatively early." I swallowed hard, finding the need to lie uncomfortable. Should I tell him that I knew? "Um... just so you know, the sonographer told me what they *think* the baby is. They said it's not a definite, and to wait for the blood test results—but do you want to know what she said?"

Axel's face flashed with a myriad of emotions. "I'm not sure I want to know."

"Oh. Well, they were probably wrong anyway." Though the sonographer had seemed pretty certain, I didn't want to tell Axel that.

He suddenly jumped to his feet. "But you know, and now I want to know because you know."

I pressed my lips together, so I didn't laugh out loud. "I'll tell you, but you can't get your hopes up in case it's wrong."

He stepped away a little, then walked back. "How long before the blood test results?"

"They said a week, so by Wednesday, hopefully." I wanted the results so I could absolutely reassure myself that everything was fine with the little one.

He sat down again next to me and this time he put his arm around me properly. "I can wait a few more days then."

"Awesome." I put my head down on his shoulder and just enjoyed being with him. No phones ringing, no classes, no nausea. I closed my eyes then yawned.

Axel chuckled. "You sure you don't want that nap? I'd love to just hold you for a while before I go home."

I lifted my head and stared up at him. My sex drive was extremely low at the moment, especially after the roller coaster of emotions I'd been through lately. But just being with him? Being held by him? That was something that might chase away the depression that had been pulling me down into a hole the past twenty-four hours. "That would be really nice."

"Let's go, then." Axel held out his hand, tugged me to my feet, then walked me back to the apartment building.

"I wasn't sure I'd ever come back here," I said to him as we walked into our bedroom, and he turned back the blankets.

"Why?" he asked.

"Well, I suppose I wasn't sure if we were going to make it, so I thought I may never see this place again."

Axel frowned at me. "Just because I made a mistake and we had a fight, doesn't mean we're done. Please know that. I'll work through practically any problem with you."

It was exactly what I needed to hear. "Well, you are my first real relationship. I guess I kind of jumped straight off the deep end, and I'm sorry for that."

"It's okay." He grinned. "I've got a bit more experience with this stuff, so maybe I can guide you a little." He unbuttoned his shirt and tugged the tails out of his jeans.

My mouth watered at the sight of him as more and more golden skin was revealed. His shirt disappeared. Then his jeans. I stared. I couldn't help it. He was so beautiful.

"Are we still just napping?" Axel asked, quirking an eyebrow at me.

I knelt on the bed and crawled across the mattress towards him. Maybe it was the fact we hadn't been together for ages. Or the fact that we were officially, definitely still together. Maybe it was the fact that he was a gorgeous specimen of a man, and my femininity didn't have a chance at fighting the lust that passed over me.

I didn't know and I didn't care. I wanted him. I reached the other side of the bed and knelt in front of him.

He quirked an eyebrow. "Are you sure?"

I nodded and reached out for him. "Kiss me. Please."

He groaned as he surged forward, cupping my face and pressing his lips to mine.

I moaned with relief. We were finally together again.

He pushed me back, but I had too many clothes on to lie down. "Hang on." I slid off the mattress and got rid of my leggings and t-shirt, bra and panties. Finally free of all the layers and warmth against my over-heated flesh, I jumped at him, kissing him, touching him. Wanting him on me, in me, and all over me. We fell in a heap on the bed, and I opened my legs for him. "Please. Just, now."

I wrapped my legs around him and he surged against me. I kissed his lips, moaning as I felt the head of his cock nudge my entrance. More. I wanted more. I flexed my hips up, taking him inside me. It stretched me, but I didn't want him to stop. I dug my nails into his back and as he pulled away, I gripped him and tugged him toward me.

He started off slowly, kissing me and rocking inside of me. My body relaxed, then he began to move faster, harder. Thrusting me into the bed, filling my body with his.

Again and again, I screamed out—wanting him, needing him. All the angst of the week was washing over me, making me so grateful for this moment. That we were back together. My stomach began to tighten and tremble. I closed my eyes and focused on the pleasure centered between my legs.

Axel dropped his head and whispered into my ear, "I love you, Chastity. I love you so much."

And his words sent me soaring into the stratosphere and beyond.

36

AXEL

Chastity fell asleep after our session and I held her for hours. There was no way I could sleep. My head was a whirl with possibilities and hope. She loved me, and our baby was strong and healthy. Would it be a boy or a girl? Which one did I want, anyway?

When no answer immediately came forth, I realized I actually didn't care. Lots of men wanted a boy, a male to carry on the family name and to take to football practice. But for me, as someone who wasn't sure I'd ever have my own child, either would be amazing. Though I did hope to have at least two. Growing up as an only child hadn't been fun, and I hoped Chastity felt the same way.

Eventually she stirred, moaning softly and lifting her head from my chest.

"Hello, sleepyhead," I said, kissing the top of her hair.

"Mmm... hey." She rolled onto her back and stretched her arms over her hair, affording me an awesome view of her gorgeous, darkened nipples and extra plump breasts.

"You've lost weight, but these look bigger," I said, running my fingers over her nipples gently.

She rolled onto her side and faced me. "Yeah, they are. I think I'm up two cup sizes already."

I rolled onto my side to face her as well. "Are you planning on breast feeding?"

"Yeah, of course." she said, then bit her lip. "I mean, as long as I can. I don't know much about it yet."

I leaned forward and kissed her lips. "We have time to learn, and whatever specialist you want to talk to, just say the word."

Her cheeks blushed pink. "Thanks."

"Hey, I know its early to even ask this, but how do you feel about a bigger family?"

"How big are we talking?" she asked with a grin.

I laughed. "Not ten or anything. But I hated growing up as an only child, so I suppose at least two. Just so they have at least one playmate."

Her eyes shone with happiness as she stared back at me. "Oh, at least two. I always hoped I'd have four, actually. Because I hated being an only child too. It sucked, big time."

I leaned forward and kissed her again, loving the feel of her warmth on my mouth. Then I pulled back. "Let's start with two and see how we're doing." I had a lot of friends who'd assumed they wanted a whole tribe of kids, only to find out that two was more than enough.

My phone began to buzz so I grabbed for it where it lay on the nightstand. It was the driver. I picked up my phone and answered, "Yeah, I'll be down in fifteen. Thanks." I hung up and stared back at Chastity. "I'm sorry, I have to go. If I didn't have some international meetings online tonight, I'd stay."

She sat up and slid off the bed. "It's totally fine. I appreciate you coming all this way just for a few hours." She ran off towards the bathroom and I watched her gorgeous ass as she went, then she shut the door.

I sighed, wanting to stay. I didn't want to spend two hours in a car working, to then work all night as well. "Wow," I muttered to myself. "I am changing." I laughed and shook my head, then forced myself to get dressed. I'd never really thought I'd find anything as important as my company and my goals.

When she walked back out still completely naked, I couldn't help myself. I rushed straight over to her and grabbed her up in my arms. "Damn, you're beautiful."

She laughed and grabbed for me, squeezing me tightly. "I'm going to miss you."

I pulled back, making an instant decision. "I'll come back next weekend, okay? You probably shouldn't be traveling too much with all your studies, so how about I commit to coming up here every weekend until graduation?"

Her jaw dropped. "You'd do that?"

"Of course." I nodded my head. I'd make sure I could. "Unless you decide you want to come to the city to visit friends or whatever, and then I'll send a driver for you, okay?"

She nodded, her eyes filling with tears. "That would be great. I think it's going to get harder to be apart now."

I pulled her into me and hugged her close. "I agree. So, I'll be back next weekend, I promise. And hopefully I'll have another new manager hired, and I won't need to fire him for being incompetent."

She giggled as she pulled back, wiping her nose. "I bet you're a tough taskmaster at work."

I nodded my head. "Only way to be successful, especially at the executive level."

She cupped my jaw for a moment then went and grabbed her clothes. I should have been packing to leave, but I watched as her delicious body disappeared from sight.

Once she was done, I grabbed my clothes, packed my stuff, and took her hand. "I have to go, but I'll call you tomorrow. Okay?"

She nodded. "I'll walk down with you. I need to get back to my dorm. Exams to study for."

We walked down together, and even though every part of me was saying I should stay and luxuriate in her body and her love some more, I got in the car, and we drove away.

37

AXEL

The start of the week went well. Taylor, the new manager Cheryl had hired, was a gun at finance and numbers and had already taken over two of my major accounts. I'd interviewed two other managers from Cheryl's list but hadn't clicked with either of them.

It was Wednesday morning, the day we got our IPSI test results, that Taylor turned to me. "Can I ask a slightly off-topic question?"

"Of course," I said, not looking up from my computer.

"Are you still looking for managers?"

"Yes. I need at least three more I think, to make it possible for me to take off the time I need in October."

"Are you going away?"

Oh. I hadn't told anyone.

I turned towards her, but she seemed to take in my mood and instantly apologized. "I'm sorry. I just realized that's a personal question."

Well, Pat and Kaiti knew. I had yet to call my parents but

would do that after the results came in today. "No. It's okay. We're starting to tell people. My girlfriend is pregnant and she's due in October. I've promised her that I'll take some time off after the birth."

Taylor nodded. "Congratulations."

"Is there a reason you were asking?"

She nodded and twisted around in her chair to look straight at me. "Yes, well... I was hoping I could help you there. I was in an incredible class at Yale, and several of the people who graduated in the same year as me aren't happy with their current positions. We had a social event on Friday night and so many of them aren't reaching their full potential. If you wanted some recommendations, I could easily tell you who is best suited to which department."

I hadn't even thought about Taylor's contacts. "That would be great, actually. I'll make a list of what I need, and you book them in around the calendar."

Taylor grinned at me. "Done." Then she got back to her work and the weight on my shoulders felt instantly lighter. If Taylor could create a team of highly talented, trainable people, then she could save my family life in one fell swoop.

My phone rang around lunchtime, and I grabbed for it. "It's Chastity," I told Taylor. "Would you excuse us?"

"Of course," she said, grabbing her bag. "I'll go get some lunch now."

I picked up the phone. "Hey, sweetheart, how's your day going?"

"Good," she said, all happiness and sunshine in her voice. "How's your day going?"

"Well, it's good, actually. Taylor, my new manager, just told me she knows several people from grad school who might fit in here, so she's going to set up some interviews for the team."

"She sounds great," Chastity said, and although there wasn't the jealousy from before, I knew she wasn't too happy.

"You'll really like her," I told Chastity. "Maybe when we're settled, we can invite her and her partner over to our place?"

"Oh, I'd love that!" Chastity beamed. "They're around my age, aren't they?"

I laughed. "Yeah, I didn't check her resume, but I'd say she's twenty-five or six."

Chastity huffed. "Better than a sixty-year-old like those guys at dinner."

I leaned back in my chair and grinned to myself. "You're right. So, tell me, have you got the results of the blood test?"

"Yes! That's why I'm calling."

I waited, but she didn't say anything else.

"Well?" I pushed. "What does it say?"

"The baby's healthy. No chromosome abnormalities or anything like that, which is such a relief."

"That's great," I said, feeling her relief wash over me. "And you? How were your vitamin levels and things?"

"Oh, I need some iron supplements, but that's okay. I can get them over the counter at any drug store."

"And?" I said, wanting to know the rest of the results.

"And what?" she asked.

I groaned. "Does it tell us the sex of the baby?"

She laughed. "It does. Do you want to know?"

Hmmmm. "I do, now that you know."

"I can keep it to myself if you want the surprise."

I wasn't sure about that. "I'm not sure that's possible. You'll buy blue paint or a pink blanket, and the surprise will go out the window."

"Well, it does mean we can prepare the nursery and buy clothes and blankets and things."

I ran my hand through my hair. "Maybe you should tell me this weekend when I see you."

"We can do that," she said. "I can buy a gender reveal cake or something."

"What's that?"

"It's when you ask a baker to make a cake and ice it so you can't see the inside color, but when you cut it open, you see the pink or blue cake."

I didn't think that was very me.

"Oh, or I've seen Online people do balloons, or lights, or all sorts of different things.

"Forget it. Tell me," I said. I wasn't into those games or stupid party gimmicks.

"You sure?"

"Yes! This is our baby. Tell me what we're having so we can plan accordingly." And it may make me feel more connected to the little black and white smudge on the screen once it had a name and an identity.

"We're having a girl," she whispered.

"A girl?" I repeated. "Did you say we're having a girl?"

"Yes. Are you happy?"

Wonder filled me. *A baby girl.* "Yes, I am," I told her, swallowing the lump in my throat. "A baby with your smile, Chastity, will be the most beautiful thing in the world to me."

She squealed a little bit. "I'm so glad, because I'm so happy too! I can't wait to paint her nursery and buy her cute little things. Is it okay if I tell my parents?"

"Of course," I said. "We should take them out for dinner together and celebrate."

"Oh, yeah. Thank you. When Mom and I have sorted our shit, I'll organize it."

"Okay, sweetheart."

Chastity went on about all things pink and girly, but I couldn't keep up. My heart was full.

I was going to be a dad. *A girl dad.* Nothing had ever been so perfect! And I couldn't wait for what the future held for us—as a family. *My family.* I just prayed I didn't screw this up...

THE END of book 2.

Read on for the final book in the ***Axel and Chastity*** trilogy.
Download: HERE

THE BILLIONAIRE'S BABY

1

CHASTITY

Two weeks had passed since I'd last spoken to my mom, and I was dying to tell her our good news. My baby was healthy, and my mom was going to have a granddaughter. I hoped she'd be happy for me. But I didn't want to just call up and blurt it out. Not like the initial announcement.

I wanted to do it right this time and tell her face to face, mother to daughter. This called for some planning. So, I called my dad and coordinated with him to organize a dinner for all four of us. Axel and I would meet him and Mom at a restaurant in the city.

When Saturday arrived, Axel sent a car to get me and I met him at his apartment so I could shower, wash my hair and change into an outfit more suitable for a nice dinner.

"I can't believe how nervous I am," I told him while I was applying my lip gloss in the bathroom, my stomach aflutter with butterflies. I'd bought a new simple black dress that was flowy around the boobs and waist. My tummy was starting to pop, and I was almost fifteen weeks along. Nothing fit me right, especially around the middle, so new clothes seemed like the best option.

"You look beautiful," Axel said from behind me.

I glanced up in the mirror to where his reflection was staring back at me. "And you're beyond handsome," I said, sighing at how amazing he looked in a simple pair of slacks and a shirt. Even without a tie or structured jacket, his shoulders were broad and gorgeous.

Axel flicked his wrist up and glanced at his watch. "We should go. You ready?"

"Yeah." I checked my reflection once more, then lifted my hand to stare down at the ring adorning my ring finger on my right hand. "I'm not sure I've ever really told you just how much I love my ring. I wear it every day and I've never taken it off."

"Never?" he asked, coming forward to stand behind me.

I shook my head slowly, leaning into his warmth and staring at his face reflected in the mirror. "Never. Not even when I thought we would break up." At the time I had been so angry at him for missing the sonogram I could barely breathe.

He kissed my hair. "Let's go, babe."

We took the elevator down to the garage and got into his car.

"Still nervous?" he asked.

I folded my hands together over my stomach. "Absolutely."

"Why?" he pressed. "Are you worried your mom will start another fight?"

"Oh, she definitely will," I told him with a grin. "That's just her way. With both you and Dad there tonight? I can only imagine what she's going to say."

Her pregnancy hormones were most likely all over the place, which I completely understood. Mine were still kicking my butt! The sickness had all but subsided, thankfully, but I was snappy, teary and horny. *What a combination.*

"Then if it's not that, what is it?" Axel asked as we drove out the garage door and toward the restaurant.

"It's just..." I sighed, trying to think about the right way to put it. "I think I just worry that she won't want to know about our baby. That she'll decide it's all too difficult and she doesn't want to be a grandma." Hot tears filled my eyes and I waved at them while blinking rapidly. I was wearing more makeup than usual, and I didn't want it ruined and dramatically running down my face.

"I doubt that will be her response," Axel said, attempting to calm my nerves. "But even if it is, I've heard things change once the baby arrives."

I glanced across the interior at him. "How do you know that?" I'd read the same thing, but how had he heard of it?

Axel shrugged as he pulled into a valet spot outside the restaurant and turned off the ignition. "I'm twenty years older than you, sweetheart. I've had friends have babies fifty times over. One of my best buddies had a baby before he even finished high school, so I've heard my fair share of stories. And one of the main themes has always been that no matter how the parents react when they initially find out about the pregnancy, they're very different when they actually have a real baby to hold and love."

He reached across and picked up one of my hands, bringing my fingers to his lips to kiss. "So, don't worry, things will work out, especially once they see our baby girl. She'll win them over."

"You haven't told my father we're having a girl yet, have you?" I asked.

He shook his head adamantly. "No. I wasn't sure you wanted to share that with anyone just yet."

The valet rushed over to the car, so we both climbed out.

Axel tossed the keys to the guy who looked about my age, and we headed into the restaurant.

"I thought we would tell them tonight," I said. "Since we know the results were pretty much one hundred percent accurate, I figure, why not?" The IPSI test made me feel a lot better about thinking of our baby as a girl. We hadn't talked names or anything like that yet, but I was feeling more comfortable every day with the little being growing inside me. With a hopeful smile I tucked my hand into the crook of Axel's elbow.

He glanced down at me. "Okay. Let's do it."

We walked into the restaurant, and I glanced around. It was spectacularly beautiful, with dimmed lighting, pristine white tablecloths and classical music tinkling away in the background. "This place is lovely." I sighed.

"I thought it would be nice to go somewhere we could talk and hear each other," Axel said.

The maître'd took our name then escorted us over to a round table with four seats.

"Yes, it's definitely quiet," I all but whispered. There were only about ten tables in the whole place, and everyone was quietly sipping on their wine and eating their food. Slowly. It was a little strange, and in stark comparison to the cafeteria I ate at every day, with conversation at a dull roar and the constant din of clanking plates and dropped silverware.

I was just about to ask Axel more about his new managerial team when my parents walked into the room. I waved at them excitedly.

They smiled at me as they walked over. There was no running or hugging, or any of the elation I'd hoped for in my daydreams about this special moment. But they'd come. That was the important thing.

"Hi, Mom. Hi, Dad."

They both smiled and sat, Mom next to me, my father next to Axel without a word.

Axel stood up and shook my father's hand.

Our gathering felt a little stilted to me, like we'd already started off on the wrong foot somehow.

"Congratulations, Katherine," Axel said, looking at my mother. "How are you feeling?"

She brushed her hair back behind her ear and sighed. "Well, nervous. We have our twelve-week sonogram this week, and then more blood tests."

"Why are you nervous, Mom?" I asked, before a horrible thought occurred to me. *What if something was wrong with their baby? How could we ever be happy if my mom lost hers?* It would destroy my parents and us...

She cleared her throat. "You know, the usual. The doctors keep referring to my mature age like it's some sort of disease. I'll feel a lot better once the amniocentesis is done. Did you have to have one of those?" She asked, looking straight at me.

"Oh, ah..." I faltered.

"No, I don't think you did," Axel said, jumping in to save me from the awkward moment. "You just had the blood test, right?"

I nodded. "Yes. We got the IPSI done."

"Oh?" Mom asked, her tone dead serious and nowhere near sounding like my mother. "How did it go?"

I grinned at her and glanced over at Axel.

He nodded at me, returning my enthusiasm.

"It went really well," I began. "The baby's healthy, no anomalies to speak of, and we found out the sex!"

"Oh, we don't want to know. Please don't tell us," she said, shaking her head emphatically and grabbing my dad's hand above the table.

"Um, okay," I managed, feeling my heart fall sickeningly low inside my chest. I had been looking forward to this moment. I wanted to share. I thought my announcement would be met with enthusiasm and support. Instead, it felt liked I'd run face first into a brick wall. I glanced over at Axel, at a total loss. *Why wouldn't they want to know?*

Axel turned back to my parents in an attempt to salvage our evening. "Are you two finding out what you're having? Or would you rather not?"

"Oh, we'll find out," Mom assured him. "But we won't tell anyone. I think that should be kept private, until the day the baby arrives, and then you can announce it."

I was flabbergasted. What a ridiculous thing to say to us. What she wanted to do with her pregnancy was up to her. But this was my pregnancy and my news. What right did she have to spoil it like this? Already hurt and exasperated, I looked over to my father.

He grimaced apologetically, a worried expression on his face. Then he turned to Axel. "Shall we order some wine?"

"Definitely." Axel lifted his hand to summon service.

A waiter hurried over and took their order.

Mom and I ordered sparkling water.

To distract myself from the crippling disappointment simmering within my heart, I picked up the menu, examining it for the prices. There were none. "Axel..."

"Just order anything you'd like."

"But..." I hated not knowing how much anything cost. It always made me feel uncomfortable. It seemed dishonest, like a trap.

He reached for my hand and did his hand kissing trick. It worked every time.

I slowly relaxed and returned to perusing the menu. I was starving, and low in iron. I didn't really feel like red meat, but I needed it. *Our daughter needs it*, I reminded myself. "I think I'll go with the steak. Can you recommend which one would be the best?" I asked the waiter.

"Absolutely."

Suddenly my mom piped up, obviously seeing my issue with the menu. "How are we supposed to know what this is going to cost us if there are no prices?"

I sighed and glanced at Dad. This was *fun*.

"Dinners on me," Axel said smoothly. "I owed Pat dinner

from his birthday, and I thought we could double up with the joint celebration of our babies."

My mother's aggravated frown said it all, but at least she kept whatever was whirling around inside her head to herself.

We eventually managed to order even though my mother asked the poor waiter twenty questions and embarrassingly ended up requesting a meal that wasn't really on the menu, anyway.

When that was finally done, I really felt like a drink but that wasn't going to happen. Not for a while yet. Our baby came first. My annoyance and disappointment would have to find others way to cool off. I decided to steer the conversation into hopefully safer waters. "Axel, how's the new management team going? I didn't get to ask you before we came in."

"Management team?" my dad repeated.

Axel shifted on his chair, seemingly uncomfortable.

I frowned. Hadn't he told my father about this team yet?

"Well, I was going to ask you about it, actually Pat. On our run tomorrow."

"Ask me what?"

"Well," Axel began, and glanced over to me. "It's been pointed out to me by a few people, who shall remain nameless, that I'm a bit of a workaholic."

Patrick chuckled and picked up his glass of red wine. "Can't argue that."

"So, Cheryl at my office has been working on hiring me a group of managers to take over some of my workload, which will leave free me up to pursue new accounts and perform the executive tasks that I prefer."

I watched my father's face as Axel spoke, and his surprise was obvious.

"Seriously?" Dad asked, his brow crooked. "You're hiring managers to take on some of your responsibilities?"

"He's delegating," I said with a grin.

My dad's eyebrows dropped. "I realize that, I'm just surprised."

Axel reached over and grabbed my hand, threading our fingers and holding my hand where everyone could see. "I want to slow down for Chastity and the baby. I want to be able to be there for her when she needs me."

"So, how many managers are we talking about?" my father asked, his tone very business-like considering Axel had just said the most amazing thing about his dedication to me and our baby.

"I've hired three so far. All graduates from the same year."

"Oh, that's right," I said, joining in on the conversation. "You mentioned Taylor wanted you to interview some of her classmates."

"Yes," Axel said, grinning back at me. "And it's working out fantastically. They're all specialized and work really well together."

"So, what did you want to talk to me about?" Dad prompted again.

Axel squeezed my hand. "I haven't actually mentioned it to anyone yet, but would you consider coming to work with me?"

I glanced over at my mom, whose eyebrows had narrowed.

"In what capacity?" my father asked. "Because we always said we wouldn't work together."

I squeezed Axel's hand. "You and Dad have wanted to work together before?"

He nodded. "Yeah, we always said it wouldn't work. But since we're sort of family now, I thought I'd ask."

I gaped at him. *Oh, God.* Mom was going to have a fit over this!

2

AXEL

The tension around me was worse than the most hostile takeover meeting. What had I said that was so wrong that everyone at the table was looking at me like I was insane? "What's wrong?" I asked.

Patrick shook himself as though getting rid of bad thoughts. "In what capacity?"

"As my second in command," I said. I'd been thinking about it a lot, and I couldn't see any good reason why Pat shouldn't work for me. He was terrific at what he did. "You'd oversee all the new managers I've hired," I continued. "They're mid-twenties and could use your experience to coach them and keep them from doing anything stupid."

"Tell me about them," Pat requested.

I gave him a quick rundown of the three new hires; two women and one guy. Between them, they spoke a half dozen languages and specialized in business, finance, and economics.

"I'll come by tomorrow and meet them, if that works for you?" Patrick's face was thoughtful, his eyebrows drawn together.

"There's no pressure at all. You don't have to say yes," I told him. "But I need more managers, and you'd be a perfect fit. If you don't think you can work with me..."

"You mean *for* you, right?" Katherine interrupted, correcting me.

I slid my gaze over to the woman who'd twice managed to get accidentally pregnant by my best friend, twenty years apart. "Sorry?"

"You keep saying you want Patrick to work with you, but you mean you want him to work under you."

I frowned in consternation at Pat's partner and Chastity's mom. What was wrong with her? Was it just pregnancy hormones? "I'm offering my best friend a job that he would be brilliant at and pays twice as well as his current position."

I was rounding down, actually. My new managers made more than Pat, and I'd pay twice their salary for an executive manager of his skill and work ethic. I'd never offered before because we'd made an agreement not to mix our friendship with business. But it didn't make sense anymore. Not with our current familial connections.

Chastity squeezed my hand. "That's so thoughtful of you, Axel. Thank you."

I could see she was grateful, and I wasn't going to say it out loud now, not with Katherine out for blood, but it had been Chastity's recommendation in the first place that I look to her father for a manger that had me thinking about it again. "I should have done it years ago," I admitted, feeling a little embarrassed. I probably should have offered him the job at a different time. When we were alone or over the phone, so he had time to think it over without the social pressures of a family dinner.

"Why didn't you?" Katherine shot out, clearly still on the warpath. "Or, maybe the question is, *why* are you offering now? For Chastity's benefit? Because it's certainly not for ours."

"Kaiti..." Pat whispered at his partner, staring at her with a grimace rippling over his face.

Katherine just glared back at him, unperturbed.

I sat up straighter, regretting the offer completely or at least its timing. "Look, I didn't mean to upset anyone. Maybe we can talk about this another time, Patrick?"

"Yeah. Good idea," my best friend answered.

Chastity took her hand out of mine and reached for her soda. "So, what's your problem, Mom?"

Uh-oh. "Um, Chastity, maybe we should leave it?"

"No. I want to know." Chastity stared at her mom, unflinching. "Well?"

"Well, what?" Katherine barked back, her glare now trained on her daughter.

"What's your problem tonight? You know there's no paid maternity leave in America, right? So, why wouldn't you encourage Dad to get a better job? A higher paying job?"

That was a good point, but I wasn't sure it was one Katherine was going to consider. If there was one thing I knew about her, it was that she was bitter and prideful to a fault. She always had been.

"You don't need to concern yourself with our finances, Chastity," Katherine snapped, sticking her nose in the air. "We're perfectly fine, thank you. A lot more comfortable than we were when we had you."

"Good," Chastity said. "Then you won't be guilting this baby into thinking it's his or her fault you don't get to do anything."

Whoa. Okay. "Sweetheart..." This whole dinner was going south at an exponential rate. Luckily for me, since I had no idea what I was about to say next, two waiters turned up with our dinners, serving all four of us at once. I stared down at my prawn risotto and picked up my fork. This was now awkward as hell.

"Enjoy your meals," the waiter said, and took their leave.

Katherine's eyes were flaming with anger. "How dare you?" she hissed at Chastity.

My future bride's hand tightened into a fist on the table before she hissed right back. "How dare I what?"

"How dare you think you can tell us what to do! You're the one who's repeating all the same mistakes we did, and you think you know better. Well, you don't. You barely know this man, and you're too young to have any baby, let alone his. *There*. I said it." Katherine threw herself back in her chair and crossed her arms over her chest.

I stared at her with my mouth open, shocked she'd actually had the lack of decorum as an adult to say such a thing—especially in public over dinner. I glanced at the mother of my child.

Chastity was beginning to boil with anger. Her face was flushing redder and redder by the moment.

I looked straight at Pat and wished I could whisper to him. *"What the fuck do we do?"* But he was just staring at me with the same hopeless feeling I had pushing through my chest. Did I intervene, or did I let this blow up the way it was meant to?

Maybe I could offer Chastity some support or help? "Sweetheart..."

Chastity pushed herself to her feet and glared down at her mother. "So, you think I'm too young to have this baby? Well, newsflash! I'm older than you were with me, and in a thousand times better financial position. So, you are wrong, Mom. *Totally* wrong."

"You should be going to chiropractic school, Chastity. Chasing your dream! Not letting one mistake ruin your future," she fired back.

"Ah—" I started to interject, but Chastity exploded beside me.

"This isn't a mistake!" she practically screamed in the quiet restaurant. "You're the one making mistakes, getting pregnant at forty-three! But I at least supported you when you shared your surprise."

Katherine got to her feet too, not to be outdone by her daughter's theatrics. "This baby is our second chance. To be together, to be a real family."

I glanced across at Pat and saw the hurt on his face that I knew would be mirrored in Chastity's. She'd always felt like she was a burden to her parents, and now her mother was telling her that she was finally getting the baby she actually wanted. That was going to hurt—and bad. It was a fucking rotten thing of her mother to say.

I reached for Chastity's hand, but she shook me off.

"You and me, Mom—we're done. Enjoy your baby, because you're never going to get to see this one, or me, again. She's just a *mistake*, anyway. I guess we have that in common!" Chastity cupped her belly, framing her swelling stomach with her hands. "Axel, let's go."

My stomach grumbled with hunger, but this place didn't do takeout meals. So, as Chastity grabbed all her stuff and twisted around to stomp towards the door, I followed after her.

I made sure the maître'd knew the dinner was on me, instructing him to use the corporate account they had on file for me, then trailed Chastity outside and into the cool night air.

She was standing on the sidewalk breathing heavily, tears in her eyes.

"Are you okay?" I asked her, though it was obvious that she wasn't.

Chastity swiped at her eyes. "Did you hear what she said?" Her voice wobbled as she spoke.

It broke my heart to see her like that, but surely, she had to see what I saw? That her mother was just acting out irrationally. It didn't mean anything in the long run. She was just letting off some steam. "Of course, I did, but she's just upset and hormonal.

I'm sure she's going to regret what she said to you, so please try not to be too angry. You can't take everything she says to heart. We all say shit in anger we don't mean." I glanced back into the restaurant and saw Pat walking out to us.

I leaned forward and pulled open the external door for him. He walked straight through and grabbed his daughter, pulling her into his welcoming arms. "I'm sorry, Chastity."

Chastity broke into sobs then and Patrick squeezed her tight.

I took a step back so I could look through the glass doors and see Katherine inside the restaurant.

She was still sitting at her table, alone, mechanically chewing as though she were trying to enjoy her meal.

She probably is. The food here is delicious.

Pat pulled back, holding onto Chastity's upper arms. "I have to get back in there before she blows another valve. The doctor said her blood pressure's too high already and we have to keep her calm."

Chastity sobbed out a laugh. "Yeah, good luck with that."

Pat held out his hand to me. "I appreciate the job offer and I'll be over tomorrow, around one PM, if that's okay?"

I shook his hand and nodded. "I'll clear my schedule. Thank you."

My best friend nodded and went back into the restaurant to try and calm his wife.

I turned to Chastity. "Let's go and get something to eat, sweetheart. And you can tell me why you're so upset."

"Because," Chastity began, then stopped, swallowing awkwardly. "Because..."

She couldn't speak, so I gave the valet the card for our car and took her hand. "Where would you like to go for dinner? We can go anywhere you want."

She sniffed and wiped at her eyes, "Anywhere?"

"Anywhere." I might regret the offer later, but I could always order in something if I was still hungry and didn't like her choice.

My car pulled up in front of us and the driver got out and tossed me the keys.

"Where to, beautiful?" I opened her door and made sure she was buckled in before I rounded the hood. Once settled in my seat, I glanced over at my beautiful girl, who was red and smudged, and who I loved more than anything in the world.

"Home," she said.

"Uh, which home?" I asked, because that could mean her dorm, the apartment, my apartment, or even her mom's house.

Chastity laughed softly. "Can we go back to your apartment, order in some Thai food, and eat in bed?" There was a twinkle in her eye that I hadn't seen in months.

"Of course. Let's go!"

"What do you want?" she asked, pulling out her cell and ordering via a phone app.

I mentioned a few appetizers and main dishes I was partial to.

Chastity tapped it all in and sent the order off. "Great. Should be at our place in about half an hour." She relaxed into the seat as I drove through the streets and sighed. "I can't believe I actually thought my mom would get her head around this and be happy for us."

"Well, she does have a lot to deal with herself," I pointed out. "The pregnancy, and her and Pat. Maybe things aren't great between them and she's lashing out." I didn't think it was that, but I had to throw some option up in the air so that Chastity didn't think it was her fault.

"Let's not talk about my parents anymore," she said, sighing again. "I want to just go home, have a long shower, eat our food, and make love all night long like we used to."

I glanced across at her to make sure she wasn't joking. We

were only about five minutes from home and my body was already reacting to her promising words.

"Make love all night like we used to? Are you sure?"

She twisted in her seat to smile at me. "Oh, yeah. I've been missing you so much this week and my body is definitely back to where it was hunger-wise."

I turned the last corner and sped down the street as fast as was legal. "Think we can fit in a session before the food arrives?" I winked.

Chastity laughed and checked her phone. "Twenty-two minutes until arrival. What do you think?"

I pulled the car into the parking garage and turned the engine off. "I think we better hurry or hope the Uber guy is late." I hadn't made love to Chastity in so long, I had blue balls just thinking about how good it was going to be. Grabbing her hand, I hurried her to the elevator doors, her delighted giggles ringing in my ears.

3

CHASTITY

Mom was a being a bitch. She always had the capacity, especially if you crossed her, but I'd never really been on the receiving end before. I didn't like to admit it, but I'd still spent my whole life wanting to please her, constantly chasing her approval. And a large part of me still felt like I owed her for all the sacrifices she'd made for me when I was a child.

But that still didn't give her the right to tell me I shouldn't have my own baby now. I was fifteen weeks along, and it was a bit late to be telling me she thought I was making a mistake. Especially when I would never say the same thing to her about her pregnancy. Her baby was a miracle statistically and would be the second chance she wanted with my dad. I could see that, and even though she'd thrown it in my face, I could understand where she was coming from. That didn't mean I wasn't angry. I was furious. But for tonight, she was no longer my focus.

As soon as we got into the elevator, I grabbed for Axel and kissed him hard, throwing my passion into the kiss. I felt his lust surge against mine, like two cresting waves crashing against one another.

He pressed me up against the cold, mirrored wall.

I gasped at the contrast of his warmth at my front and the cold at my back.

The doors dinged open, and Axel pulled me out of the elevator and into the apartment. He tugged at my dress in need.

But I was too impatient to wait for him to take it off. Instead, I stepped back from him to grab my dress around the waist and pulled it up and over my head, myself, before dropping it to the floor beside me.

Axel's eyes widened as he scanned my changing body, still clad in the nice black underwear I'd bought just for tonight. When his gaze met mine, lust was written all over his face, from his darkened eyes to his mouth where he licked his lips with hunger. He dove toward me.

I tangled my arms around his neck, swept up in the storm of his passion. When he lifted me against his body, I wrapped my legs around his waist, planting kisses on his face and neck, holding on for the ride.

He walked us into the bedroom and there he set me on my feet and pulled his shirt over his head. "Strip off and get on your hands and knees on the edge of the bed," he ordered.

I was too excited to argue and simply obeyed.

He got rid of the rest of his clothes in moments.

Meanwhile, I pushed my panties down my legs and tore my bra off. Then turned around and knelt on the edge of the bed like he'd requested, going down on my hands so I was in a position that gave him total access to me. My heart pounded faster than it should as I waited for him, glancing over my shoulder to watch him move behind me.

"I got you a present. Do you want it now?" he asked, running his hand up and down my back.

I shivered at the caress. Not exactly what I'd been expecting him to say. "Ah... do I need it now?"

He grinned, disappeared for a minute and returned with a small, white box. "It's a clit vibe. It's the highest rated one in the shop where I bought it. Want to try it?"

I was pretty sure I was wet enough already, but why not? "Sure!" The last thing I wanted to do was turn down a gift from him and ruin the mood. Plus, I'd never tried anything like it before.

He handed me a small, pink, silicone tube that looked a bit like lipstick. He then pressed a button on its base, and I took it from him, the thing vibrating in my hand.

"I'm going to lick you, then enter you," Axel said, staring straight at me. "Set this next to your clit when I'm inside you, all right?"

I nodded, swallowing the groan that rose in my throat at his hot words. I loved it when he spoke direct and dirty to me like that.

He knelt down behind me and used his hands to open my thighs.

I turned away, dropping my head to relax my back.

Then he set his mouth on me. Sensations pulsed over my flesh as his lips suckled my clit.

"Oh! Axel... *wow*."

Then he ran his tongue up my pussy and thrust it inside me.

I screamed out in pleasure, then bucked against his mouth, unable to stop the involuntary jerk of my hips. From that angle, his mouth felt totally different and pressed on my pussy in new and amazing ways I'd never experienced before.

He stood up too soon and pressed his hard cock against me. "Fuck, you're too hot."

All my focus shifted to the space between my legs where he ran the soft skin of the head of his cock over me. From my swollen, throbbing clit, past my pussy, all the way up to my ass then back again. I moaned as the pleasure washed over me and closed my eyes. "Please fuck me," I whispered.

He pressed the head to my opening and thrust in just a little, teasing me.

It made me gasp and ache for more.

"Say that again," he growled.

I pushed back against him.

Not hearing what he desired, He withdrew completely.

Shit! I whimpered and groaned out in frustration, giving him what he wanted. "Please fuck me!" I begged.

He grabbed both of my hips and pulled me back, pressing his cock into me again. "Now, put the vibe on your clit."

I'd totally forgotten about that little thing. "Okay," I breathed. Resting my weight on my left elbow, I extended my right arm under my body to touch the little vibrator to my clit. I cried out at that first magical touch of vibration against my already sensitized flesh. My clit exploded with immediate ecstasy.

Axel plowed his thick cock straight into me, driving deep.

I came instantly, screaming out at the clenching tightness within my belly.

Axel groaned as he hardened his grip on my hips. "Damn," he hissed. "You almost made me come right then with you."

I hung my head with a moan and tilted my hips back for him, wanting more.

Axel read my move perfectly, pulling back and piercing me again.

I cried out, again, totally unable to deal with all the pounding while the vibe pressed perfectly against my clit, giving me the ultimate in sensation immersion. The ache inside my belly began to build again and with every stroke of Axel's cock, it pushed me higher and higher. I gasped and groaned, desperately bucking against him. The harder he thrust, the more I craved.

Together, we raced towards the final climax, pushing harder and faster up the hill to the precipice of bliss.

Just as my clit felt like it couldn't take a single moment more, Axel thrust deep inside of me and swore as he succumbed to his desire. He came, and heat flooded my belly, setting off my final orgasm.

I screamed, closing my eyes as wave after wave of pleasure rolled over me.

Axel pulled out and collapsed onto the bed beside me, sweaty and flushed. "Oh my God. That was so hot, baby," he breathed, a broad smile on his face.

I grinned at him. "So hot," I agreed. It had been perfect, but damn I was even more hungry now. "Do you think the Thai guy dropped the food and ran?" I asked.

Axel laughed. "Probably. I'll go check." He jumped up and walked out of the room. The perfect future husband.

I rolled onto my back and held up the little vibe so I could press the button at its base and turn it off. "Now, that's a great present," I said to myself with a satisfied sigh.

When Axel came back, he was still naked and had bags of Thai in his hands. "Picnic in bed?"

"Oh, absolutely!" That sounded perfect after amazing sex, and it's exactly what I wanted. I shuffled to the top of the mattress and sat up against the headboard, cupping my belly with my hand. I was getting bigger by the day, and I was loving it. I couldn't wait to wear those tight spandex tops that would show off my big, swollen stomach.

"Here you go." Axel handed me some cutlery then spread out the takeout containers for us to eat from.

"This is my idea of Heaven," I said, grabbing some noodles and opening the lid of the container. "Just you and me, in our bed, talking, and eating. What else could you want?" I took a bite of the chicken stir fry and groaned. "God, this is good."

We ate quickly, barely talking as we were both so hungry. But after some rice, chicken, noodles, and soup, I sat back and sighed, sated. "Thank you for that. It was great."

"You ordered it through your phone, which means *you* paid for dinner," Axel said with a frown. "I'll transfer some money over for you." He reached for his phone.

I swatted at him. "Don't you dare. You paid for dinner tonight and it was my fault we didn't get to eat it. I'm sorry about that." What a waste it had been. Our delicious meals would have sat there looking so sad and lonely without us. "Do you think Dad would have eaten our dinner too?" I asked, suddenly imagining my father's expression when he realized we weren't coming back.

Axel, who was still eating his prawn rice noodles, shrugged. "Probably. I've seen him put away three steaks in a sitting before."

I sighed and snuggled under the blankets. "I wish I didn't have to go back tomorrow. I'd rather just stay here and watch movies and relax." But knowing Axel would be working for most of the day made staying a moot point. I didn't want to relax alone.

"Well, I don't have to do much until six-ish. We could go out for brunch, then chill together for the afternoon?" He offered.

"Seriously?" I asked him, putting my head on the pillow.

He lifted the food containers off the bed and slowly closed them up. "Yes, seriously. I told you I want to slow down and enjoy life, and there's only one way to do that."

He certainly sounded serious. I needed to do some studying, but at the moment, I didn't care about anything other than getting the rest my body craved. "You're right. We need to get used to spending Sundays together," I announced. "Family days. Brunch and movies."

"And more sex," he added with a sexy grin.

I most certainly wasn't going to argue that. "Oh, definitely!" I said, then yawned, my tiredness getting the better of me. "That clit thing was amazing. Thank you for buying it for me." Axel really was an amazing fiancé. How many guys were confident and secure enough in themselves to buy their girlfriend a sex toy?

"You're welcome," he said, gathering all the containers up in his hands. "Give me a minute to clean up and I'll be back to sleep with you soon."

"Take your time," I whispered, settling into the pillow.

With his arms full, Axel disappeared into the kitchen.

I closed my eyes. Tomorrow, I'd enjoy spending time with Axel, but for now, I needed sleep.

4

AXEL

Sunday with Chastity was fantastic, and so much more relaxing than I'd expected. We had great sex, then a huge brunch. More hot sex, then watched a movie on the couch in my apartment. Well, I watched the movie while mentally planning my workday for Monday. Lists. Emails. Meetings. The usual.

Chastity watched the first ten minutes of the movie with her head resting on my shoulder and her hand on my leg, then fell asleep.

When the movie finally ended, I turned the TV off and the sound changing seemed to wake her up.

"Oh... I missed the ending." She groaned with disappointment as she lifted her head off my chest and sat up.

I rolled my shoulder where it had gone numb half an hour ago. I'd been too afraid to wake her, so I'd stayed put. "You missed most of it, sweetheart, but at least you got some rest." I stood up and stretched my back, extending my hand to her to help her to her feet. "How about we order a late lunch? What time is the driver taking you back to school?"

She rubbed her eyes and yawned. "I asked him to come around four PM. What's the time, now?"

I glanced at my watch. "Ah... about three forty-five."

"Oh, shit." She raced for my bedroom, calling out as she went. "I've got to pee, then pack, then go!"

I walked over to the bedroom and spoke through the closed bathroom door. "I can ask him to come back in a couple of hours if you want to go out for dinner before you go?" The extra time for me to work would be helpful of course, but I wanted her to know that we always had flexibility with our drivers. I paid for the privilege.

She stepped back into the bedroom from the ensuite and started picking up her things. Her cell, her bag, and her clothes. "That sounds so lovely, Axel. Thank you. I wish I could. But I really need to get back. We've got finals coming up," she said, stuffing all of her things into the large overnight bag she'd brought.

I grinned at her. She was happy to go back to school, which meant she was content with us. "Okay. Great. Is there anything else I can do for you?" I asked.

She launched herself at me, a grin on her face. She was practically glowing.

I swept her up into a hug, pulling her hard into my body.

"Nothing," she squealed. "You've been amazing. Thank you so much."

I walked her to the elevator and kissed her goodbye, wishing she didn't have to go.

As she was stepping into the lift, she put her hand against the door, stopping them from closing. "Hey, I just want you to know how much I appreciate you asking my dad to come work for you. It was really good of you. I know he'll love it."

I glanced down at the marble floor and ran a hand through my hair. I didn't know why it embarrassed me to have her be grateful for such a thing, but it did. "I'm doing it for all of us," I told her. "Pat is amazing in his field, and I think he'd be an asset to my company. I can pay him a lot more than he currently makes, which will benefit your mom and him." I'd happily just transfer a million dollars straight into his account if it would make his life easier, but Patrick was proud, and I knew he'd prefer to earn it. And I understood that.

She grinned at me, happiness twinkling in her eyes, "I know you're justifying your kindness by saying the decision was made purely on its merits, but I know you're doing it to help him. And my mother. And me."

I smiled at her, grateful for her understanding. "I need someone I trust at the helm with me. And Pat fits the bill." He was the only man on the planet I truly trusted. He had integrity and a great work ethic. Time would tell if we could be friends, family, and work colleagues.

Unfortunately, I'd heard some horror stories about mixing the two over the years, but it was time to step out of my comfort zone. I'd never gotten anywhere by staying inside the box, anyway.

"I love you," Chastity chimed as she stepped back into the elevator and let the doors close in front of her.

I held my hand up in farewell. "I love you too," though I wasn't sure if she heard me as the doors closed on my words. I sighed and glanced around. The apartment was so quiet now. So empty. Exactly how I used to love it. Not so much anymore, I realized, as the silence sank down on me like a weight around my neck.

I sighed once more and wandered into the kitchen, cleaned up, made myself a protein shake, and headed for the office. It was midnight when I next checked the time. I'd gotten a lot of work done and was prepared for the week, including Patrick's impromptu interview.

~

The following day, I was up and gone by six. I went to the gym, had breakfast, and was in the office by eight AM. My new managers were already in, working away in the conference room Cheryl had allocated for them until we could find the right space to put them all.

I liked having them close by my office, and them being together meant they brainstormed and bounced ideas off each other, which benefited everyone. "How are they doing?" I asked Cheryl as I stood by her desk, staring at the trio through the glass windows of the meeting room.

Cheryl gave me a rare, approving smile. "They're doing very well. A little too enthusiastic at times, but I can't fault their work. Or their intent. What are you going to do about them?"

"What do you mean?"

"They need a leader. You and I know that. And you can't do it. You're too busy."

I grinned at my office manager. Always one step ahead. "I have Pat coming in today to meet them. I've offered him the job."

"Patrick Johnson? Your friend?"

"Yes, that's him. And Chastity's father, too."

Cheryl's mouth dropped open, then she snapped it up again.

Damn, where was the camera when you needed one? That was the first and probably last chance I'd ever have of capturing a moment when I shocked Cheryl.

"I didn't know that was the connection," she admitted.

I grinned, suppressing the laugh that rose. "When we met, we didn't know the connection either. And once we did, well, it was too late."

And thank God for that. If I'd met Chastity as Pat's daughter, I would never have looked at her as anything more than the daughter of a friend.

"How is her pregnancy going?" Cheryl asked, her tone all business polite.

"Good," I answered in the same tone. "Fifteen weeks along so far, I think. The baby's healthy and she's healthy." Another thing I thanked the universe for.

"And college? When does she graduate?" Cheryl asked again.

I glanced at my office manager, who'd never shown more than a professional interest in my personal life before. "A month or two. Not long now."

"Hm. Okay. I'll get back to work and bring Patrick around to you when he arrives."

I stopped myself from responding with a "thanks, boss." Sometimes it truly felt like I worked for Cheryl, not the other way around. "Thanks."

Cheryl headed off and I went back to work.

At one pm, there was a knock on my office door and Patrick walked in. "Those three are going to take over this company, Axel. You're in trouble."

I laughed and closed my laptop. "You've been here less than a minute and you've already worked that out?"

"I got here half an hour ago and have just been hanging out with Cheryl and listening in on the three of them. They swap between English, French, and some other language I didn't quite pick up on."

I grinned at him and gestured to the chair in front of me. "You want to sit and chat?"

"Nah. I was thinking we could go out for lunch and talk there. I'm starving and I know you haven't eaten yet."

I stood up and walked around the desk. "Would you like to take the three vicious babies along?"

He shook his head with a smile. "No. I already know I want to work with them."

"So, you're in?"

Pat thrust his hands into his pants pockets and nodded his head.

"Don't you want to know the salary? Benefits?"

Patrick laughed and shook his head. "Axel, I know how generous you are. I know I give you hell for your success and your money, and all that shit, but..."

"Hey, look. Don't get soft on me. Here." I turned around and picked up the contract I'd had written up and handed it to him. "This is only the initial offer." With anyone else, I would never have told them such a thing, but this was Pat. I half expected him to shove the contract back at me.

Instead, he took it, then sat in the chair by my desk.

Okay, so we weren't going straight to lunch. I sat back on my chair and waited for him to finish reading.

"A car?" he asked.

"Yes." Any car he liked under a hundred thousand.

"Top tier health benefits?"

"Yes. For you and your family." Which would mean that hopefully Katherine's pregnancy would be covered, though I hadn't checked up on it.

"My salary—" Pat began.

"Not enough?" I asked. I had room to move. "We could set some bonuses based on performance."

Patrick's gaze flicked up to meet mine. "I need two weeks to tie up some loose ends at work, then I can start."

"As easy as that?" I couldn't believe it.

Pat nodded. "Yeah. As easy as that. You got a pen?"

I pushed a pen across the desk towards him.

He picked it up and signed on the dotted line. "Done."

I shook my head. "I can't believe we're finally going to work together."

"Even though we said we never would." Patrick chuckled, passing the signed document back across the desk.

I stood up and walked around the desk, grabbing my jacket. "Lunch to celebrate?"

"On you," my buddy said with a grin.

"Of course." And it always would be from now on, and my friend couldn't complain.

An hour later we'd downed a bottle of red wine and eaten a couple of steaks and were sitting in one of our favorite restaurants on a Monday afternoon.

"Don't you have to get back to work?" Pat asked, taking a sip of his water after four glasses of wine.

"Don't you?" I asked him.

He shrugged. "I took the afternoon off."

"Then I will too!" I declared, then ordered another bottle of red. "I still owe you that birthday meal, and since the other night got shot to hell, we can pretend this is your birthday lunch."

Pat groaned and ran both hands over his face. "Fuck, that was ridiculous. Kaiti is so worried about everything at the moment, and it makes her crazy."

Yeah, makes her a crazy bitch. "Can I ask you something?"

"Sure," Pat said, taking the bottle of red from the waiter and pouring us both another glass. "At this point in time, I don't think we should have any secrets."

"Why now?" I asked. I'd thought we were pretty solid as friends before.

He mock glared at me. "Because you got my daughter pregnant, and I saw you two naked in your apartment. I don't think we can get much closer, man."

I burst out laughing. I couldn't help it. "Okay, but I just wanted to know how you're doing with the pregnancy. Katherine's, I mean. You happy about being a dad again?"

"Are you happy about being a dad for the first time ever?"

I stared at him and let my joy spread over my face in a massive grin. "I couldn't be happier. That baby is the best thing that ever happened to me, except for Chastity, of course, and it's not even here yet."

"She's not even here yet," Patrick corrected, then sighed heavily. "I'm going to have a granddaughter. I can't really believe it."

I huffed out a laugh. "I can't believe my daughter is going to be your granddaughter, man. But, hey... stranger things have happened."

"Name one."

I couldn't, and Pat and I spent the rest of the afternoon drinking and laughing about it. We sealed our new working relationship with wine and good conversation, and it was truly one of the most enjoyable days I'd had in a very long time.

5

CHASTITY

The next month flew by. I was super busy at school, and Axel's workload was hectic. But he still drove down every weekend to spend time with me or more accurately, he was driven. I liked to joke with him that he was turning into a regular old billionaire now, having a full-time driver; but he just laughed and said it was my fault. I'd told him to delegate some jobs so he could work more effectively, and allegedly, driving was one of them.

My dad and I chatted every other day, and he and Axel were getting on well at work. They were both men who tended to be masters of the understatement, especially when it came to their own accomplishments. But if I had to guess, I'd say they were killing it together. In fact, it was time I checked on it.

My driver arrived, thanks to Axel's protectiveness, now that I was twenty weeks to drive me to my sonogram in the city. I'd offered to be closer to him so he could make it easily from work. As we set off, I put my bag on the seat next to me and picked up my phone, calling Axel's office.

A familiar voice answered the phone and I grinned. "Hi, Cheryl, it's Chastity!"

"Hello, young lady. How are you feeling today?"

"Great, actually. A bit nervous about my sonogram, but I'm sure everything will be fine." One hand went to my basketball of a belly as I said the words.

I'd read so many horror stories Online about women losing their babies later in pregnancy. I didn't know how I'd cope if I lost my daughter now, especially since I could feel her kicking and shifting. Being able to physically feel her moving around in there made it even more real; and I felt very attached to the little being inside of me.

"I'm sure you will be fine," Cheryl said, in her mothering tone. "And I'll make sure Axel doesn't miss it, even if I have to drive him there myself."

I laughed out loud at the image her words evoked. "I love you, Cheryl. You're awesome."

"Well, you're a good girl, Chastity, and I'm very grateful Axel has found someone like you."

We were silent for a moment, and I enjoyed the glow between us.

I'd never met, nor spoken to Axel's mother. By all accounts, she was a cold, horrible woman. So, in some ways, I think Cheryl's presence in Axel's world was a little motherly. I certainly got that vibe from her. She was professional to a fault, but she had a big heart and was fiercely loyal.

On the other hand, my own mother didn't want to talk to me, and for the sake of our health and our babies', I'd decided it was best not to try and contact her. Dad kept me up to date with any pertinent information, and I had to assume he did the same with her in regard to me.

So, as far as I could see, Cheryl was the only maternal influence either of us had at the moment in our lives, so it was nice to hear her such beautiful things.

"Thank you, Cheryl. I appreciate it."

"So, that being said, what can I do for you, young lady?"

I grinned. And there she was. The business manager was back.

"I'd like a report, please."

"A report?" she asked, sounding confused.

I grinned. "Yes. I want to know how my dad and Axel are getting along. Neither of them will tell me the truth. They only say it's going fine, but I know you'll tell me, Cheryl."

"I'm going to put you on hold for a moment, okay?"

"Of course." Was she running to another room so we could gossip without all her staff listening in?

Within a minute she was back on the line. "Thanks for holding, I had to move from where I was."

"That's no problem, Cheryl." Of course, she had to move. I knew it. *She has gossip.*

"I'm not sure I should report in on my boss, Chastity."

Yeah, right. "I don't need specifics, Cheryl. I just want to make sure there isn't going to be some big blow-up. You know, with them being nearly related because of me, best friends, and now work colleagues I've been extremely nervous about how they're getting along, but neither of them will say much about how things are going."

Cheryl laughed softly. "I can tell you that things are going much better than even I anticipated, and I had great hopes for the alliance."

"Really?" I asked, happiness filtering through my chest like sunlight. "Are they getting along that well?" Did they have lunch together? Brainstorm ideas? Did Dad have an office next door to Axel's now?

Cheryl chuckled. "Well, they don't spend a lot of time

together. Patrick oversees the managers and takes responsibilities from Axel, which leaves him to do more CEO-related tasks. So, he ends up walking around and talking to them instead. I'm finding it... funny."

She was finding it funny? "How is it funny?" She would probably be the only one that found it humorous that Axel was out of his depth.

She huffed out a laugh. "Yes. I don't think he quite knows what to do with himself some days. The younger managers are doing a fantastic job, and your father oversees them well. He teaches them while he's guiding them. I think he'll help Axel take the whole company to the next level—if Axel's ready for it."

I frowned. "Why wouldn't Axel be ready for it?" He worked harder than anyone else I knew and had achieved so much in his lifetime already.

"I'm not saying he's not, but it would require a lot of time and dedication on his part, and I think his focus has shifted."

"I..." I didn't know what to say. I knew his focus had shifted. He had a life now. A partner and a baby on the way.

"Don't get me wrong, Chastity, I'm glad he's changed priorities and has you. But you should know that his business model has the capacity to double and triple his revenue if it grows the way he's always planned for. And with your father at his side, I think they can do truly amazing things."

I nodded to myself with pursed lips. "Thanks, Cheryl." It wasn't exactly the report I'd wanted, but she'd given me an honest one, that was for sure.

"I better go," Cheryl said. "Good luck with the scan this afternoon. It's two PM, correct?"

"Yes." And in a rare moment of worry about Axel, I'd actually forgotten about the scan entirely. That's what *I* needed to focus on. My baby. Our life together. Not the worries that came with being engaged to a billionaire.

Cheryl said goodbye and hung up.

I put my phone down on the seat next to me, deflated. I'd gone into the conversation looking for gossip and something happy to focus on, but instead I felt..... sad.

Cheryl was saying that Axel and my dad worked brilliantly together. So brilliantly, in fact, that they could push past some corporate glass ceiling and beyond. But only if I got out of the way.

Was that true? Was that what Axel wanted? To live to work. Or was I being unfair in making him choose? I didn't know either way, but I had to talk to him about it and soon.

The car trip took longer than I thought it would, probably because instead of studying, I spent the time worrying. But soon enough, I was in the waiting room filling out another form when Axel walked in.

"Hey, sweetheart," he greeted me, sitting down on the chair next to me. "How's your day been?" He wore an expensive suit and looked powerful. Hot, in fact.

What was the question again? *My day?* "Oh, fine," I said, loving the way his hand slid straight onto my thigh. Protective. Possessive. I reached for his hand to hold, my stomach churning. "Hey, Axel?"

"Yeah?"

How did I ask this without causing waves? "Am I holding you back?"

He twisted in his chair to stare at me. "What are you talking about?"

"I mean... your business is doing so well, and you and Dad are doing great things. And well, I don't want to be the reason you don't achieve the goals you've set for yourself."

Axel frowned at me. "Chastity, I'm confused."

And he should be. I'd gone out of my way to make sure he

worked less, and now I was having second thoughts? "I'm sorry, it's just... are you happy?"

"Of course, I'm happy," he said, squeezing my hand and smiling at me.

"I know, but have I ruined work for you?"

He sighed. "Look, work is strange at the moment. The management team has taken *so* much of my workload, at times I'm not sure what I should be doing."

I grinned at him, needing to make a joke. "Yeah, but you needed four people just to take over some of your work. What does that say about how much you were doing?"

Axel chuckled. "Well, yeah, there's that."

"Chastity?" The receptionist called.

I stood up. It was time. "Come on, Daddy," I said to Axel. "Let's go see our baby."

Axel stood with a grin, and we walked into that small, white room.

I lay on my back and lifted my top, used to the routine of scans, already.

The sonographer smiled at me as she got the lubricant ready. "This is a longer scan as we're looking at all the anatomy. So... here we go," she said, setting the probe on my belly.

I looked towards the screen, the black and white lines soon wriggling into the shapes that I knew so well. "There she is," I whispered and glanced towards Axel.

He was staring at the screen with an intense look on his face.

"You know it's a girl?" the sonographer asked.

"Yes." I grinned. "The blood test said the baby's a girl. Are they ever wrong?"

"Let's just check," the sonographer said, swiping the probe over my belly. "No, they weren't wrong. That's a little girl."

Axel sat down in the chair next to me and grinned. "She's beautiful."

I stared at him, feeling my love grow bigger and stronger. "She is."

"So, there's the head. Let's just measure the circumference." The sonographer went on the measure the whole baby, noting that she was healthy and well. No anomalies and was measuring exactly to term.

When we left, I was filled with happiness and clutching more pictures for my wall. "I'm so glad you were here to see her," I told Axel as we walked outside into the fresh air. "Do you want some of the pictures?"

He nodded. "Yes. Can I have the hand one?"

I laughed at him. "Of course!" It was my favorite too, but I wasn't going to stop him from taking the one he wanted. I sorted through the little stack of printouts and handed it to him. "There's something special about her little hands, isn't there?"

He took the picture, then nodded. "Yes. She's perfect." Then he glanced back at me. "Are you going to stick around so we can have dinner together?"

I put my hand on his arm and sighed. "I'd love to. Do you have the time?"

"Of course, I do. We could go back to the apartment and spend a couple of hours in bed?"

My lower belly clenched at the suggestive tone of his voice. "Oh, yes, please."

He wrapped his hands around my waist and drew me into him.

I went with him, wanting to be as close to his warmth as possible, sliding my hands around his neck and pulling him down to me for a kiss.

An afternoon of sex and food sounded like Heaven to me and a great way to distract me from my troubled thoughts.

6

AXEL

I stood in the central area of my main business floor—a sea of low walled cubicles—and glanced around the office filled with people, marveling at the amount of work being done. Patrick was in the conference room yelling at someone, and everywhere I looked, people were on the phone, staring at computers, or rushing to their next meeting.

"Surveying your kingdom?" Cheryl asked deadpan as she walked up to stand beside me.

"Well, yeah." I assumed she was joking, of course. But in a way, I suppose I was looking at what I'd created. What my business sustained. Lots of people with jobs, supporting themselves, and possibly families. That was an achievement. And what I liked about it the most was the fact I'd built it up from nothing. My parents hadn't given me squat. "Can you believe it was just you and me in the beginning?"

Cheryl rolled her eyes. "I had to bring coffee mugs from home because there was no money for extras."

A laugh burst out of me at the memory. "Yeah, I remember that." Twenty years had changed many things, but not my appreciation for Cheryl. I stared at her as she glanced around, checking on the staff like a mother hen watching over her chicks. Perhaps it was time to show my appreciation in a bigger way than a simple "thank you."

"I was hoping to talk to you, actually. Do you have time now, Cheryl?"

Cheryl met my gaze as though assessing my intent, then nodded once. "Yes, I've got five minutes."

I chuckled to myself as I walked back to my office, Cheryl trailing behind me. She had five minutes to spare me, did she? *Better not keep her then.* I walked over to my desk, turned around, and leaned against the edge. This wasn't a meeting, and I didn't need to sit in my executive chair. "I won't keep you long, but I wanted to tell you that I appreciate everything you've done for me and for this company."

Cheryl narrowed her eyes at me. "Why does it sound like you're about to fire me?"

"Oh God, no!" I cried, shaking my head. "You couldn't be more wrong."

She stood patiently, eyeing me with suspicion.

It suddenly occurred to me she was waiting for me to continue. But the problem was, I didn't have anything planned. *Time to think on my feet.* "Well, I want to know how I can best reward you for your loyalty and hard work, Cheryl. A yearly bonus, perhaps? A raise? Tell me what you want and it's yours."

I already paid Cheryl well, but nowhere near what I paid my Ivy League managers, which didn't make sense when I thought about it. Without her, this place probably wouldn't exist.

Cheryl shook her head at me. "I'm not really comfortable talking about raises and such, Mr. Patterson. You've always been very generous with my yearly increments."

I stood up from the desk I leaned on and stared at the woman before me. "Can I ask you about your retirement plans, Cheryl? How many years do I have you for, before you leave me?"

Cheryl smiled, though it was tight. "Well, my youngest is still in college, and the bills for that are still coming in. So, I'm hoping to be here another ten years or so."

Perfect. "You have two children, correct?" We didn't talk about a lot of personal stuff, Cheryl and I, but I'd heard enough to know she was married with two sons.

"Yes. Michael is twenty-seven and Tommy is twenty-one."

"What's the balance of his tuition fees and boarding?" I asked.

Cheryl didn't answer, but her eyes went wide as though she were already a step ahead and on to my plan.

I just crossed my arms over my chest and smiled at her. "I can guess, if you want me to."

She swallowed hard, her throat working. "It's close to a hundred thousand, I believe. But we're happy to do it, of course. Anything to help the boys succeed."

The perfect mother. Something I'd never had. I walked around my desk and pulled out my checkbook from my top drawer. "Cheryl, without you, I would never have made it past the first year. Without you, I would never have found Taylor or hired Patrick."

I sat down in the chair and grabbed a pen. "You have been a mentor to me in many ways, so please take this as a bonus for all your hard work." I wrote out a check for a hundred grand, tore it off, then got up again and walked over to her. "With my heartfelt thanks." I held it out.

Cheryl's bottom lip quivered. "Mr. Patterson, I couldn't possibly—"

"You can, and you will. Or I'll just send it over to your house in cash. Unless you'd prefer that?"

"No... I..." Her gaze darted from the paper to me and back

again. She seemed to finally realize I was serious and her hand shook as she reached for the check and put her fingers on the paper. "Axel, I don't know what to say."

Cheryl rarely used my first name, and it tugged at my heart when she did. "Just don't leave me yet. Not until I figure out what I'm going to do next. With work and Chastity. Everything."

Cheryl swiped at the tear that rolled down her cheek, then she nodded. "No. We still have a lot to do before I can retire."

I leaned back on my desk and smiled at the woman who was still standing in the middle of my office, nearly speechless. "That's all I needed to tell you, Cheryl. If you want to go to the bank before they close, maybe leave early today?"

She nodded slowly, her lip doing that quivering thing like she was about to cry, then she turned on the ball of her foot and walked out without saying another word.

I sat and relaxed back into my chair and sighed. That had been well overdue. And it felt great to reward her in a way that truly mattered. I reached for my mouse and began scrolling through emails. I needed a bigger fish, a larger project. Patrick had the managers under control, and the manager trio had most of my work covered. I needed more.

MORE CAME the week Chastity graduated. She got through her exams, packed her stuff and drove back to the city in her car. The door opened and she called out, "I'm here!"

I jumped at the sound, then grinned. I was going to have to get used to that since she was moving in. I got up from my computer and walked out into the living room. "Welcome home."

Chastity dropped her bag on the floor and stretched her arms out wide. "To my million-dollar apartment? Ha." She rubbed her belly and glanced around.

More like 5 million, but I wasn't going to correct her. "How's my baby?" I asked, walking up and putting my hands on either side of Chastity's belly the way she liked. I cupped the solid flesh that felt almost like she'd stuck a basketball under her t-shirt.

"She's wonderful," Chastity answered, then leaned forward and kissed me, tasting of sweetness and love.

I picked up her one bag. "Should I call the concierge to get your other bags from the car?"

"Yeah, that would be great. Thanks."

I made the call and soon enough, Chastity's bags were piled up in my bedroom and she was sitting on the couch, rubbing her stomach. We needed to work out where she was going to put everything. My bedroom closet was full.

I glanced at the time. It was only three PM. "We've got a few hours before dinner. Are you okay if I keep working?" Should I even ask that in my home? *Our home?* I corrected myself. What was the protocol here?

Chastity answered for me. She just stood up, cupped my face and kissed me quickly. "Do whatever you need to do. I'm going to have a quick nap because my feet are killing me. Then I'll shower and unpack maybe. See you in a few hours." She headed off towards the bedroom, a hand on the small of her back.

I sighed. I wouldn't mind having a lie down either, but when was the last time I had a nap in the afternoon? I turned towards the study, the email I was halfway through calling my name.

Then I heard Chastity groan and sigh and I stopped. "Screw it." I unbuttoned my shirt and walked into the bedroom.

Chastity was pulling back the covers, wearing nothing but panties and a thin tank top. "Oh, are you joining me?" she asked.

I unzipped my pants and slid them off. "Yes, I think I will."

Chastity laughed happily as she slid into bed, surrounded by pillows, one between her legs and one in front of her.

"You've built yourself a bit of a pillow wall," I remarked, sliding onto the mattress.

She made a contented noise. "Hmm... Not behind me, though."

I cuddled in behind her, sliding a hand over her hip and closing my eyes. "I've missed you." Especially at night. Sleeping without her was impossible. I always slipped back into bad habits, getting only three or four hours most nights.

"I hope so, because you're not getting rid of me now."

I kissed her neck. "Thank God for that," I whispered,

She fell asleep almost immediately.

I didn't think I would. Sleeping during the day had never been my thing. Sleeping, full stop, had never been my thing. But sleep, I did. And when I woke up, Chastity was still there, my baby kicking away beneath my palm. "Oh, wow, she's moving," I said, loving the feel of the shifting and pushing against my hand.

Chastity groaned, rolling onto her back. "Sorry, I have to move. My hips are killing me."

I ran my hand over her bump, marveling at the movement going on. "This is incredible."

"Yeah, it is." Chastity smiled, lying happily in my arms. "What are we doing for dinner?"

It was Saturday night and there were a hundred places we could go, probably more. "We could go out if you're up for it? Japanese? Italian, maybe?"

"I'd love to go out and celebrate a little. We didn't get to do anything after my graduation."

"I'm sorry, sweetheart. I had to fly to France, and well..." I hadn't gone to her graduation for several reasons, but mostly because I wanted Chastity to enjoy her achievement, and not worry about what sort of fight her mom and I were going to get into.

Chastity and her mother still weren't really talking, but

Katherine had gone to the ceremony, mostly because Patrick had dragged her there.

"You wanted to let my parents have the moment, I get it. I just missed you. I wanted you to be proud of me too."

Love filled my chest. "I *am* proud of you, sweetheart. I'm very proud of you. I would have completely understood if you decided to just quit school to have the baby; but here you are, a college graduate."

"And five months pregnant," she said with glee, rubbing her hands over her belly again.

"Yes, you are." I pressed my lips to her belly, then rolled out of bed. "Let's go then. Dinner."

"Shower first," she said, getting up slowly. "Are you going to join me?" She glanced over her shoulder with a sultry expression.

Damn. I'd missed that look. Heat flooded my groin and my cock hardened, rearing for action. "Hell, yeah," I said and followed her into the bathroom.

She shrugged off her tank and panties, shaking her ass for me playfully.

"How are you going to be most comfortable?" I asked, jumping straight to it. "From behind?"

She turned the water on and wiggled her ass again. "Say, is that vibe thing waterproof?"

"Yes it is." I walked out of the bathroom to fetch the clit vibe and some lube from the nightstand. I didn't want to hurt her, and her body was changing every day. When I walked back into the ensuite, my cock was throbbing. I grabbed some lube and worked my shaft, loving the way she stared at me as I did it. "Damn, I've missed you," I told her. "Have you missed me?"

She nodded, the water cascading over her rounded body. "Yes."

"Have you missed my cock in your pussy?"

She groaned and cupped her hands around her breasts, squeezing her darkened nipples. "Oh my God, *yes*."

I walked forward and grabbed her, kissing her hard.

Her arms came around my body, then moved down to my cock, squeezing the head and stroking it.

I turned her away from me, deciding to test out a theory I had. She liked me talking dirty to her, or at least telling her what I wanted to do to her. She always flushed pink when I did. "Put your hands on the wall and stick your ass back if you want me to fuck you."

She gasped and did exactly as I'd ordered. Her fingers splayed over the grey tiles, she bent forward, sticking her ass back and spreading her legs for me.

I pressed the button on the clit vibe and slid it around her hip. "Use this. I want you to get yourself nice and ready for me."

"Oh, I'm ready." She gasped as she pressed the vibe to her clit. Then She sashayed her hips, tempting me.

I put my hands on her thighs and rubbed my cock between her spread legs, and over her lips, driving us both crazy. "Tell me what you want."

"You," she panted, pressing back.

I would have laughed if I hadn't been so horny. "Do you like me telling you how much I want to fuck you?"

There was a soft pause, then she moaned. "Yes."

Then I was right, and I'd make sure I told her a lot more often. "We're going to discuss that later, what you want me to say to you. But for now, I want your pussy to squeeze me so tightly I come in you."

"Yes. Oh, yes, please." She panted, hanging her head forward.

I slid my hand between her legs, thrusting a finger deep into her pussy, testing how ready she was for me.

She moaned and wriggled on my finger.

My sweet Chastity was nice and juicy, so I withdrew it and

replaced it with my cock, thrusting deep with one solid stroke. "Oh, God, yes. My beautiful girl," I groaned out, rocking into her perfect heat again and again.

She came almost instantly, squeezing my cock hard as I worked in tandem with the vibe to overwhelm her senses.

"Oh God..." I closed my eyes and held tight to my control, fucking her through the ripples of ecstasy, and then up that mountain of desire again. Deep and hard and fast, I plowed; until we were both screaming in raw bliss, the hot water running over our satisfied bodies.

7

CHASTITY

Moving in with Axel was both strange and natural at the same time. Asking him for space to be cleared in the closet took some time, but soon enough he'd sorted out what he needed on a daily basis, and we split the walk-in space. And I moved his extra items to the closet in the spare bedroom.

"Maybe we should have his and hers closets at the new house," he'd joked, which inspired me to go on a house hunt.

I was heading towards six months pregnant, and now that school was finished, I had nothing to fill my time with except for keeping an eye on my health and planning for the future—our future.

Axel left for work around seven AM and often didn't get home until dinner time.

One night he'd asked me how my day was, and I begrudgingly admitted, "I'm bored."

He stared at me like he'd never heard the word before. "Ah... sorry. You'll need to define that better for me."

I sighed and dropped my fork. "I don't know what to do all day while you're at work. I feel like I need a job or something. I'm going a little stir-crazy here."

Axel's mouth opened and shut. "But you're six months pregnant," he finally said.

I ran my hands through my hair, then pulled it up into a bun on top of my head. "I've been looking at houses for us, and I found one I really like. It's got lots of character and is in a great location. It's close to your work and my parents."

Mom and I had started occasionally texting each other, but we really needed to have it out properly. She'd need my support when her baby came, and I certainly needed her now.

"That's fantastic. When can we see it?" Axel asked.

I jumped up from the table, feeling my perkiness returning. "I'll get my laptop and show you right now!" I heard his chuckle as I tried to race to the bedroom, though running while waddling wasn't the most elegant thing.

When I returned, he'd cleared the table, and I sat down to search for what I'd found earlier. "I'm not sure if this is the sort of thing you're going to like. It's not super modern and it needs a little work, but I'd really like the project. I could paint the baby's room, and maybe hire contractors and oversee the renovations." I'd never done anything like it before, but I was sure with Axel's connections and money, I could certainly learn.

"Show me," Axel said.

So, I did. "It's four bedrooms, with a study as well," I told him, showing him the layout of the house. "The lot is huge for the area, but the house needs new carpets, and maybe a new kitchen."

"On Patterson Drive?" Axel asked, his lips quirking up at the irony. "Is that going to be weird, or is it meant to be?"

I grinned up at him. "I think it's meant to be."

"Can I have a quick look?" he asked, gesturing to the laptop.

"Of course." I pushed the computer at him.

He clicked and scrolled and scanned what I'd found, holding his chin as he did in thought.

"I've looked at hundreds of listings," I told him, feeling the need to fill the silence with my chatter. "From inner-city apartments to huge blocks out of town."

"And this was your favorite?" he asked, still staring at the computer screen intently.

"Well, yes. There are more finished, more expensive properties, of course." Though this one was still insanely expensive. I'd had a heart attack over the prices in my first few days of searching, but after a chat with Cheryl that Axel didn't know about, she'd told me not to even look at the price and just choose the house that my heart wanted.

After all, it was Axel's money. He was the one who should say if it was too expensive or not, and that was a direct quote from Cheryl.

"I like it," Axel finally said. "I've always wanted a pool in my family home, so we'll need to see if there's room for one in the backyard."

"Oh, yeah, that would be amazing. I just thought with the house being so expensive, we'd need to wait to do those sorts of improvements."

Axel leaned forward and kissed me. "We don't have to wait."

I threw my arms around his neck and burrowed my head into his shoulder, tears filling my eyes.

"Hey, are you okay?" he asked, pulling me back.

I had to look down and blink away the tears. "Yeah, I'm fine. It's just the hormones," I admitted, fanning my face with my hands dramatically. "I'm too emotional lately. It's ridiculous."

He grinned at me then kissed me again. "You're perfect. Now, do you want me to call the real estate agent?"

"Could you?" I asked, knowing Axel would do a much better job at organizing something that big and important than me. "You do know your way around that kind of stuff."

He nodded. "Give me ten minutes." Axel took out his cell phone, grabbed the number of the real estate agent off the screen, and walked away to the office.

I sat on the chair, wanting to squeal out aloud but held it in. We were going to buy a house to raise our daughter in, together. It was unbelievable! Moments later, I could hear Axel chatting to someone on the phone, so to keep busy, I quickly rinsed the dishes and loaded the dishwasher.

He was back soon after. "Well, I have some good news," he said with a grin.

"Tell me!" I was practically ready to bounce out of my skin with excitement.

"The house is empty and the owners are wanting a quick sale, so we'll be able to negotiate a lower price. So, once we see it and it passes inspection, we may be able to get going on the renovations sooner than expected."

"Before the baby's born?" I asked, this time my voice rising to the squeak I'd been afraid of.

He grinned at me. "Yes."

I launched myself at him, hugging him tightly, even though my baby bump made it entertainingly awkward. "I was afraid that would never happen," I admitted. "That we'd wait too long and then have to move with an infant." And that sounded like an absolute nightmare to me. Especially if I ended up with a C-section or complications that required major rest time afterwards.

Axel pulled back. "We haven't seen it yet but if there's any structural damage, then we'll have to move on to something safer. Try not to get your hopes up too high, okay?"

I nodded enthusiastically and clapped my hands.

He sighed, but smiled as if I was incorrigible. "They're high already, aren't they?"

I bit my lip and grinned. I'd already driven past the house and planned out all the flowers I would plant in the front yard and already envisioned the swing on the porch. "When can we go see the inside?" I asked.

"Tomorrow, around lunchtime. I'll clear my schedule from noon til one."

I hugged him again. "Oh, thank you, thank you, thank you, Axel."

He kissed my forehead and sighed again. "Just be careful not to fall in love with it too quickly. I've been bitten by that bug before, only to find out it's not the right one."

"Okay, I'll try," I reassured him, but I don't think I convinced him.

He walked off for a shower, shaking his head in good humor.

It was too late though, I was totally in love with the place. And I was going to be heartbroken if I found that my dream home wasn't my dream at all.

THE NEXT DAY I drove to the house in my little car, talking to the baby the whole way. "Your room is the one behind ours. I'll be able to run in and help you anytime you need me. And there's a park just down the street, and a massive backyard for you to play in. Although, Daddy wants a pool, so the backyard might end up pretty small. But then we'll have a pool, so, either way, it'll be awesome. We can teach you how to swim!"

I knew I probably sounded insane to anyone looking in from the outside, but it was how things were with me now. My whole world was centered around the baby who made my back ache and my belly bulge and my hormones a complete mess. She was my everything. And I couldn't wait to meet her and be her mom.

I arrived early and parked down the street a short way so I could check out the neighbors. The blocks were all large with relatively new houses. It was zoned for residential homes and had no apartment buildings. The existing homes were grand houses and took my breath away, which meant they were all well taken care of, and the owners took pride in their residences here.

When twelve o'clock struck, a blonde woman parked in the driveway and hustled up to the front door wearing a short skirt and a jacket.

I wasn't sure I should approach her. There was something about her demeanor I didn't like. But I was sure Axel would handle her so I wouldn't have to. I checked my phone and there was a text from Axel.

Two mins away. Just caught a red light.

I smiled as I put my cell phone away. Ever since the debacle around the twelve-week scan, Axel had been extremely thoughtful about messaging me when he was late, which I appreciated to no end. So, I waited. I wasn't going in by myself.

Then his black sports car pulled up and I walked over, grinning as Axel hopped out of the driver's seat.

"You drove yourself for once?" I teased.

He laughed. "I wanted to see how far it was from the office for myself."

"And?" I asked.

He grinned. "Twelve minutes on the nose."

"Brilliant," I said.

He grabbed hold of my hand and started walking towards the front door. "It's a great street," he remarked. "The front lawn needs some work, and a new fence."

"Yeah, a higher one, preferably," I agreed. "So, I can bring her around the front and not worry she'll run out onto the street."

Axel smiled at me. "Are we going to name her yet?"

I shook my head. "No. Not yet, please. I feel... I don't know. I can't really explain it. But it seems like bad luck to name her before she arrives."

Axel sighed. "No problem. But maybe we can discuss options, so that we're prepared?"

"Okay," I agreed. "We can do that." I already had a list of my top ten names memorized.

Axel rang the doorbell, and we could hear the rushing of heels clattering on the floor to the door to open it. "Axel Patterson?" the blonde asked, her eyes set on Axel's handsome face and her bright smile firmly in place.

"Yes, and this is my partner, Chastity," he said, gesturing to me.

The blonde's eyes fell on me, and I saw a shift in her face when her gaze fell on my belly.

I rubbed it for good measure. "I'm due in October and we're looking for a family home."

"Oh, well yes! This home is perfect for you then. Come on in," she said, falling straight back into professional mode. "The owners are very motivated to sell and are happy to commit to a quick closing. The house has seen better days, but the position is incredible."

"You go with her, I'm going to wander and take a look around," I told Axel, dislodging my hand from his grip.

The blonde didn't miss a beat and went off on her own tour, still talking away about the noble qualities of the home.

Axel grinned at me. "Okay."

I walked into the first room, the one I'd already planned to use as Axel's office. It was the smallest, and now that I saw it in person, it was perfect. Great light, and no built-in closet. I worked my way through the house, noting the need for new paint, new carpets, even a new kitchen and bathrooms long-term. But the space really was amazing. It was twice as big as Axel's apartment, and three times as big as my mom's house. We would have so much freedom here; to work, live, and play.

"Shall we check out the backyard, beautiful?" Axel asked as I joined the other two in the huge living room.

"Yes, please."

Axel turned towards the blonde. "Would you mind calling your office now and enquire about that home inspection, please? I'd like to speak to Chastity for a minute."

"Of course, sir," she said, and bustled off officiously.

"Thank you," I said. "She's a bit full on for me."

Axel shrugged. "Most real estate agents are like that, But I'm used to it." He opened the French doors and we walked into the backyard. "So... what do you think?"

I glanced around at the huge, open space. There was lots of grass, a garden shed, and a huge oak tree right in the middle of the backyard. "I think this is the best backyard I've ever seen for child to grow up in."

Axel stepped behind me and put his arms around my waist. "Good job keeping your enthusiasm in check in front of the agent, by the way. But what do you think about the house, really?"

I closed my eyes and rested my head back against him. "I love it."

He kissed my hair. "I do too."

I twisted around in his arms, my eyes wide. "What does that mean?" I asked cautiously with bated breath. My heart was beating a little too fast, and although I was afraid of the answer to come, I was also so excited I could barely breathe.

Axel leaned forward and rubbed his nose with mine. "It means, assuming it passes several different inspections, we'll buy it and move in as soon as possible."

"You mean it?" I whispered, already envisioning the baby's

room in a kaleidoscope of pink—with a vintage rocking horse, an antique crib, and beautiful, restored rocking chair.

"Of course, I do," he said, kissing me softly. "But let's find out where we stand structure-wise before we make an offer, okay?"

"Okay." I agreed, crossing all my fingers and toes. This is the right house. I could just feel it!

8

CHASTITY

It was a tense week while we waited on the pest and structural inspections, and Axel got quotes for a pool and renovations to the kitchen.

I was sitting on the couch with my swollen feet up when he arrived home early.

"Chastity!" he called out, his voice loud and happy as it echoed through the living room.

I glanced up from my cell phone. It was barely five PM. "I'm here!" I called back. "Just reading." A pregnancy and birth book, as usual.

He walked into the room, grinning from ear to ear.

I swung my legs off the couch and stood up. "Everything okay?" It certainly looked like it, but he wasn't saying anything, so it felt natural to ask.

He schooled his features into a calmer expression, then nodded. "Yes. Everything is great."

My breath caught in my throat. "Did you get news about the house?" I asked, my pulse quickening.

"I did. Everything passed inspection, so I put an offer in, and they accepted."

I stared at him, speechless. Did that mean what I thought it meant? "What does that..."

"It means the house is ours, beautiful."

My hands flew to my mouth as I gasped, shocked. *We have a home!* I could explode with glee.

Axel continued. "We've agreed to a thirty-day settlement, and because the house is vacant, they're also allowing us to go over to get measurements and quotes so the renovations can start as soon as we take possession."

I squealed and rushed forward, hugging him tightly, tears filling my eyes. "I can't believe it." He'd bought us a house for our family to grow in. It was beyond my wildest dreams.

Axel held me against him as he heaved a sigh of relief. "You and me both. I was really worried I was going to have to tell you it failed inspection, and I knew you had your heart set on it."

I laughed as I gently withdrew, wiping away the tears and reaching for a tissue to blow my nose. "Yeah, I tried not to get attached to it, but I fell in love with that house *so* quickly."

"It's going to be a big change, Chastity. No concierge. No elevator," Axel said, glancing around at his apartment.

It would be a change for him, but for me? I couldn't wait to get my feet back on solid ground. I wanted to plant a tree and wiggle my toes in the grass of my own backyard. I wanted to peg washing and carry a basket on my hip. I wanted normalcy; a down-to-earth home for our daughter to grow up in. "It's going to be amazing, Axel. I don't know how to thank you."

He smiled as he knelt down in front of me and kissed the baby bump. "I just want you two to be happy. That's all that's important to me."

I lifted my left hand and ran my fingers through his thick hair, staring down at his handsome face. "Thank you."

He got to his feet again and started chatting about dinner plans.

I tried to nod and talk, but all I could think about was the house. I got my laptop out and stared at all the photos for the hundredth time. The floorplan and the yard. "Can I tell you what I'm thinking of for the house? You know, like which bedrooms for what use, etc?"

Axel chuckled as he opened a bottle of sparkling water. "Please do. Tell me what you're thinking."

I told him which room I wanted for the nursery, and how I wanted to decorate it. Then I went on to describe every room's purpose and design.

Axel hummed and laughed and smiled.

He was really listening to me, and I felt heard and loved. It was one of the most fun and happy nights I'd ever had. It felt like such a monumental step toward our future together as a family.

Now, if only I could sort out the issues I was having with my mother.

THE NEXT THIRTY days passed in a whirlwind. I was almost thirty weeks pregnant, and I'd spent the month with architects, designers, and contractors. The sheer amount of money Axel was throwing at this project was dizzying, but I tried not to focus on it. My weight was down, and my energy was zapped, but there was only one way forward, and that was to keep working toward our goal.

I walked into the real estate office to pick up the keys from the blonde who'd sold us the house. Axel and the previous owners had signed all the papers this morning, but Axel had organized for me to pick up the keys.

Her smile, as always, was bright and fake.

The baby kicked me hard as if to show her own excitement.

"Ow, baby girl. Relax." I rubbed the spot where she'd kicked me and thanked the blonde agent.

"Good luck with the new house," she said. "You'll all be very happy there, I'm sure."

"We will," I said with pride, sticking my nose in the air. "Axel's already planned out everything we need for renovations, so I'm very lucky."

"You are," the blonde snapped with a tightness in her voice I didn't understand. "Not all of us can get pregnant to billionaires."

I stared at her, shocked by her underhanded words. *So, she knows who Axel is, does she?* I could have justified my pregnancy, told her Axel had happily started our family earlier than expected, and loved me more than anything. But I didn't. I'd had enough of her crap. "Well, not all of us are massive bitches, so it takes all sorts, doesn't it?" And I walked out of the real estate office with my head held high. Axel and I knew the truth about our relationship, and I wasn't justifying it to anyone else. *Fuck that bitch,* I thought as I walked out into the sunshine.

Harry, my driver, held open the car door. "To the new house?"

I grinned at him and got into the car, my belly now so large it was difficult to sit behind the wheel myself. "Yes, please, Harry. Thank you."

He shut the door and we arrived at the new house within five minutes.

I'd been there many times over the past month, but never as the owner. I eased myself out of the car and walked up the sidewalk, glancing around at the huge front yard and fence that would soon be torn down. *So much work still to do,* I mused. But we'd move in soon enough, hopefully within the month and then the next chapter of our lives as a family would truly begin.

And that was exactly what we did. Between Axel and me, we managed to get the house ready for move-in. We scheduled painters, had the kitchen gutted and remodeled, and all the furniture delivered.

I didn't really like handing off the job of decorating the baby's room to anyone else, but with my blood pressure getting higher and my energy running low, I ended up finding a satisfying compromise.

I located a decorator who hand painted the baby's room and let me watch and chat, allowing me to be as much a part of it as possible. I still hadn't been able to sort things out with my mom, but it was becoming clear that I needed her, and I was sad she was missing all of this.

Although my dad was always around, at the apartment or on the phone, I wanted my mom. The day we moved into the new house, I called her.

"Chastity, hello," she greeted as she answered the phone. She didn't sound surprised to hear from me, but she didn't exactly sound excited, either.

"Hey, Mom. How are you doing?"

"I'm fine," she said, but didn't ask about me or offer anything further.

"That's great," I said. "Dad told me that you finished work up early to rest. How's that going?"

Mom's blood pressure had been so high, her doctor put her on bed rest for a month. She was now well enough to go about her normal life if she was careful, but there was no returning to work.

"It's tedious," Mom admitted, then sighed. "Did you take possession of the new house yet?"

My mouth dropped open, shocked. Then I realized that she would know everything Dad did.

"Yeah, we closed a month ago, and its finally ready to move in. I was wondering if you wanted to come over and see it?" I held my breath as I waited. Would my mother want to see the sort of house Axel had bought for me?

"I'd like that," she said finally. "What time suits you?"

I glanced around the empty room. "Anytime today, if you want. Axel won't be home until dinnertime. Do you want me to send a car around to pick you up?"

There was a pause.

I knew Mom wasn't supposed to drive herself. She was over thirty weeks with blood pressure concerns, and I was close to thirty-four weeks now. I hadn't seen her in person since my graduation. We'd both look quite different now than we did back then.

"Yes. That would be good."

"Okay, great. His name is Harry and I'll call him now. He'll probably be around soon."

She hung up.

A thrill of excitement shot through me. I was going to see my mom again and show her our new house. A house I was *so* proud to call our home. A house that in the past would have only been something I would have seen in a magazine.

I called Harry and he said he could pick my mother up in half an hour. Axel had hired him to be our full-time driver the past few months. It seemed overly excessive to have someone on call just to drive Axel and me around, especially when we had our own vehicles. But at times like this, I was grateful for Axel's protective streak.

I raced around the house for the next forty-five minutes. Well, raced is probably an exaggeration, but I changed clothes, brushed my hair, and tidied up, wanting to make a good impression. I put some healthy snacks out on the new granite kitchen island and waited with bated breath for her to arrive.

When my phone rang and it was my father, I jumped on answering it. "Hey, Dad!"

"Hey, sweetie. Ah... have you invited your mom over for a chat?"

I rolled my eyes. "Obviously she already told you, so what's wrong?" He wouldn't have called me just to wish me luck.

"Well, I just want to warn you that she hasn't been in the best of moods lately. She might bite your head off over the smallest thing, so please tread carefully."

I rubbed my hand over my wiggly little girl and sighed. "So, are you... what are you saying exactly, Dad? That I shouldn't have invited her over?"

"No. I'm glad you did. She's been harassing me for months for photos and details of you and your life. Now, she can see for herself."

I put a hand on my hip. "If she wanted to see me or our house, why didn't she just ask?"

"You know why, Chastity."

I sighed and stared down at my swollen feet. "She's missed my whole pregnancy, Dad."

"I know. And you're missing hers." His words hung in the air, then the doorbell rang throughout the house.

I twisted around and stared down the long hallway to the large doorway. "I think she's here."

"Okay. Well, just be careful, Chastity. You're both the most important people in the world to me, and I don't want either of you hurt or upset."

"I'll try not to upset her, Dad, but to be honest? I'm a bit sick of dancing around her. I feel like I've been doing it my *whole* life."

He sighed. "Yeah, I understand that, honey. And any other time, I'd tell you to just go for it, and hash it out with her. But right now, well... you'll see. She's not her normal self."

"Okay, Dad. I better go. Love you."

The doorbell chimed again, and I sighed. Okay, so I had to be on my best behavior, even though everything inside of me considered our time apart my mother's fault. *Come on, Chastity. You're about to be a mother. You can do this,* I scolded myself. *Take the high ground.* With a deep breath I walked towards my front door and opened it onto the next chapter of my life.

9

CHASTITY

I opened the door, and my mom was standing on the other side—on my porch. "Hi, Mom." My heart ached at the sight of her.

She was pale and gaunt. Her eyes had dark circles underneath them and she was compensating with way too much makeup. "This is a nice area," she said casually, glancing around. "You were lucky to be able to buy on this street."

"We were," I agreed. "Very lucky." Lucky that it came on the market, lucky I found it, and lucky Axel had the money to purchase it for us. "Come in," I said, standing back and beckoning her inside. "We only moved in officially a few days ago, so we're not quite unpacked yet." I didn't know why I was making excuses for the house, it was a piece of art. The interior designers had done an incredible job.

Mom walked in, slowly, moving carefully.

"Are you okay, Mom?"

"Yes. " She answered, though I could tell by the gingerly way she moved, she was in pain.

"Do you want the tour?" I asked.

"Sure," she said. "Where can I leave my bag?"

"Oh, let's go straight to the kitchen and you can put it down there." I directed her into the huge open kitchen and dining space.

She walked in and stood near the granite island, staring at the room in something akin to wonder. "This is—" she coughed to clear her throat. "—beautiful, Chastity."

"Thanks, Mom," I said, surprised to hear a compliment already out of her mouth. "The house was in need of a bit of love when we bought it. Everything was a little sad. The walls, the kitchen, the carpets. Everything needed to be replaced."

"You're lucky Axel can afford to do everything all at once."

I bristled at the first shot fired, then soothed myself. It was true. We were. "Yeah, I know. I can't believe this is our first house, though it could be our last, too. I can't imagine moving."

My mother wandered over to the windows that looked out over the huge backyard. "You haven't done much in the way of landscaping yet," she observed.

"No, not yet. Axel wants to put in a pool."

She twisted around to look at me. "Aren't you a spoiled one?"

I put a fake smile on my face. "Are you jealous?" I calmly asked her.

She crossed her arms over her chest, making her huge belly more prominent beneath the flowing black dress she wore. "Why would I be jealous?"

"You shouldn't be," I told her. "But I can see it on your face. So, you tell me, Mom, why would you be jealous? I know you had it tough, but your life is great now. You have Dad, and a new baby on the way. Why the bitterness?"

She turned away, facing out toward the backyard once more.

When she didn't respond, I walked closer to her and reached out, but I didn't touch her. Too much had passed between us over the last six months, and I wasn't quite ready to just sweep it all under the rug. In fact, I thought we needed to put it on the table, once and for all. "You need to tell me, Mom. What's the real problem here? Is it Axel? You hate him, I suppose, because he's rich and too old for me?"

She didn't even turn to look at me, she just rubbed her belly in slow circles. "I don't hate Axel."

I crossed my arms over my chest. "Good. Because he's wonderful to me and makes me very happy."

My mother didn't say anything.

So, I pushed on. "Okay, so it's not Axel. It must be that you still think I've ruined my life by getting pregnant. You feel that I've thrown away my future because I'm not continuing on to chiropractic school."

She turned around to me slowly, and her eyes were red. "I know you haven't ruined your future, Chastity. Axel will look after you no matter what happens between you, and that sort of financial security is something I never had raising you."

I sighed and let my arms drop to my sides. "I know that, Mom. But I didn't get pregnant on purpose, and I didn't choose Axel because he's rich."

"I know."

"Then what did I do wrong?" I burst out. "You've barely spoken to me for six months, and now that you're here, you still won't talk to me..."

Mom swayed on her feet.

In a panic, I rushed forward, grabbing her arm. "Are you okay?"

She nodded, but I could see the sweat on her brow.

"Quick. Let's get you sitting down." I led my mother to the couch and made sure she was reclined with her feet up before I left her to get something to drink. "What would you like? Cold water? Orange juice?"

"Juice would be nice," she said, though her voice was barely loud enough to hear.

I poured both of us a drink and rushed back to the couch. "What's going on with you, Mom?" I sat on the couch opposite her, wincing at the pinch in my hip and trying to find a comfortable spot for the baby and me.

"Lots of things are wrong with me." She sighed heavily. "I'm forty-three and having my second baby. The hospital staff treat me like I'm some sort of... oddball, because I dared to get pregnant naturally at my age."

I grinned at her. "Yeah, I suppose most of the women who get pregnant in their forties do so through IVF."

She nodded, then took a sip of her juice. "I have high blood pressure and they're pretty sure I'll get pre-eclampsia; which means they'll have to deliver the baby via C-section as soon as it gets too dangerous for the both of us."

I gasped, my breath catching in my throat. *How horrible.* "Oh, Mom, that's terrible. How are you feeling about that? I'm so sorry."

"I hate it," she confessed. "I was still jogging five miles a day when I was eight months pregnant with you. This one though..." She rubbed her belly thoughtfully. "This one is taking everything I've got, plus some."

"But is the baby healthy?" I asked, a question I often asked my dad, but wanted to hear it from her as well.

"Yes. The doctors are happy with the baby's progress, it's just my body that's struggling."

I blinked quickly as hot tears filled my eyes. "I'm so sorry, Mom. I didn't realize. I had no idea."

"No," she said clearly, sighing again, her strength returning a little. "I'm sorry, sweetheart. I've been so... stupid. I shouldn't have reacted the way I did when you told me you were pregnant.

I was just so angry for you. That you were going to miss out on so much, making the same mistake I did."

"But I'm not, Mom." I gestured to my new home. "Look around. This is my new life. A man who loves me, a new house, and baby girl who will hopefully be born in a month or so. I know this isn't what we planned, but it's what I want."

My mother stared at me, then nodded slowly. "It's not what we talked about nor planned for you. But I can see how happy you are, sweetheart. And I'm sorry I couldn't be here to help you or share in your joys."

I swallowed hard against the wave of emotion that rose in my throat, clogging my nose and making it difficult to talk. "I didn't need your help, Mom. I just wanted you to be happy for me. Especially with my baby girl. I'm—" I had to stop and swallow again, the tears getting the better of me now. "I'm so happy I'm pregnant. I really am."

She smiled, and this time I could make out some of the warmth in her eyes that I'd been hoping to see. "I know, sweetheart. Having a daughter, especially when you have one like I did, is a wonderful thing."

"Thanks, Mom." I reached for a tissue and wiped my eyes. "Do you know what you're having?"

She shook her head. "No. We decided not to find out."

I didn't bother bringing up what she'd said at dinner. All of it was in the past. It didn't matter anymore. What mattered was moving forward, together, as a family. "So, are we okay? I mean, can we go back to being in each other's lives? I want you to come here, and I want to be able to see you. I want to go out shopping for baby things. All of that good stuff."

She grinned this time and it was a relief to see the brightness return to her eyes. "Yes. I'd like that."

"Great!" I said, clapping my hands. "Are you hungry? I can

make us something to eat." I groaned as I hauled myself to my feet.

"I'm not really hungry," she protested.

I laughed. "Me neither. But my specialist is worried about my weight, so I've got to eat a bit more." I waddle-walked into the kitchen and pulled out some chocolate that I was sure would tempt her. Carrying them back, I offered her the box. "I know you like these."

"Thank you," Mom said as she took one.

I grabbed one too, then sat back down on the couch.

"You do look a bit thin, Chastity." She frowned.

I laughed. "Yeah. Thin. Right! I'm *huge*."

Mom shook her head. "No. Your cheeks are sunken, and your arms are too thin."

I sighed. "Well, I didn't mean to lose weight. It's just been difficult to eat, and with all the stress..."

"Make sure you look after yourself," she said. "I'm sure the doctor is right."

I popped the chocolate into my mouth and chewed, savoring the sweet, milk chocolate. "Have you got a good doctor, too? Axel said that Dad's insurance should have kicked in for you."

She nodded, the light in her eyes dimming. "Yes, it did. I didn't really want to change doctors, I liked mine. But when the pregnancy became high risk, Patrick thought it was better..." She trailed off into silence.

I felt the bone of contention grow. "So, you're still not happy about Dad and Axel working together?" I asked. May as well talk about everything that was upsetting her, now. No point leaving it for another day. I wanted everything sorted out as quickly as possible.

"It's not that I'm not happy."

"Then what is it?" I asked, forcing myself to reach for the chocolate box I'd set on the coffee table and grab another one for myself. "It's obvious you're not happy about your private health insurance, and that is certainly something I do not understand."

"It's not that I'm not grateful," she replied defensively.

I laughed at the expression on her face. "You don't look grateful, Mom. You look like that chocolate in your mouth just turned to ash and you're too polite to spit it out."

Her face twisted up into a bit of a wry half-smile, half sneer. "I can't help it."

"You can't help what?"

"That I don't like the way we're so entwined in each other's business all of a sudden. Patrick's boss is his best friend but could also become his son-in-law. It's too messy. If something goes wrong between you two, or those two, it's going to royally screw up everything. In our lives, Axel's business, Patrick's confidence... just everything."

I leaned back against the couch cushion and rubbed my belly, loving the feel of my daughter kicking softly against my left hand as if reassuring me. "And if nothing goes wrong, then Dad and Axel are both happy," I countered.

My mom frowned at me. "Axel's been too generous. I don't know what to say about all the money he's been throwing at Patrick."

I laughed at that one. "I'm sure you had a lot to say about it at the time, Mom."

"He shouldn't get preferential treatment because they're friends. That's just a recipe for disaster."

I grinned, feeling totally at ease now. My mother had been worried about nothing. She'd probably been sitting at home alone all day, twisting herself in knots. "Mom, Axel told me that he offered Dad the exact amount he would pay any executive manager. The car, the insurance, it's all standard compensation. If it's a lot more than Dad used to make, then he was wasted in his former role."

Mom was silent for a minute, then nodded. "I told him the same thing about his old job. He worked far too hard for too little."

I grabbed my phone and glanced up at her. "Well, the guys won't be home for hours still. How about we order some take-out and watch a movie?"

Her eyes glistened with unshed tears, then she nodded. "Sounds like fun. What do you want to watch?"

I waggled my eyebrows at her. "What about Father of the Bride, Part 2?"

She laughed at me thinking I was joking.

But I wasn't! So, we spent the rest of the afternoon eating popcorn and chocolate, watching movies, and catching up on the months we'd been apart.

And when Axel eventually called to say he was going to be late, I didn't even mind, because Mom stayed with me. And that's when I knew she'd missed me too.

10

AXEL

At six PM I texted Chastity to tell her I was going to be late and blamed work for needing to stay back. But when I couldn't concentrate for a single minute more, I went to the gym to work out instead. I was so furious at Pat I couldn't think straight. He'd advised against taking on a new, pet project that I'd spent a month getting access to. He wanted me to throw all my work away and give up on this deal.

No one had ever spoken to me the way he had, rejecting my idea and telling me it wasn't good enough to invest my time in.

My initial reaction was an explosion of words, and I don't even remember what I said; but I think I might have threatened to fire him. Considering he was my best friend and future father-in-law, everything was far more complicated. Why did he have to challenge me the way he did? Did he want my company? Did he want us to fail? Did he want to just be a giant pain in my ass for no goddamn reason?

I pumped iron until my arms shook and my chest heaved with the strain. Then I drove around the city until my temper calmed and I felt like it was safe to go home. When I got there, I sat outside my house for far too long in the car. Who am I going to talk to about this? I couldn't go to Chastity or Pat. Maybe Cheryl will listen?

I dropped my head back against the headrest. Fucking hell. I'd dropped to a new low. I was the boss. I wasn't supposed to be looking for people to whine to. I needed to suck it up and deal with this myself. Growling with annoyance, I got out of the car and walked towards our new home, my temper dropping as I stepped into the light cast through the front door glass panels. The house had come together beautifully, and Chastity was happy and well. I should be counting my blessings.

But what would happen to us if Patrick and I couldn't sort out our differences? Had hiring him as my second in charge been the right thing to do? I stood on my doorstep and took a deep breath. I wanted to talk to Chastity about my problem, but how?

The door opened suddenly, and Chastity's beaming face welcomed me home. "You're back!" Her gaze swept my clothes. "Did you go to the gym?"

I shrugged, feeling guilty about lying to her, so I told the truth. "Yeah, I had a bad day, so instead of bringing that shit mood home, I tried to work it out myself."

She opened the door wider, her smile not faltering for even a second. "Thank you for that. It gave me more time with my mother."

I walked into the hall and put my briefcase down, then realized what she'd said. "Your mother? Did you see her today?" They hadn't been seeing eye-to-eye for months now.

"She's still here. Come and say hello." Chastity grabbed my hand and pulled me down the hallway. "She loves the baby's room, by the way."

I was tugged into our living room, where a woman I barely recognized was sitting at the kitchen table holding her pregnant belly. She was thin and pale and looked nothing like her usual self.

I nodded at her. "Katherine, it's nice to see you."

She smiled at me, and there was more warmth in her face than I'd ever seen directed at me. "Are you okay, Axel?" she asked.

I frowned at her. "Why wouldn't I be?"

"Patrick called. He's worried about you."

I groaned, then went straight to the fridge to pull out a cold beer, all pretense gone. I'd hoped to avoid this exact conversation, but Pat dropped me straight into it. "What did he say?" I asked, on edge again.

"You didn't tell me Dad was worried about Axel," Chastity said to her mother.

Katherine didn't respond.

I chugged back some beer, needing the fortification for this conversation. "I didn't want to bring this home to you," I told Chastity, then shook my head. "Church and state." But it was difficult when things between us were so intricately connected.

Katherine stood up, pale and wan, her belly bulging almost bigger than Chastity's.

"Go on," I said to her. "Tell me that I made a mistake, Katherine. That I should never have hired my best friend, the man that will be my father-in-law." I took another long chug of beer. "I fucked up."

Katherine shook her head. "No. You didn't. You gave Patrick the job he needed. He's been bored for so many years. And you —" she stopped and swallowed. "You gave him the chance to do more. Be more."

I ran a hand through my hair. So now she's on my side? And when I didn't necessarily even want her to be.

"Katherine, that is generous of you. But it doesn't change the fact that Pat is trying to destroy the biggest deal I've ever made.

He's making me second-guess everything I've worked so hard for."

Katherine grinned at me and rubbed her belly. "And?"

"What do you mean, and?" Surely, she could see the problem with that.

"I mean, he's your second in charge. He loves you more than anyone."

I put both hands on the counter and stared down at the white marble. "What are you trying to say, Katherine?"

"I'm saying that Patrick's intentions are only to support you. To be worth the money you pay him. If he's telling you to stop and look again, maybe you should heed his warning."

I glanced up and glared at her. "Seriously? You think he knows better than me what is good for my company?"

Katherine's gaze was steady as she stared at me, looking remarkably like her daughter in that moment. "What reason would he have to want you to fail? Your company puts food on the table in our house and feeds his daughter, too." She laughed a little to emphasize the point she thought I was dense. She turned towards Chastity. "It's time for me to go. Can you call your driver for me, sweetheart?"

I hung my head, defeated but still angry. Maybe Katherine was right, and I needed to speak to my second in charge again. "No. Call Pat to come pick you up. He hasn't seen the house yet," I said, choking back my pigheadedness.

"You want Dad to come to the house now?" Chastity asked, biting her lip as though worried.

I nodded. "Yes. Tell him to come in if he wants to talk. If he doesn't, he can still pick your mom up."

"Okay. Sure." Katherine turned away to use her cell phone.

Chastity crept up next to me.

"Are you okay?" she asked, putting her hand on my arm.

I nodded. "Yeah, I think so. Things at work have just been

intense lately." I'd been going after things too hard, again. That was becoming clear by the headache building behind my eyes. Chasing those bigger fish that Cheryl had talked about. But with Chastity at home waiting for me every night, I had to leave earlier than I should. I had to get more done on weekends or stay up through the night while Chastity slept.

It wasn't easy to balance everything. The company. A partner. Family. I shook myself and turned towards my beautiful woman, putting my hands around her belly. "How's our baby today? Has she been giving you grief again?"

Chastity slid her hands over mine, moving them to where the baby was kicking. "She's fine. Just getting too big for me to carry her around like this."

"Not long now," I said, leaning forward to kiss Chastity on the lips.

There was another reason I'd been pushing so hard. I wanted everything tied up and settled before the baby was born. Chastity would need me at home, with her. And I wanted to be that support for her. I wanted to be everything she wanted. But currently, I had no idea how I was going to do it all. It all felt beyond my reach; but I was no quitter. "I need a shower," I said, feeling hot and bothered. I was still covered in dried sweat from the gym and felt tacky.

Katherine walked back over to us, her hand pressed to her back. "Patrick said he'll come over and pick me up. He'll be about twenty minutes."

"Perfect timing for me to have a shower, then." I kissed Chastity once more, taking courage and patience from her lips. "I'll be back soon." I walked into our bedroom and shut the door, feeling tired to my very bones. Maybe it was time for a rejuvenating vacation. Somewhere warm, with no internet access. Does such a place exist? What did Chastity call a vacation at this point? A babymoon? One last holiday before our lives changed forever.

I pulled off my t-shirt and workout sweats, going straight into the newly renovated bathroom. It was clean and bright, and the shower was big enough for Chastity and me to have sex against multiple walls. It was by far one of my favorite places inside the house. The backyard was next—a pool for leisure and exercise.

I stepped beneath the hot spray and sighed at the sensation, wishing the water could wash away all my worries. Had it been the wrong choice to pursue this deal? Was Pat right? It hadn't felt like it today when we'd been discussing it. I'd wanted to throttle him for second guessing me, for calling me a fool.

I'd regretted hiring him at that moment and had immediately worried what Chastity would think of me for firing her father. It would have ruined so many relationships. Pat's and mine, and perhaps Chastity's and mine. I wasn't sure having him work with me was worth the benefits, risks, or the stress. I just didn't know anymore.

After wallowing in how pathetic I was for a few minutes, I scrubbed myself clean, washed my hair, and even shaved. May as well face the future well groomed. When I stepped into the bedroom with a towel wrapped around my waist, Chastity was there, sitting on the bed with the door shut. I ran my fingers through my still damp hair. "Why do I feel like I'm about to be told off?"

She shook her head. "Oh no, this isn't that at all. I came in to tell you I support you and love you, no matter what. Okay?"

I pulled the towel off my body, quickly dried my hair, then threw it towards the laundry basket. When I walked towards the closet, I couldn't help but notice the way Chastity's gaze swept over my body. Even in moments of high stress, I loved the connection we shared. "What do you mean, sweetheart?" I grabbed a shirt and a comfortable pair of jeans, then pulled the jeans on.

"I mean... you seem to be more worried about the relationships involved in this than the work. I think you're right. You need to separate the two if you can."

I put my arms through the sleeves of my shirt, then began to button it up. "I don't know if I can, sweetheart. If I want to fire your father, what's that going to do to our relationship? There's a reason Pat and I never worked together before, and that was because I was concerned I'd lose his friendship. Now, we're so much more intertwined than a simple friendship ever could be."

He was our baby's grandfather, among other things.

Chastity stood up and walked towards me. "You need to do whatever you need to do," she assured me. "You've been a success because you've worked your ass off and followed your instincts. If you think Dad's wrong, tell him. If you need to fire him, fire him. I'm sure you wouldn't just throw him out on the street with nothing."

"No, of course, not. I could get him a job with some contacts tomorrow."

She smiled at me and lifted her hands to cup my jaw. "Then what are you worried about?"

"I..." What was I worried about the most? "Us. I don't want anything I say or do with my company to affect you and me."

She kissed me. "It won't. I'll make sure of it. I'm proud of you. So do what you've got to do."

The doorbell rang and I turned towards it, sucking in a deep breath. "Your dad's here."

She nodded and took my hand in hers. "Let's go, then."

11

AXEL

Chastity walked ahead to the front door and opened it for her father.

He spoke to her quietly, so quietly I couldn't hear what he was saying.

My gut churned. What the hell was I going to do about this? Part of me wanted to leave—to avoid the whole situation—but the bigger part of me told me to man up and face whatever needed to be done.

"Come see the baby's room," Chastity invited. "It's my favorite place to be in the house. Although, the kitchen is pretty amazing, too." My future fiancé waxed lyrical about her happiness with the house. She told her dad about the new floors, the plans for the backyard, and everything else she had planned to make our home perfect for our family.

And I still hadn't stepped out of my bedroom. I took a breath and was just about to join them when Katherine pushed open the door to pop her head in.

"Are you still in here?" she asked.

"Yeah, why?"

She smiled at me, and there was a hesitancy in the smile I didn't usually see from her. "You're really worried about this, aren't you?"

I glanced away, still not sure about this woman or whether I trusted the new side of her I was experiencing. "Yeah, I am," I admitted.

"Why?"

"Why?" I repeated, feeling exasperated. "Because everything I care about is on the line. Chastity, Pat, my company."

She smiled serenely this time, rubbing her belly in rhythmic circular motions. "I like your list of priorities, Axel. That's how it should be."

I frowned at her. "What do you mean?"

"You said, 'Chastity, Patrick... then your company.' It may have been accidental, but that's your order of importance. And that's how it *should* be. Your wife, or partner. Your best friend. Then your job thirdly. Not first."

I sighed and scrubbed my hands over my face. "Katherine, I—"

"No, wait. Axel. I'm trying to pay you a compliment, not upset you. I..." She stopped, then frowned. "It's no secret I haven't always liked you."

I huffed out a laugh at that one. "Really? No way."

"You're the sort of man who tends to chew on girls and spit them out, and I was scared for Chastity in the beginning."

I opened my mouth to rebuke her, but she spoke over the top of me.

"But I was wrong."

My jaw dropped.

She grinned at me. "There. I said it. I was wrong. About you. About you and Chastity. My daughter is the happiest I've ever seen her, and you're obviously a good man. A good provider. And a great friend, or Patrick wouldn't have kept you around for a decade."

I sighed. "Why do I feel like there's a but coming?"

"No but," she said, shaking her head. "I just ask that you listen to Patrick the same way you have on all the other issues you two have faced together. He loves you. My daughter loves you. And my granddaughter is going to love you too." Katherine stopped talking then.

I could see the tears shimmering in her eyes. A strange tightness wove its way around my chest, and I nodded at the woman who I'd been at odds with since the moment I met her. "Thank you, Katherine."

She nodded and she may have wanted to say more, but Chastity and Pat had found us.

"What are you two doing in the bedroom?" Pat asked, his face lighting up with humor. "If I didn't know you both so well, I might be jealous."

"You?" Chastity huffed at him, nudging her mom out of the way softly to come stand next to me. "I could start to worry that Axel has a thing for pregnant women—and it's not just me!"

I wrapped my arms around her and kissed her hair. "It's just you, sweetheart. It'll only ever be you."

She cuddled in, then silence fell over us.

When I looked up, Pat was sharing a strange look with Katherine.

"Should we take this party back to the living room?" he suggested.

"Sure," I agreed. "And how about a beer?"

"Yeah, that would be great," Pat said.

We all walked back into the living room and the atmosphere was much more settled than I'd even hoped for.

I got us a couple of beers from the fridge and the women sat on the couches, both holding their large bellies in that sweet, protective way new mothers always did. I handed Pat the bottle with an awkward grimace, not entirely sure how this interaction would play out.

"How about you show me the backyard?" he said, accepting the beverage. "Chastity mentioned you want to put in a pool?"

"Yeah." I sighed with relief. "That's a good idea."

Get away from the girls and have a proper talk. Man to man.

I opened the French doors, let Patrick through, then shut them behind us. "There's chairs beneath the tree," I told him. "If you want somewhere quiet." It would be dark too, which would help both of us to speak freely.

We wandered off the back porch and took a seat on either side of the massive tree in the backyard. The sun had gone down, and the shroud of night fell around us.

"It's a beautiful house, Axel. Chastity is very lucky," my future father-in-law said, breaking the ice.

I glanced over at my best friend. "I'm the lucky one, Pat. She's amazing."

Silence fell again.

Should I start, or would he? When he didn't speak, I decided to forge ahead. After all, I was his boss. "Pat, I'm sorry about what happened today. I behaved poorly." And I had. I'd never yelled at an employee like that before.

Pat sighed as he drank his beer. "You might be right. Perhaps working together and being family might be too much."

I settled further in the chair, relaxing against the back. "How do people do it? Keep everything separate?"

"I don't think that's so much the key," Patrick said quietly. "Some of the best teams in the world are related. Fathers and sons or brothers. They make it work *because* they're related, not in spite of it."

It sounded like he'd thought about this a fair bit. "What do you mean?" I ventured.

"Well, our friendship makes me more honest with you, more likely to tell you the truth."

That didn't really help. "Pat—"

"No. Think about it. You can hire any guy to be your second. You can pay him a fortune to bow and scrape and work his ass off. But ultimately, he doesn't care if you lose twenty million dollars. He doesn't care if your company goes ass up in the end. He'll just move on to the next job. It's no skin off his nose. But you're my family, Axel. Your success feeds my daughter. It will pay for my granddaughter's education. And I'll be damned if I stand by and let you make a mistake that could ruin you. I won't do it. You can fire me for being a stubborn asshole who won't let you make a deal I think is shit. I won't lie to you. I won't give in or feed your ego. I won't do it, Axel."

I swallowed hard and set the beer bottle on the grass next to the chair. I opened my mouth to speak, then swallowed and shut my mouth again. *Is he right?* Would Taylor have stuck her neck out and risked the chopping block when I'd yelled that I wanted the deal? Probably not. But Pat had... and would continue to do so. I groaned. "Do you really think it's that bad a deal?"

"Hell, yes, I do. I ran the numbers. Let me show you tomorrow. If I'm wrong, you can fire me."

I turned toward him. "I don't want to fire you, but I'm not sure I can stop myself from yelling at you if you go up against me like that again." I'd been *so* angry. I'd treated my friend like shit, and I hated myself for the things I'd said.

Pat chuckled. "Yeah? And?"

"I don't want it to be like that between us. Yelling and screaming. Feeling..."

"What? Angry?" he prompted.

"Yes!" I hated feeling so out of control.

He laughed. "Bud, you're my best friend. I don't care if you yell and scream or throw a damn chair at me. I'm going to tell you straight up what I think. It's up to you if you want someone kissing your ass or covering it. Because I'm only here to do one of those things."

I stood up and reached my hand out to my friend in a gesture of good will. "So, you'll keep working for me?"

Pat put his hand in mine.

I pulled him to his feet. "Yes. But only if you can handle me giving you the truth, because I'm not going lie to you, Axel. Not for any amount of money."

Pulling him in close, I hugged him hard. "You're a good friend, Pat."

"And you're a great boss, Axel. But you need to learn to take advice."

We turned and walked back towards the house.

"Yeah, I do. And I could probably use a little more." I stepped up onto the porch and glanced inside.

Chastity was laughing, chatting away happily with her mom. The light made her hair glow gold, and her skin looked luminescent.

"Tell me what you need," Pat said, standing next to me on the porch.

Shoulder to shoulder, he was my brother in arms.

"I need to... slow down. But I don't know how. I hired the terrifying trio to take my workload down a notch, then got you to take the rest of the stress. But Cheryl started funneling these new projects to me and I saw the potential for growth and—"

"You can't stop, Axel. You're a workaholic. I've always said it."

I punched my friend in the shoulder. "Shut up. I said I needed your help, not your shit."

Pat chuckled loudly. "Look, you need a straight-up vacation, friend. It's obvious. You're about to have a baby and you're killing yourself for what... another million or ten? Take Chastity away to

Hawaii or something. Get some well-deserved rest. I promise you, your empire will still be here and standing strong when you get back."

I scrubbed my hands over my face for the second time that night. "Fuck, Pat. How have you done this for so many years? Managed a kid and work?" And the truth was he'd done more than that. He'd stayed healthy and fit. Found time to dated women, as well as climb the corporate ladder.

He laughed. "I didn't manage an entire company the way you do, but yeah, it's fucking hard, man." He reached for the handle and opened the door. "Now, you tell Chastity you're going to take her for a vacation, and I'll convince Cheryl to back off for a few years until my granddaughter is old enough."

He opened the door.

That's when we heard a pained moan and a shout. "Dad! *Quick!*"

We bolted inside and Chastity was standing over her mother, where Katherine was leaning over on her side, clutching at her belly.

"Something's wrong!" Katherine cried. "Pat! The baby!"

"I'm calling an ambulance," I said aloud, jumping into action.

Pat knelt next to his woman.

I put the cell phone to my ear and dialed nine-one-one, Katherine's moans turning to screams in my ears.

They came within five minutes, buckling Katherine onto a gurney.

Pat jumped into the ambulance with her without a second's hesitation.

Chastity began to cry as soon as they left, tears streaking her lovely face.

I held her tightly, thanking God for our blessings and the healthy baby still safely tucked away in Chastity's belly.

"What if the baby dies?" Chastity whispered to me an hour

later. Katherine had wanted Chastity to stay home, and rest and the uncertainty was fast getting to her. She wanted to know what was going on with her baby sibling and her mom.

Patrick had promised to call as soon as he had news, but if Katherine was taken into surgery, I knew Chastity would want to go to the hospital as soon as possible. So, we waited on the couch, having not moved from where we'd collapsed after they left, our anxiety filling the room.

"Don't talk like that," I told her. "They'll call soon. You'll see."

When my cell phone rang, we both jumped. It was Patrick's name on the screen. I reached for it and answered as calmly as I could manage. "Pat. Talk to me. Is everything okay?"

12

CHASTITY

My heart was thundering in my chest as I stared at the cell phone. It was Dad. "Oh, please have news on Mom," I whispered.

Axel continued talking to my dad.

I signaled to him that I wanted to hear, too.

"Hey, let me put you on speaker, Pat." Then he pressed the button and held the cell phone out in front of him so I could be a part of the conversation. "Is everything okay?" he prompted.

"How's Mom? How's the baby?" I called out over the top of him, digging my nails into Axel's arm where I sat on the couch, pressed into his side.

"They're okay for the moment," Dad assured us.

I exhaled, relief flowing over me in a massive wave. "Oh, thank God." I reached for the phone and took it out of Axel's hand. "What happened, Dad?"

"It was false labor, they think. The baby isn't doing so well, and Kaiti has pre-eclampsia, which we already knew was going to be a risk. But as Kaiti's only thirty weeks they're going to try and keep the baby in there as long as possible."

My hand flew up to my mouth. "What does that mean? Is she home?" Hopefully she was already in bed with a book or curled up watching a movie.

"No. They're going to keep her here at the hospital, on forced bed rest. They'll try and keep her hydrated, monitor the baby, as well as Kaiti's blood pressure. If anything happens or she gets worse... well..."

"Well, what?" I demanded, standing up so I could move around and use up my anxious energy. "What are they going to do?" I'd read a little on pre-eclampsia and it was supposedly terrible for the baby and the mother.

"They said they'll do an emergency C-section and get the baby out," my father said hastily. He sounded stressed, and judging by the situation, he had every right to be.

My eyes filled with tears. "But she's only thirty weeks." The baby would only weigh one and a half, to maybe two pounds at this stage. He or she would have a tough road ahead if the delivery was this early.

"Yeah, but your mom's strong. And thanks to the healthcare Axel gave us when I took the job, the hospital said they can keep her in and look after her until she delivers. Whether that's tomorrow, or in two months' time."

I looked toward my beautiful man and gave him a grateful smile. "Then I suppose Axel's job did come in handy, Dad." I leaned down and kissed my man where he still sat on the couch. He'd made sure my parents were taken care of, even if they hadn't always seen eye to eye.

Axel shrugged, ever the modest one.

Dad chuckled softly. "It's come in more than handy, sweetheart. We bought a new house a month back, thanks to this job. I can finally give your mom the family home she's always wanted. So, yeah, I owe Axel more than he knows. Which, by the way, friend, if you're still listening, is more proof of why I'd never lie to you or mislead you. I would never have been able to afford the house we wanted on my old salary, and my old health insurance would never have covered Kaiti's condition. So, thank you."

Axel stared at me, obviously overwhelmed by the compliment.

I shoved the phone at him. "Say something," I whispered.

Axel coughed to clear his throat. "Yeah. Of course. No problem, Pat. Take whatever time off you need to."

"No need," Dad said. "I have to go home and pack a bag for Kaiti, then I'm on my own until they call me. I'll go crazy waiting at home, and Kaiti doesn't want me in the hospital twenty-four-seven anyway, so I'll see you tomorrow. I rather keep myself busy, than be pacing aimlessly, waiting for a phone call."

Axel coughed again. "Send Katherine our best wishes, Pat. I'm sure everything's going to be okay."

"Yeah, me too. Anyway, I better go. I've got to get Kaiti her hospital bag. Lucky she's already packed it! I'll see you tomorrow."

Dad hung up and I collapsed back on the couch next to Axel.

He ran his hand over our baby bump protectively.

I cupped our baby too. "We're so lucky, Axel. I know I've complained about being sick and exhausted, and the size of a whale, but Mom is really unwell. And the baby could die. Preeclampsia can be really serious if it isn't managed properly."

"But it *is* being managed," Axel said, though he continued to press his hands to my belly. "Though you're right, we are lucky, sweetheart. Lucky to have each other, and lucky for this little miracle." He bent his head and kissed my bump, then stood up. "God, what a day. I think I'm ready for an early night."

I glanced across the room at the wall clock. "It's only ten o'clock."

He twisted around to stare at me. "Do you want to stay up?"

"No." I sighed, pushing myself to my feet. I napped every day just so I could stay awake long enough to see him after work. "No, I'd love an early night to be honest. But I know you've been getting up to work through the nights and dealing with early mornings too. I was just checking that you're okay to go to bed now."

Axel stared at me like he was shocked by what I'd said.

"What?" I asked.

"I didn't realize you knew."

"Knew what? That you leave bed in the middle of the night to go work? Of course, I did." I barely slept an unbroken hour before needing to wake up, readjust the pillows, roll over, or go to the toilet. I knew he left, and I knew he was working. I could hear the clickity click of his typing in the quiet of the night.

"Why didn't you say something?" he asked.

I shrugged. "It wasn't a big deal." I took his hand and tugged him towards the bedroom. "Let's go get ready for bed." I walked into our huge master bedroom and began to undress, sighing when I unhooked my bra and let my heavy breasts fall against my belly. "My boobs are *so* big now."

Axel chuckled from his side of the room. "One of the many things I love about your pregnant body."

"Oh?" I lifted an eyebrow at him. "What else do you like about it? The swollen ankles? The huge belly? The acne?" My pimples had gone nuts, and I couldn't even bend over to tie my shoelaces anymore. All of my flexibility in sex was gone—which I hated. With another sigh, I pulled back the covers and climbed into bed naked and feeling hot.

Axel slid in too, pulling me into his arms. "I love your huge belly," he whispered into my ear, running his hand over the distended flesh. "And I'd take you right this minute, if you'd let me. You're as sexy as ever and none of my attraction for you has abated." He thrust against me to make his point, his cock hard against my ass.

I closed my eyes, a small smile tugging at my lips. "I love you."

He laughed and kissed my hair, knowing that I'd gone well past my sex opportunity window.

My body refused to obey my will by around nine pm, unfortunately. It just wanted rest, and lots of it.

"I love you, too," he said back.

We lay in silence for a minute, and just as I was beginning to fall into the darkness of sleep, Axel started up a conversation.

"Hey, how come you haven't said anything about my working so much? I thought you'd be annoyed or something."

I pulled myself up from the depths of sleep with effort. I had to focus, because Axel's tone told me he needed to talk, but I couldn't open my eyes. "I'm not annoyed. How could I be?" I asked him with a soft laugh. "You bought this incredible house for us, and you provide for a hundred other families as well." *Like my parents.*

When I realized that Axel had been deliberately hiding the amount of work he did, I'd felt terrible. He shouldn't have to pretend he had balance in his life when he didn't. He had to work a stupid number of hours to be the success he was, and I was proud of him.

When he didn't say anything, I continued. "I'm sorry I made you feel like you had to hide your work." I ran my hand over his fingers where he gripped my hip. "I'm so proud of you and your success. And I'm sorry I was such a bitch about it all those months ago. I was selfish to think that I could have all your time when so many people count on you."

And work made Axel happy, that was obvious. If I tried to take that away from him, what sort of partner would that make me? He was one of those people who thrived on progress and chasing goals. And I had no interest in changing him. I loved him just the way he was—workaholic mentality and all.

"Thank you for saying that" Axel whispered, and this time I heard the sadness in his voice.

I groaned with the strain but managed to roll onto my back, then roll again to face him. "What's wrong? You sound... sad." Which wasn't like Axel, not at all.

"I'm not sad, it's just—" He stopped and sighed.

"What's going on, hon?" I asked, leaning forward to kiss his lips. "You can tell me anything. You know that right?" And I would try not to argue or get mad, even if he suddenly wanted to go back to working all weekend, every weekend again. I wouldn't like it, but I wouldn't complain. He did too much for us for me to pull that shit.

"It's just that, I suppose, I'm feeling a bit lost at work. Since hiring all the support staff, I don't feel like I have enough to do."

"What do you mean?" I asked, confused. "What are you doing at three AM on the computer if you're not working?" Because this, I had to know!

"No, I'm working," he said. "I didn't mean it like that. I've found new things to do, but I'm just not enjoying it as much as I used to. I don't think I've figured out where I want to be yet."

I absorbed what he said and took a minute to piece it all together. "Is that why you and Dad got into a fight at work?"

"Sort of," he admitted begrudgingly. "I wanted to move ahead with a deal that I'd been putting together for months, and he thought it was a bad idea. So, I suppose it's a symptom of me feeling completely lost."

"Let me see if I've got this straight," I said slowly. "You've set up this awesome company and have delegated your responsibilities to people that seem to be more than capable of doing them, but now you're not sure what to do with yourself?"

He sighed. "Kind of. Yeah. I don't know. Maybe it's time for a vacation."

I grinned in the darkness. "A babymoon?" I asked,

"You know we haven't even gone on a honeymoon yet," he reminded me.

I laughed. "Yeah, we've done things a little backwards, but that's okay! So, you think you could really take a couple of days off to relax and maybe decide what you want to do next?"

I was dying to get away and spend some quality time with Axel. It had been months since we'd had more than a few minutes here and there, snatches of time around all the renovating, studying, and work.

"I'd need to speak to Pat, make sure he's okay with us going, considering your mom's current status."

"Oh, yeah, you're right," I said, biting my lip. "I don't want to miss the baby being born, especially if the timing is unexpected."

"We could stay local, or at least within a few hours' travel time if it'd make you feel better. Cancun, maybe?" Axel suggested. "Then, if they need us, we could fly straight back."

I gasped aloud. "Really? You think I'm bikini-ready?"

He reached over and cupped my face. "Absolutely. You always have been. I'll organize it tomorrow and we can leave as soon as possible."

I tried not to squeal with excitement as I nodded. "Oh, yes, please. I love our new home, but I miss spending time with you! So, if we could go away and relax just for a bit before the baby comes, I'd love it *so* much."

"It's a good idea," he whispered. "It'd give me time to reassess a few things, and time to enjoy just us before we officially become a family."

"Perfect," I said, feeling tears prickling at my eyes again. How had I gotten so lucky?

Then he kissed me and in that one beautiful moment, it truly felt like everything was going to be okay.

13

CHASTITY

Within thirty-six hours, we were packed and on a private plane, flying down to Cancun for our babymoon.

"I can't believe this!" I cried happily, staring out the window. "We're really going on a vacation." Together. Just us! It was our last chance before the baby came.

There had been a few boxes to tick before we left, but we'd gotten everything organized in record time. Mom was stable and her doctor didn't anticipate having to act for at least a few more weeks, barring complications.

Dad and the management trio eagerly took on the task of looking after the company in Axel's absence—under the watchful eye of Cheryl, of course. And I'd gotten my specialist's okay to fly at almost thirty-five weeks, because we said we'd be back in five days or less.

"Have you spoken to Dad today?" I asked him.

"Yeah, I called before we left. Your mom's medication seems to be working and her blood pressure is down, but they're still keeping her at the hospital."

I grinned at him. "Yeah, she messaged me this morning. I think she's driving everyone nuts, but I'm glad she's there and being taken care of." She would have preferred to be home of course, but she was in the safest place for her and the baby right now. And she knew it. "Thank you again for making sure she has the best care."

Axel smiled. "It's my pleasure, sweetheart."

The flight to Cancun was quick and easy, and before long we were sitting on lounges beside the resort pool with drinks. Axel had some sort of whiskey cocktail, and I had a pretty layered mocktail decorated with a pineapple chunk and a tiny umbrella.

"Ahh, this is paradise." I sighed, closing my eyes and loving the feel of the warm sunshine on my stretched belly. Axel had somehow convinced me to wear the bikini I'd brought along as a joke. Even though my boobs overflowed the cups, and my belly was huge, I was wearing it and it felt great to be so free. Axel said he loved how I looked and who was I to argue with him? After all, nothing said "this guy is taken" more than a heavily pregnant woman in an ill-fitting bikini glued to his side.

"Would you like anything to eat, ma'am?" a man asked someone close by.

I lifted my hat off my head and glanced up.

The guy with the tray was talking to me.

"Oh, no, thank you."

He nodded and walked away.

I looked around the resort, noticing the lack of people. "Is this place usually so quiet?" I asked.

"Well, it is September, which is the low season," Axel explained. "But this resort does have lower numbers due to their large suites."

"So, you spent more to stay at a place that has exclusively limited rooms and therefore limited clientele?" I think I was starting to figure him out.

"Yeah, that's about right," he said with a shrug, his naked shoulders moving in a sexy way that had my lower body warming up for later.

I grinned at him. "That's fine by me." I lay back, put my hat over my face again and soaked in the atmosphere.

At dinner we enjoyed fresh seafood and more drinks and chatted just like we used to. "I've missed you," I told him.

His face fell like he was upset.

I reached over the table and grabbed his hand. "I didn't mean it in a bad way. It's just, you know... we spent so much time together over Christmas break, then with my studying, and your job, time was harder to find. Then there were the renovations and everything. It's amazing, though," I assured him. "And I love our life. But I miss just sitting with you and talking, that's all. It wasn't meant to be a negative."

He twirled his fingers around so I could hold his hand properly. "I know what you meant. It was easy in the beginning. Just enjoying each other's company, thinking we only had a week or two together."

"I'm much happier now, knowing we have forever," I told him, grinning from ear to ear. "But I just wanted to say thank you for this. I know work has your head in a bit of a spin, but you're still taking this time out to spend with me, and it means a lot."

The baby chose that moment to kick.

I ran a hand over her little feet. "Ouch! She's getting so strong."

Axel smiled at me, but I could feel the tension in him hadn't eased.

"Hey, I'm sorry if I upset you. I didn't mean to." *Quite the opposite, actually.*

"No, you didn't. It's okay. I'm just in a bit of a strange place at the moment. I'm sorry."

I squeezed his hand. "How about we go back to our room after dinner? I want to show you something."

"Oh, yeah?" he asked, taking a sip of his beer and cocking a brow.

I nodded and crunched down on the crispy green salad in front of me. I'd been aching for intimacy with Axel for a few days. I wanted to fuck like we used to, when I was able to adore his body and make him cry out in ecstasy. I wasn't sure he'd want that from me, with this big belly distracting his thoughts and attention, but I was going to try.

"Well, I'm pretty much done here," Axel said, his eyes burning with the desire I'd been so desperately hoping to see. "You ready to show me?"

I nodded, biting my lower lip. "Yep. Let's go!" I pushed my plate away and stood up, grabbing my man's hand.

We hurried through the restaurant, found the elevator and stepped inside.

"Are you going to give me a clue?" Axel whispered into my ear as he pushed the button for our floor. "Is it a new watch or something I can wear?" he joked.

I laughed at him. "Just because you gave me a credit card to pay the food bills with, doesn't mean I'm going to spend it on anything else."

He drew back and blinked at me. "What do you mean?"

I swallowed hard. "I mean... I'm sorry. No, I haven't bought you anything."

"Because you didn't think you had access to money yet? Shit. I am so sorry, Chastity." He stepped back and ran a frazzled hand through his hair. "I thought you understood that card was for anything you wanted to buy. Stuff for the baby. Clothes. A gym membership. Anything."

I frowned at him. "Thanks, but I'm not really comfortable spending your money like that."

The doors dinged open and my reason for coming upstairs was fast losing its appeal.

Axel took my hand and tugged me out of the elevator and toward the large, red door that was the entrance to our suite. "Sweetheart, you can't work now, and probably won't want to work until the baby is much older. I hope so, anyway. My money is officially *your* money now. Everything that is mine, is yours," he finished as he opened the door.

I walked into the suite. This conversation was officially one I didn't want to have. I just wanted to be on my knees, sucking his cock, and enjoying the pure joy of his body—not talking about bloody money! The door shut behind me and I took action. I untied the halter dress from behind my neck and let it shimmy down my curvy pregnant body until it hit the floor. Then I spun around, ready to get on my knees to prove just how much I loved him.

But he was already on his knees, staring at me. He wasn't undressed, he still wore his shirt and slacks and was down on the ground.

"Um, what are you—"

He pulled a small black box out of his pants pocket and held it in his hand. "Chastity, I love you more than anything in this world."

I swallowed hard, wanting to cover up my nakedness, but feeling like that would destroy the atmosphere he was trying to create. "I love you too," I whispered, stepping closer. Was he really doing what I thought he was doing?

"No one has ever loved me, or challenged me, or made me smile the way you do. You're the most beautiful person, inside and out," he said as he opened the ring box.

I gasped, covering my mouth with my hand. "Oh my God, Axel."

Inside the box was the most glorious engagement ring I'd ever seen. It had a huge, round white diamond at its center, and was completely surrounded by perfect tiny pink diamonds. It looked almost like a flower and my heart melted.

"Chastity, will you marry me? I would be honored if you'd be my wife, as you're already the mother of our child."

Tears welled up in my eyes as my heart picked up its melty bits and soared. It was too soon, wasn't it?

But our daughter kicked up a storm inside my belly, reminding me that it wasn't.

We were a family already, and Axel wanted us to be husband and wife. What could be more perfect than that? "Yes," I whispered, nodding my head as emotion overcame me. "Yes. *Of course*, I'll marry you!"

He jumped to his feet and rushed me, kissing me hard and passionately.

I sobbed with joy against his lips.

"Thank you" he whispered, pulling back to take the ring from its box, before taking my left hand. "I went a little bigger on the sizing just in case, but we can get it resized anytime you like." He slid the ring onto my finger, where it lay snug against my knuckle.

"It's perfect," I breathed. I was absolutely touched that he'd even thought to concern himself with the potential factor of pregnancy swelling. He had really wanted this moment to be special.

"No. You're perfect," he said, reaching over to cup my face and kiss me again. "Now, our house will be our home. My money will be our money. And our daughter will have my name. I hope?"

I grinned at him. "Only if I get it, too."

He chuckled. "Of course."

"Oh, Axel." I threw my arms around him. "A baby, a house, and a proposal in less than a year. Are we crazy?"

He hugged me tightly. "Yep. We're totally crazy and I wouldn't change a damn thing. Now... what were you going to show me?" He drew back and raised an eyebrow at me in question.

"Oh!" I dropped to my knees and unbuttoned and unzipped his trousers. I wanted him now more than ever.

"What are you—?"

I looked up at him and grinned as I took his cock out. "Showing you how much I love you." I wrapped my left hand around his girth, admiring the way my new ring twinkled in the lights, then I sucked the head into my mouth, loving the taste of him.

He groaned, sliding his hand into my hair. "That's amazing, but you don't have to do that. Are you even comfortable down there?"

I came off and looked up at him. "Very comfortable, actually. But I can stop if you like?"

He shook his head from side to side, unable to hide his smile. "No. Please..." He tugged on my hair in encouragement.

I grinned as I moved forward once more. I was more than comfortable on my knees, and as I took him back into my mouth and pleasured him, I listened to the sound of his moans. All too soon, I got squirmy. Need grew inside me, and I felt wet between my legs.

Dropping one hand between my thighs, I ran my fingers over my panties, enjoying the sensations of pleasure pulsing up from my clit.

Axel groaned and tugged my hair back so that I was forced to look at him. "Bed?"

I shook my head. "No. Right here." I sat quickly on the floor, pushed my panties down my legs and past my ankles, then rolled over and stuck my ass in the air. It felt deliciously scandalous to be so heavily pregnant and down on all fours like a wild thing, ready to be taken and claimed.

It was dirty and fast, but Axel didn't disappoint me. He never did. He knelt down behind me and slid his cock between my thighs, dragging it over my throbbing flesh, checking for my readiness.

I ached for him so badly it was maddening. "Come on! Please!" I urged, wiggling back against him desperately.

He pressed the head of his cock to my slit and thrust in with one powerful, balls-deep stroke.

I gasped at the pleasure and the intense pressure as he forged inside of me. I rocked back on his cock, sheathing and unsheathing him; loving the sensation of him filling me once more.

"You okay, baby?" he ground out as he gripped my hips.

I nodded emphatically and moaned. "Yes. Don't stop!"

And so, he took me right there there—hard and fast—on the carpet.

Writhing with an aching need, I bowed my back and clawed at the floor. I couldn't remember wanting him so badly!

He fucked me with the raw desire of his beautiful, fit body until we were both screaming, and our orgasms exploded one after the other like fireworks in the night sky.

Best proposal night ever!

14

AXEL

After I proposed and fucked Chastity on the ground like some sort of wild animal, we lay on the carpet, trying to catch our breath.

Fuck, that was hot but so unexpected. And probably incredibly uncomfortable for my very pregnant fiancé. I pulled her into my arms. "Are you okay? Did I hurt you?"

She turned to look up at me, her face pink, sweaty, and radiant. "Not at all. That was amazing." She groaned as she rolled onto her hands and knees again. "But I think I need to get up. Can we move this celebration to the bed?"

I jumped to my feet and offered her my hand.

"Oh, I'm okay," she insisted. "It's easier if I do it." Carefully, and slowly, balancing her weight, Chastity got to her feet. "Phew!"

I gestured to the carpet. "Are you sure that was okay?" I was feeling guilty as hell about our passionate romp, even though I was pretty sure she'd been the one to instigate it all. The details were a little fuzzy now, to be honest. *That orgasm was insane.*

She laughed. "Are you kidding me? I was the one on my

knees, too impatient to get to bed. So, thank you for ignoring the whole pregnant belly thing and just, you know..." She faded off.

It was my turn to laugh. "What? You're thanking me for just fucking you?" I grabbed her and kissed her. "The pleasure was all mine."

She giggled as she walked towards the bedroom. "I'm just going to pee, then I'll meet you in bed."

"Okay, sweetheart." I was so tempted to use the energy buzz currently pumping through my bloodstream for something else. A gym session? Work, maybe? But this was a vacation, and I was trying to learn how to relax. I heard the toilet flush, so I grabbed some bottles of water and headed toward the bed.

"You want me to put a movie on?" I asked, grabbing the remote and pointing it towards the huge smart TV opposite the bed.

"Sure," she said, flopping onto the California king mattress. "But don't expect me to stay awake for it. That orgasm was *awesome.* It was so strong it destroyed me. I can barely keep my eyes open!" She crawled up the bed and put her head on the fluffy white pillows. She looked like a goddess lying amongst the blankets. A rounded, heavily pregnant, glowing goddess.

"Damn, you're beautiful," I said, sitting on the mattress and running my hand over her ass and up the curve of her spine, simply admiring her.

"Hmm, I love you," she answered. "Can we call everyone in the morning and tell them?"

Tell everyone? *Oh, right.* "You mean about us being engaged? Absolutely." I crawled over and lay down facing her, then swept her long hair off her face. "We could steal off to Vegas and get married this week, if you want."

Her eyes opened slowly, though they were unfocused. "You want to be married to me that badly?" she murmured.

"Yes," I said honestly. "The sooner, the better." I'd wanted to propose for months. But I'd wanted her to be happy, and in a good place mentally before I popped the question.

Her eyes closed as she sighed. "I love that. Thank you. But I'd really want my parents there for such a once in a lifetime occasion."

I kissed her cheek. "Okay, beautiful. Just sleep."

"Are you going to work?" she whispered.

"No, I'll just lay here," I said. "I'm jumping out of my skin withexcitement, though." Chastity was going to be my wife! I'd never felt better.

"Okay. But I don't mind. You do whatever you've got to do. I do need to sleep though, I'm sorry."

I glanced down at her and kissed her again. "Sleep, beautiful. No apologies necessary."

And she did, she was snoring softly within moments.

I grinned to myself. There was nothing like a strong orgasm to knock you out and guarantee a good night's sleep. Usually I'd be right alongside her, ready to pass out from the bliss. But tonight, I was jumping. I felt pumped!

I got up and got dressed, buzzing to do something constructive with the energy. *Maybe a run? Yeah. Why not?* I hadn't gone for a run in weeks, choosing instead to train for intervals of twenty minutes, and then get back to work. But I'd done too much of that lately, And I was making mistakes; like that deal Pat had saved me from closing on. He'd been right. I'd gone into work yesterday and he spelled it out.

The business I'd wanted to buy was secretly drowning in so much debt, it was possible I wouldn't have been able to dig myself out of it for a very long time if I'd committed. Pat may have very well saved my whole company.

And although I was more grateful than I could say, I owed Pat that house he wanted for his family. It was the wake-up call I'd needed. I had the people to delegate to, and while I found my footing in my new CEO role, I had to take a step back and reassess my goals.

So, why did I keep pushing so hard? I'd reached all the goals I'd set for myself years ago. But as with all goal setting, once the bar was reached, there was always something else to shoot for. A higher profit. More staff. Bigger fish.

But was that something I still wanted to chase now that I had Chastity? I was going to be married, with a baby daughter. I wanted to stay fit and healthy for them. I wanted to provide for them, but that didn't mean being absent at home.

Chastity had started saying that she now accepted that I needed to work my ass off to keep my company at its best, but did I really? Did I have to kill myself to keep the status quo? To pay off my house? To put food on the table? *No.* I had enough money to never work again. To have five children, provide them all with an Ivy League education, and buy them houses, too. So, did I really need to die on the sword of the corporate world?

I pulled on some joggers, a clean t-shirt, and some running shoes, then headed out. I attracted a lot of weird, confused looks from staff and other guests, probably assuming I didn't belong at a resort of this caliber. But I just popped my air pods into my ears, cranked up the music, and took off.

It was just coming to sunset, and the sun was melding into the rippling water in a mess of spectacular oranges and yellows. Jogging over the brush and onto the beach, I hit my stride and took off down the beach while some techno instrumental played in my ears.

Why do I work the way I do? I wondered. I'd always put it down to a simple drive to succeed. It was a desire to earn money and dominate, to excel at what I was good at. But was it really that? Could I walk away tomorrow? Sell the company, pay any debts owing, and invest what was left? I certainly had the assets to do it. *But would that make me happy?* Would Chastity be content with me just being around the house all day. What would I even do?

I reached the natural end of the beach, stopped, and turned to look back at the way I had come. I had no idea how far I'd run, but my brow was slick with sweat, my breathing was labored, and my heart banged like a bongo drum in my chest. "Time to go back," I said to myself.

My legs didn't want to move, but I pushed them to start going again, and once I found my rhythm on the wet sand, it was easy to follow my footprints back to the hotel. I'd run much further than I'd realized, so I took a moment and simply sat on the beach, staring up at the moon. *So beautiful.*

Pulling my phone from my pocket, I checked it. Chastity hadn't messaged or called. *Good.* Hopefully she was still fast asleep and resting that gorgeous body of hers.

I rested back on my hands, digging them into the sand and took a few deep breaths. Could I get rid of all my current responsibilities and live day to day without work? Would I find a hobby? Or a renovation project, maybe? Was that something that interested me? What about mentoring another young businessperson? Or trading on the stock market?

I groaned at the possibilities rolling around in my head. I loved my job and my company. I didn't want to sell it or stop working. Not now, anyway. Maybe once the baby arrived, I'd feel different? But at the moment, it just felt like everything was more difficult and was no longer giving me the same satisfaction it once did—before I'd hired help.

Maybe I needed to back off on the big acquisitions, and just manage? Work more closely with Pat? He had great instincts, but I still didn't know what I really wanted. What I needed was to talk to Chastity. She seemed to have a better insight into business and life than even I did sometimes. How? I had no clue. Maybe it was the advantage of youth? Either way, right now, I wanted to be with my girl—my fiancé.

I got up and brushed the sand from my pants. This had been a good idea; to come down to Cancun. To rest, relax, and reassess. Chastity had come here with the goal to enjoy her last few weeks as a woman before she became a mother, which luckily for me, gave me a lot of opportunity to spoil her.

I went back to the hotel, up to our suite, and had a long shower in the main bathroom, avoiding the en suite so I didn't wake her. The place we'd gotten was a three-bedroom suite. None of the one-bedrooms were available when I'd booked, and they tended to be too small anyway.

When I was clean, dry, and finally tired, I crept back into our bedroom.

Chastity was still soundly asleep.

I stood in the doorway, wondering if it was best that I go to another room. The last thing I wanted to do on our babymoon was to disturb her; that's not what she needed. I turned toward the other bedrooms.

"Hey. Are you coming to sleep now?" Chastity called out.

I twisted back to see her smiling face. "Are you sure you're okay with me sleeping here? I don't want to disturb you."

She flicked back the covers. "Are you kidding me? This bed is *huge*. Jump in."

I walked across the room, my naked feet sinking into the plush carpet.

"Plus, you just proposed, remember?" she said, rolling over to present her ass to me. "I think that requires at least a few cuddles to celebrate."

I chuckled as I snuggled up behind her, pressing myself into her warmth. "I think so, too."

"I love you," she said, pushing her ass back at me.

"I love you, too," I whispered, sliding my hand around her waist to cup her belly. "Both of you."

"Mm... Night," she sighed, and fell asleep again.

I lay there counting my blessings. One. Two. The two girls in front of me were the two most important things in my life now and they always would be. I needed to sort out what I wanted to do for work, but it wasn't a pressing issue. I had plenty of everything, so perhaps I could slow down for a little bit. It wouldn't kill me, right?

I closed my eyes and soon drifted off to sleep, a childhood memory tugging at me just long enough to pique my curiosity, but not concrete enough to sink my teeth into. I'd work it out in the morning.

15

CHASTITY

Axel spoiled me tremendously over the next few days as we enjoyed our vacation in Cancun. Our resort was near a large, upscale mall, so we went shopping and bought beautiful clothes for the baby. He also purchased several things for me, even though I thought it was a waste of money to buy maternity clothes at this stage of my pregnancy. Axel was adamant and still wanted me to be comfortable—and happy.

That's what he said, all the time. "I want you to be happy." It blew my mind that my happiness was his goal, and I was happy. Deliriously happy in fact. How could I not be? I had a man who loved me, and he'd surprised me with a proposal of marriage on our impromptu babymoon! He was the man I loved, who had fathered the daughter still growing safe and sound in my womb. Things literally couldn't be better.

On the last morning before we left to return home, we were sitting at breakfast when Axel brought up a topic that I felt he'd been keeping inside for far too long.

"Can I chat with you about something before we head back?"

"Sounds serious," I said, my stomach swooping in an anxious way. "Is this about us?"

He shook his head. "No, not at all. I want your advice about something."

"Of course," I said, relief sweeping over me as I took a sip of my freshly squeezed pineapple juice. "Tell me what's going on."

He sighed and leaned forward, gripping the small table with both hands. "I... don't know what to do about work. I'm feeling useless there, in my own company. It's strange and I don't like it."

I gaped at him, then put my glass down. "Useless? You?" I fluffed my new pink dress over my baby bump and settled my hands over my daughter. "How is that possible?" I settled into the chair, trying to find a more comfortable position. This was going to be a long conversation. I could already tell.

We had six hours before we had to get to the airport, so we had time to hash this out. And with the waiters hovering around, we also had as much food and drinks available as we wanted to consume.

"Yes, me," he said, dropping his head and running an agitated hand through his hair. "I walk around the office, watching everyone else perform the tasks I used to do. Coupled with the fact that I'm finding I don't have as may responsibilities now, it's weird."

I grinned at him. "You've delegated too well, is that what you're saying?"

"Well, yes. I think so."

I reached for a grape and popped it into my mouth, the sweetness exploding in my mouth the moment I chewed down on it. "You do realize you had to hire *three* new graduates *plus* a kick-ass manager to do the work you used to do as one person? That's insane. You should be proud you kept everything afloat so well on your own!"

He laughed and pushed himself back in the chair. "I know,

you've joked about it before. They're killing it, though. Doing all of my jobs and doing them well. I've heard from Cheryl that the four of them don't even need to work weekends, which is great for them."

He didn't sound happy about it though. "But what? You're missing it? The hours? The weekends, the nights, the huge amount of work you used to do?"

Axel ran a hand over his face and groaned like he was frustrated.

I opened my legs, so I scooch move forward on my chair, my belly too big now to sit comfortably practically anywhere now. "Look, I get it. It was your life for, what, twenty years? Of course, you're going to miss it. The adrenaline, the success; ticking off jobs and dealing with international meetings, travel, and..." I threw my hands around. "All the *millions* of other things you do that I don't know about."

He chuckled. "I do miss it all. But I love you, Chastity. I want to be around for you and the baby. I just need to figure out how to achieve a reasonable balance." He tapped the side of his head with his knuckles. "Up here, more than anywhere else," he admitted. "It's like I need to retrain my brain."

"Okay, well tell me more about what you miss," I encouraged, wanting to know more. "What did you love about doing four people's jobs?"

Axel scrubbed his hands over his face. "I don't know. I can't really put it into words."

"Well, why did you want to be successful in the first place? Do you remember?" Surely there was a reason for his drive?

"What do you mean?" he asked, frowning at me. "Everyone wants to be successful in business."

"Yeah, I know. But you're *so* driven. More than anyone I've ever met. And it's not like you had a wife or a baby to care for, like my dad. So, what made you so determined?" I asked, pushing him towards a resolution for which he may not know the answer. "You know. What was the real reason you wanted to work so hard?"

"For you. For the baby!" he snapped at me, seemingly frustrated.

I put my hands up. "I'm not accusing you of anything, honey. You're amazing in every way. But if you want me to help you, then please, talk it out with me."

He sighed. "I'm Sorry. Okay. What do you mean?"

"I mean... what drove you? Back then, especially? What made you come out of graduate school and build an empire? Surely, that takes a special sort of person."

He shrugged, like he didn't know.

"If you don't want to talk about it, that's totally fine." I said, grinning at him. "I'm happy to discuss the wedding or something else."

We'd mutually decided not to call my parents and tell them about the engagement. Mom was finally stable and settled, and Dad was stressed at work. We decided to tell them when we returned home, which was more personal than over the phone, anyway.

I extended my arm and sighed as I stared down at my hand. "I love my ring so much." It was so large, it bordered on almost being gawdy. But the pink diamonds surrounding the white diamond in the middle made it so happy and bright. I was honestly filled with glee every single time I looked at it.

"I'm glad," Axel said, though his voice was soft, thoughtful.

I glanced back up. "Do you want to talk about it now?"

He met my gaze with an intensity that surprised me, then nodded.

"Okay. So, tell me. What was it?"

Axel crossed his arms over his chest and leaned back in his chair. "I needed to be a success," he answered.

"Says, who?" I asked.

"Says me. My parents."

"Your parents? What do they have to do with it?" I pushed. *Now we're getting somewhere.*

He gestured to a waiter, who hurried over.

"Yes, sir?"

"I need another coffee," he said. "Cappuccino, please."

The waiter glanced my way.

I shook my head with a smile. "I'm fine. Thank you."

Once the waiter left, I glanced back at Axel. "Go on." I wasn't going to let the ordering of coffee distract me from this much needed resolution. This situation was annoying him and had been for a while. And now that he finally wanted to talk to me about it, I wasn't going to let him slip away.

"You were talking about your parents," I prompted.

He sighed, shifting in his chair. "My parents are wealthy. They come from old money. They paid for my education—boarding schools and Ivy League—but made it clear that they wouldn't have a hand in supporting me afterward. Not that I would have ever asked them to, but they drilled it into me from a very young age that once I graduated, I was on my own." He exhaled slowly, sounding almost relieved at the confession.

"I suppose that's pretty normal," I said, shrugging. "Most parents want their kids to stand on their own two feet after college. I know mine did."

"Yeah, but yours would have helped you if you needed it. Let you go home to stay with them while you found a job, or at least made you feel like they wanted you to succeed even when you faced hiccups or hardships."

"They didn't want you to succeed?" I repeated. "You really think that?"

He looked at me like he couldn't believe he'd just said it. "Ah, yeah. I uh..."

"You don't know? Don't remember?"

"They..." he frowned. "I don't know."

"You do," I pushed. "You think they set you out in the world, well-armed with a good education, but you think they wanted you to fail, don't you? And with them wanting you to fail, they cut you off completely, didn't they?"

He nodded. "Ah, yeah. They... yeah."

I was putting it together now, slowly. But it was becoming clearer. "So, your absentee parents paid for school, then cut you off, expecting you to fail, and what? Come home to them? Admit defeat?"

Pain crossed his face. "They never said anything, but I got that impression from time to time. Yes"

I sat forward, my lower back aching. "So, you're twenty-three, twenty-four, broke, and needing a job. What do you do?"

Axle glanced away. "I bunked in with a friend and his parents and got a job. Fast. Developed my own clients, went out on my own, found Cheryl, and the rest is history."

I rubbed my belly, the baby kicking out from under my ribs. "And when along that road did you think to yourself, 'I'm going to show them I can succeed on my own, and I'm never going to ask them for help?'"

Because that made perfect sense. That a guy who had been cut off, kicked out, and left to fend for himself had decided to conquer all expectations and work harder than anyone had ever imagined.

"I didn't decide," Axel said, blinking rapidly.

"I kind of think you did," I told him. "Maybe not in those exact words. But I suspect your drive to succeed comes from your parents, indirectly."

He shuddered. "I'd hate to think that. I don't want them to be the reason for my success."

"They aren't." I shook my head. "*You* are the reason you're successful. It's been all your hard work. But maybe it's time to look at whether it still makes you happy? Or even just sit back and look at what you've achieved? You don't need to prove anything to anyone anymore, Axel. Least of all, them."

They sounded like complete assholes.

"I need to think about it," Axel said.

I nodded at him. "Sure. I'm only spit-balling. I could be wrong."

Axel drank his coffee, deep in thought.

Meanwhile, I ate the rest of my fruit. I didn't bother bringing up the topic again, and tried not to be offended by the fact he withdrew and didn't talk to me for some time after that.

He was thinking about why he was so driven, and how closely knit his success was to his parents' behavior, when he'd probably thought they were completely separate issues. He needed space to figure it all out, and I understood that. It was a heavy and deeply personal topic.

We ended up leaving early for the airport, arrived with time to spare, and were soon on our way home again.

This time, as a newly engaged couple.

16

AXEL

We flew home, got picked up by one of the drivers, then went back to our new house. I tried to chat with Chastity while we traveled, but even I knew I was being distant. I couldn't help it. My head was in a downward spiral the whole time, trying to make sense of our last conversation.

The denial I felt was overwhelming. Everything inside of me screamed she was wrong. I didn't want to even consider the fact that some of my success might have *anything* to do with my parents. My horrible, narcissistic, totally-abandoned-me and-made-m-feel-unwanted-my-whole-life, parents. They couldn't be my driving force to succeed. *They can't be.* The very idea sullied the best part of my life, outside of Chastity and our little one, of course.

My newly engaged fiancé went straight to our bedroom to have a nap as soon as we'd dropped our bags by the front door.

I needed to distract myself, so I went to the office and logged onto the computer, feeling a sense of calm fall over me with the familiarity of the move. I checked emails and got straight back to work. I was pleasantly surprised to read the day's report from

Patrick and Cheryl. Everything was totally under control, but they wanted my help with something they couldn't do themselves. *That's* what I wanted to hear. That I was needed at my own company. Finally.

Sometime later, after a quick dinner, we headed into the hospital to visit Chastity's mom. Katherine had a private room on the third floor, and as soon as we reached the door, Chastity cried out, "Mom!" and rushed to her side. Chastity leaned over to hug her mother, both of them groaning with the effort. Their swollen bellies made the task strangely jigsaw-like, the pieces just not fitting into place the way the ladies wanted them to.

"How was your vacation?" Katherine asked, a smile on her face as her eyes raked over her daughter. Then she grabbed Chastity's left hand, her eyes bulging out of her head. "Is that what I think it is?" she gasped.

Chastity glanced over at me, her eyes lit with happiness. "Yes. Axel proposed on the trip, and I wanted to tell you and Dad in person."

Katherine released Chastity's hand to grimace and rub the sides of her belly. "Congratulations to both of you. You look very happy."

I walked up and stood next to Chastity. "We are. Thank you, Katherine. But how are you? That's why we're here, after all."

Katherine swatted her hand through the air dismissively. "Oh, don't worry about me. I have a hundred doctors and nurses fluffing around to make sure I stay on my ass and don't move. At this rate, I'll be three hundred pounds by the time I deliver."

Chastity ran her hand over her mother's shoulder. "Actually, I hate to be the one to say it, Mom, it looks like you've lost weight." And she had. There was no way she was putting on any weight, even being as sedentary as she was forced to be.

"It's the medication. It keeps the fluids down. I'd gotten really puffy for a while there." Katherine patted her cheeks.

Chastity and I exchanged worried looks. Katherine didn't look well.

I moved over to a chair on the other side of the room and sat down to give them a little space for mother-daughter time.

Chastity sat right next to her mom. Two women. Two big bellies. They were a beautiful sight, really, though it was quite unusual to have a mother and daughter pregnant simultaneously.

"We should have organized a photo shoot for you two," I said, off the cuff. "Both of you pregnant at the same time. It's a marvel."

Chastity laughed and glanced at Katherine. "Oh, yeah. Imagine that."

Katherine blinked at me as if a realization was dawning upon her. "I don't think I have any photos of this pregnancy. None. I had a ton of me when I was pregnant with Chastity."

I pulled out my phone and held it up. "Do you want one now? I can snap a few pictures. Or I can arrange for a photographer. They can come here if you want?"

Katherine pulled back the blankets and slowly moved her legs to the side of the bed. "Now. Here. In front of that plant in the corner," she said, pointing over near the window.

"Okay," Chastity agreed as they both stood and waddled over to the only green thing in the room.

"I like this color on you," Katherine said to Chastity, motioning to her new pink dress.

"Thanks, Mom." Chastity glanced at me with a grateful smile. I'd encouraged her to buy a few new things while we'd been away. I'd been shocked to know that she hadn't bought enough clothes for herself through her pregnancy, not wanting to spend my money.

They stood by the only non-hospital looking wall, side by side, belly to belly, looking at me, smiling.

I lifted my phone and took a photo, then feeling creative I

said, "Can you stand facing one another so we get the bellies together?"

Chastity laughed but moved to turn towards her mother, grabbing the underside of her stomach to accentuate the curve.

Katherine flinched as though in pain but turned also, holding her belly tight. Even though Chastity was four weeks ahead of Katherine in gestation, Chastity's belly was smaller.

I wasn't sure how that was possible, but what did I know about pregnancies? "Smile," I said.

Katherine was getting paler by the minute.

I snapped a few shots quickly, then rushed forward to take her hand and offer my support. "I think it's time to get back into bed. At least you have that memory, now. You can relax."

She nodded and didn't fight me as I held her arm and helped her the few steps back to her bed.

That's when Pat walked in, his gaze narrowing immediately. "What happened?"

"I don't know," I told him.

He rushed forward to flick back the blankets for his wife.

"She stood up to have a photo with Chastity, then went pale."

He pressed the call button for the nurse and began fussing over Katherine as she climbed back onto the hospital bed. "You know you're not supposed to get up."

She sighed. "I still have to go to the toilet and shower myself, you know."

But from the looks of it, she may not even be doing that much longer. She was as pale as the sheets surrounding her.

The nurse came in and we gave her the short story of what happened.

"Let me check your blood pressure," the nurse said, then shook her head. "Your blood pressure is too low."

"Yeah, those stupid meds are working *too* well," Katherine

grumbled. "Pre-eclampsia is supposed to have me fainting from high blood pressure, not the other way around."

The nurse made a note in her chart. "I'm going to talk to the doctor. I'll be back as soon as I can." She excused herself and left.

Patrick sighed and visibly shook himself. "Okay... so, how are you two? How was the vacation?"

"Amazing," Chastity said, then stepped forward, arm extended and wiggling her fingers. "And look."

Patrick took her hand and stared down at the ring I'd chosen for his daughter.

He glanced my way with a smile. "Congratulations." He stuck his hand out.

I shook it. "Thanks," I mumbled, happiness spread through me. Technically, I probably should have asked Pat's permission, again. But he'd given me the green light months ago, I'd just been waiting for the right time. And the right time being the time I thought she might actually say yes.

"Do you have a wedding date?" he asked, sitting down on one side of Katherine's bed.

Chastity sat down on the opposite side.

I glanced at my fiancé for a concrete answer. We hadn't even discussed it really, yet.

She shrugged. "No idea! I'm just enjoying the moment and being engaged. It's awesome." She happily rubbed her belly.

I just stared at her in genuine awe. She was truly the most beautiful woman I'd ever seen in my life. "We haven't talked about it, but I'd like to get married as soon as possible. So, it really depends on if you want a maternity wedding dress or not."

Chastity stared at me, then blinked a few times in rapid succession. "You want to get married in the next four weeks?" she breathed in shock.

I grinned and thrust my hands into my pockets. "Well, I'd marry you tomorrow, if you'd let me."

I heard Katherine's groan and glanced up. She was shaking her head. "Seriously. These two are nauseating," she joked deadpan.

I laughed, how could I not? "I'm sure you two are just as bad in private."

Katherine and Pat glanced at each other, and for the first time, I saw a spark of something I'd never seen before. A deep love. An understanding. Gratitude.

I stepped closer to Chastity and took her hand when she reached for me. "So?" I asked. "What do you say?"

"What do I say to what?"

"To getting married sooner rather than later."

Her eyes widened. "You were being serious?"

"Of course, I was. But I totally understand if you want to wait until after the baby is born."

Chastity's eyes sparkled as she grinned at me. "She'd be cute as a flower girl."

"She would," I agreed, though the idea of waiting years to marry the woman I loved felt like a kick to the gut. I bent forward to kiss her fingers, then moved back to my chair.

"You okay?" she called out to me.

I nodded and forced myself to wipe the disappointment from my face. I was absolutely bursting to tie myself to Chastity in every way possible, and yet she didn't seem worried at all. Perhaps it was the age difference and a matter of perception? From her point of view, she probably thought she had all the time in the world.

For me, I felt like I'd waited my whole adult life—*decades*—to find her. I didn't want to wait a minute more to marry her.

"How's work been, Pat?" I asked. "Now that we're back, if you need time off..."

"No. It's fine for the moment." Patrick reached onto the bed and grabbed for Katherine's hand. "I think I'd drive Kaiti nuts if I was here all day."

"Oh, he would," she confirmed. "Believe me, he's *worse* than the bloody doctors."

"Well, you're the most important thing in the world to me," Pat said, showing a rare insight into their relationship. "And I don't know what I'd do if something happened to you."

Instead of responding with her casual cold wit, Katherine teared up, her eyes glistening with unshed tears.

Everyone was quiet.

I looked at Chastity, who was tearing up too. *Oh, no.* "Well, I'll be back in the office tomorrow, so if you need to leave at any time, you can," I said, forcing the words into the uncomfortable silence.

Patrick looked my way, then grinned. "You're busting to get back to work, aren't you, buddy?"

I nodded. "Definitely."

"Did you at least take some time off while you were away?" he asked.

"I did!" I told him proudly. "Ask Chastity. I barely opened my laptop."

"I don't believe it," he said, blinking at me.

"It's true," Chastity said. "I was totally spoiled. We had sleep-ins and long lunches, and lots of shopping, and drinks by the pool. Axel didn't work at all, really."

Pat laughed. "Well, good for you. But I know my best friend, and you'll be busting balls to get in there tomorrow. You're the very definition of a workaholic, and I've always admired you for your drive."

I willed a smile to my face. "So, I'll see you tomorrow, bright and early?"

"You will."

The conversation happily moved away from work, and back

to the impending babies' arrivals. I nodded and smiled when required, but Chastity mostly carried the conversation, so I had time to sit back and think some more.

I had been a workaholic for so long and loved every minute of it. Had I changed? Or was the true reason behind my drive to succeed that I wanted to prove my parents wrong? Had I simply just been desperate to prove that I could do it on my own?

Now, that I had Chastity, I didn't feel like I had to prove anything to *anyone*. But what did that mean for my future?

17

CHASTITY

Axel wanted to marry me now? Like this? Thirty-five weeks pregnant, swollen and uncomfortable? *Seriously?* My head was spinning with the implications of what he'd said. Where would we get married? What about flowers? A dress? A reception?

When the doctor came in to talk to Mom about her medication, I hugged her tightly and left with the promise to drop by the next day.

As soon as we were home, I couldn't hold the words in any longer. "Were you serious about getting married so soon?"

He hung the car keys on the hook by the front door and locked the door behind him. "Yeah, I was."

"But seriously?" How was that possible? Surely, he wanted to wait a few years, until I was finished breastfeeding and had gotten my body back?

He pulled me gently into his arms. "I would marry you today. Tomorrow. Whenever you say the word. It's your choice if you want to wait until after the baby's born."

"But I'm a whale," I whined, sliding my arms up around his neck. "I won't fit into any dress."

He leaned forward and kissed my lips. "You are more beautiful now, than ever before, Chastity. And I would be so proud to marry you, even nine months pregnant. I actually love the idea of it."

I frowned. "What do you mean?"

"I mean, a baby is the ultimate commitment to one another, and the wedding will celebrate that."

He was serious. Suddenly I could see it. A long, long dress flowing over my round bump, pink roses in my hair. "How do you want to do it? Small? Big? Reception? No reception?" I asked.

He grinned at me. "I want whatever you want. Money's no object, of course. Book anything, buy anything, I just want you to be happy."

I turned on the side to get my belly out of the way, then leaned against him to hug him. "Can I think about it some more?" I wasn't sure I had the energy after all the renovations to plan an event like that.

He chuckled and kissed the top of my head. "Of course. There's no pressure at all, sweetheart. I just... thought it might be romantic, that's all," he said, then placed a soft kiss on my lips.

"Thank you. I'll talk to my mother about it, I think." She'd probably think I was utterly crazy.

"I think that's a great idea. It'd give her something to plan and have control from her hospital bed," Axel said, then kissed me once more before walking into the kitchen to grab two bottles of water from the fridge.

"That's another thing," I said. "Mom could be in hospital for months yet. I can't get married without her there." Irrespective of the falling out we'd had, and any past baggage we shared, I couldn't enjoy the biggest day of my life without her there cheering me on.

"That's true. I hadn't thought of that," Axel admitted, cracking open the bottle and taking a few chugs of the water. "Sorry, baby. I wasn't thinking."

I shrugged. "It's all good. You want to marry me, that's all that's important."

"So true," he said, walking over to put his hands around my non-existent waist. "How about we go to bed, and I show you just how much I love you?"

Heat unfurled inside my belly in response, shooting preemptive bolts of pleasure along my veins. "Yes, please."

"You're not too tired?"

"For you?" I giggled. "Definitely not." I stepped back and took his hand, tugging him to the bedroom where he took me to the stars and back again.

THE NEXT DAY I went into the hospital after lunch to discuss my ideas with my mother. I'd been Online all morning looking at wedding dresses and venues. If anyone was going talk me out of this crazy plan—it was her.

"Hey, sweetie!" She greeted me as I knocked on the door frame, then entered. She was looking pale but otherwise well.

"Hi, Mom. How are you doing today?"

"Not bad," she said, then swallowed hard. "Thirty-one weeks today, so that's really good. The baby is getting bigger by the minute and the longer he or she stays in there, the better." Mom rubbed her huge belly and shifted in the bed as though she was uncomfortable. "You're thirty-five weeks along now, right?" she asked.

I nodded. "Yeah. I have a check-up with my specialist tomorrow, actually." I grabbed the yoga ball in the corner of the room and rolled it over to the bed, then sat on it with a groan.

"This is great. I can see why people like to sit on them during labor."

"Yeah, they are," she agreed, then cocked her head to the side. "What's up? You look like you need to tell me something."

I laughed. She always knew. It was one of the many reasons I'd stayed away and didn't visit her during my first trimester. She would have known I had a secret from the moment I walked in the door.

"I've been considering Axel's proposal that we get married while I'm still pregnant, but there are so many things to consider and worry about, and I want your advice."

She pushed herself more upright, then settled with both hands on her belly. "What's there to worry about?"

"You, for one thing!" I said, gesturing to my sibling in her belly. "I need you there. I could never enjoy my day without you, but what if you're still in hospital?"

Her smile was tight. "When were you planning on the event?"

"Well," I began, "I spoke to a wedding planner this morning who said she could throw something together in four weeks, which would make me thirty-nine weeks. I know that sounds *crazy*. If I went into labor that week, it could ruin everything." The more I talked, the crazier it sounded. Babies came anytime, and they were considered full term at thirty-seven weeks. I could go even go into labor on the day of the wedding!

Mom cackled with laughter. "You don't do things by halves, do you, sweetheart?"

I frowned at her. "Why aren't you trying to talk me out of this? Don't you think it's insane?" I'd been prepared for her frowns and disapproval, and even a scream here and there. But this happy look she had on her face? I was *not* prepared for that. Maybe she hadn't heard me correctly? "Mom, seriously. Do you think it's smart to throw some expensive party together the week before I'm due?"

"Well, you were ten days late, so you know you could go way over your due date yet, Chastity."

My mouth dropped open. "Over?"

"Of course. A normal gestation is considered anywhere between thirty-seven to forty-two weeks. There's wiggle room aplenty."

I groaned and leaned forward on the bed. "Oh my God," I exclaimed. "Forty-two weeks? Imagine that!" I couldn't. *Another seven weeks of this?* Getting bigger every day? "I'd be the size of a house."

Mom laughed again. "To answer your question, I do think it's insanity, but everything about you and Axel is insane. The way you fell in love around your dad, your age-gap, you managing to finish school and all the other pressures on you like your pregnancy and the house. Everything has been done at lightning speed and yet I've never seen you look so happy, and Patrick said he's never seen Axel so happy either. So, I think you should go with your instincts on this one, sweetheart. What's your heart telling you?"

Tears swam in my eyes and my throat tightened with emotion and heat. "Um... that getting married heavily pregnant would be amazing. Like a sign of how much we love each other. The commitment we have to be a family." It was so old-school, in lots of ways. With marriage you could marry someone, then divorce them and never have to see them again. But once you had a child together? You had to see that person for at least the first eighteen years of the child's life. It was serious. Nothing said commitment like a baby.

"Then do it!" she said. "Risk it. If you have to cancel due to the baby or a complication, who cares? It's not like Axel can't afford the cost."

"Mom!" I grimaced at her.

"It's true!" she said with a smile. "He won't care at all, and everything could just be postponed to a month or so afterwards in the worst-case scenario."

Excitement began to creep into my belly, then reality hit me hard again. "But what about you? You could still be here in four weeks' time. I can't get married without you there, holding my hand. I just can't! I won't, Mom."

Mom's eyes filled with tears, but she blinked them away as she reached for my hand. "I'll be there, sweetheart. And, although he may not be able to attend in person, your little brother will be there too."

"What?!" I croaked. "You're having a boy? I thought you didn't know?"

Mom hiccupped out a laugh, then swiped at the tears that ran down her face. "We weren't going to, but we've had *so* many scans due to my high-risk status, now, that it was becoming very obvious." She grinned at me.

I lifted my hand then pressed my palm gently against the roundness of her belly. "I'm going to have little brother. I can't believe it, Mom."

"Your dad is so happy," she said, her face now beaming with an infectious smile. Then she became serious, the tears welling once more. "I just hope he's healthy. The scans all say he's big and strong, but so much can go wrong now. Especially with my age. The doctors and nurses do nothing but refer to my age like it's a disease." She *tsked*.

I grinned at her. "Ignore them. Your baby's a miracle, Mom. You just need to keep him in there a little longer."

She nodded, then squeezed my hand. "Show me what dresses you're looking at. Do you have any ideas of what you want to do?"

"I do. I was thinking of something small and intimate, maybe fifty people. I found some hotels I like the look of, with great gardens for the wedding, and I did find a dress, but it is so expensive!"

She smiled, then brushed away another tear. "I'm sure Axel told you that you could have anything you like."

I nodded. "He did."

"And your father will want to help with the wedding or the honeymoon. I'm not sure, but he'll want to pay for something."

"Thanks, Mom." In the past I would have stressed about where Dad would get the money, whereas now I knew that Axel's company was paying him well, so I tried not to worry. I pulled out my phone and began searching for the photos I'd collected for this exact conversation. "Can I show you what I've found so far?"

"Definitely. Show me."

We spent the whole afternoon talking about wedding stuff. Dresses, flowers, reception packages, and the celebrant. We laughed, we cried, and Mom even made some phone calls for me and booked the wedding planner, so I didn't have to stress so much.

It was a total luxury, an un-necessary expense, but I couldn't imagine doing it all myself. Not at the scale I wanted, and not in four weeks. By the time I left the hospital, I was desperately in need of a nap, but my heart was full to bursting. My mom was totally on board with me getting married in a month, and I would have a baby brother soon.

Life was good.

Now I just had to tell Axel and my dad the news! Everything was full steam ahead.

18

AXEL

It was a bit of a surprise when Chastity told me she wanted to get married on September twenty-sixth, the week before the baby was born. I couldn't believe she'd agreed on my soon-as-possible concept! But the shock soon wore off, and excitement set in. She would be my wife, and soon.

Within a few days, Chastity had met with a wedding planner she'd seen on Instagram, and the plans for our "special day" were underway. The hotel reception was booked, the celebrant called, and Chastity was up to her eyeballs in magazines and notebooks full of quotes, dates, and pictures of dresses and bridal bouquets.

The other amazing thing was that Katherine was still pregnant, still fighting the nurses, and holding onto her sanity—although barely, according to Patrick. Despite their differences, Chastity's happiness was very much entwined with her parents' approval. Which brought me back to my job for the day.

I needed to call my parents. The wedding invitations had gone out, and I wanted to tell them myself before they received their silver and white envelope. I picked up my cell phone once everyone else had left the office and hit the button to dial them.

My mother picked up the phone. "Hello, Axel, this is a surprise."

Of course, it was. It wasn't Christmas or someone's birthday. "Hello, Mother, how are you?"

"I'm well, how are you?" she answered, her voice typically cold.

I forced a smile to my face so that my tone was pleasant. "I'm really good actually, and I wanted to share some news with you. Two pieces of news, actually." Now that I thought about it, I hadn't even told them I was going to be a father. "Is Dad around? Would you mind putting me on loudspeaker so that he can hear me as well?"

"Very well. Give me a moment." She seemed to put the cell phone down because there was a strange crackle, then the sound of her footsteps as she walked away.

I waited. Then there were muffled voices in the background and the phone was picked up again.

"Hello, son," my father's big voice boomed through my cell phone.

"Hi, Dad. How are you?"

"Fine, thank you. How can we help you?"

I closed my eyes for a moment, anger simmering in my gut. I got friendlier, more personal service at the restaurants I frequented. And I didn't need their damn help. *Just tell them and hang up*, my inner voice advised. "I wanted to share some great news with you both. I'm getting married."

There was a soft gasp at the other end of the phone. "To whom?" my mother asked.

"Her name is Chastity, she's the daughter of one of my oldest friends. We met last year and she's definitely the one." I nodded to myself as the un-rehearsed words just popped out. That sounded right. Good. The was a long pause on the other end of the line. "You two still there?"

"Yes. We're here," my father said.

"Congratulations," Mother added, her tone of voice high and pitchy. "When's the big day?"

"Well, assuming things go to plan, about three weeks."

"Three weeks? What's the rush?" she asked.

Not that it was any of her business. "I want to be married to her as soon as possible, that's the rush," I answered back. "She would have preferred to wait until after the baby was born, but I want her as my wife as soon as yesterday."

"The baby?" Mother squeaked.

"Yes. She's pregnant and due in October." With a baby girl that is going to have her daddy wrapped around her little finger in no time, I was sure of it. More silence followed. *For fuck's sake.* "Well, I just wanted to let you both know before the invitation reached you. So, yeah."

My parents were still mute. What was going on in the background, I had no idea, but anger was beginning to build from deep within my belly. They were being told that their only son was happy, getting married, and finally at the age of forty-three, becoming a father.

I pinched the bridge of my nose, knowing that I should hang up the phone and not delve into my childhood, but the need to get some answers outweighed my common sense. "Hey, before I go, do either of you remember why I wanted to run my own company? Did I always want to be rich?" I hated the word when I talked to most people, when it came to my parents, it was an easy descriptor.

Mom groaned. "No need to be so crude about money, Axel."

It also served to annoy them, which was always a bonus.

My father coughed to clear his throat. "You wanted to own your own business because I always did. You also grew up in a wealthy household, Axel. Why wouldn't you want to have the same things as an adult?"

"I suppose you're right," I gritted out. "So, as far as you're concerned, I'm just copying you, Father. Is that right?" The very idea galled me. As if I owned a company because my father did. He wasn't my hero, nor someone I aspired to be.

"Not copying, no," he replied, his tone haughty. "Why does it sound like you're provoking an argument, Axel?"

"I'm not," I declared, even though I could feel in the pit of my stomach that I was. I just couldn't help myself. "I've just been wondering lately why I still work so hard. After all, it isn't necessary." I stopped for a moment, chewing on the thought, but my parents didn't speak, so I continued my monologue, "I think it's because you two refused to help me, kicked me out after college, and made me practically homeless. Despite your wealth, you decided I needed to do it all on my own."

It was coming together in my mind the more I thought about it. They'd barely been parents when I needed them as a child, then they'd gotten rid of me as soon as they physically could when I was grown.

"We paid for all of your education, including college," Mother defended. "That's the best foundation one can have in life. A good education, debt-free. You were much better off than any of your friends, even then. Now, look at you."

"Yes, look at me," I said, clenching my left hand into a fist where it lay on the desk in front of me. "A success in business, and now I'll have a wife, and a daughter. What more could a man want? Right?" *Other than the respect and acceptance of his parents.*

"You've done well, Axel," Mother said, her voice frosty despite the polite words. "We always knew you would."

Of course, they did. "Bet on the breeding, right?" I snarked.

"Don't be crass, Axel." She didn't correct me, though. They took full credit for my success, which made me furious enough to throw my phone at the wall.

I took a deep breath, similar to those I'd heard Chastity practicing lately. *Calm. Stay calm. They're not worth it.* I'd had enough of this conversation. I was never going to get what I needed from my parents, so it was time to let go of the grudge I still held towards them and move on. I have my own family now. There was no need to lament the loss of the one I came from.

"Thank you for my education," I told my parents. "But it's been twenty years now since you influenced any part of my life. I'm a success because of my own talent and perseverance."

"Axel—" Mother rushed in to say.

"Goodbye, Mother, Father."

"Axel!" Dad ground out, angry apparently.

I didn't care. I hung up. There was an unfamiliar sting in my nose and throat that I chose to ignore, and when my phone vibrated—my parents calling back—I rejected their call and packed up to go home.

I arrived at my front door, not really remembering the drive home. I shook myself. That wasn't safe. *Shit.* Maybe I should have called the driver? But it didn't matter now, I was home. I took an extra moment before I walked inside, to just absorb where I was. I didn't live in a bachelor pad anymore, with a revolving door for the women walking in or out. I didn't sleep alone every night, and I wasn't single. Far from it. I lifted my hand and opened my door, calling out to my soon-to-be wife. "Honey, I'm home!"

"Hey!" she called back. "I'm in the kitchen! Did you eat yet? There's food in the fridge. I had some meals delivered today for us."

I walked into the kitchen and saw my gorgeous blonde angel sitting at the kitchen table that she now used as a wedding preparation station.

She glanced up at me, a smile on her face.

My heart ached and my eyes filled with tears.

"Hey... you okay?" she asked, frowning at me, immediately sensing something was off.

I gulped and nodded, blinking the emotions away quickly. "Yeah. I'm fine."

She pushed herself to her feet and flicked out her black dress that clung to her baby bump. "You don't look fine." Then she did something perfect. She walked over to me and wrapped her arms around my waist and pressed her head into my chest, hugging me tightly.

I put my arms around her and rested my chin on her head, holding her close. My heart was still pounding too hard, but with Chastity's arms around me, it began to slow, to even out. Peace fell over me. I exhaled and sighed. This was my family. This was my home. The past was gone, and if my parents didn't want to be part of my future, they didn't have to be. I had to stop trying to make them fit.

When Chastity pulled away, she didn't talk to me immediately. She went to the fridge and showed me the meals that had been delivered. Lasagna and other pasta dishes, chicken breasts with vegetable sides, and a container of Beef Stroganoff.

I chose the chicken and veggies.

She heated it up, plated it, and pushed it towards me on the island counter.

I sat on the stool and dug into the food, my empty stomach grateful for the meal.

Once I'd finished, Chastity pushed a beer across the counter, then said, "Talk."

I laughed. She'd done well to wait this long. "I spoke with my parents tonight and told them about the wedding and the baby."

Chastity's eyes almost bugged out of her head. "You hadn't told them yet?"

I shrugged. "It wasn't intentional. I just... we don't really speak. We call for Christmas and birthdays, and that's about it."

She frowned and rubbed her huge belly. “Really? Wow. I can’t even go a week without talking to my parents.”

I grinned at her. “I know, but your parents love you, sweetheart.”

She tilted her head at me. “You don’t think your parents love you?”

I glanced down at the cold beer bottle pressed between my palms and took a drink. Did I? “No, I don’t.”

She didn’t come around the island or touch me, for which I was grateful. I needed a minute.

“Is there anything I can do for you, my love?”

I glanced up and stared at my whole world. “You’re already doing it. You’re giving me a family, sweetheart. I just need to rethink my whole life, that’s all.” I huffed out a laugh and ran my fingers through my hair.

“What do you mean?”

“I mean… I think I’ve always worked the way I do to prove to them that I could do it. You know, succeed without their help. And then it became a habit. I don’t know.”

That was when Chastity came around and sat next to me. She didn’t talk, she just leaned her head against my shoulder and sighed.

“I love you, and I know they’re not exactly the right age to be your parents, but you know you can share mine. And my grandparents, and my aunts, and uncles. If you want more of a family, I’ve got lots who will care about you.”

I chuckled and sighed. “Thank you. I appreciate the offer.”

Chastity was more than enough for me, but I needed to talk to Pat and Cheryl. Maybe it was time for me to shift my work paradigm a bit. It didn’t need to be the way I defined myself as a person, or a man. I provided for my family, and I knew Chastity wanted me. My time. My help. Maybe it was time to stop lying about trying to slow down, and actually do it.

19

CHASTITY

The wedding planner turned out to be amazing. She took *all* the stress off me with the planning and did most of the correspondence via text. It was like having some awesome, knowledgeable best friend who sent me pictures of colors, flowers, table settings, and invitation patterns.

My belly was still rather high, making it difficult to breathe, but the doctor said I was measuring right on schedule. So, it was full steam ahead for the wedding plans. My back and hips ached a little, but with regular chiropractic adjustments and short walks around the block, I was managing the pain okay.

I found a gorgeous wedding dress I loved at a reasonable price. It was simple in design, ivory, with a lace trim around the bodice, and it flowed over my baby bump and right down to the floor.

We were having the reception at an old hotel a short way out of the city, with period features, a beautiful garden, and an old-world charm that I simply adored. We just had to hope and pray that we made it to the Big Day without any issues.

~

Two weeks out from the wedding, I was thirty-seven weeks pregnant and sitting at the kitchen table when I got a phone call from my mom around nine AM.

"Hey, Mom, I was just going to take a shower, but I'll be there soon." I'd been visiting almost every day, just to break up her day and to keep her in the loop about all the wedding plans.

"It might be better to come in later with Axel," she said, sounding anxious.

"Why, what's up?"

"They're taking me into the O.R, soon."

I stood up, my hand shaking as I lifted my arm to rest my hand on my belly. "Why? What's wrong?"

"Nothing's actually wrong. Really. I've hit thirty-two weeks, and the baby is healthy enough to come out. My body just isn't coping as well as they want anymore, so it's time. Don't worry, sweetheart. Everything will be fine."

Tears welled up in my eyes and I pressed my hand to my mouth so I wouldn't cry out. She reassured me that she would be fine, and she was the one about to go into surgery.

"Chastity?" Mom asked quietly. "Are you still there?"

I nodded, even though she couldn't see me, and swiped at the tears that leaked down my face. "I'm here, Mom. Okay. Okay... we have to just but our faith in the doctors, I suppose. If they say you and the baby are better off, then, that's great! It's definitely better to be safe than sorry." I swallowed hard, injecting some enthusiasm into my voice. "You'll have your beautiful baby boy by the end of the day!" Was it *really* safe for the baby to come out at thirty-two weeks? It didn't seem long enough.

"Yes. God willing," she whispered.

I almost broke down again. The tears flowed and my throat

ached. "You'll be fine, Mom. The baby will be fine, too. Get Dad to call me when we can come visit, okay?"

"Okay. I think I have to hang up, they're here."

"Is Dad there for you?" I asked urgently, suddenly realizing he wasn't in the background of the phone call.

"He's here. He's getting ready with surgical scrubs."

Thank God. "I love you, Mom. I'll see you soon."

"Love you too, sweetheart. See you later." And she hung up.

I collapsed back onto the chair, tears flowing freely down my cheeks. I let myself cry for a minute, needing the release from all the stress and overwhelming nature of what was going on. But once the sobs subsided, I walked to my bedroom for some tissues, blew my nose, washed my face in the en suite basin, and went in search of my phone again.

Axel picked up after just one ring. "I was just about to call you. How are you doing?"

The tingling in my nose started up again, but this time I pushed the feelings away. "I'm okay. Do you know what's happening with my mom?"

"I've been in meetings all morning, sweetheart, but I just got a message from Cheryl that Pat had to run off to the hospital. Katherine's having the baby today, is that right?"

"Yes," I said, swallowing hard to push the sadness down again. "She's only thirty-two weeks, but the doctors said that they'll both be better off if the baby is delivered now."

"Well, let's hope they're right," Axel said.

I nodded, unable to speak. What if something happened to my mom? Or my brother? How would Dad ever recover?

"Sweetheart," Axel said, when I didn't re-join the conversation, "your mom has the best care money can buy, but I know you'll be worrying non-stop until they're both okay. If you give me an hour, I'll pack up and come home to be with you."

I bit my lip. I wasn't sure that us sitting at home freaking out together was the right thing to do, plus, an hour was a long time to be alone before he got home. "How about I message Harry and ask him to pick me up? I can meet you at the office."

"You want to come here?" he asked, his shock obvious now.

I put my hand on my hip. "Are you embarrassed by your big, fat fiancé, Axel Patterson?"

He laughed. "You're gorgeous! I thought last night would have proven to you how beautiful I think you are."

Heat flushed my cheeks at the mention of last night. Axel had licked, probed, and suckled my pussy with his tongue until I'd come over him; then made love to me slowly until we'd both finished together. I was getting big and awkward, but it didn't stop Axel's desire to get me into the bedroom. If anything, he was making me lazy by doing everything for me.

"Yes, you did." I grinned, even though he couldn't see me. "So, is it okay if I come to you? I might even get Harry to drive me to a baby store so I can buy a gift for the baby. I haven't gotten anything yet because I thought we had more time." And now that I knew they were having a boy, I could buy some awesome little blue things. Our own nursery was nothing but pink, from the curtains to the blankets, to the toys and the rug. It was absolutely pink perfection. It'd be nice to shop for something else, though.

"That sounds like a great plan," Axel agreed. "Go shopping, then head on over to the office when you're done. But if things change and you need to go to the hospital, just message me, and I'll meet you there."

"Thanks, hon. I love you."

"I love you too."

I hung up to let Axel go, because more than likely he was now run off his feet at work. My dad was his main manager and had left work with no notice. I took a settling breath and texted Harry. Luckily, he was actually out running an errand, so would only be ten minutes away. I took that time to pack some food and bottles of water into my new bag and was waiting for Harry when he arrived.

"Where would you like to go first?" he asked as he opened the car door for me.

"Well, I'm not sure what it's called, but there's a little baby boutique on the same street as the hospital. Down near the intersection."

He nodded. "I know the one. Let's go."

I got in the car, clutching my cell phone in my hands and checked the volume was set on loud three times as Harry drove us into town.

"Everything okay?" he asked suddenly.

I burst out with a nervous laugh. Harry didn't make conversation often, even when I tried to engage him. So, the fact he was asking a question out of the blue made me feel like I was being far too transparent with my anxiety.

"Oh, ah. Yes. Thanks for asking," I managed.

Harry went back to being quiet.

And I suddenly needed to talk to someone. "My mom was just taken in for her C-section, and she's only thirty-two weeks, so I'm a little worried for her and the baby."

"That's understandable," Harry said. "Is that why you want to go shopping? For your new sibling."

I grinned at Harry, still clinging to my cell and praying for a message from my dad to say everything was okay.

"Yes. Exactly. And hopefully by the time I've found something for the baby, my father will have messaged me to say they're out of surgery."

"I hope that happens," Harry said, and we lapsed back into silence.

As luck would have it, things worked out exactly how I'd hoped. I was paying for my baby brother's gift when my phone rang loudly. "Oh, oh. Here. I've got to answer this." I shoved my credit card at the woman behind the counter, who'd heard the whole story over the half hour I'd been shopping and answered the call. "Hey, Dad! Is everything okay?"

"Yes. Your mom's fine and so is the baby. You have a new baby brother."

My hand flew up to my mouth, the knot in my stomach that had been making me feel sick for the past hour releasing in a flash like a balloon let go. "Oh, Dad, that's so amazing! How's the baby? How big is he?"

"He weighs almost four pounds and he's doing very well. They've taken him straight to the NICU in case he gets jaundice, but the doctors said that he should only be in there for a few days, hopefully. But he's safe, that's the main thing."

I held my breath and was almost afraid to speak. "And what about Mom?"

"She's okay," Dad said, but it didn't sound like he meant it.

"What happened?"

"Well, her blood pressure skyrocketed during surgery, and she lost a lot of blood. She's still in there, getting stitched up. I had to come out with the baby."

I pressed my lips together hard. "Um..." I panicked.

"She'll be okay, Chastity. We just have to wait for her to come out of surgery."

"I'm just down the street," I told him, taking back my credit card and gathering the bag with all the baby's goodies in it. "How about I come straight to the hospital now?" 'Thank you,' I mouthed to the woman who'd helped me in the boutique.

She waved me off with a big, encouraging smile.

"If you want to," Dad said.

"Yes. I do."

"I don't want you to be stressed, Chastity."

I walked out of the shop, rolling my eyes heavenward. "Dad.

I'm going to be worried about Mom no matter what. I'd rather sit with you than worry alone at home."

"Okay. See you soon."

We hung up.

Harry opened the door for me. "Jump in. I'll drive you down to the hospital."

I considered walking the two blocks, but my nerves got the best of me. "Thanks, Harry." I sent Axel a message in the car.

The baby is here! A little boy, almost 4lbs, and healthy. Mom is still in surgery, so I'm going to the hospital to sit with Dad. See you there!

In the two minutes it took for Harry to drive me to the front of the hospital, Axel texted back.

Congratulations! That's great. I'll get out as soon as I can. See you at the hospital. Take care of yourself, beautiful.

I grabbed the gift bags, thanked Harry, and rushed into the hospital. I found my father on level three, in Mom's room. She wasn't back yet, but I put my arms up and hugged him. "Congratulations, Dad. You have a son!"

He pulled back and smiled at me. "And he's amazing. Do you want to see him?"

I gaped at him. "Can I?" I put the gift bags down and tucked my cell phone into the pocket of my pregnancy leggings.

"You need to wear some special gear, but you definitely can. We can go now if you like?"

I nodded and walked with dad towards the door. "Have you heard any more about Mom?"

He shook his head, lines creasing around his eyes, showing his worry. "No. But they said they'd tell me as soon as they have news."

I grabbed his arm, holding my huge belly with my other hand. "Then let's go see my baby brother."

20

CHASTITY

My heart ached as I stared through the glass window of the special care nursery. I'd been told that the contact was limited to only my dad today, but I could come back in a few days to visit my brother.

He looked so tiny, attached to all the monitors and the oxygen. He was beautiful and perfect but seeing him there filled me with fear.

I put my hand up on the window, the cold pressing into my palm. *Poor baby.*

My daughter kicked out at me inside my belly.

I rubbed the spot where she'd made contact. "Your uncle made it out into the world before you, baby girl," I said, joking with her quietly. "He's going to be competitive. I can already tell."

My father stepped out of the nursery and shut the door behind him.

"He's so beautiful, Dad. Do you have a name chosen for him yet?"

He turned to stare back into the room. "We've narrowed it

down to a few, but your mom and I haven't agreed yet." He swallowed hard, his throat muscles working. "When she wakes up, we'll decide together."

I turned towards him and put my arms out, giving him a quick hug before he pulled back. He didn't really seem happy to have me here, but I wanted to be supportive. It was entirely possible he was just overwhelmed and didn't know how to feel or express himself right now. So, I needed to be patient and understanding. I'd certainly want the same if our situations were reversed.

"Maybe we should go back to Kaiti's room and wait," he suggested after a moment.

"Okay, Dad." I held my belly as I waddled down the hall and into the elevator, then headed back to her room. It would be my turn soon, to be in this hospital, having our baby. I shivered, then pushed away the expected fear that came with thoughts of labor as a first-time mom. I glanced across at my dad as we walked. He was really worried about my mother, more worried than I'd ever seen him about anything before.

"Chastity!"

I looked up and saw Axel sprinting along the corridor.

"You're here. Thank God. I've been looking everywhere for you. I think your phone's off."

"Oh, no. The battery must have died," I said, tugging my cell out of my pocket. The screen was dead, even when I pushed the buttons. "Shit. I'm so sorry, honey, I didn't realize." I kissed Axel quickly and smiled at him. "I'm okay and my brother is doing great. We're just waiting on the doctor to tell us how Mom's doing."

Axel smiled suddenly, then tugged on my hand to encourage us to follow him into Mom's hospital room. "Oh, haven't you heard? They came in before while I was waiting for you. Katherine's out of surgery and in recovery."

"How is she?" Dad asked, stepping closer and grabbing Axel's arm.

Axel didn't miss a beat. "They said she's doing really well."

My father staggered sideways.

Axel lunged and took hold of him, then gently directed him back into a chair to sit down.

"You okay, Dad?" I asked, noting the paleness of his cheeks.

He nodded. "Yeah. Just… um, give me a minute."

Axel and I exchanged worried glances.

"How about I go get you a bottle of water, Dad?" I said, sensing he might need a moment with his oldest friend. "There's a vending machine down the hall."

"That's a great idea, sweetheart," Axel said, before my dad could protest. "Can you grab a few extra?"

"Definitely. I'll be back in a few minutes." I hurried down the hall and grabbed some water and a few snacks. I was getting a little nauseous, which meant I had to eat. My little girl was sure taking a lot out of me at this point.

When I got back to the room, there was a nurse there speaking to my father. I'd missed the conversation, obviously, but everyone was smiling, so that was a good sign. When the nurse left, I hurried up with the water and snacks. "What's going on?"

Dad turned to me. "Basically, your mother lost a lot of blood, and they had to put her under fully and operate on her further after the C-section."

My hand flew to my mouth. "Oh, God."

"She's okay though," he said calmly. "They assured me it's a relatively common side effect, especially given her age and the pre-eclampsia. She'll be waking up in a few hours, so they said we should all go home, get some sleep, and come back tomorrow."

"Are you going to do that?" I asked Dad.

He laughed. "No way. I'm not leaving her. But you two

should. Go get some sleep and come back tomorrow when your mom is awake and feeling a little better."

I wasn't sure my mother would feel very well at all the day immediately after major surgery, but I wanted to see her anyway. "All right. I'll be back in the morning, Dad." I gave him a quick reassuring hug.

Axel extended his arm for a handshake. "Congratulations again, Pat. I can't wait to meet your little man."

"And I can't wait to meet my granddaughter," my father said with a big grin.

When our farewells were done, we went home together.

My heart felt heavy, but knowing mom had made it through the surgery successfully was an immense weight off my mind.

Axel and I ate an early dinner, and I had a long bath to relax before bed. Just as I was beginning to get all prune-like, and was readying myself to get out of the tub, Axel walked in.

"You okay in here?" he asked gently.

I chuckled and nodded. "Yeah, I'm fine, honey. Just relaxing." And what else did I have to do? More nesting? Shopping? Planning. *No.* My wedding was officially screwed up. And I didn't care, or I shouldn't care. What else should I have expected, wanting to get married with both my mom and I in our third trimester?

Axel put the lid down and sat on the toilet, then faced me. "You don't look relaxed, Chastity. In fact, you look... well, kind of angry."

I glanced away, trying to clear my features of the feelings coursing through me, but it was impossible.

"Talk to me. What's wrong?" he prompted.

I groaned and allowed myself to sink back into the bath, grateful for the huge, deep tub that allowed the water to cover all of me. "I'm not angry. Or I suppose I'm angry, but it's at myself for being so selfish. All I can think about at the moment is the fact that we're going to have to cancel our wedding." Even just saying the words out aloud made me tear up, and I dashed them away.

"I should be just grateful that my mom and baby brother are here, and they're both going to be okay. And yet, I can't believe I'm admitting it, but I'm actually upset we have to postpone our wedding. How stupid is that?"

"It's not stupid or selfish at all," Axel reassured me, his gaze filled with love and understanding. "Is it the first thing you thought of?"

I frowned at him. "Of course not. I didn't even think about the wedding until after we got home."

He smiled at me. "Then don't be too hard on yourself. Your initial reaction was concern for your mother and brother. You've just realized that today has a flow on effect on the rest of our life."

I pouted now. "Yeah, I know."

"You're allowed to be disappointed, sweetheart. You've been planning the whole day, and looking forward to it, and so have I. Remember, your mom has been looking forward to it too. She'll be disappointed as well. But in the long run, it doesn't matter. If we have to postpone it for a few months..." He shrugged. "So be it."

I nodded, blinking quickly and sending more tears down my face. *So stupid.*

"Hey, don't beat yourself up over this. You're almost thirty-eight weeks pregnant and have had a very stressful day." He went down onto his knees, kneeling next to the tub. "Do you want to know how selfish my thoughts have been today?"

I nodded. Anything to help me feel better about myself would be great round about now.

"I couldn't stop thinking about how lucky I was that you and the baby were healthy."

I rolled my eyes. "That's not selfish."

"It is when my best friend's wife is in the hospital and their baby's in the NICU. I was just so grateful that it wasn't you," he said, his expression marred by worry.

I couldn't help it; I twisted around in the water with the grace of an elephant and kissed him. "I love you."

"And I love you too," he replied, helping me out of the bath.

We were soon wrapped up in each other's arms, naked and quiet in our bed.

"I hope Mom and the baby are okay," I whispered into the dark.

"They will be," Axel said. "Katherine's strong, and that baby boy will have Pat's fire, I know it."

I squeezed him tighter, nuzzling into the nook of his shoulder where I was cuddled. "I'm so grateful for you, you know that?"

He kissed the top of my head. "Ditto, sweetheart. Now sleep, then in the morning you can go visit your new brother."

I didn't think I'd be able to sleep. Not with all the shitty, selfish thoughts and constant worrying about my mother whirling around in my mind. But eventually, I did.

THE NEXT MORNING, I went into the hospital and Axel went to work. My heart was in my throat when I walked into my mom's room, but I was greeted by a beautiful sight.

My mother was sitting up in bed, sipping on a cup of tea. "Chastity."

"Oh, Mom. You look wonderful," I said, rushing to her side. She was deathly pale still, but there was a brightness in her eyes that I hadn't seen for a long time.

"I feel a little strange," she admitted, "but there's no pain—thanks to all the meds they have me on. But how are you doing, sweetheart?"

"I'm good," I said, sitting in the chair next to her bed like I had every day for the past two weeks. "Your tummy is half gone and you look so good," I observed.

She shrugged. "I'm recovering well enough, so I'll still be able to make your wedding in a few weeks."

I gaped at her in disbelief. "Seriously? I was going to cancel it until you were fully recovered. Maybe post-pone it until next year some time?"

"No way," she said, shaking her head. "I'll be discharged soon enough, and the doctors have said the baby is doing really well. He's a little fighter. So, assuming he starts feeding properly and doesn't have jaundice, we'll both be home soon."

Tears burned in my eyes. "That's too much pressure on you, Mom. You don't need to—"

My mother put her hand out to stop whatever words were coming out of my mouth next. "I want to. Look... I know I haven't always been a fan of Axel's. Right from the start, I know I was a bitch to him."

I glanced down at her hand resting on my arm and didn't know what to say.

"But he's a good man, Chastity, and he's good for you. I never thought I'd say this, but he deserves you, sweetheart. With all of your beauty and sweetness, and intelligence and heart, I wasn't sure you'd find the guy that completed you. But you have. And you both deserve to have the day you planned."

I swallowed hard. "I want you there, Mom. It wouldn't be my special day without you."

Glancing up, I found my mom smiling down at me. "I'll be there, and God willing, so will your brother. Even if I have to roll down the aisle in a wheelchair and carry him with me."

I put my hand out and grabbed hers. "Oh, Mom, I couldn't ask you to do that."

She laughed. "Mark my words, Chastity, I'll be there; so, don't you dare cancel anything."

My baby kicked and rolled inside my belly.

"It was crazy of me to even attempt a wedding this close to the end of my pregnancy, let alone yours."

"You'll be fine," she said. "And I can't wait to see you walking down the aisle on your father's arm. It's going to be amazing. You'll be the most radiant bride there ever was."

I exhaled slowly. "Are you really sure? I already called the wedding planner to cancel everything, but she was tied up and hasn't gotten back to me yet."

"You're not canceling anything on account of me, do you hear me?" Mom said once again.

"You're really, *really* sure?" I stressed.

"Yes!"

My phone began to vibrate, and I glanced down to look at the screen. "It's the wedding planner."

"Well, tell her that's nothing's changed, then you can go see the baby."

I grinned at her, letting the phone buzz a while longer. "What did you end up naming him?"

She leaned back on her pillow with a smile. "Grayson Patrick."

I stood up with the phone still vibrating away in my hand. "That's beautiful, Mom. I really like it."

"Good. Now answer the phone and go see him. He's beautiful!"

"I will!" I walked away to take the call, my heart singing a song that only I could hear.

My mother was well, my brother was here, and my wedding was still on. Just one week to go. All my daughter had to do was stay put and not make an early entrance like her uncle!

21

CHASTITY

Just over a week after my mother gave birth to Grayson, our wedding day arrived. I was thankfully still very pregnant, and our baby girl was still giving my ribs a daily beating.

I woke up at the hotel where we were getting married, blinking my eyes awake. For a moment I was confused, because I was alone and the dark drapes weren't the ones we had in our house, then I realized where I was. "Oh my God... we made it!" I groaned as I rolled over, stretching my arms above my head before attempting to get out of bed.

It took a try or three, my belly making it difficult to get moving in the morning, but once I was on my feet, I waddled to the bathroom to pee and have a shower. I washed my hair and shaved under my arms, amazed we'd gotten this far. I'd stayed awake for hours last night, hands pressed against my belly, waiting for the tell-tale signs I was going into labor.

I'd felt sure if anything could go wrong, that it would. But I didn't. Instead, it was officially my wedding day, and I was still pregnant. Thirty-nine weeks today. When I stepped out of the shower, I was grinning to myself, and happiness was pulsing through me with every beat of my heart. "Baby girl, thank you so much for waiting for us to have this day. I really, *really* appreciate it."

"Chastity? You awake yet?" my mother called out from my bedroom.

I pulled the robe over my body and tied the belt above my huge belly. "Yeah, Mom. Just in the bathroom." I opened the door and walked out, finding her already dressed and smiling in the main room, baby Grayson in a tight wrap around her chest.

Mom and Dad were big into the attachment parenting idea, especially with a preemie. The constant heat and contact meant Grayson was thriving, already well above his initial birth weight.

Mom clapped her hands together. "I've ordered some room service, so breakfast should be here soon. Then the hairdresser and makeup artist will arrive. It's all systems go!"

I sat down on the bed, envying her energy and flat tummy. "How come you're all bouncy already, Mom?"

She laughed. "Well, it *is* my only daughter's wedding day."

"Yeah, but you had major surgery recently, and you look amazing!"

She smiled a secret type of smile. "Your dad's been looking after me at home, and I've been lucky with my recovery. I feel so much better than I did while I was pregnant, so even with the pain, my body is rebuilding and I'm feeling stronger by the day." She rubbed her hands over Grayson's back protectively, the very picture of maternal bliss.

I sighed, leaning back on my hands to try and relieve some of the pressure under my ribs. "I can't wait for this baby to come out. Last week I wasn't really feeling it, but today... I'm so done."

My mother grinned at me. "You only need to make it through today, then my granddaughter can come out and meet us all whenever she's ready."

Tears filled my eyes and I blinked them away. So many feelings today. "I'm so glad you're here."

"I wouldn't have missed it for anything." There was a knock on the door and Mom's face lit up. She loved room service. "I'll go get that." And she hustled off to get the breakfast cart.

I managed to get to my feet and decided it was time to get dressed. I had pretty underwear to put on, a silk dressing gown, and a lot of beautiful food to eat. And that's how the morning went. Surrounded by food and mocktails, chatting women, and beauty.

The makeup artist did my makeup exactly how I wanted it—heavy enough to look good with lots of photos, but natural enough so I looked like myself. Just a good version of myself.

The hairdresser dried then curled my hair using a wand, then arranged half of it on top of my head while leaving the rest to flow down my back. Axel loved my long hair, so I wanted to wear it at least partly out for him.

My wedding flowers were mostly roses, red and white, so the hairdresser threaded some white roses into my hair. It looked both romantic, elegant, and whimsical.

"Oh, you look beautiful, sweetheart," my mother said, looking at me from across the hotel room.

I glanced in the mirror one more time, pleased with how everything was turning out. "Thanks, Mom. So do you."

Her hair was blow dried straight and her makeup looked great, too.

"Time to put your dress on?" Mom asked. "Your dad and the photographer will be here soon."

"Oh, you're right," I said, glancing at the time. "Yikes!" I got to my feet gracelessly and gathered my dress up in my arms. "I might need your help to put it on, Mom."

"Oh, no problem." she said, placing a swaddled Grayson very gently in his portable bassinet.

I dropped the dressing gown on the bed and slipped the bridal gown over my head, my mom helping to bring the fabric down over my belly, before she started on the drawstrings at the back.

"I'm glad you chose this type of closure. It's so much better than a zipper or buttons," she commented.

I chuckled. "Yeah, the dressmaker suggested it since we really didn't know how big I was going to get. I liked the idea of the flexibility."

Soon my mother finished tying me up.

I turned towards the mirror.

"You look absolutely beautiful." She squeezed my hand in delight.

"Thanks, Mom." I took a deep breath, then exhaled slowly. "This is really exciting, but I also feel very nervous."

She just grinned at me.

"What if he changes his mind at the last minute?" I whispered.

My mother cackled with laughter. "Changes his mind? Then he'd be officially crazy, and you wouldn't want him anyway!"

I didn't think that would be the case, but hopefully it was a moot point. "What's the time?" I asked.

She was saved from answering because Dad knocked, then walked in the room. "How's my family doing?" Then he stopped and stared at me. "Nervous?"

I nodded. "A little, but more in a 'I hope he doesn't change his mind' kind of way. Not in an 'I think I want to cancel' sort of way." I shuddered at the very idea.

"Oh, he's not changing his mind," my father said with a grin. "He just about kicked me down the aisle to come get you. He's waiting by the metaphorical alter, as we speak."

Mom handed me my bouquet.

I squealed softly, unable to stop the jolt of excitement that pulsed through my belly. "Let's go."

"Okay." Mom gathered the baby up and tucked him into the wrap she wore, holding him close and tight against her body.

As a small family, we walked out of the room, down the hall and out to the patio that led into the rear gardens.

Axel had rented out the whole hotel for the weekend, so we had complete privacy and all our family and friends could stay the night.

I looked around, soaking in the grandeur and pure beauty of the gardens. A white carpet runner stretched before me, decorated with crimson rose petals.

"I'll go find my seat and see you both at the front." Mom kissed me quickly on the cheek, then kissed Dad too.

"Bye, Mom. Thank you."

She disappeared around the side with her precious cargo.

Dad held out his elbow to me. "Shall we?" he asked, his eyes shining.

I nodded and reached for his elbow with my left hand, my right gripping tightly to my custom bouquet. "Yes. Let's do it!"

22

AXEL

Waiting for Chastity to walk down that aisle was one of the most exciting, terrifying, and heart-stopping moments of my life.

My parents were sitting in front of me, in the first row. I'd greeted them when they'd arrived, and they said they would be staying for the night. I was pleased they were here, but that was about as far as my feelings went on the subject. I honestly hadn't expected them to make an appearance after where we left off.

It was Cheryl, whose eyes were shining with tears and love as she stared at me, who gave me the feeling that my true family was already here, supporting me.

As the music began, everyone rose to their feet and turned to look down the aisle as one. Ribbons and roses adorned the bridal walk and the venue looked magnificent. Chastity had truly outdone herself and my soul swelled with pride and love.

I stared dead ahead, my heart thundering in my chest as I stood next to the female celebrant we'd hired to perform and officiate our ceremony.

The doors to the hotel opened and two people emerged in the

distance. A beautiful woman dressed all in white and her suited father beside her. As they walked closer, the sheer perfection of Chastity's shining face hit me like a lightning bolt to the heart. The smile on her face and the love in her eyes were everything I'd ever dreamed of and so much more; a woman to love and cherish, who loved me in return, and an eternity to spend together.

My gaze dropped to the curvaceous swell of her belly, the luxe fabric hugged her tummy like a glove, before spilling and flowing over it like a waterfall of ivory. Our precious daughter still waiting to make her grand and much awaited entrance into the world. She'd be here soon, and we'd be a family. One filled with laughter and playtime together with memories of local schools. My children would never be shipped off to boarding school like I was. We were going to be close to our children. It's what we both wanted—it's what they deserved.

I smiled at my wife-to-be, a lump clogging my throat as she stepped even nearer.

Pat lowered his arm then took her hand, lifting it for me to grasp.

I did eagerly, feeling the solid warmth of her fingers in mine, popping the dream-like quality of the vision and making it all the more amazing because it was *real*. "Thank you, Pat." *Thank you for trusting me with your baby girl.*

Patrick smiled; his expression filled with nothing but happiness and trust as the unspoken moment passed between us.

"Thanks, Dad," Chastity whispered, then squeezed my hand and stepped up beside me.

Pat stepped aside and one of Chastity's college friends in a sleek red dress emerged from the front row discreetly and relieved the bride of her bouquet until we reached the end of our vows.

Chastity turned toward me and held out her hands for me to hold.

I faced her square on, gripping both of her hands in mine, ready to declare to the world and everyone around us that I would love her until the day I died.

The ceremony went quickly but was beautiful. Chastity had truly pulled off a miracle! *What a woman.* I was in awe. She could do anything she set her mind to. Then, before I knew it, it was time for our vows.

"The couple has written their own vows and would like to declare them now," announced the celebrant with a nod and a soft smile.

Chastity beamed up at me, gripping my hands tightly. "Axel, I love you more than anything in the world. Thank you for the gift of our daughter, our beautiful home, and the incredible life you're creating for us. I am grateful for you every single day. You make me so happy, and I know you're going to be the most amazing daddy to our little girl."

I had to look away as heat burned my eyes, but I pulled it together because it was my turn. There wasn't a single sound around us, the quiet almost deafening. I coughed to clear my throat, then laughed. "I should have gone first."

That broke the tension and the people around us laughed.

I blew out a breath and smiled at my woman, plucking up the most important courage of my life. "Chastity, I adore you. From the very first moment I met you, I knew you were special, like sunshine in a dark world, truly beautiful where others only pretend to be. We've gone through so much together this year, but we are stronger for it. There's nothing that we can't overcome together. And I know you will be an amazing mother to our baby, and I cannot wait to spend the rest of my life loving you."

Two single tears slipped down Chastity's lovely face, but she didn't wipe them away, and her lip quivered when she tried bravely to smile.

The celebrant spoke next, moving the ceremony along to its

eventual conclusion. "With the power vested in me by the state of Florida, I pronounce you man and wife. You may kiss the bride."

I reached for Chastity's face, cupping her rosy cheeks, then leaning over her perfect belly I kissed her gently, infusing the timeless moment with all of my love.

In front of our whole world, her parents and mine, as well as her friends and mine, we were finally married. Mr. and Mrs. Patterson.

Together, we turned toward the crowd of our loved ones who cheered and jumped to their feet in celebration of our nuptials.

I looked to Chastity and grinned, feeling more elated than I could ever remember being. "Now, it's time to party, sweetheart!"

23

CHASTITY

The wedding reception went through the afternoon and well into the night. We had official photos taken around the old hotel, then jumped straight into the decadent food and drinks, dancing the night away to the music the DJ mixed.

It was fun for all, but it was hell on my feet. And even though I'd found the most perfect white, flat, comfortable shoes for the wedding, my feet and ankles still swelled uncomfortably. But all in all, it was a perfect day.

I finally met Axel's parents, who, to be honest, were as cold as ice. I would never have thought it was possible that they were the ones responsible for creating a man as warm, loving, and amazing as Axel. It blew me away.

I began getting small cramps just after dinner but didn't let on to anyone. It wasn't much at first, just gentle little tightenings around my belly, similar to period cramps. Then, when it got too difficult to keep up with the conversations around me, I just sat down and told everyone I needed a rest and couldn't dance anymore. And luckily since I was thirty-nine weeks pregnant and the bride, no one questioned me.

There were a few short speeches and then we cut the exquisite wedding cake I'd had designed by a local baker. Four layers of extravagantly moist and delicious chocolate cake decorated with edible white and red roses to match my bouquet. They were truly to die for and everyone seemed to enjoy it.

Then the drinking and partying really began, at least for my guests who weren't fighting back the panic slowly taking them over. If I was in real labor, what should I do? Leave my own wedding? No, I couldn't do that.

Mom came and sat with me to keep me company for a while.

And although I tried, it became impossible to hide the pain rippling through me from her attentive gaze. "Oh..." I gripped my belly and held my breath through the pain, then when I realized what I was doing, forced myself to exhale.

I'd read so many books on natural birthing, hypnobirthing, and theories that promoted a woman's power and right to give birth the way she wanted to. Which for me, was hopefully as naturally as possible.

But it was my mother who'd told me that the pain was like a wave. She said that it would swell up, become crazy intense, then drop away and disappear. She'd told me to ride the wave and not fight it, but fuck, that wasn't easy to do!

"Hey. Are you okay?" Mom asked, turning towards me.

I nodded, feeling the pain wave begin to subside and within thirty seconds, it was like it had never been. I sighed with relief then rubbed one side of my bump where the pain was particularly bad. "Yeah, just getting some cramping. It's probably all the dancing." I rubbed my whole belly now and relaxed into my chair. *God, that's better...*

She gave me the side-eye. "And how long exactly has this been going on?"

I shrugged. No point in lying now. "Since dinner or a little after."

Mom checked her cell phone. "So, three hours or so?"

I nodded, feeling the tightening in my belly beginning again, a little gentler this time.

Her lips kicked up at the edges. "I think you're in labor."

My heart thumped a little faster. I'd been thinking it too for a couple of hours now, but had been trying to ignore it. Hearing someone else say it aloud made the possibility so much more real. "I was hoping it was just Braxton Hicks," I said, rubbing the hardening flesh of my belly. It was like a drum again. *Damn.*

Mom nodded. "Well, most first labors take about twelve hours from start to finish, so there's no need to rush to the hospital. You just enjoy the rest of your party, and if you need to leave because it all becomes too much, tell me, and I'll smuggle you back to your room for a bath."

"A bath?" I repeated.

Mom nodded. "Or a shower. The hot water is great for pain relief. I spent most of your labor in a shower."

"Okay." Sounded odd to me, but what did I know? And I was all for natural pain relief where possible.

Mom reached out a hand and squeezed my arm. "Just remember what I said. Don't fight the pain, it's doing something amazing and functional. And make sure you rest in between every contraction. You'll need your strength for the last hour. Labor is a marathon, not a sprint."

Another cramp hit me, and I closed my eyes, visualizing the wave going up, going up, going up, *BREATHE.* Then all of a sudden it fell away, subsiding, and just as fast as it had come it was gone. I opened my eyes and grinned at her. "Yep. I can do this."

"Of course, you can." She smiled at me. "You're one of the strongest people I know, Chastity, and I'm so proud of you."

The words were unexpected and brought a smile to my face. "Thanks, Mom. I love you too." Another wave of pain hit, and I worked my way through it. I managed another hour before Axel dropped by to see how I was, and I couldn't hide it anymore. In fact, I didn't want to.

"Hey, beautiful. How are you doing?"

I stared up at him, admiring how gorgeous he looked, slightly sweaty and smiling brightly. "We... well, I think I'm in labor."

Axel stared down at me, his eyes wide and immediately terrified. "W-what?" he stuttered.

"She's definitely in labor," my mother agreed sagely. "Contractions are every five to seven minutes. They're a bit irregular still, but they're getting stronger."

Axel hurried around the table and sat down next to me. "Why didn't you tell me earlier?"

I shrugged. There was no rush. "Because I didn't want to leave yet. The first stages of labor can take hours." *And hours and hours.* "Plus, if it's a false start, we would have left our own wedding for nothing."

Axel reached for my hand. "Let's go now, then. Is it straight to the hospital? Or?"

"No. We have to call the doctor's service first to let them know we need the doctor to meet us there. Plus, Dr. Martinez said to stay at home until I can't stand it anymore." The last piece of advice she gave me at my thirty-eight-week appointment last week.

"So, what do we do?" he pressed.

I didn't really know. Pain hit me and I bent forward, closing my eyes and gripping my belly, focusing on the wave, but finding it more difficult now.

"You could try a shower," Mom suggested. "Back at your room. Or maybe the hospital is the right place to be. Wherever you think you'll be more comfortable."

I blew out my breath. *Where is my hospital bag? I* wondered. "Um... I think I want to go to the hospital." I'd feel so much better once I was there, I was sure. "But I left my bag at home."

It was filled with my clothes and toiletries, pads and baby clothes, and a hundred other little tips and tricks I'd taken off Instagram.

"I'll have your father get that for you. I've got to look after the baby. Hang on." Mom darted off to find Dad.

I shared a look with Axel, pain tightening in my back. "Not the way we planned to spend our wedding night, is it?" I joked.

Axel gripped my hand, his gaze full of attentive empathy.

I squeezed back, finding some relief from the pain.

"Watching you bring our first child into the world?" Axel asked. "Sounds like you've turned the best day of my life into the best night of my life, too."

"First child, huh?" I repeated, shifting on the seat to find a comfortable position. Everything was aching now. My back, my legs, my whole belly. "How many are we having?"

He laughed. "Now probably isn't the time to have that conversation. But I was an only child, and I was kind of hoping we'd have at least two, so they would always have each other."

I nodded, enjoying the fleeting moments of relief in between contractions. "I always wanted three." *Or four.* But I wasn't saying that at the moment. *Let's see how I handle this one, first!* I told myself.

He smiled. "That sounds amazing."

I gasped as another wave of pain hit me. *Yep.* I wanted to go to the hospital, now. Screw the shower. "I want to go, now," I said, launching myself to my feet. And that's when my water broke. "Oh crap," I whispered as warm fluid gushed down between my legs. "That's really gross." And it was. *What a weird feeling.*

Mom came back with Dad, who had his car keys in hand. "Where's your hospital bag? I'll go get it and meet you there."

"In our room," I said. "Next to the bed. It's a pink suitcase."

I glanced at my mother. "Ah, my water just broke two seconds ago."

Her smile was massive now. She was definitely excited about her first grandchild. "Time for the hospital," she declared.

Axel was freaking out, I could tell, because he wasn't speaking, but he was kind of *vibrating*.

"Axel?" I prompted. "Honey?"

"Yes!" he almost shouted unexpectedly. "Yes... car."

Dad swung his keys around his finger. "I'm off to your house. I know where the spare key is. I'll see you at the hospital."

He slapped Axel on the shoulder. "It's go time, buddy."

I grabbed my phone and took my husband's hand, a little calmer now. "I think I want to get changed first. I'm feeling a bit yucky."

"Oh, yes. Of course," he said, then put his hand against the small of my back and walked me slowly through the crowd and into the elevator.

A contraction hit me as we were going to our room, and I had to stop, press against the wall with my hands for a moment, and breathe deeply. When it was over, I shook myself and kept waddling like a determined mama duck. I wanted my cotton dress that I'd packed for tomorrow. It was meant to be for our post-wedding breakfast, but that obviously wasn't going to happen now. Our little girl had chosen to make her grand entrance as grand as it could possibly be!

I glanced at the man I could now legally call my husband. "Looks like everyone will be having tomorrow's breakfast without us."

Axel chuckled nervously. "Yeah, I suppose they will."

We got to our room, and I felt calmer. Seeing Axel so freaked out made me immediately relax for some strange reason. One of us had to be level-headed during all of this.

"What should I do?" Axel asked me, hovering anxiously.

"Untie my dress for me," I said, turning around and giving him instructions on how to loosen the dress. Once it was undone, it slithered off my arms and dropped to the floor. I groaned with relief as my breasts were finally free. "Oh my God, that feels *so* much better."

Axel was staring at me like I'd gone insane.

I had to tell him what to do, it seemed. "I'm going to have a really quick shower. You call Harry or whoever and tell them we need a lift to the hospital. Just give me fifteen minutes, okay?" That should be long enough.

"Okay." Axel took out his phone and started pressing at the touch screen.

I managed to kick my shoes and underwear off as I waited for the water to warm up, then stepped under the shower's spray. It was bliss. My mother had been so right. Beneath the hot water the contractions felt infinitely more manageable. "I've definitely got to use the shower at the hospital if they let me." I called out to Axel. "This feels awesome."

Axel stuck his head into the shower, worry creasing his brow. "Are you okay if I quickly change clothes too?"

I nodded. "Of course. I'll just stay in here a little longer."

I pulled the pins out of my hair, the dull headache I'd been holding all day ceasing as soon as my hair was finally down. Next was my makeup. I scrubbed my face and washed all the grime away.

Four contractions later, I was clean and ready to get dressed. I turned off the water and waddled into the bedroom. "It's so strange that when there are no contractions, the pain is gone." Like it had never been there.

"That's good," Axel said. "Yeah?"

I nodded. "Yeah. Give me two minutes to get dressed, then we can go." I pulled on my cotton dress but didn't bother with underwear. I was pretty sure I was getting naked as soon as we got to the hospital. A contraction hit, snatching my breath away, and I bent in half, huffing and puffing through the wave until I could finally stand again.

Axel was there with me, a hand rubbing my lower back. "Are you okay?"

I nodded and straightened up. "Yep. But let's go before they get any worse." They were getting stronger but were still relatively far apart. "Let's go, *husband.*" I beamed up at Axel.

My husband finally smiled back properly. "Okay, wife. Let's go to the hospital."

"Let's go have our baby," I added, walking out of the room and toward the elevator once more. "It's strange to think I'm going to waddle into the hospital like this and come out holding our daughter."

Axel kissed my lips as the elevator doors opened. "This really will be the best day of my life."

I blinked back the tears. "Mine, too," I sniffled.

We got in the car and headed toward the hospital, ready for our lives to change forever.

24

CHASTITY

By the time we arrived, I could barely walk from the pain. The cramps were coming hard and fast, wrapping around my stomach and refusing to let go. The tears had also started to flow as pain and doubt pulled me down. "I can't do this. I can't do this!" I sobbed as I held tightly to Axel's arm.

"Do you want me to carry you?" he asked.

Panic set in. "God, no! I'm too heavy." And even if he could pick me up, what if he dropped me? No... just *no*. This wasn't some stupid comedy act. I was getting in there on my own two feet under my own power, like countless women who had come before me.

There was a short break, where the pain wave moved away and back out to the deep swell, leaving me on the proverbial beach of relief. "It's stopped. Quick, let's go," I panted.

We staggered forward together and made our way into the hospital.

Axel checked us in, rushing through all the necessary paperwork.

Meanwhile I was taken into a free room and put on my back.

"We're just going to check the dilation of your cervix, and then we'll know more about how long you've got to go," said the nurse. "You'll feel some pressure." Then she shoved her fingers up into my cervix and

The pain was excruciating, and I screamed.

She removed her fingers and disposed of her gloves.

The pain was still pulsing inside of me even in her absence and I gripped the bed sheets with white knuckles, my breath hitched in my throat and my eyes wide.

"You're already seven centimeters. Well done," she said pleasantly.

"Well done," I groaned out. "She says well done?"

"It won't be long now. I'll let the doctor know."

Not long? How long is not long? "Can I have a shower?" I asked, launching myself up to sit where I'd been lying down.

"If you'd like to," the nurse said with a smile. "There are two shower heads so you can have one on your belly and one on your back if you need it."

"Thank you," I groaned, standing up and stripping straight out of my dress. Another contraction came my way and I braced myself by grabbing onto the bed and breathing through the intense cramping that gripped at my belly with its sharp claws. As soon as it began to subside, I shuffled towards the shower and flicked on the taps. "Oh my God," I moaned. "No wonder women ask for an epidural." I stepped beneath the shower and hit my lower back with the heat, sighing as the pain immediately decreased to a more manageable level.

"Did you say you want an epidural?" Axel chimed in from the door. "Do you want me to call someone?"

I shook my head adamantly. "No. Seven centimeters is almost there. I can do this. Plus, I'm pretty sure there comes a point where it's too late, anyway." And this was the point at which I'd be asking for it, but I was okay. The less drugs, the faster the recovery, and the less chance of complications for the baby and me. *Fingers crossed!*

"Oh, please." Another wave hit me and this one hurt like hell. I cried out, whimpering as the panic that I'd felt earlier walking from the car began to set in. Then my stomach did something completely different, and I vomited without warning in the shower. I retched and spat on the tiles, then turned the shower head towards the puddle of unpleasantness to wash it all away.

"Oh my God, I am so sorry," I said to Axel, washing my mouth out with water. "That is not something you should have to see."

Axel's eyes were kind and full of love as he stared back at me. "You're doing amazing, sweetheart. Just keep going."

It only got harder from there. The pain became more and more debilitatingly intense until I could no longer stand. "I... I... need to lie down," I said, staggering back towards the bed, then the strangest sensation came over me. "No, I need to go to the toilet!" But I didn't want to sit on the toilet. *What if I push the baby out? No!*

The feeling was still there though, which was ridiculous but true. "I want to go to the toilet," I whined in frustration.

"So, go," Axel said, indicating toward the toilet.

I shook my head. "No. I can't." I didn't want to sit on it. Then another contraction hit me, and I cried out and dropped to my knees on the floor. Suddenly terrified, the pain overwhelmed me. There was no wave to ride anymore. There was only a great wall of pain and darkness. "Argh! Please make it stop. *Please.* Get this baby out! I can't do this anymore."

"I'll get the doctor," Axel said, reaching out his hand to pull me up, but I shook my head, remaining on my hands and knees, finding the position comforting somehow. My belly was dropped low now, and I could relax my neck.

The door opened and people walked in. Who was there, I

had no fucking idea. I didn't care who it was at this point. I just wanted the pain to end. How did women do this?

"I heard congratulations are in order," a woman's voice said. It sounded like Dr. Martinez.

"Ah, yes," Axel said. "We were married this afternoon."

Was it really still our wedding day?

"So, how are we doing Chastity?" the doctor asked just as more pain hit me.

I clawed the floor and cried out like a feral cat, so ridiculously grateful when it was finally over.

Axel's hand was in my hair, his voice in my ear.

I wasn't sure what he was saying, but I knew he was being supportive.

"How about we get you up on the bed so I can take a look at how far along you are."

I shook my head. Nope. No way. Not happening.

"Come on, sweetheart," Axel coaxed.

"No." I began to bear down, pushing back, then freaked out and stopped. "Oh my God, I want to push. Am I allowed to push?" Was I allowed to? Wasn't there a rule about waiting until they said so? Was I dilated properly? Was I going to screw everything up?

The nurse was suddenly beside me on the floor. "Lift your legs. That's it, one at a time. I'm just going to get this birthing mat under you, Chastity."

I was shaking my head, but I did what she asked, letting them shove a thick, padded mat beneath me. "What do I... Can I..." *What do I do?* I was getting no answers!

Axel was down on his knees beside me, his hand in my hair. "It's okay, sweetheart. The doctor is coming."

Where'd she go? I wondered vaguely. *And why?*

"You're doing so well, Chastity. *So* well. I love you so, so much, beautiful girl," Axel murmured in my ear.

Dr Martinez's voice was suddenly behind me. "Chastity, if you want to push, then push. When the contraction comes, bear down, slowly. Not one big push, just gently. Okay?"

I nodded without answering, getting ready to focus. Pressing my hands into the mat, I prepared to push back. When the next contraction struck, it was a relief to be able to do *something* with the pressure. I didn't have to just endure it; I used the pain and pushed. There was a shift inside of me. Flesh moving within mine.

"Very good," the doctor said. "Now, take a breather for a minute. Then do the same thing when the next contraction comes, just push a little more."

So, I did. When the pain swelled, I pushed back, feeling the twist of my daughter inside of me. It stole the breath from my lungs.

"I can see the head," I heard the doctor say from what seemed like very far away.

I couldn't help the guttural cries now emanating from my throat. The ring of fire was a real thing and it burned! I wanted it over with as quickly as possible. Steeling myself, I dredged up whatever I had left in me, and with one big, last push, my daughter twisted free.

I dropped my head, needing a minute as the release from pain washed over me, instant and tangible. I couldn't open my eyes just yet, but there was movement around me.

"You're so amazing, sweetheart," Axel cooed in my ear. "Do you want to turn over and hold our daughter?"

I forced my eyes open and managed to roll over onto my back on the mat on the bathroom floor.

The doctor handed me my naked, blood-smeared little one.

I put her on my chest, still struggling to breathe, and looked down at her with reverent awe. She'd been crying when she was handed to me, but as soon as she was set on my chest, she'd stopped crying and snuggled in as if it were the most natural thing in the world—and it was. "Wow," I breathed, putting both hands on her, cupping her tiny little head and running my fingers down her spine to her adorable little backside. "You're finally here. Hi, beautiful."

"Let's get you up on the bed so you can both be comfortable," the doctor suggested. "We just need to deliver the placenta, then you can stand up and move into bed."

It didn't sound pleasant, but I knew it was an important and necessary part of the birthing process. It felt weird with the nurse palpating my belly to assist in its passing, but once done, I began to buzz with a euphoria the likes of which I'd never felt before.

"How about you give the baby to Dad, and we get you up?" said the nurse. She put a pink, white, and blue blanket over Axel's arms, then she carefully picked up my baby and transferred her into Axel's care.

His face filled with wonder and when he put his finger out toward her little hand and she gripped it, his eyes filled with tears.

Love hit me so hard, I was left breathless. This was what it meant to be a family; to be parents and love a little someone more than anything else in the whole world.

The nurse helped me to my feet and out of the bathroom.

I gratefully climbed into the hospital bed, absolutely exhausted.

They covered me in blankets, ensuring that I was as comfortable as possible.

Axel came to sit beside me. "Do you want her back?" he asked, not moving to give her to me.

I grinned at him, nestling into the pillows and sighing. "I've held her for nine long months. I think it's your turn."

He chuckled and gingerly pulled her higher up his chest so that he could kiss the top of her head.

The doctor did her final examinations and once they were

sure I was in good health, nothing but some minor grazing, we were left alone.

"I'll be back to weigh and measure her," the nurse had said as she smiled and left the room.

I nodded, not worried in the slightest. It was the weirdest thing to go from feeling like you were going to die if the pain kept going, and then all of a sudden, it was gone—like it had never even existed in the first place.

"What do you want to call her?" I asked my husband, the man who'd turned my life inside out and back to front. Who had changed every plan I'd made for myself and re-made them with me a hundred times better.

He glanced up at me. "I thought we'd settled on Janie?"

I grinned at him. "I agreed with that as part of the joke, after our parents had done such a stellar job with our weird names. But what do you *really* want to call her?" I asked.

"I always liked the name Margaret," he whispered, staring down at his tiny daughter, fast asleep in her father's arms. "Maggie for short," he added.

"Is that a family name?" I asked him. It was quite traditional, the polar opposite of both our names.

"No," he admitted. "I just like it."

"Maggie," I repeated, staring down at her face. Her eyes were softly closed, and she had the most angelic little lips, and mass of dark hair like Axel's.

"Margaret Jane Patterson?" I asked with a grin.

He laughed. "Do you like any names you want to tell me?"

I shook my head. "I did, but now that she's here, none of the names I liked originally suit her." And I loved names that could be shortened or changed with a person's age. She could be Maggie, Mags, 'M', or Margaret. Whatever she wanted. It was a queen's name for our little princess. I glanced at the clock. Three AM. "It's probably too early to call Mom and Dad."

Axel glanced at the time, too. "Your mother could very well be up feeding. Why don't you send them a text?"

It was a great idea, so I did. I took a photo of Axel with the baby and sent it to my mom.

"Baby's first photo," I said with a smile as it flew off into the ether. I closed my eyes and sighed. "Axel, I'm getting tired now."

"Then sleep, sweetheart. You did the most magnificent job. I'm so proud of you."

I forced my eyes open to see Axel staring back at me. "Who would have thought that this would happen? That a year ago when I saw you at the health club, we'd end up here?"

His smile was full of love and hope. "I would never have dared think it, but I dreamed of you; of a woman with your heart. And I prayed that you would find me, so that I could love you."

Tears of happiness spilled down my cheeks as I pulled myself up.

My husband leaned forward to kiss me, our daughter—a piece of my heart—nestled between us.

EPILOGUE

CHASTITY

5 years later.

I cradled our newborn son in my arms, watching him root around, looking for a nipple to latch onto. He made the cutest little sounds, similar to a piglet, snorting and grunting away.

"Hang on a moment, little man. Give me a second." I moved my maternity top aside, unclipped my bra, and put my hungry little bundle onto my breast. I gasped a little at the ferociousness of his attachment, then sighed when the pain vanished as he began to drink.

Leo was only ten days old, so my nipples were still getting used to being fed on again, but he was doing amazing overall. He was sleeping and feeding well. Motherhood was so much easier the third time around. The pregnancy, the birth, everything had just been easier. I was so much more relaxed this time and was finding myself enjoying Leo more because of how little I worried.

I'd kept my other two alive—I could do it again.

I heard a little shriek and looked up to see my eldest torturing her brother. I narrowed my gaze at the birthday girl and called out, "Maggie, share the trucks! You know they're his."

Maggie was a fiery little five-year-old and Thomas was my naughty little three-year-old. They were my whole world, even on the days they drove me insane. Our children were the best thing I'd ever done, except maybe choosing Axel as my husband. They came in a pretty close tie for first.

"Hey, beautiful," Axel said as he stepped out onto the back patio and kissed the top of my head. "How's your morning been?"

"Great. But the kids have been waiting for you to get home."

He slid into the lounge chair next to me quietly, since the two eldest hadn't spotted him yet. "For any particular reason? Or just because I'm the easy one?"

I grinned at him. "They're desperate to go in the pool."

We'd had the pool put in about six months after Maggie was born and the kids were good swimmers because of it.

His face lit up. "Oh, definitely!" He stood up and yelled out to the kids, who were playing in the shade of the huge central tree in our yard. "Who wants to go swimming?"

"Me!" They both cried and ran for their father.

He leaned down and scooped them up into his arms, chatting animatedly as they told him all about their morning.

Leo popped off my boob, his little milk drunk face absolutely perfect.

I put him over my shoulder and gently rubbed his back, so he'd burp. "Their swimmers are in the chest next to the door, hon," I said, knowing he was more than capable of looking after them.

He winked at me and went about getting them ready for a swim with him.

"How was the meeting this morning?" I asked, since he'd just arrived back from a quick trip into the office. It was a Saturday and although Axel had slowed down so much over the past five years, he still did the occasional weekend or all-nighter. Not today, though.

"Fine," he answered. "Pat had some strategies he wanted to go over, which were all good. He said they'll be over later for cake and maybe dinner. I was thinking of ordering in Chinese, if you want?"

I grinned at him. "I love that idea. Thank you."

It was Maggie's fifth birthday, but we'd gone low-key this year. With Leo just born, and Maggie due to start school next year, we'd decided to just have a cake and a chill night with our closest family.

"Great. I'll text him to confirm," Axel said and began wrangling the kids into their swimmers.

I lay back in the lounge with the baby over my shoulder and marveled at how amazing our life now was.

Axel had lessened his expectations of his own duties and had gone into more of a co-executive role with my dad. They worked together on an equal standing, and Axel shared his old responsibilities. He was happy, healthy, and slept eight hours most nights. He was also the most incredible father. Attentive, patient, calm, and present.

I watched in awe as he opened the gate to the pool and jumped in with the kids. Maggie was a proficient swimmer already, and although Thomas was confident, he still swam with his floaties and vest on as they splashed and played.

I relaxed in the lounge with a sigh enjoying the warmth of the baby on my chest, moving his little sleeping form lower so I could cuddle him properly. I'd never thought I could be this content and happy. It was an amazing feeling and one I was grateful for every single day.

A few hours later, the kids had been bathed and were now dressed in their party clothes. For Maggie, that was a princess tutu dress with rainbow sparkles.

For Thomas, it was a spiderman costume, and I wasn't fighting either of them on their choices. They looked utterly adorable and it was, after all, their party.

The doorbell rang and Axel trotted off to open the door for my parents. I'd put out a few platters of food, and Maggie's cake was front and center. A princess castle cake, three tiers high, just like she wanted.

"Auntie C!" Grayson cried, running full tilt into the kitchen to greet me.

"Mr. Grayson!" I cried back, scooping up the gorgeous little brother that I adored with all my heart and soul. "How are you doing today?"

"Great!" he said, looking mighty pleased with himself. "I made Maggie a card. Do you want to see?" He held up the piece of paper with perfect little squiggly drawings all over it.

"That's perfect, buddy. How about you go show her?" I set Grayson down on the ground and he took off to find the other kids. The three of them got along famously and it made our lives so much easier.

Mom walked into the room carrying two bottles of white wine, one in each hand. "I know you can't drink, but I need one," she announced, setting them both on the kitchen counter.

I laughed at her dramatic expression and pulled out a glass for her. "Why? What's wrong?"

She shook her head and slid onto the nearest kitchen stool. "Oh, nothing. Grayson is the most healthy, energetic boy the pediatrician has ever seen. He has a perfect bill of health." And yet my mother looked miserable.

"Then why do you look like you sucked on a lemon?" I teased, opening the bottle of wine and pouring her a glass.

She picked the glass up by the stem and took a sip. "Because I'm exhausted. He runs me off my feet every damn day."

I sighed in understanding. "He goes to school next year, Mom. Things will get easier, I promise."

"Yeah. Probably," she agreed, before she drank some more.

I sighed again. Maggie was energetic and loved to be on the go, but she also liked to color and paint, be quiet and read. Boys weren't like that, they were *all* 'go', and I could imagine that by the time Thomas was her age, I'd be praying for school to start too!

My father came into the kitchen and gave me a hug, a pink box tucked under his arm. "Where's my little princess?"

"Here I am, Papa!" Maggie cried, waving her arm madly.

Dad grinned at me and went to greet the birthday girl.

I stared after him, grinning at the picture they made together. Papa and his own little girl. "She's surrounded by boys," I said, nodding at Maggie with her father, brother, her uncle, and her grandfather.

Mom turned to look at the three kids playing on the mat. "They're perfect, Chastity. And speaking of perfect, where's my little Leo?"

"In his bassinet," I said, jerking my head toward his room.

Mom hopped up and headed straight for her newest grandchild, wine forgotten.

I shook my head and grabbed a bottle of water from the fridge. My mother may complain about how energetic the kids were, but she was great with them. She even had Maggie and Thomas over at her place once or twice a week, just so I could run my errands.

We'd fallen into a great pattern, my parents and I, especially with them living only about a ten-minute drive out of the city. We caught up every week socially, shared childcare, and Dad and Axel worked together still, of course.

Everything had turned out so much better than we ever expected, even if Grayson was wearing my poor mom out.

"How about we do the cake?" I called out to the group, and everyone responded with cheering.

"Great!" I grabbed the lighter and headed over to the table while Maggie jumped up on the chair so she could blow the candles out. "Remember, it's Maggie's birthday. You can have a turn at the candles later," I reminded her brother and uncle Grayson—who we referred to as her cousin most of the time. The semantics were just too complicated for two five-year-olds.

Mom walked out of the nursery holding baby Leo in her arms, rocking side to side as she came to join us.

Axel stood at the other end of the table holding up his phone to take photos and a video... I hoped.

"Ready? Happy birthday to you..." We sang.

Maggie, my gorgeous little blonde cherub, grinned like she was the luckiest girl on the planet. And she was. She had a family that loved her more than anything, and she had a smile that could melt your soul.

The song ended and I leaned in to whisper, "Blow out the candles, baby girl."

She blew hard and got them all out in one shot.

We all cheered together.,

My dad was clapping and whistling loudly.

Meanwhile, the boys began fussing to have a go at the candles.

"Okay, okay. Grayson's turn, then Thomas's turn, all right? Then we can cut the cake," I said, quieting them.

We had to do two more lightings and blowings out of the candles, by time they were done, I wasn't sure anyone would want to eat the cake. But the kids had a fabulous time anyway.

Since they insisted, I cut the cake up and served it to the kids only. Once they were finished and wiped down, we all sat outside on the deck to watch the kids playing under the tree and on the swings.

"Happy?" Axel asked, rubbing my hand from his place to my right.

I nodded. "So very much. Everything is just perfect."

Then Thomas screamed.

Maggie yelled.

And my parents went running to break up the next sibling fight.

Perfect chaos, I mused. That was my life now, and I wouldn't change a thing. With my handsome husband, and brand-new baby, I had the three darlings I'd always wanted, and things couldn't get any sweeter.

THE END.

〜

Thank you so much for reading the last of ***Axel and Chastity's trilogy***, but guess what? The saga continues with Patrick and Katherine's story!

I've written this trilogy from Katherine and Patrick's point of view so you can better understand how their romance unfolded...

You can download book 4:
https://books2read.com/u/4X6XML

Or read on for a sneak peak into Katherine and Patrick's Second Chance!

〜

1

PATRICK

Walking in on my daughter, naked, in the arms of my best friend was not something I'd ever imagined happening to me. Not even in my worst nightmares.

Had I thought I'd one day accidentally catch Axel fucking some woman in his apartment or on his desk at work? *Sure.* He was a player, and a rich one at that. He had a different woman in his bed every other night.

But my daughter...? Never!

I used my key and walked into Axel's apartment a few days after Christmas day, expecting to find my best friend hard at work like he always was—the eternal workaholic. His parents were cold as ice and lived on the other side of the world, so he wouldn't be busy with family stuff, that was for sure.

To be honest, I'd been worried about him. He'd sounded like absolute shit when I last spoke to him the day after Christmas, and I wanted to make sure he was doing okay.

I froze when I saw Axel naked and kissing a girl perched on the edge of the marble countertop in his kitchen. My first instinct was to turn around and walk away. No one wanted to be *that guy* who ruined a mate's hookup. But then I'd heard the young woman's familiar giggle, and her blonde hair caught my eye as being disturbingly similar to my daughter's.

Oh, hell no! Rage instantly consumed me. "Chastity!" I roared. "What the hell are you doing here?"

She gasped and covered her chest with her arms, her face stricken. "Dad!"

Axel turned his back to cover my daughter. "Pat, go wait in the living room."

I gaped at him. "Axel. What the fuck?" He was ordering me about like I was some subordinate who worked for him? *Fuck that for a joke!*

"Just go," he commanded again. "We'll be there in a minute."

Steam and fury poured through me, but the very last thing I wanted to see was the two of them, naked, doing the walk of shame back to the bedroom to re-dress. *Gross.* I stomped off to the living room so I couldn't see them any longer. I could hear their footsteps on the floors, then a door shut.

I sat on the couch and buried my face in my hands, equal parts enraged and physically ill. How long had this been going on? Had they met at my birthday party? Was this the girl Axel had been telling me about? *Oh God. Oh... shit!*

I ran my hands through my hair and lifted my head, inhaling deeply and praying for divine intervention. Surely, I was dreaming, right? I wasn't actually sitting in my best friend's living room, waiting for my daughter and best friend to return and explain why they were about to have sex in his kitchen. It just... couldn't be my reality. It couldn't!

A minute or more later, they walked back into the room. Dressed once more, thank the heavens.

I stayed sitting in the armchair and watched them approach, my disgust barely contained. I felt like a grenade with the pin pulled, ready to explode.

Chastity was pale and drawn, her lower lip trembling like she was going to cry.

I steeled myself against the soft emotions within me that always gave in to her when she pouted like that.

Chastity sat on the sofa to my right, hand twisted in her lap.

Axel stood over near the sofa on my left.

Bastard. "So," I managed to say, taking a deep breath and trying to remain calm. "How long has this been going on? Since my birthday?" If they met there and started dating immediately after, that would be the biggest insult. I hadn't seen them talking all that much that night, but that didn't mean anything, necessarily.

"No!" Chastity quickly denied. "We met at the gym, and we had no idea who each other was. We went on a few dates and *then* found out that you two knew each other."

I sat up straighter and slid to the edge of the chair. "And when you found out Axel was my best friend, what did you do, Chastity?" Surely that must have come as a shock to them?

"We, ah..." She stared at me with tears in her eyes. "We broke up."

Bullshit! I jumped to my feet, anger exploding inside my gut with scarcely restrained fire. "Then what the fuck is going on here?" I yelled.

Chastity sobbed, then covered her mouth with her hand, obviously overcome in the moment and unsure of how to proceed.

Axel, the traitor, got to his feet slowly. "Pat, look. I'm sorry you found out this way. It's not ideal in any way."

I stared at Axel, stupefied. I thought he was smarter than that. He was a billionaire businessman for fuck's sake! He must have a brain cell between his two ears! "Not ideal?" I repeated. "You were up here *fucking* my daughter, Axel."

Axel put his hands up in surrender. "I'm sorry, Pat."

"You're not sorry," I ground out, sinking back onto the lounge. *Fucking liar.*

Axel opened his mouth to speak again.

I put up my hand to stop him from apologizing again. "And don't even start! You have no idea how I feel, Axel. *No* idea!"

"No, I don't," Axel agreed, his tone calm.

Too calm for my liking. I was fucking furious over here and he was... what? Relaxed about the fact our friendship was over? Just chill about the worst situation I'd encountered in my life? "No, you don't. Because you don't have any kids," I hissed at him. "And why don't you?"

"I'm sure you're going to tell me," Axel muttered, staring down at the carpet at his feet.

I ignored his childish behavior and yelled the truth in his face. "Because you're a selfish, narcissistic asshole!"

"Dad!" Chastity protested, jumping to her feet. "You can't talk to him like that."

I whirled on my daughter, my only child. "I've known Axel since you were in elementary school, sweetheart. You don't get to tell me how I speak to him."

Tears filled her eyes again. "But, Dad—"

"No!" I growled at her. "I'm disgusted with you. Disgusted with you both." Then I turned on Axel. "You're twenty years older than her, for fuck's sake!" Why did neither of them realize this was a problem? A *massive* problem.

"We know that," Axel explained softly. "This was only meant to be a holiday fling. Nothing serious."

Did he just say that? Did he seriously just fucking say that to my damn face? I marched up to him and shoved Axel in the chest with both hands. "You bastard. You take my daughter... *my daughter*, and convince her to have some slutty affair? She's better than that, Axel, and you know it!"

"It wasn't his fault, Dad," Chastity said. "I was the one who begged him to date me for the couple of weeks I was here. He didn't want to go on after we found out the connection, but I—"

I flicked my hand to dismiss her. "You're a child, Chastity. You don't know anything about this guy."

"Excuse me?" Chastity said, her cheeks flushed red.

I ignored her, my anger directed at my former best friend. I pointed my finger at Axel. "You and I are done, you got it? Come on, Chastity. We're going home."

"Dad, please stop. I know this is a shock, but I'm almost twenty-two. And I like Axel. He's been great for me!"

I turned towards my daughter, amazed by the words coming out of her mouth. *How could she be so naïve?* So stupid. "You have no idea how I'm feeling, Chastity. Shock doesn't even come close to covering it. And as for Axel, I fail to see how some rich player who's slept with half the women in the city can be *good* for you. You've got your whole life ahead of you!"

"Dad, stop!" Chastity gasped. "You have no idea about our relationship, or how amazing Axel has been to me."

Amazing? Give me a break. "Yeah," I rolled my eyes. "I'm sure he turned on the charm to get in your pants, Chastity. But don't expect him to stick around. He created the saying, '*hit it and quit it*'."

"Stop!" Chastity yelled back, anger flashing in her eyes.

I flinched.

"I love him, Dad. I love him! He's amazing. And even if this fling lasts only two weeks, I'm happy. How can you not see that?"

I stared at my daughter, my young, beautiful and apparently, very naïve daughter. *Is she serious?*

"What?" Chastity repeated, flicking her hair indignantly like a model in a commercial.

I swallowed hard, my nightmare continuing. "Did you just say you *love* him?"

"Uh..." Chastity faltered. "Yeah... I..."

That bastard! I turned on Axel. I'd known he liked to play around, but he'd always shown respect to the women he slept with at least. He made sure they knew what they were signing up for and didn't get hurt. But this...? I hadn't thought he was capable of this. It was a new low for the man I'd considered my best friend. I threw my hands up in the air. "Now she loves you? Fucking hell, man! Why'd you have to go and screw with my daughter, of all people?"

Axel turned on my daughter, his expression stoic. "That wasn't the deal, Chastity."

I shoved Axel again. "What did you just say? She says she loves you and you say that wasn't the deal?" Surely, Axel must have known that by sleeping with an innocent, her feelings were going to become involved? He wasn't that fucking daft, was he?

For the first time, Axel glared at me. "It wasn't! I told her what was on offer, and she said she was happy with it."

I swung before I made the conscious decision to hit him. Hard and fast, my fist shot out *in rage, at the injustice of the vile words spilling from his lips. Cr-aaack!* Impact. Pain exploded up my wrist. "You're a smug bastard," I accused with venom. I grabbed Chastity's arm. "Let's go."

"Axel..." she whispered.

Axel wiped at the blood dripping from his lip. "Go."

"But—" she began.

"Chastity. Go. There's nothing more to say."

I looked away. The off-beat love scene was making me sick.

"Wait! Let me grab my bag," Chastity said, pulling away.

"Where is it?" I asked, curious about their set-up.

"The bedroom," she answered.

I laughed. "How was it sleeping in that bed by yourself all night? Bit lonely?" It was a cruel thing to say, but I wasn't feeling particularly charitable at the moment.

She turned and frowned at me. "What do you mean?"

I crossed my arms over my chest. "Everyone knows Axel won't sleep with his women. He spends more time in the guest room than his own bedroom." Something I'd always considered a genius move, from a male perspective. A bastard move.

Chastity stared straight at me. "Well, that shows just how much you don't know him, Dad. Axel's slept with me, all night, every night we've been together."

My mouth dropped open. *He... what? No. That meant— Oh, no.* I turned on my best friend, who was still wiping his bleeding mouth. "Is she telling the truth, Axel?"

He lifted his head, locking gazes with me. "Yeah," he returned. "So what?"

"So what?" I repeated, surprised once more about how stupid this guy really was capable of being. "So that means—" I took a breath. "Oh my God. You love her too!" I would have slammed my head into a wall if there was one close enough, and for the second time in a matter of minutes, I wanted to punch Axel in his damn face.

Chastity walked back into the room with a bag in hand.

"You ready?" I asked her, though I was still reeling from what I'd just learned. That meant Axel hadn't been just playing with Chastity, he was in love with her.

And she thought she was in love with him, which meant this whole scenario was even more fucked up than I first thought.

"Uh, yeah."

We walked into the elevator and went down to the parking garage.

My head was whirling with impossible words and feelings, and all of it was too much to deal with.

Chastity and I didn't speak the whole time. We walked to the car in silence and drove to her mom's house.

Her eyes were shiny like she was trying not to cry, but a tear trailed down her cheek as she opened the front door.

I walked up behind her, something I hadn't done since she was in pre-school. I opened my mouth to speak to her, but she was gone before I'd gotten my thoughts in order.

She left the door hanging open, and that's when my ex-wife walked out, confusion written all over her tired face. "Patrick? What's wrong? What are you doing here?"

I groaned, a little part of me dying inside. Now, this was going to take some telling.

~

Keep reading, download:
https://books2read.com/u/4X6XML